MONTANA
3
MARRIAGES

Wildflower Bride

MARY CONNEALY

MONTANA
MARRIAGES
3

Wildflower
Bride

BARBOUR
PUBLISHING

OTHER BOOKS BY MARY CONNEALY

Montana Marriages series:
Montana Rose
The Husband Tree

Lassoed in Texas series:
Petticoat Ranch
Calico Canyon
Gingham Mountain

Alaska Brides (a romance collection)
Black Hills Blessing (a romance collection)
Cowboy Christmas

Dedication

This book is dedicated to my husband, Ivan. He worked so hard for so many years while I was raising our four daughters: Josie, Wendy, Shelly, and Katy. The long hours, early mornings, hard labor, relentless work outside with the cattle in bitter cold and blazing heat—all to support us while I stayed home with the girls. We both really believed it was the right thing to do. Or as Ivan is fond of saying, "I don't suppose it hurt them any to have you around."

So now the girls are grown, and I can help a little more with the money. He still works in the bitter cold and blazing heat. But maybe now he only works as hard as one and a half men instead of two.

Ivan, you are my hero.

"The LORD is my light and my salvation;
whom shall I fear?"
PSALM 27:1

CHAPTER 1

Montana Territory, 1877

Gunfire jerked Wade Sawyer awake.

His feet hit the floor before he made a conscious decision to move. Grabbing his rifle mounted over the door, he rammed his back to the wall, jacked a shell into the chamber, and listened.

Another shot fired, then another. The volley went on and on. Many guns blazing.

Even as he figured that out, he realized the gunfire wasn't close. Wade yanked the shack's door open. In the heavy woods and the dim light of approaching dawn, there wasn't much to see, but he knew the ruckus wasn't aimed at him. It had another target, and from the direction of the sound, he knew what...or rather who.

Glowing Sun. And her village.

Already dressed because he slept in his clothes, he yanked his boots on. Snagging his heavily lined buckskin coat off the peg on the wall, he dashed toward his horse, yanking the jacket on while he ran.

Living in a meadow Wade had penned off, his chestnut gelding had his head up, alerted by the shooting, staring toward the noise. Wade lassoed the horse and had leather slapped onto the animal within two minutes. Wade swung up and slid his rifle into the boot of the saddle. Letting loose a yell that'd make a rebel soldier proud, Wade kicked his horse and charged toward death.

The shots kept ringing, echoing from the Flathead village set in the meadow high on the mountaintop.

His horse was game, and terror goaded Wade to risk the treacherous trails at a breakneck pace.

But it was too far. Racing up a deer trail, he knew, no matter how fast he rode and how much he risked, he'd be too late. He was already too late when the shooting started.

The hail of bullets ended. Wade galloped on. The weapons falling silent only made Wade surer that whatever damage was being done was over. In the gray of dawn, that silence ate at him, interrupted only by his horse's thundering hoofbeats. He reached the base of the rise surrounding the Flathead village and tore up the mountainside.

A horse skylined itself, a masked rider atop it. A struggling woman thrown over his lap, screaming, clawing, kicking. A blond woman dressed in Indian garb, her hair catching the rising sun. Screaming as only Glowing Sun could scream.

She was still alive. Wade felt a wash of relief mixed with rage and terror as he goaded his horse forward. He could rescue her. Save her. He was in time.

Wade closed the distance, his horse blowing hard as it galloped up the rugged hillside, hooves thundering. Still a long upward quarter of a mile away, Wade wasn't close enough yet to open fire. Afraid he'd hit Glowing Sun, Wade drew his rifle and carefully fired over the man's head.

At the instant he pulled the trigger, three masked riders topped the hill, riding at full speed.

Wade's bullet slammed the first one backward. The man shouted. His horse reared. A splash of bright red bloomed on the man's shirt. Grabbing at the saddle horn, the outlaw showed great skill by keeping his seat. But he lost control of his mount and plowed into the horse bearing Glowing Sun and her abductor.

Shocked and sickened to have shot a man, Wade grimly raced on toward Glowing Sun.

The masked man just behind the one Wade had wounded swung his gun at Wade in a way that struck Wade as awkward or somehow wrong. The shooter hesitated; then, without firing a shot, he abandoned the fight, whirled, and raced his horse back the way he'd come.

The third man, skinny, but beyond that unrecognizable behind his kerchief, turned to face Wade's gunfire. The instant he saw Wade, he turned coyote like the other outlaw and ran, leaving behind his wounded friend and the man who had Glowing Sun.

Cowards.

Glowing Sun gave an impossible twist of her body and an earsplitting shriek. She kicked herself over backward, landing a bare foot in the man's face.

He must have yanked on the reins, because the horse reared, neighing and fighting the bit, skidding and spinning. As the horse threatened to go over backward, the man threw himself to the ground.

Glowing Sun went with him, screaming but not with fear or pain. It sounded like fury, killing-mean rage. And it sounded strong. Wade prayed she hadn't been hurt.

Wade, still galloping full ahead up the long slope, leveled his rifle one-handedly and fired again, even higher this time.

The man Wade had shot gained control of his horse, wheeled, and dashed after the other bandits.

The fallen man leapt to his feet, still holding on to Glowing Sun. Then Wade realized the masked man wasn't holding her...he was fighting her off.

Shouting Flathead words Wade didn't understand, she had one hand jammed into the man's throat as she slashed with her knife.

With the sharp *smack* of his backhand on Glowing Sun's face, the man broke her grip. Her blade slashed, catching a flare of light from the first beams of the rising sun, cutting the man across his arm and chest. The outlaw yowled in pain.

Staggering back, Glowing Sun screamed an Indian battle cry and dove at him. She caught his kerchief and pulled it down. Then her fingers slipped. She fell and slid down the steep hillside on her back.

Wade fired again, his horse thundering forward.

Stay alive. Stay alive.

He'd be there in seconds. But one bullet, one slash of a blade could rob the world—and Wade—of Glowing Sun's courage and beauty and indomitable spirit.

The outlaw jerked his gun free and shot at Wade. There was no blast. The gun jammed or was empty. Wade thought of the volley of gunfire that had awakened him and suspected the man had emptied his gun already.

Fury twisting his face, the man, his mask dangling around his neck, gave Wade one wild look. Wade saw his face plainly. Blood poured over his thick black beard and down the front of his heavy sheepskin coat. The outlaw snatched up his horse's reins and threw himself into the saddle, and in two leaping strides, his horse vanished over the rim, following the other outlaws into the Flathead valley.

Wade reined hard as he reached Glowing Sun. His horse nearly sat down as it slid to a stop. Wade swung to the ground and raced to Glowing Sun's side.

Blood soaked the front of her dress, coated her hands. She jumped to her feet as he got there.

"Where are you hurt?" Frantic, Wade tried to force her onto the ground.

She fought to stay on her feet and slashed the knife.

He knew her well enough to duck. "It's me! Glowing Sun, it's Wade. Let me help you!" He knew what he must look like. He hadn't shaved all winter or cut his hair. Or bathed for that matter. He had no business expecting her to recognize the wild man he'd become.

She froze. Her knife was raised to strike. Her eyes locked on his face. "Wade?" The rage switched to relief. The knife fell from her fingers and she launched herself into Wade's arms.

He staggered down the hill a few feet as he caught her hard against his chest.

Dear God, dear God, thank You. She's alive. Holding her feels like a taste of heaven. Thank You. Thank You.

Wade's head cleared from the knee-weakening relief. "Where are you bleeding? Were you shot? Did those men hurt you?" She felt vital and strong in his arms, not like a wounded woman should. His hands went to her shoulders, to push her back so he could see where she'd been hurt.

Before he could accomplish that, the smell hit him. Wade whirled with her still in his arms. Her feet flew out as she swung from his neck. He carried her as he dashed to the crest of the rise to see. . .

Devastation.

Smoke and bodies.

The tepees in flames.

Glowing Sun's village laid to waste, people sprawled everywhere. A dozen, maybe two dozen, all still. As death.

Gasping in horror, Wade looked at the village.

He'd made a habit of riding up here through the winter. This was the summer hunting grounds for Glowing Sun's people, and he'd watched and waited for her to return from her village's winter camp. He knew, even as he'd done it, the behavior was too much like what he'd done to Cassie Dawson a few years ago. But he couldn't seem to help it. He'd needed to see Glowing Sun.

As spring had come on, he'd been more careful. Ghosting his way to the rim to study the high mountain valley to see if the Flatheads had returned. Only a week ago he'd ridden up here to find they'd come back. He'd dropped behind a scrub pine and watched until he caught a glimpse of her, alive and well and as beautiful as a dream. Then he'd slunk away like a low-down coyote.

Now, movement caught his eye. The men who'd taken Glowing Sun galloped far across the shallow bowl where this small group of Flatheads, roaming far from their reservation home, spent their summers. Wade's hand clutched at his gun, but he was too far away for a shot.

A shot. He'd shot a man. His stomach churned. He fought nausea.

A wail of torment from Glowing Sun stopped him from dropping to his knees and emptying his stomach. He wanted to get on his horse and run from what he'd done. But he couldn't leave Glowing Sun with this devastation.

A flash of Glowing Sun fighting for her life ran vividly through his mind. What choice did he have but to fight for her? But it left him heartsick.

Then he looked again at the smoldering ruins of the peaceful village. Men, women, children. Killed by those four men. They'd come with rifles and handguns. The Indians were, more often than not, unarmed, at least unarmed beyond knives and spears. The Flatheads were a peaceful people. Their meager weapons were nothing against heavily armed men with repeating rifles.

Wade should be proud he'd shot one of those murdering scum. He should want to kill them all. The shame of that thought made his stomach twist again, and he thought he might vomit. He knew being able to kill wasn't the sign of a man. He'd grown enough in his faith to understand that, but his common sense was fighting a battle with his upbringing.

"Why did this happen?" Wade asked God aloud.

Glowing Sun answered. "A massacre." She still clung to him, but she'd lifted her head and turned to look at the butchery. She'd spoken in Wade's language. He'd taught her English, or rather helped her rediscover her first tongue.

Wade blocked her view of the nightmare by turning and putting his body between her and the destruction. Thinking of her distracted him from his nausea.

Wildflower Bride

Before he could check her for injuries, a cry of pain rose from the village nearly half a mile away in the valley.

Whirling to follow the sound, his weak stomach forgotten, he released Glowing Sun and grabbed at his horse's reins. He jumped on, held his hand out to her. Her hand slapped into his with a sharp *clap*. He swung her up in front of him, remembering how she'd liked to ride.

They raced down the hill and waded into a bloodbath.

Glowing Sun snagged the reins away and swung her leg over the horse's head. She jumped to the ground before the chestnut stopped and raced toward the loudest cries of pain.

Wade followed, relieved to see her moving and unhurt despite the blood.

Glowing Sun dropped to her knees. "Mama!"

Wade's stomach twisted with dread as he saw two gunshot wounds bleeding from the woman's chest. The woman opened her eyes, but they seemed unfocused. She grabbed at Glowing Sun as if fighting her off, screaming.

"No, Mama. Let us help you."

The older woman kept screaming, fighting.

"Flathead, Glowing Sun. Speak Flathead to her."

Glowing Sun looked up, confused.

"You're speaking English." Wade pulled off his coat then tore off his shirt and grabbed his knife out of its sheath in his boot.

Glowing Sun shook her head then turned back to the woman.

"*Ten*. . .Mama. . .*Ten*."

Ten? Did that mean "mother"? Wade should have learned the language of the tribes around him. Why had he never tried? His father hated the idea. Indians were to be driven off, not treated as neighbors.

Glowing Sun spoke in the guttural tribal language.

The injured woman calmed and seemed to recognize Glowing Sun. Instead of screaming, she began a chant.

"We've got to get the bleeding stopped." Wade dropped beside Glowing Sun. The chances of saving Glowing Sun's mother were slim, but they had to try. With a loud tearing sound, Wade's shirt split under his blade. Wade handed strips to Glowing Sun, who pressed them against the gushing wounds.

Glowing Sun began to pray in English, frantic petitions to God for mercy. Wade glanced up and saw love in Glowing Sun's eyes. The kind of love Wade had known for his mother. A long-lost love.

Wade knew nothing of the Flathead language, but to him the woman's chant was a dirge. To the extent he could understand, it sounded wordless, just syllables of mourning.

He joined Glowing Sun in her prayers, asking for a miracle, because only a miracle would spare this woman.

"God, please spare her life. Guide our hands. Wisdom, Lord, give us wisdom to know what to do, how to help."

The two of them worked in desperation, one on each side of the stout woman. Stemming the bleeding, binding the wounds. Long black braids, streaked heavily with gray, hung limp. The woman's dark eyes seemed to look beyond the sky. A cry rang from her lips. Her eyes flickered closed, but the dirge continued.

"Press harder." Wade shoved a wad of cloth on top of the one soaked with blood. He moved Glowing Sun's crimson-stained fingers.

The woman didn't react to what had to be excruciating pain. She continued her death chant.

Glowing Sun's mother's song became weaker, quieter, sadder.

At last the noise ended. Wade felt the moment life left the woman and her spirit left her body.

With a cry of grief, Glowing Sun stopped her futile medical treatment and flung herself on the woman.

Wade eased back, staying close but knowing nothing he could say or do would help. Only then did he hear other moans. Other cries for help.

Wildflower Bride

He lurched to his feet, his knees numb from the long time on the ground. How long had they worked on the dying woman? Were there others they'd neglected in their futile fight to save Glowing Sun's Flathead mother?

He hated to leave Glowing Sun. He couldn't insist she come. He faltered. "I've got to see if there are others who need help."

She didn't raise her eyes. Instead she started her own death chant.

Without even waiting to see if she heard him over her cries of grief, he turned and rushed toward the sound of pain.

CHAPTER 2

W ade dressed the wounds of five people. Three he expected to die within hours. They were gut shot and there was nothing that could be done. Two others had a chance, if infection didn't set in.

He'd counted nineteen dead.

The two who were less seriously wounded were still bad off. One, a half-grown boy, had a bad bullet graze cutting his leg and a gunshot wound in his shoulder. The other was an older woman, gray haired and whipcord lean. She bled from her temple. Wade had figured her for dead until she began moaning. Wade noticed when the moans at last penetrated Glowing Sun's grief.

Wade was surprised she remembered as much English as she did. Though she'd rediscovered much of the language of her birth while they'd been together in the fall, now she seemed to speak it with little effort. He wondered if she'd secretly practiced it over the winter. He also wondered if she'd thought about him.

Glowing Sun ended her chant and lurched to her feet, leaving her mother's side for the first time, turning toward the others who were hurt. "I didn't know anyone else was alive." She rushed toward the old woman just as Wade got to the woman's side and dropped to his knees.

One whole side of the woman's head was matted with blood.

"We need more bandages." Glowing Sun pulled her knife from behind her back and slit the soft doeskin of her skirt. Wade hadn't seen the knife since she'd slashed at her kidnapper.

The woman's eyes fluttered open. She focused on Glowing Sun and struck.

A hard blow knocked Glowing Sun backward. The woman rolled to her side and lunged, shouting words Wade couldn't understand.

Wade caught the woman by the waist and flipped her onto her back on the ground. Assuming she was panicking as Glowing Sun's mother had been, Wade spoke soothing words to the struggling woman. "Glowing Sun, talk to her in Flathead."

Glowing Sun lay on her back as if dazed.

The woman swung a clawed hand at Wade's face.

He caught her wrist in midair and she swung with her other hand. Wade was close enough that the blow landed on his back and did no harm. "Glowing Sun! Make her understand I want to help her."

Then Wade realized the woman, swinging her free fist, pounding on his back as he wrestled with her, was looking at Glowing Sun with clear eyes. Not like Glowing Sun's mother, who was delirious. This woman was absolutely clearheaded in her attempt to hurt both of them. But mainly Glowing Sun.

"What's the matter with her?"

Glowing Sun regained her place at the woman's side and shouted harsh words at the woman.

The woman yelled back.

Pinning the woman's free hand, Glowing Sun continued her war of words.

The woman struggled, kicking and wrenching her body wildly. She screamed as if they were killing her. Wade held on doggedly. Only her wounds kept the woman from possibly winning this fight against both of them. She was older than they but wiry and strong and fierce. At last she quit fighting them. Her muscles went lax and she fell silent.

Glowing Sun spoke more calmly.

The woman listened then replied.

Glowing Sun's face crumpled as if the words stabbed knife wounds into her soul. Releasing her hold on the woman, Glowing Sun looked at Wade. "Let her go."

Wade arched a brow at Glowing Sun and held on. There was no attack from the woman's free hand, so warily, Wade did the same and leaned back on his heels.

The woman closed her eyes, covered her bloody face with both hands, and began the wailing that sounded like grief, much like Glowing Sun's mother had. But Wade knew this woman wasn't crying for her own impending death, but for the death of her people.

Glowing Sun jerked her head in a way that asked Wade to step away from the woman. They moved to the other wounded, accompanied by the death song.

Two of the surviving Flathead people had died while they worked on the angry woman. Wade prayed over the third but held out hope only if God supplied a miracle. As they finished binding the leg of the half-grown boy, Wade finally asked, "What was that back there?"

Glowing Sun gestured and Wade followed her to the far end of the village, away from the singing. "That is the mother of my. . . my. . ." Glowing Sun furrowed her brow as if searching for the English term. "*Naw'*."

"'Naw'? What's that?"

Hesitantly she said, "Husband?"

Wade controlled his expression only because this day had been so laced with shocks he was numb. He remembered all too well Glowing Sun swinging up on the back of a horse and riding away last fall. He'd come only moments after she and Wade shared their first and last kiss. As she rode away, she had looked back with longing, but still she'd made her choice.

It had cut Wade's heart out. He looked around at the devastation and found the man he sought. Dead, sprawled on his back, a tomahawk in his hand and so many bullet wounds it was clear it had taken a lot to kill him. "And she's angry at you?"

"She blames this massacre on me because they didn't hurt me. Instead they tried to take me with them."

"That's ridiculous. If they did leave you alive, they had terrible plans for you. And this killing is because they're evil. That's not your fault."

Glowing Sun looked at the death surrounding them and caught a handful of her white-blond hair, twisting it as if to yank it out of her head.

Wade knew no one could deny what he'd said. The evil was too huge, too ugly. "She's got no reason to hate you."

Glowing Sun yanked that razor-sharp knife with the slender blade from behind her back. "She has objected to me joining her family from the first."

"So you are married? Were married?"

She raised the knife to hack at her hair.

"Stop!" He caught her wrist.

Glowing Sun pulled against his iron grip. "Why do you stop me? Do you wish to *own* me because of my hair? Or *love* me? Or *hate* me because of it? I would rip it from my head, cut it away."

"No, I don't love you because of your hair." Before this morning's madness he would have said he loved her because of her heart, her fiery spirit, her courage, and, yes. . .her beauty. But he'd seen a savage side of Glowing Sun today as she'd slashed at her kidnapper. He realized he didn't know her well enough to claim something as deep and profound as love. But he wanted to know her. Wanted to love her.

"We don't have time for you to fuss with it. Let's bury your dead and tend to the injured." Wade wanted to ask about her husband. Had they been married before he'd rescued her from kidnappers last fall? And what did it matter anyway? Except that it meant he'd kissed a married woman. And more important, at least as it showed her character, the married woman had kissed him back.

"Where did you come from?" Glowing Sun dropped her hair without slashing it off.

"I've been living in the mountains. In a miner's shack."

"Nearby?"

"Near enough to hear the gunfire."

Glowing Sun looked around the village until her eyes landed on her husband. "Wild Eagle." Tears filled Glowing Sun's eyes as she looked away. The tears overflowed as she pointed at two children lying dead, side by side. "And that is my brother and my sister." Her voice broke.

She lifted her chin as if drawing courage straight from her spine. "My father is dead beside him. Better my mother is dead now than to face life without her beloved husband and children."

"And what of you? Now you face life without anyone." Except him. Glowing Sun had him whether she knew it or not.

"You speak truth. There is no time now for anything but seeing to my people."

The sun rose high as they worked, exchanging few words. Glowing Sun carried water as her patients cried out with thirst and pain.

The older woman roused herself soon enough and, despite her ugly head injury, began tending the boy who had a chance at survival. She refused to let Glowing Sun or Wade near him.

The smoke dissipated as the tepees finally burned to the ground, leaving only the reek of ash and the scent of blood.

"We need to bury them." Wade turned from the living to face the dead. "What can we use for a shovel?"

Glowing Sun nodded then squared her shoulders and approached her mother-in-law. They began to speak quickly. Wade wasn't sure anymore if the words they exchanged were harsh or if the guttural language just sounded like it to his untutored ears.

At last Glowing Sun returned to his side, tears in her eyes that told him all he needed to know. "She refuses to let us touch them. She said she needs to go to the Bitterroot Valley and fetch a holy man to sing for them."

"We can't just go away and leave them lying here."

"It is more the way of my people than to bury them. We believe people return to the earth when they die. Some tribes burn their dead on pyres. Some leave bodies to the elements, allowing the earth to reclaim them."

"Which will you do?"

Glowing Sun shook her head. "It isn't for me to say. She believes they died murdered, their souls stolen. I believe they died in battle. That is a noble death. It will be up to the holy man."

Wade didn't like it. But he wasn't about to add to Glowing Sun's distress. He walked to the side of the unconscious woman who lingered despite her devastating wounds.

"I'll respect your traditions, Glowing Sun." The sun lowered in the sky, and Wade knew it was too late in the day to begin the journey. "We'll head for the Bitterroot Valley tomorrow."

"Do not call me Glowing Sun," she snapped. "Wild Eagle's mother told me I've dishonored the name and my tribe." She walked along beside Wade and knelt by the injured woman's side, glancing over her shoulder to see if this would earn her a rebuke. "I remember my white name and will only answer to it from now on. Abby. I don't remember the rest of it, but maybe it will come back."

Glowing Sun's. . .Abby's. . .mother-in-law ignored them, as if she knew the woman they hovered over was beyond being hurt by them. "She can do this, Glow. . .uh . . .Abby? She can decide how to treat *your* parents after their deaths? Decide to strip you of your name?"

"We respect age. To defy her now would only deepen her contempt and anger. And she's badly hurt, despite her refusal to let me help with the boy. I won't make things harder for her."

As they knelt, Wade realized that the woman's shallow breathing had ceased. Her tenacious hold on life had been severed. Glowing Sun drew a blanket over the face of the young woman who had never regained consciousness.

"We've done all we can." Wade rose and came around the woman to Abby's side.

"You would leave me?" Abby looked desperately at him.

"No!" Shocked that she'd even think it, Wade rested his hand on her shoulder. "Let's get some sleep and set out in the morning."

"Set out where?"

"The Bitterroot Valley." Wade would see Abby home, though it hurt to send her so far away.

"Have you nowhere you need to be? Don't you own a ranch?"

"My father owned a ranch, not me. No, I can go along with you and see you safely home."

Abby looked at her village.

High mountains rose up on the north and a waterfall cascaded down into the valley, feeding the stream that cut through the center of the village. That stream flowed red with blood. The smoldering ruins of the village made a mockery of the lush grass and newly leafed forest that grew along the valley's rim.

"There's nothing left here." Wade resisted the urge to pull her into his arms and comfort her. "Not for you, not for anyone."

Sid Garver charged his horse up the last hard mile of the trail into his canyon hideout.

The animal faltered, heaving, exhausted from the hard run as Sid spurred it on, desperate to get under cover after being seen at the Indian village. As he neared the well-concealed crevice that led into the heart of this mountain, he heard a shout from behind.

He reined his horse in, fighting the bit of the mustang that he'd been pushing past its limit for two hours.

Hoofbeats behind him stopped. He wheeled his horse to see Harvey wriggling on the ground like a landed trout.

"How 'bout I just shoot him, Sid?" Paddy O'Donnell had a big smile on his face. He swiped his mouth like the thought of emptying his gun into a friend made him drool with pleasure. "He's gonna be heavy to haul inside, and he's slowing us down."

They hadn't been slowed down at all. Harvey had stuck his saddle for this wild ride away from the Flatheads they'd slaughtered. But Sid wasn't entirely opposed to Harv dying. Harv had bought into this fight by grabbing that woman. They should've killed her like the rest. They could have cleaned out that trash then rode away and come back in a month. No one would have tied them to that massacre.

Sid swung down off his horse, nearly kicking the quiver and arrows that hung from his saddle horn. He'd grabbed them on an impulse, stripped them off the body of a big warrior. It had suited him, taking this trophy of their kill. Sid could understand the bloodlust that led a man to take scalps.

Ground-hitching his horse, Sid strode to Harv's side. It was obvious the man had been bleeding like a stuck pig the whole time they'd been riding. Sid hadn't looked back or offered to help.

Leaning over Harv's blood-soaked form, Sid thought about that beautiful critter this dumb ox had grabbed. All that blond hair stuck there in the middle of that Flathead village. Young and beautiful and feisty and hair glowing like gold.

Hard to blame Harv when Sid had wanted her himself.

But there was golden hair and there was just plain gold. Sid would have killed the woman without hesitation to clear the way to the gold. But he'd wanted those Flathead cleared out of there more and for the only reason Sid was gonna keep Harv alive.

"Grab him, Paddy." Sid didn't bother to ask Boog. The man had a bullet in his shoulder. Sid had been half afraid Boog would fall off his horse before they got home, too. But Boog was a hard man to bring down.

Paddy giggled as he swung down. He came up beside Harv. On opposite sides, the two of them hoisted Harv to his feet.

Harv clenched his jaw—his jaw slit by that wild woman's knife. She'd cut his face and his arm, and she'd opened up wounds on his chest and neck, too. Harvey had to know he was lucky to be alive. "She got my mask off, Sid." Harv grabbed Sid's shirtfront in a death grip. "I'm done riding with you if we can't shut her up."

"You mean she can identify you?" Sid hadn't so much as looked at Harv until they'd crossed the Flathead village and gone over the rim of that valley. Sid assumed Harv had pulled his mask down himself, though none of the rest of them did until they were well clear.

Sid's fingers itched to put a bullet in Harv right now. But Harv had the whole gang over a barrel and knew it. "Yep, we have to shut her up." It went against his grain to kill a woman. But if it came down to life and death, Sid reckoned he could do whatever was necessary.

Boog rode up beside them, his left arm hanging motionless at his side, blood soaking his shirtfront. His face was sheet white, but he still sat tall and steady in the saddle. "The man who shot me and saved the wild woman saw you, too."

Sid's jaw tensed. "You're sure? No one's gonna pay much attention to a half-wild woman been living with the Flatheads. But if a white man saw him. . ."

"I'm sure."

"You'll have to lie low awhile, Harv, till we make sure it's safe." Unless the cut turned septic and killed him. Save Sid the trouble but lose him a fortune.

Now someone had seen Harv's face. If the man who'd shot Boog had a sharp eye, he might recognize them even with their faces covered. Western men knew details—boots, guns, saddles, brands. You didn't always have to see a man's face to recognize him later.

Wildflower Bride

A gritty sound of pain escaped, but Harvey held his own weight and headed silently for his horse, which Boog had caught and led back. Nursing one arm, Harvey nearly fell as he struggled to remount.

"Just a coupla more miles and we can patch you up."

Harvey nodded, but he didn't unclench his jaw to speak.

Sid set a slower pace. There'd been no sign of pursuit, and they'd put hours and mountains between them and that village. They'd circled around the whole mountain valley because the man coming along had forced them to run for it to the west, but this canyon was on the east side of the Flathead village.

But now they could rest.

And plan.

CHAPTER 3

She was no longer Glowing Sun.

Her eyes flickered open at that thought. She didn't know how to be anyone else.

Abby. No last name to her recollection. Just Abby. She'd been ten. Surely she'd known her last name. But her life with her white family had faded completely.

A flash of her white father laid out in his grave came from somewhere deep in her memory, and she wondered how much else was there.

She pushed back the blanket salvaged from the wreckage of her village. As she sat up from where she'd slept near Wild Eagle's mother, she saw Wade sleeping on the far side of the fire. And no one else. "She's gone!"

Wade was on his feet, his gun drawn, before Abby had finished speaking. Looking around, seeing no gunmen, he holstered his weapon and rubbed his eyes. "Who's gone?" But he figured it out before she could answer. "She must have started out for the Bitterroot without us. They can't go back alone. She's hurt. The boy couldn't even walk yesterday."

"I suppose she decided she'd rather risk death than travel

with me." Abby pulled her knees up to her chest and leaned her face against them, closing her eyes against the pain. She'd known she wasn't her mother-in-law's choice for Wild Eagle. But Wild Eagle had wanted her, and the woman had accepted it. Only now did the woman show contempt. Maybe with the death of her family, all Wild Eagle's mother had left was hate and she'd needed to aim it at someone. Abby would never know.

"We'll catch up to them." Wade began packing his bedroll. "You can go to the larger village to live." Wade appeared eager to be rid of her.

"I won't return to the Salish people. That life is dead to me." She reached for her hair. Usually she carefully tended it, running a comb through it and braiding it every night. Then upon waking, she let the braid free, combing and braiding it again.

It reached nearly to her waist, and she'd had it unbraided when the men attacked yesterday morning. She'd washed it in the cold creek the night before the attack and let it dry in the spring breeze. Then all day yesterday, after Wild Eagle's mother's cruel words, she'd ignored it, hated it. She'd never given a thought to ridding it of its knots. She might as well have a rat's nest on her head for the snarls.

A sudden bitter wildness gripped her, and she pulled her knife. Hating her hair. Hating that her difference had separated her from the life she loved. She slashed a chunk of snarls away and grabbed for another.

Wade's running footsteps warned her, and she turned. He caught her hand. "Stop!"

"You like my hair, then?" She slammed the hank of white snarls against his chest. "Take it. I'd been kidnapped for it last time we met. My village had been slaughtered for it. Wild Eagle's mother hates me for it. My yellow hair affects white men like it is truly gold. It makes you all act like fools. So of course you like it, too, Wade."

"Glowing Sun, I didn't—" Wade held on to her knife-wielding hand.

"No!" She pulled against his grip, eager to fight, to rage instead of hurt. "My name is *Abby*. I will *never* answer to my Salish name again. Strike it from your mind."

Before she could attack, the sound of hoofbeats pulled her eyes toward the rim of the mountain valley.

Two horsemen appeared.

Wade shoved her behind him and pulled his gun with the soft *whoosh* of leather against steel.

They rode silhouetted against the morning sun and appeared only as black shapes, faceless. One led a packhorse behind him.

"Perhaps the men from yesterday have returned." Abby stepped to his left side. "Perhaps the gold of my hair is too much for the fools to resist."

Wade reached for her then looked at her knife. A smile spread across his face. A handsome face, Abby realized, though it was lost behind whiskers. And she remembered she'd thought so when they'd been together last fall. And now he seemed to approve of, even enjoy the fact that she'd drawn a knife.

What a strange heart for a white man. Not a brutish coward like those who had attacked her village. She well remembered from last fall that he'd also been kind when other white men had tried to take her from her village. Wade had come along and protected her. Not that she wasn't doing well at protecting herself, but he'd helped. And he'd been so kind. It was his kindness that had captivated her far more than his looks. His kindness had made her long to stay with him when she was promised to Wild Eagle.

And now he looked like a crazy man, his dark hair flowing, his beard covering every inch of his face. But his kindness was still there in every word and deed.

The disloyalty to Wild Eagle, only hours dead, shocked her into raising her knife toward the men.

"Wade!" one of the men called out.

"Stop!" With a lightning-quick move, Wade caught her hand as she prepared to send her knife whizzing at the intruders. "I know one of them. He's a friend. Red Dawson. These aren't the men who attacked you."

"He is white." She twisted, trying to escape his grip. "He cannot be trusted. You cannot be trusted."

"You trust me already, Abby. You're just mad. I don't blame you." Wade hung on gamely to Abby's wrist with his left hand while he holstered his gun with his right. "They mean us no harm."

Abby had to give Wade credit for not trusting her, because he wrested her knife away from her.

"Ow." He looked at a quarter-inch slit in his thumb, wiped the blood on his shirt, and arched one brow at her as he tucked the knife into his boot. "Behave yourself."

Abby wanted to claw his eyes out. The arrival of the two men intervened.

Red pulled up beside Wade and swung down, the other man just a moment behind him. "What happened here?"

The men studied the carnage and the long row of covered bodies stretched out alongside the stream. "Let me go and give me back my knife. Your friends are safe enough."

Wade gave her a penetrating look then released her and plucked the knife from his boot. "It was a massacre of Glowing Sun's. . .uh. . .Abby's. . ." Wade shook his head and ran his hand through his tousled hair. "This was a Flathead village. This woman, Abby, lived with them and was one of the few left alive." As Wade quickly told them the rest, Abby noticed he'd smeared blood on his forehead; his finger was cut more deeply than she'd realized.

"Glowing Sun?" The other man looked at Abby as he removed his hat. His long brown hair reminded Abby of Wild Eagle. Of course her Salish man's hair had been longer, but it was as thick.

"I've heard of you. I'm Silas Harden. I'm married to Belle Tanner Harden. Some drovers who helped with our cattle drive last fall told of a white woman named Glowing Sun who lived with the Flathead. It must be you."

"My name is no longer Glowing Sun." Abby's eyes narrowed. "With the slaughter of my village, I leave my Salish name behind. My name is Abby. The white name I was born with."

"So Buck made it to help with the drive?" Wade extended his hand. "I sent him. I'm Wade Sawyer."

Silas shook Wade's hand. "Yes, Buck, Roy, Shorty. Roy ended up marrying my daughter Lindsay."

"Honest?" Wade noticed he was bleeding when he left a streak of blood on Silas's hand. "He was just a boy."

Pulling out a handkerchief, Wade pressed the cloth to his wound. Disgusted with his fumbling efforts, Abby jerked the kerchief away from him and tied it tightly against the paltry cut.

"I know." Silas shook his head and crossed his arms in disgust. "And my daughter was too young. But we couldn't talk any sense into 'em."

When Abby was done with her bandaging, she looked up into Wade's eyes. He'd watched her, his head bent low. Now they were too close. Abby stepped back and to his side.

Silas looked at Abby, but there was no evil in his eyes, not like in the men who'd come yesterday. "They told us about the kidnapping and that Wade had gone after you when you ran off. I'm sorry about your village. Who did this?"

Abby shook her head silently.

"We don't know." Wade rubbed his bandaged thumb. "We haven't had time to turn our thoughts to tracking them down. There were wounded to tend. Two other survivors headed back to the main Flathead village in the Bitterroot Valley. What brings you out this way?"

The redheaded man pulled off his hat. Glowing Sun saw his serious expression and knew this wasn't a show of manners so much as a sign of respect for whatever news he carried.

"There's been an accident, Wade. Your pa's hurt bad. He asked for you. There've been people out looking for weeks. No one had seen a sign of you. Then the gap finally opened to the Tanner Ranch—"

"The Harden Ranch," Silas interrupted. "How long do you think it's gonna take for you to remember Belle's married?"

"It's not that I forget she's married. You're standing right here, after all. It's just hard to break the habit of wondering whether one of her husbands will last." Red shrugged one shoulder sheepishly.

One of her husbands will last? Abby had a sudden desire to meet this woman.

"You and half the other people around here." Silas shook his head, looking disgusted.

"Sorry."

"Work on it."

Red turned back to Wade. "Silas knew you'd been up in this country late last winter. The two of us've been scouting around for a week. This morning we finally found a trail and backtracked you here. You need to come home, Wade."

"That's not my home. Not anymore."

Abby was struck by how much Wade sounded like her.

"His back is busted up. He got thrown by a mustang out riding alone and lay there through a cold night."

"My pa fell off his horse?" Wade sounded incredulous.

"He hasn't been able to walk since. He's asking for you."

Wade shook his head. "Not interested."

Red rested one gloved hand on Wade's shoulder. "You can always leave again. Going to see him now is the right thing to do."

"I've told you what he's like. He's the one who—"

"Wade," Red said, cutting him off, "honor your mother and your father. It's as simple as that. Nowhere in that commandment does it say they have to deserve it. He's a broken man. Come, if only to say good-bye. He doesn't have long to live."

"That spiteful old man will live forever."

For the first time, Glowing Sun realized how young Wade was. She'd thought little of his age. But his words now were the words of a boy, not a man. Abby turned and glared at him. "Your father has asked for a chance to say good-bye. I have lost two fathers. You should cherish the father you still have."

"Cherish my father?" Wade looked at her, the kindness gone. It made him a different man, cold and empty, a stranger. "My father was a tyrant who. . .who. . ."

Wade sighed so deeply, Abby could see his whole body nearly empty of breath. He shook his head as if to clear it and shrugged. "Yes, of course I'll go. Let's get packed up."

"We can split what's left of our supplies between us and let Abby ride our packhorse."

He reached for Abby's arm but she evaded his touch. "I have no place with you. Ride away and return to your life."

Wade froze. "No. If you won't go with me, then I'll stay. I won't leave you here alone."

"I am alone, no matter where I go now. I cannot return to my village and I will not fit into the white world."

Wade squared off in front of her, as solid and unmoving as the mountains that surrounded them. "I won't leave you."

Abby stared at him. Their gazes held a long time. Too long. She knew he meant it. And she knew he needed to go home. Well, she'd ride along with him, then, and leave when he was busy saying good-bye to his father. With a snort of pure disgust, she said, "Fine."

They packed up in minutes.

"Don't you want us to stay and bury them?" Red asked.

"Glowing. . .uh. . .Abby. . .said her people would have a special rite for the dead. They'll be back to see to them."

Red looked doubtful, but after a long hesitation, he settled his Stetson firmly on his head and swung up onto his buckskin gelding.

"You've left Cassie alone at the ranch for a week?" Wade asked as he mounted his chestnut.

"I left her to visit Belle."

Wade blew a long, low whistle through his lips. "Do you know Belle Tanner?"

"Harden," Silas said through clenched teeth as he mounted his roan.

"Sure, I know Belle." Red sounded kind of sad.

Wade shook his head. "Cassie's never gonna be the same."

The men looked at each other for a long moment then started laughing.

Abby had no idea why.

They fell into line as the trail narrowed over the edge of the valley. She took one look back. This was the second life taken from her. It must be something about her. God must have created her to be alone.

Well, fine. She'd be alone. That suited her.

As they crested the valley walls, Red took the lead, glancing at Wade as he passed him. "You look like a wild man, Wade. You'd better shave and cut your hair before your pa sees you."

Without comment, Wade fell into place behind Red. He ran one hand into his beard, nodding. "I haven't given it a thought all winter."

Abby noticed that Silas brought up the rear. She wondered if that was because they thought she'd run. She ran her hand across the knife she'd hidden in the pouch at the small of her back. Well, they had the right of it. She would run. But not now. Not until she'd seen Wade home. He'd saved her from that awful murderous brute. In fact, he'd saved her last fall, too. So she was indebted to him, and that didn't sit right.

She'd see him home because she knew he wouldn't go otherwise.

And then they'd be even. She'd owe no white man.

CHAPTER 4

A bull charged straight for Cassie Dawson. She screamed, dropped her lasso, and threw herself sideways. The bull missed her by inches.

Landing on her backside, Cassie whirled around to see the bull skidding and wheeling around. She scrambled to her feet. Her hair came loose from its braid and the dark, waist-length strands blinded her.

Screaming again, she thought, *The fence. I have to get to the fence.*

The bull charged. Its hooves thundered.

There wasn't time. Cassie staggered back.

A rope flashed past Cassie's face so close she felt more than heard the whip of it. The noose snagged the bull around the neck. The animal jerked to a halt instantly, only inches from Cassie.

Cassie staggered backward then turned to see the fence not that far away. On shaky legs, she ran for it. She would have climbed over, but Belle Harden's voice stopped her as surely as if Belle had roped her, too.

"What did I tell you about getting in that pen?"

Cassie turned, pulling her hair back and out of her eyes, an apology already forming on her lips. But Cassie couldn't speak for the fire in Belle's eyes.

Belle finished hog-tying the bull then stood and strode toward Cassie. "Why'd you come in this pen alone?"

"I. . .I wanted to practice."

"After I told you how William died, gored by a bull?"

"Yes, but that isn't really a bull." She pointed to the calf struggling against the pigging strings.

Emma Harden, Belle's thirteen-year-old daughter, untied the little bull and it jumped to its feet and pawed the ground.

"Git!" Emma waved her arms. "Hiyah!"

The calf bawled like a little spanked baby, turned tail, and ran.

Cassie looked at Belle.

Belle narrowed her eyes. "Just because he's only a couple months old doesn't mean he can't knock you down and stomp you into the dirt. He proved it."

Cassie dusted the back of her skirt.

"Red would skin me alive if he found out you were in here alone. He's gonna be mad just findin' out I taught you to rope."

"Dinner's ready." Sarah's voice mercifully pulled attention away from Cassie. Belle's nine-year-old daughter stood just outside the door of the gracious log cabin with the long porch. The house was less than a year old, and Silas had built it big enough to leave room for company. . .or a growing family.

Belle's little girl Betsy clung to Sarah's skirt on one side. Cassie's firstborn, Susannah, had a hold on Sarah's other side. The two girls looked almost like twins. Both had curly black hair. Betsy's from her Italian daddy, Anthony Santoni, Belle's third husband, now mercifully dead. Susannah's hair came straight from Cassie, passed down from her grandmother, a Spanish countess. Susannah was just a few months older than Betsy.

With toddlers clinging to her knees, Sarah held the two babies in her arms. Little Michael, with bright red hair just like Red's, was perched on Sarah's hip. The other, Belle's newborn son,

Tanner, was cradled in Sarah's arm. Even at two weeks old, the child was the image of his pa, Silas Harden.

"I'm sorry. I shouldn't have come in this pen without you." Cassie had to choke out the apology. Honestly, Belle was bossier than Red.

"What'd I tell you, Cassie Dawson?" Belle jammed her fists on her hips.

Cassie suddenly wanted to laugh, but she wasn't going to. Belle had taught her better than that. She lifted her chin and forced herself to glare right into Belle's eyes. "I made a decision that I could handle that calf. Yes, I fell over, but I would have been fine. You"—she jabbed her index finger straight at Belle's chest—"are *not* going to speak to me like I'm a child."

Belle grinned.

"Nice work." Emma patted Cassie on the shoulder. "Real scary."

"Thanks, Em." Cassie's cheeks warmed up she was so pleased with the compliment on her dangerousness.

Belle rolled her eyes.

Sarah, with an entire nursery of children, approached enough to hear Cassie practice using her backbone. "That's real fierce. I'm not funnin' neither. I'd mind you right quick. Wouldn't you, Susannah?"

Susannah, nearly two, poked the fingers of both hands in her mouth as she nodded. Through her drooly fingers, she giggled and said, "Mama scary."

"Good." Belle smiled down at Cassie's little girl. "It's settled. Your mama is as fierce as can be." She turned back to Cassie. "We're getting you toughened up. You may never get onto roping a calf, but you're learning to push back when someone pushes you. That's a good lesson. You won't have Red riding roughshod over you anymore."

"Red's pretty sweet, Belle." Cassie knew it was wrong to think of Belle as her mother. Belle was only about ten years older. But the woman was fifty years smarter and a hundred years stronger. Still, they should be friends. But Belle treated thirteen-year-old Emma like more of an equal than Cassie. "He really doesn't ride roughshod over me."

"Best to be prepared just in case he starts. Now, promise me you'll practice with the calf I built you"—Belle pointed to a sawhorse with a longhorn skull hanging from one end—"instead of going in the pen."

"I promise." Long gone were the days when Cassie sat demurely in her mansion embroidering pillowcases and keeping her skirts tidy while she waited for her tyrant first husband, Lester Griffin, to come home. Since Griff had died and she'd married Red, she worked alongside him whenever possible. Of course, they had two children now and that slowed her down some. And Red had never let her so much as swing a rope, let alone try to hog-tie a steer.

Belle cleared her throat.

Cassie pulled her thoughts back to the lessons Belle was trying to teach her. "I mean, I promise because I *want* to, not because I'm taking orders from anyone." Cassie felt her cheeks heat up. It was just plain embarrassing to speak so rudely, but Belle insisted.

"Good girl." Belle patted her shoulder. "Try it without blushing next time. And you're getting better at roping, too."

"I can drop the rope over the fake calf every time now. From a moving horse, too. That's why I decided it was time to try a real critter."

"Red may be gone for weeks hunting that worthless Wade Sawyer."

"Wade's not worthless. I told you he's changed."

The noise Belle made in response definitely qualified as rude, and there wasn't a single speck of pink on Belle's cheeks. Cassie intended to learn that exact grunting noise.

"We'll work on roping and busting steers and the other chores any decent woman oughta know. It's unbelievable you've never learned bronc riding. What is Red thinking? If we don't get finished, maybe I'll start coming for a visit from time to time. Have you ever cracked a bullwhip?"

Cassie shook her head. She'd never even seen one. "I'd love to have you visit."

Reaching Sarah's side, Cassie took her precious son, Michael, into her arms and smiled down at Susannah. Her skin was as white as a porcelain doll with perfect pink blush painted on. Cassie had that same skin and the cheeks that wanted to blush at the least little provocation. "Hi, sweetie." Every time Cassie saw Michael's riot of red curls, she wanted to laugh and dance a jig. This little boy who looked like Red and her little girl who looked like her—her family was a gift straight from God.

"Hi, Scary Mama." Susannah hugged Cassie's knees.

Cassie laughed.

Emma swung Betsy up into her arms and tickled the dark-eyed toddler who giggled and squirmed.

Belle took her new little son, Tanner, in her arms and ran one gentle finger down his cheek.

Cassie patted Sarah, who had long red curls escaping her braid, thanks to Belle's second husband, Gerald O'Rourke, long dead and not mourned. Sarah and Michael looked like brother and sister though they shared no blood. The Irish bred true. "You're cooking for a crowd with me and my children here. I appreciate it."

"The three of you together don't eat as much as Pa. It's fun having company." Sarah, her arms empty, picked up Susannah.

The bunch of them went inside.

"What are we going to practice on next?" Cassie pulled out a chair for Susannah.

Sarah set the little girl down and tied a towel around her tummy to keep her from falling. Cassie took the chair next to her daughter, holding Michael on her lap.

"Have you ever branded and cut a calf? It's the time of year for it."

"Ma"—Emma washed her hands at the tidy sink—"Pa said

you're not to start branding while he's gone. He said it's too soon after the baby."

"We could just do a few for practice. He'd understand."

Emma wiped her hands, her head shaking. "I'm telling."

"Like he wouldn't notice anyway." Belle smiled. "How about I let you teach Cassie how to handle a branding iron and castrate a calf?"

"That'll work." Emma hung up the towel and went to the stove.

Sarah set a steaming hot bowl on the table. Emma added a teetering mountain of lightly browned biscuits.

"What's *castrated* mean?" Cassie began ladling the chicken stew Sarah had prepared, careful of Michael's grabbing fingers.

"I'll tell you after dinner." Belle sat down at the head of the table with her son tucked into the crook of her elbow.

"Why not now?"

"You need to finish your meal first."

"No, I don't. Tell me what it means?"

Belle stopped reaching for her fork and raised her eyes at Cassie, giving her a level look so daunting Cassie couldn't imagine ever standing up to Belle unless Belle gave permission. . .which wasn't really standing up to her at all. "Trust me, Cassie."

Cassie wondered if this was one of those times she should be rude and pushy. Something sparked in Belle's eyes that helped her decide to be patient. And anyway, the stew smelled good and she was starving.

Dinner got over.

Belle explained.

Cassie decided she'd never question Belle again.

❧

"The bleeding started up the minute I moved this morning." Boog unstrapped his arm, held in a sling by his belt. "We might as well use the branding iron. Get the fire red hot."

Sid didn't think Boog's arm was broken, but Sid was no doctor. He watched Boog grit his teeth as he pulled off his bloody shirt. The blood had soaked through the heavy padding they'd bandaged him with. The man didn't so much as moan. He was tough, no denying it.

Harv had complained all night like a little girl. His cuts were bad, especially where that wild woman had slit his chin, nearly cutting Harv a new smile in his chin hair. But Boog had a bullet pass through his shoulder and he'd never made a sound.

Sid shoved the iron deep into the flames.

"Don't you come near me with that thing." Harv scooted away from the fire, a dirty kerchief tied around his jaw to staunch the bleeding from his face.

"It'd help, Harv."

"No one's gonna close a wound on my face with a runnin' iron."

The running iron with its hooked tip could be used to alter any brand. They didn't rustle big-time, just enough for some odd cash. Sid had a lot bigger dreams than rustling. He aimed to rustle an empire from Mort Sawyer.

But money got tight for whiskey, so sometimes they'd grab a few calves, drive 'em in this dead-end canyon. They'd fix the brands then let 'em grow awhile before they sold 'em so the brand healed and looked pretty good. They'd even registered brands that were easy to twist around and turned Sawyer's M Bar S, Linscott's Double L, and Dawson's D Bar into the brands the gang claimed. Now that the gap had melted and they could get into that high valley the Harden Ranch claimed, they could run off a few cows from there, too.

"It's not like you're purdy'r nuthin'." Paddy laughed as he leaned back against a tree trunk that sat alongside their campfire, looking at Harv.

Harv's fingers twitched, and for a second Sid thought Paddy had pushed himself right into the business end of a shootout. But

Harv didn't draw, and Paddy was too busy laughing to notice he'd almost died.

Boog, who didn't miss much, slid his cold eyes between the two, his six-gun strapped down. His shooting hand still worked just fine. "Let's get this over and done." Boog sat down by the fire and reached for the iron.

"I'll do it." Sid needed Boog, make no mistake about it. He needed Harv, too, and that gnawed at his gut because Harv was slowing them down. "You can't burn your own wound."

"I have before." Boog's ice blue eyes, as cold and dead as coffin nails, flickered away from the iron and steadied on Sid's face.

Sid felt death whisper across his skin like sleet. Sid moved cautiously, as if Boog was a ten-foot rattler. "So you want help or not?"

Boog nodded.

The dull rasp of the iron against the burning wood brought Harv forward, eyes riveted on the red-hot metal. Even Paddy shut up and got serious.

Carefully, Sid barely touched the oozing wound then pulled back the instant Boog's skin hissed.

The four of them were silent as Boog closed his eyes, his teeth clamped shut against any sound of pain. The smell of burnt flesh burrowed into Sid's nose.

Boog looked up at Sid. Killing-mean eyes. Sid's stomach churned. One wrong move right now and Sid would be dead on the ground just because Boog hurt so bad he needed to hurt someone else.

"Now do the other hole." Boog's voice sounded like a thousand miles of jagged rock.

Sid swallowed his fear as he moved around to stab this dangerous man in the back. Again the hiss. Again the silence. Sid had a new appreciation for the steel at the core of his saddle partner.

Sid set the running iron aside and went back to his place by the fire while they all waited silently for Boog to stop wanting to kill someone.

At last Boog spoke. "We need. . .need to get back to Sawyer's." His faltering speech was the only concession he'd make to the pain. "We've been gone long enough. Questions will be asked if we're away longer. But I'll be laid up a couple more days."

Sid suspected Boog should have been laid up in bed, with a doctor's care, for two weeks. Instead he asked for two days.

"I'll go back now with Paddy." Sid was glad for the excuse to be rid of both wounded men. "We'll leave you and Harv here to heal and tell the cowhands you got sidetracked and'll be along shortly."

Boog's eyes slid to Harv. "No, I'm not sittin' here listenin' to Harv whine like a little girl for days. I'll kill him just to shut him up. And there goes that gold you're so hungry for, Sid. I'm going along with you. We'll tell 'em we had a run-in with rustlers. Tell 'em they dry-gulched us and got away."

"What if we see that spitfire of a girl? She can identify me." Harv plucked at the caked blood in his black beard and fell silent.

Sid had no doubt Harv wouldn't survive being left behind with a wounded, surly Boog. The only reason Sid hadn't plugged him was that gold. "We're biding our time until the boss dies. No heirs since he cut that worthless bum of a son out of his will. Once Mort is gone, I'll stake my claim to the ranch."

"There'll be some others that want it for themselves," Boog warned.

Sid nodded. "And they can fall off their horses just as easy as Mort did." Sid stood and started saddling Boog's horse. He knew better than to ask, because Boog wouldn't accept help from any man. He'd saddle his own bronc if he were hog-tied and buried up to his neck in scorpions.

Boog's eyes narrowed but he let Sid work.

"What about the gold? We don't need the ranch if we get the

gold." Harv's shifty eyes darted between Sid and Boog. He was a man without honor, so he expected none from anyone else. Sid knew that Harv realized his knowledge of that cache of gold was the only thing keeping him alive.

Sid suspected Harv had the situation with the gold and the ranch about right. "I want both. The ranch and the gold. And if Mort don't up and die pretty soon, I might just give him a shove right through the Pearly Gates."

Boog made a sound Sid had never heard from the man before. Narrowing his eyes, Sid said, "What?"

"Mort Sawyer in heaven." Boog snorted, shook his head, and then snorted with amusement again. It was as close to a laugh as Boog had ever come in Sid's presence.

CHAPTER 5

"You sure you don't want anything from your cabin?" Red asked Wade for the fourth time.

"Nothing there. Food for a few days, nothing I want."

"We can lay up at my place overnight." Silas pulled up as the four riders reached a trail that climbed up a treacherous, snaking path. "See what the womenfolk are up to."

Wade looked up that narrow trail, dreading the journey home. He'd ridden in near silence all day, switching between his imagination—dreading what his father would have to say—and prayer. The afternoon was wearing on and it'd be deep into the night before they got to Pa's ranch, if Wade rode straight through.

The June days were getting longer, but in the Rockies the sun set early if a body stood in the shade of the mountain. And the shade of the mountain was everywhere. Staying at the Tanner Ranch was a one-day reprieve. It'd give him a chance to clean up, shave, wash his clothes, and work up his nerve. "Sounds good to me."

"Agreed." Red tugged on his hat brim. "It's too far to travel to your ranch tonight."

"Pa's ranch. Not mine."

Red gave Wade a sharp look. "Tomorrow I'll go on with you, Wade. I told Mort I'd see you all the way home."

Wade couldn't hide much from Red. The Dawsons were the best friends he'd ever had in his whole miserable, friendless life. "I don't need a babysitter, Red." Wade could barely speak through a jaw that seemed permanently locked in a grim line.

"No"—Red clucked to his buckskin and headed up a trail that'd scare a mountain goat into a dead faint—"but you could use a friend."

Wade nodded silently and veered his thoughts away from whatever ugliness his father would have waiting. Red knew him well enough that no thanks were needed.

Glowing Sun. . .no, Abby. . .sat her horse quietly while the men talked. Today her name was Abby, so he'd use it, even make himself think it. Abby had to come along to Pa's ranch. Wade had to take care of her. She'd lost her whole life. So if she didn't come home with him, he wasn't going.

Silas fell in behind Red. Abby watched Silas quietly. She had a way about her of observing everything. Wade was sure the woman would be able to follow this trail back to her home without hesitation. He wondered if she had plans to do such the minute he wasn't watching. But what did "home" mean with her village wiped out?

She glanced at him, and he tipped his head for her to go next. She shrugged and started up. The trail was narrow enough that they rode single file and it was easy to stay quiet.

"Whom shall I fear?"

It was a psalm. One of Wade's favorites. The Twenty-seventh. *"The Lord is my light and my salvation; whom shall I fear? The Lord is the strength of my life; of whom shall I be afraid?"* I've spent my whole life being afraid. God, I'm sorry about that man I shot. Give me peace in my soul about pulling that trigger.

The irony was, if Wade told his pa he'd shot an outlaw, Mort Sawyer would be proud. If Wade talked about how sick it made him, Mort would be ashamed.

Everything Mort stood for and respected was completely at odds with Wade's way of thinking. And how many thousands of times had Pa made sure Wade knew what a disappointment he'd turned out to be?

Wade repeated *"Whom shall I fear?"* whenever he imagined conversations with his father, imagined rage, imagined blows. The worst was Wade's imagined blows in return. He caught himself daydreaming about venting years' worth of fury on his father.

That was the real reason it made him sick to think about putting a bullet into that brutish man. Because on a very deep level, Wade wasn't sorry. He was glad he'd shot the man. He wished he'd have killed him. Killed them all. And that bloodlust led back to his anger with his father.

A terrible sin, to imagine hurting my father. I'm sorry, God. It's driven by fear. All the anger and vengeance is based on fear. Because I know my father can hurt me. Not with his fists anymore, but his words feel like a beating. "Whom shall I fear? Whom shall I fear?"

Pa couldn't hit him. Wade was an adult. If his father, even when he was healthy, had attacked, Wade would have gotten away. He wasn't a child trapped in that house with nowhere to go. But it was so hard to leave the childish fear behind.

"Greater is he that is in you, than he that is in the world." The Bible said so. Jesus was in Wade's heart. Jesus was greater. *"Whom shall I fear?"*

Wade had stored up scriptures about fear and strength and courage since he'd become a believer. Red and Cassie had helped him search for verses that gave him strength against the things that tormented him, and now he clung to them.

And he clung also to the dream of being a light in his father's life. That would be the true test of courage. Not hitting back or shooting a bad man but speaking honestly of his love for God and of how much his father needed that love, too.

He'd already talked to his father about faith. It ended ugly.

Maybe that was why he was going home now. To try again.

After a grueling climb and descent, they approached Silas's house riding four abreast as the setting sun washed red and orange across the land. From a distance, they saw dust kicked up from a corral.

"That's Cassie. She's riding. Cassie doesn't ride." Red kicked his horse into a trot.

Wade was on Red's right, Abby next to Wade with Silas on Abby's right. They picked up the pace to stay even with Red.

Shaking his head, Wade found his first smile for a long time. "Belle must've taught her."

"My Belle knows how to train girls to handle themselves." Silas looked across Abby to smile at Red.

"But she. . .she always rode to town on my lap." Red tilted his hat back. "I kind of liked that." They closed the distance to the corral.

"There's four of you now, Red." Wade had stayed at the Dawson place for long stretches, working as a hand for Red. He well remembered carrying the baby while Red carried Cassie. The little woman was scared to death of riding. "That would've been a load for a single horse."

Wade knew that when he wasn't around, Red carried Cassie while Cassie carried Susannah with the baby on Red's back.

"She's doing good, isn't she?" Red's voice was thick with pride.

They'd drawn near enough that Wade could see Cassie twirl a rope. "Look at her with the lasso."

The noose shot out and snagged a yearling steer. Cassie's pony dug in its heels and jerked the calf off its feet. Hitting the ground, Cassie fell toward the calf, straight into the thrashing hooves.

With a cry of alarm, Red lashed his reins on the horse's shoulder, and the buckskin leapt into a flat-out run.

Wade was one second behind, goading his chestnut, charging toward the disaster.

Red pulled up at the corral and hit the ground sprinting.

Just then Cassie stood up out of the churning dust, her hands raised high in triumph.

"I did it!" Her teeth gleamed white in her dirty face as she smiled.

"Cassie!" Red vaulted the fence.

Whirling at his voice, Cassie laughed aloud. "Did you see me hog-tie that calf? I'm going to brand him then cut him. Emma's going to—"

"Belle Tanner, you get over here." Red's face turned the color of a beet. He was enraged.

Cassie had taken several running steps toward him, but she stumbled to a halt at his tone. Her arms lowered. The smile shrank off Cassie's face.

Red turned toward the group of women sitting on the fence. Wade recognized Belle and little Susannah. But the rest of the brood were strange to him—except the infant with hair the color of a carrot had to be Red's son, and he knew Belle had a brood of young'uns.

"It's Harden." Silas joined them in the pen. "Belle Harden. Try to remember that."

Wade stood outside the fence to watch the fireworks. He and Abby dismounted and shared a look.

"Belle, you promised me you wouldn't start spring branding until I got back." Silas pulled his gloves off and glared at his wife as he tucked them behind his belt buckle.

Wade whispered to Abby, "I know Belle Tanner. . .uh. . .I mean Harden, a little. Silas is a brave, brave man to talk to her that way."

Abby arched a brow at Wade.

"What'd I tell you, Cassie Dawson?" Belle climbed over the fence with economical movements, striding toward the bawling, thrashing calf. Her spurs jingled, her holstered six-gun slapped against the hip of her leather riding skirt. She released the hog-tied little guy.

Cassie nodded and marched right up to stick her nose in Red's scowling face.

Red was an easygoing man for a fact. He didn't get mad often. Wade had only seen it a few times. But when Red's temper blew, it flared as hot and red as his hair. Wade resisted the urge to go put himself between Cassie and that anger.

Red took his eyes off Belle to face his wife. "What are you—"

"Don't you speak to me that way, Red Dawson." She jabbed him right in the second button of his broadcloth shirt. "I am an adult woman, not a child. If I think a calf needs to be thrown and branded, then I'll do it."

Red's mouth formed a hard straight line as he glared down at his wife.

His wife glared right back.

It wasn't much of a standoff, because Red quit glaring and started grinning. "You roped that calf like a real cowboy, honey. And you were riding to beat all, too. Scared me half to death, which is why I blew my stack. I'm sorry. I'm so proud of you." He circled her trim waist with one arm, yanked her against him, and swooped down to fetch himself a kiss right there in front of all of them.

By the time he quit, the whole group was clapping. Cassie had her arms tight around Red's neck and her toes dangling off the ground.

"What else did Belle teach you to do while I was gone?"

"I can't wait to tell you. I missed you, Red. And Michael learned to clap his hands."

"I missed you all something fierce." He hugged her hard then set her on the ground. With his arm around her waist, they walked together toward the gathering of children.

Silas walked over to Belle. "You promised me you wouldn't start spring work. You just had a baby."

Wade thought Silas sounded more resigned than mad.

"I didn't do a thing, Silas." Belle raised both hands to shoulder level as if it were a robbery. "Emma worked with Cassie. I gave advice and watched from the fence. I kept my promise. Besides, I trusted you with the roundup. I knew you'd be back."

Silas kissed her on the nose. "Thank you."

Belle's return kiss was much warmer. "Tanner's double the size since you left."

Silas turned to look at the baby, and they headed toward the group.

Loneliness welled up inside Wade as he watched that smiling crowd fussing over babies. Red hoisted Susannah high in the air.

She squealed with laughter and yelled, "Papa's home!"

Red accepted his warm welcome-home from sweet, beautiful Cassie. Silas was welcomed just as thoroughly by that tough-as-nails Belle Tanner. . .Harden. Wade was so impressed he decided he'd try to learn the woman's new name. This husband just might last.

He looked sideways at Abby. "You want to go meet 'em all?"

Abby had been watching, too. Now she turned to Wade. Her eyes were sad, aching. He wondered if she was thinking about her Flathead village or her mother or her husband. She'd lost so much.

Soft feelings had sprung up between Abby and Wade last fall. Had she ever thought of *him* with a sad, aching look in her eyes? But why would she when she had a warrior at her side?

"Abby, when we get to my father's ranch, there's a woman there who cooks and cleans for us."

"Your mother?"

"No, my mother died a long time ago. But Gertie runs the house. She has her own private room and there'd be one for you near her. She would welcome your company. She's always been able to handle my father, and she'll teach you how, too." Wade smiled, but he didn't feel one ounce of happiness. "She could never teach me. But she spent a lot of time taking care of me after—" Wade fell silent.

Abby hesitated. "After what?"

Wade tensed and didn't answer. There was no good reason for her to go home with him. He only knew he wanted her by his side when he faced his father. "If you don't go with me, then I'll go with you, Ab. I'm not letting you just wander off alone into the wilderness." He said it as if he was worried about her, and he was. But he was almost as worried about himself.

"I will go as far as your ranch. If staying there suits me, I will stay until it no longer suits me."

"Thank you." Wade exhaled like a weight had lifted. He rested a hand on her upper arm and guided her around the corral to where the happy families congregated.

They saw Susannah squirming to get down. Red let her go and took the baby in his arms. Susannah went scurrying off toward some scrub brush nearer the cabin.

"Susannah, come back here." Cassie smiled at the active little girl and went after her.

Wade reached the group just as a rattling sound jerked everyone in the group around. Only one creature made that deadly rattle. Wade, Red, Silas, and Belle all drew their guns.

"Susannah!" Cassie was in their line of fire. With a wild leap, Cassie hurled herself forward, stretched flat, inches above the ground.

A rattlesnake uncoiled from the brush, launching itself at the toddler.

A dull *thud* and the snake's head stopped. Momentum carried the rattling end of the snake forward. The snake's coils twisted around her and Susannah.

Cassie hit the ground on her belly. The rattler's head was pinned to the ground by a narrow, razor-sharp knife.

Cassie shrieked and flailed at the snake. Red reached the two of them and swooped Susannah into his arms as he tried to get the bleeding snake off Cassie.

Wade, Silas, Belle, and Emma were only a step behind.

Cassie shoved at the moving snake, screaming.

Susannah started crying, frightened by her mother. Betsy and Michael bought into the noise, too.

The group extracted Cassie from the coils and comforted Susannah.

When Cassie was on her feet and double-checked for injuries, Silas looked at Belle. "Did you throw that?"

"Not me." Belle holstered her six-gun.

One by one, they all looked between each other then finally turned and looked at Abby. Wade noticed she only had eyes for the snake.

She strode toward the long, brownish-gray striped creature, jerked her knife free, and beheaded the serpent with a quick, ruthless swipe. Cleaning her blade by stabbing it into the ground, she returned it to the sheath at the back of her skirt waistband and picked up the rattler.

"Supper." She sounded satisfied. Hungry, too. "Enough for everyone to have a bite. I know how to prepare it so the poison doesn't—" She turned and looked at the others, all transfixed by the sight of that perfectly thrown knife and that long, still-wriggling snake. "What?" She glanced at the snake.

"You saved her," Cassie sobbed. "You saved my baby girl."

"You act surprised." Abby frowned as if Cassie wasn't talking rationally. "Far wiser to use the knife than your body. Do you know this snake is deadly if you let it bite you?"

Cassie flung her arms around Abby's neck.

Abby staggered back a step and held her arms out at her sides, obviously shocked.

"Uh, we'll probably just have beef stew." Wade carefully reached for the snake dangling from Abby's fingers. "Not rattlesnake. Okay?"

He didn't want to upset Abby; after all, she'd just saved Cassie's life. But he wasn't eating snake. If he'd been starving. . .maybe.

Abby, with Cassie hanging from her neck, shrugged. "Rattlesnake is a special treat, but if the meal is already cooking. . ."

Wade tossed the snake away with terrified energy coursing through his veins at Susannah's near miss.

"No, wait. Save the rattle. The children will enjoy playing with it."

"Let's wait to get the toy until Cassie calms down a bit." Wade patted Abby on her arm.

Chaos erupted as everyone rushed forward to thank Abby.

Wade caught Abby looking from one grateful person to another as they swamped her. She acted as if they were foreign creatures. More dangerous to her than the snake.

Before long, Belle had Abby at her side talking. The two were swapping advice on how to best skin a buck.

Cassie gave Wade a smile and yanked on his beard. "It's good to see you. I didn't recognize you at first. You look a fright." She gave him a quick kiss on his furry cheek then turned to go with the women.

"Keeping your knife razor sharp is the secret." Belle pulled her knife out of her boot.

Abby produced her own skinny blade. "My stone got left behind at my village."

"It's sharp." Belle admired it. "You did this with a stone? Can you show me? We've got a whetstone, but I haven't been able to get the edge I want with it. I always use my strop." Belle turned to Cassie. "Let's sharpen yours while we're at it."

Cassie produced a knife. Wade was too surprised to notice where it came from.

"You're carrying a knife now, honey?" Red, looking uncertain, pushed his hat back and scratched his head.

"Belle said I should. A woman has to be able to take care of herself." Cassie followed after the other women, Emma and Sarah included, leaving the men alone with two babies and Susannah.

"Why did you throw your body instead of your knife?" Abby asked Cassie.

Wade didn't hear the answer.

Red dropped back to walk beside Silas and Wade. "Uh. . .I don't know if Cassie should carry a knife. She might cut herself."

"Or you." Wade chuckled.

Silas slapped Red on the back.

Susannah slapped Red smartly on the ear. "I wanna knife, Papa."

Red groaned.

Silas started laughing.

The three men got along well. Which was a good thing, because without knowing exactly how it happened, they ended up being ousted from the house after supper to bunk down in the barn. Sure, the house was crowded, but Wade had a strong notion that Red and Silas would have liked to sleep next to their wives.

Maybe Wade wouldn't rush into learning Belle's new name after all.

CHAPTER 6

Abby watched the tension grow in Wade until she thought he might snap.

He looked more like himself with his hair cut short and his face clean shaven. It was easier to separate herself from the horror of her village riding beside Wade as he'd looked last fall. She did her best to turn her mind away from the death she'd witnessed. The gunshots still rang in her ears. The blood was there every time she closed her eyes. She tried to shut it down by focusing on Wade and this strange world of the whites.

She'd let Cassie convince her to don a gingham dress. It pushed up high on her legs as she rode her barebacked pony. Wade had urged her to use a saddle, but she'd refused to load the horse down with heavy leather and iron.

The closer they rode to Wade's ranch, the tighter his jaw clenched. Tension vibrated off him in nearly visible waves.

A rugged trail opened to lush valleys of grass edging along the mountain slopes. As they rounded an outcropping of rock, Wade pulled up and turned on the trail to face her. "You told me you were a believer, a Christian. . .is that right?"

Abby wondered what the man was fretting over now. She

thought of Wild Eagle and the steady way he faced everything. He rarely laughed, rarely got angry. He was a rock she could lean on. But a rock was hard, and she'd been hurt by that hardness many times. Abby felt like she knew every thought that went through Wade's head, and if she couldn't figure it out, she just had to wait a bit because he'd tell her.

"Yes, a Blackrobe lived among our people. He spent part of the winter with us, in our winter hunting grounds. He told us of the white man's God and how He'd given His life to save us. A beautiful story, a story only God would have written. Our small village embraced Jesus. As I learned more, I remembered stories my own parents had told me of Jesus and Christmas and Easter. When the Blackrobe heard me speak to him in his tongue, he let me say his white words to my people in their tongue."

"I noticed that you have been speaking English well. Would it be okay if we prayed right now?"

"Prayed? You and I together?"

"Yes. Once we round this bend, you'll see my father's house. I don't want to make a show of praying in front of the cowhands or my father. There aren't many believers among them. I'd like to go in there with another believer at my side." Wade shook his head. "I've been praying since Red came to tell me I had to go home. I should have let Red come along. He's a wise man. He fills in for the circuit rider in Divide, but he'd been on the trail a long time searching for me. He needed to get home."

"What is it you pray for?"

A humorless laugh escaped from Wade's lips. "Courage."

"Are you lacking courage? I had not noticed."

Wade tilted his head a bit. "Thank you. But when it comes to my father. . .I'm afraid of everything. Afraid of what he'll say. He has a cruel tongue, Abby. And there's more. I'm afraid of my own anger. Red told me I'm to honor my father, and I know that's true. God sets it down in the Good Book as a commandment. But my thoughts toward Pa are angry, even violent. I want to yell back at him all the angry words that I've got in my head, and I know that's a sin."

"Why is it a sin to tell him of your anger?"

"Because I picture myself screaming, 'I hate you.' And in my mind, while I yell that, I punch him and pay him back for all the years and years of hurt I suffered at his hands."

Abby pursed her lips. "Well, take out the screaming and the punching, but the rest is just honest. There can be no honor without honesty. The words are the same."

Wade looked at her as if he wanted to see inside her mind. "That's true. I could just be honest but without the fury. I see rage as a sign of strength. But that's from Pa. Truth is strong and needs no anger." He nodded his head then rode up beside her so they faced each other. "It would be a. . .a light. There is so much darkness on the M Bar S."

Wade tugged his hat off and hung it from his saddle horn, pulled away a single leather glove, and held out his bare hand. "Will you join me?"

Knowing it was what he expected for some reason, Abby took his hand. When he closed his eyes, she followed his lead.

It was a simple prayer. As he spoke quietly of his desire to be sinless and courageous, a sudden image of her white father kneeling beside her bed, holding her hand and praying with her, flickered and was gone. Was that a memory or her imagination? Was it just once, at the end of his life when he knew the family was dying? Or had it been a normal part of her day? For some reason she thought of bedtime and prayer together. But it was only an impression. There was no memory beyond that lightning-quick image of her father in prayer.

Wade finished his heartfelt words then looked up. Their eyes caught. Their hands held. A moment stretched too long and still neither of them looked away. Wade hadn't given much thought to riding together, only Abby and him, for a few hours. But as he looked at her, he knew it was well they weren't together longer.

At last Wade quietly dropped her hand. "Thank you, Abby."

They rode forward, and it was as Wade had said. The second she rounded the outcropping of rocks, she saw the massive log house. "What kind of fool builds such a house in this cold land?"

Wade turned to face her, his brow furrowed. "A fool? You're calling my father a fool?"

Not the best way to get along with Wade, but she reminded herself that she didn't want him touching her hand. She didn't want to look deeply into his eyes again. She had no wish to get along with Wade, so it mattered nothing if she insulted his home. "How many hours a day does he spend chopping wood to keep a fire going to warm such a monstrosity?"

Considering he was wound tight as a coiled rattler, that Wade managed to smile seemed akin to a miracle. "That's good for me to hear. My father does struggle to keep it warm. And even with hired men chopping the wood for it, it's never really comfortable in the winter."

"And winter lasts half the year." Abby sniffed her contempt. "Better to live in a tepee. One small fire would warm your entire home."

Wade squared his shoulders. He appeared to have relaxed a bit. Perhaps she should insult his father more. It seemed to agree with him.

"How many trees were cut down so your father could be so... so...grand?"

"Too many. My pa was never one to worry about what he took from the land, only what it could give him." He looked her straight in the eye. "I'm glad you decided not to stay with Belle."

"Your offer of a job was the only way I could think to take care of myself right now. I have nowhere else to go."

They rode up to the house, Wade on his chestnut, Abby on a roan mare.

Dismounting, Abby followed Wade up the four steps of the porch that stretched the length of this monster of a house.

Wildflower Bride

The door swung open. A woman as wide as she was tall moved with startling speed for one so elderly. She darted across the broad porch and flung her arms around Wade.

Her weight and enthusiasm nearly knocked Wade down the steps. He grabbed for a sturdy pillar and caught himself in time.

"My boy! My boy is home!"

Wade hugged the woman close, leaning his tall frame down to press his cheek on the gray head.

Abby had to wonder if Wade was correct about his mother being dead. It didn't seem like the kind of thing a man would be mistaken about.

"I heard about Pa."

The woman nodded her head but didn't speak, her face still buried in Wade's chest.

Abby came up beside Wade and watched the reunion. The longing she felt for this kind of contact was stunning. Her Salish... no...Flathead—that was the white word—mother had been kind to her, but the woman wasn't given to hugs. Her Flathead father had been as quiet as Wild Eagle. Abby had no memory of her own long-lost ma.

A fleeting image of a woman as thin as a sapling pulling Abby onto her lap was there in her mind. Was that her white mother?

Ma. . . Yes, thinking of the woman as Ma fit. But what other name? What first or last name? It itched inside Abby's mind that she'd so completely left her white family behind. Perhaps more would come back to her now that she had reentered the white world. As she thought of that, her anger welled up. The white world had killed her Flathead family. But now the rest of her tribe didn't want her. She belonged nowhere.

The woman pulled away from Wade, wiping her eyes on her apron. Finally, she looked up. "Mort's fit to be tied. Laid up in bed, near to thrash anyone who comes within reach. He's spitting mad that he can't move his legs. The foreman comes and takes his orders and gives reports. Besides him, I'm the only one who goes in his room. It's like trying to talk to a wounded grizzly."

Wade's shoulders slumped. Abby knew he was dreading this meeting.

"He's been shouting for someone to find you and bring you home. He won't be happy to see you, though. He'll just take more of his temper out on you, son. I'm sorry."

"I'll see him and give him a chance, Gertie." Wade slid his arm around the stocky woman's shoulders. "That's all I'll promise."

"No." Gertie's hand clamped on Wade's. "Give me more than that. We need you here, Wade. The men aren't working anymore. Most of the old reliable hands have left. And new ones have come in that. . .that scare me."

She looked hard into his eyes. Abby felt the force of the woman's will and knew this one was strong. Despite the tears and the hugs, there was an iron core in the woman.

"I can't leave your pa, and I'm afraid to stay. Afraid for both him and myself. Please promise me you won't leave, at least as long as your pa is alive. Once he's gone—the doctor says he can't live long like this—we can let the jackals take the ranch."

"Take the ranch?" Wade shook his head quickly. "It's Pa's ranch. Who's gonna take it?"

"Anyone who's strong enough, Wade. This is the West. There's no law outside the city limits of Divide. And precious little there."

"Divide's a quiet little town, Gertie."

"Not since the rustling started." Her tight bun quivered as she shook her head. "People are on edge. Mort's new hands are too quick with a gun. The old sheriff quit and moved to Helena to live with his son. The new one isn't strong enough to keep the peace. Mort either holds this place or loses it with the strength of his back and his will. And his back doesn't work anymore."

"Let's go see him."

"Promise me first."

Wade fell silent.

They stepped inside the house.

Abby's eyes widened at the huge living room stretching to her left. A set of stairs rose up along her right. Doors opened on the left side and at the far end of the massive room. Foolish whites to close in the outside then be forced to heat it and clean it. Waste. Pride. She was ashamed of the color of her skin. "Foolish."

Wade turned to her.

The old woman did, too.

"Excuse my manners. You taught me better than this, Gertie. Let me introduce Abby. We found her along the trail. Her. . .uh. . ."

Abby saw him flounder. They hadn't discussed what to tell people. Did she want the whole world to know she'd spent years with the Flathead tribe? In the gingham dress Cassie had given her, with her hair neatly braided, she outwardly fit in with the white world, even though her soul boiled with contempt for the whites, for their violence and lust for her blond hair and their stupid, immovable homes.

"My family died." She could hear the stilted tone of her voice. She had rediscovered her white language almost completely. She wondered if one day soon she wouldn't be able to remember her Indian family just as she had forgotten her white family. How did her mind do that? Separate her from her past like this? "Wade came along and helped me. I have nowhere to go."

"I told her there would be work for her. What about it, Gertie? Could you use a hand?"

Gertie looked Abby up and down. Her eyes had the sage look of the oldest women of the Flathead village. Finally, Gertie nodded. "I can always use help. I'd be glad to have you, Abby. . . ." Gertie fell silent, letting the phrase hang.

Abby shrugged.

"Salish." Wade gave Abby a look of apology like it was his fault that she'd been cornered into telling a lie. "Her name is Abby Salish."

Gertie nodded. But Abby saw those sharp eyes and knew the

strange exchange between Abby and Wade hadn't been missed. "Well, Abby, you might as well go on into the kitchen. No need for you to listen to Mort's poison."

Wade's arm snaked out and grabbed Abby. "No, I've told her about Pa, and she's been giving me a hard time for not honoring my father. I want her to see Mort Sawyer in action." Wade turned, challenging Abby with a look.

Abby lifted her chin. "I would love a chance to have my father back. You should appreciate him more."

A roar sounded from upstairs. "Gertie! Get this slop away from me!"

Wade arched his brows at Abby as if daring her to honor that angry man.

"Let's go meet your father."

CHAPTER 7

Once when he was a young teenager, Wade and a couple of cowhands he rode with had surprised some rustlers using a running iron on a calf. Wade's horse had been shot out from under him in the chaos. He'd used that dead horse as a shield from flying bullets.

Now he was the horse. Or at least he felt like the poor beast must have as he led the way up to his father's room with Gertie and Abby hiding behind him.

Pa's shouting got louder, maybe because they were closer, but Wade thought the rage was building, too.

Abby straggled behind. Wade already knew she wasn't one to hide. But Gertie very definitely had Wade smack in front of her.

The coward.

Wade reached for the doorknob.

"You get up here!" The door seemed to shake under the impact of his pa's anger.

"Gertie! Gertie, you're fired. You worthless—"

Wade stopped as the tirade grew more hateful. He looked behind him at Gertie's wide eyes.

"You get fired often?" Wade whispered, as if, if Pa didn't hear his voice, he still had a choice of running.

The threats and insults continued.

"About six times a day," Gertie whispered back. "Until he needs something. Then he starts in shouting for me to fetch for him."

Mort let loose a stream of language that made Wade want to cover Gertie's and Abby's ears. His own, too. But he was short on hands. Wade shook his head in disgust.

Then he noticed Abby's contemptuous expression. "This is how a man speaks to his woman? This is what passes for strength in a white man's world?"

Wade noticed she didn't whisper. He also noticed his father quit hollering.

"I'm not his woman," Gertie said.

Wade thought he saw a pained expression in Gertie's eyes. Had she nurtured dreams, ever, that Pa would marry her? He should have, Wade realized. Gertie had cared for Pa, his child, and his home faithfully for over a decade. But Wade had never seen so much as a breath of romance pass between the two.

Sucking in a deep breath, Wade twisted the knob and swung the door open. His father sat up in bed. Their eyes met.

Silence.

Wade stepped in, braced for the insults and threats. He decided to start first. Chances were, once Pa got wound up, he wouldn't hear anything Wade said anyway. "I heard you sent for me, Pa. Well, I'm here. Here to help if you'll have me, with your care or your ranch, wherever you need me."

Wade hadn't meant to say that. In fact, until Gertie's pleading at the front door, Wade had fully intended to come, listen to whatever spiteful things his pa had to say, and leave. Most likely he'd be ordered to leave. But Gertie had asked, and the sight of his pa in that bed was shocking. Pa's strength of will was still there, but he no longer had a body to back up his threats.

Pa was a shadow of his former self. He'd lost weight, his shoulders were narrowed, his chest caved in. Jowls hung from his cheeks. His legs were as slender as twigs under the single coverlet.

"Wade?" Pa was nearly six and a half feet tall, but his prone position stole even that commanding height from him.

Bracing himself for the explosion, Wade advanced into the room.

"Whom shall I fear? Whom shall I fear?"

Wade knew exactly whom he did fear as he watched his father's expression go from surprise to anger. He shouldn't have, not according to the Bible, but he feared his own earthly father, God forgive him.

"Decided to come home, huh, like a whipped pup?" Pa's fists clenched as if he were dreaming about throwing punches.

Doing his best not to flinch, as he would have in the past, Wade prayed silently for the courage he'd gained from knowing a better, kinder Father. God in heaven was on his side. He turned as always to Psalm 27.

"The Lord is my light and my salvation; whom shall I fear? The Lord is the strength of my life; of whom shall I be afraid?"

An almost supernatural calm eased into Wade's muscles and bones. "I came home because there is a God-given commandment to honor you, Pa. I am here out of obedience to God. Now, do you want to spend the first moments we've seen each other since you threatened me on the trail last fall telling me what a disappointment I am? Or, since I'm your only living family, should we try and talk to each other?"

Pa's fists opened and closed. His jaw clenched as if he was physically trying to hold back the rain of words. It might be the first time he had ever exerted an ounce of control over his temper, and, even doubting it would last, Wade was encouraged.

"I cut you out of my will." The words were harsh, but Pa didn't shout. "If you're here to watch me die then take over my ranch, you're wasting my time."

"Good, I'm glad you did." Wade crossed his arms to cover up

the deep pain in his belly. Not because he'd been disinherited, but because he had a father who would do such a thing. "Keep it that way. Then you'll know I'm here to help, not for the money. That's settled. Now, do you want to tell me what you need done around the ranch?"

"You don't know how to run a ranch. A ranch takes strength and guts. You've got neither."

"If you're happy with your foreman, I'll just help care for you. Give Gertie a break. I also brought someone home to help. She's—"

"You'd stay to the house like a woman?" Pa roared.

The clenched jaw hadn't held.

"You're the one who sent for me, remember? You just said you don't want me working the ranch."

"I didn't say that. I said you don't know how. I said you don't have any guts. And you just took it like a weakling."

"Being cruel to your son isn't a sign of strength, Pa. It's a sign of weakness, to my way of thinking. Being kind to an old tyrant who doesn't deserve it, doesn't want it, and doesn't thank you for it—now, *that* takes strength." Wade felt his temper slipping. His pa had taught him that anger was strength, but God had taught him better. Yes, Jesus got angry, but mostly He stood right in the face of powerful people and remained calm. There was great strength in self-control.

Pa fell silent.

Wade waited.

Gertie began straightening the covers on the massive oak-framed bed.

That's when Wade looked back at Abby. She stood by the door, studying Pa with narrow eyes.

Wade reached out his hand. "Come here. Meet my father."

Abby snorted, not quietly either.

"Who's she?"

Wade turned to see his father now watching Abby.

"Her family is dead. She needed somewhere to go. I told her she could stay here, work with Gertie."

"Now I'm running an orphanage?"

"No, you're hurt. Caring for you is more than one person can do. Gertie, you can use some help around here, right?"

Gertie grunted as she tugged on a sheet. "I've told you how things are going to the dogs around here, Mort. I've got all I can do to carry food up and down these stairs. I'm not getting my cleaning done in the rest of the house, and I can barely keep up with the laundry. I haven't planted a bit of the garden yet, and we'll be pinched for food this winter if I don't get something done. Having help will keep the rest of the house from going to wrack and ruin."

She'd always had a way with Pa that Wade couldn't understand. She didn't seem to mind his rages, his insults. She'd just soldier on, do what was asked and then some. How many times had she diverted Pa's temper and given Wade a chance to scoot into some hiding place? Then she'd come and find him and tell him to come on out. It was safe. She'd come after Wade's mother had died, and Gertie had been a mother to him in every way but blood. Of course, many times she hadn't been able to divert Pa's fury. Then she'd come and find Wade and bandage his wounds.

"I'll be dead by next winter anyway."

Abby made the rude noise again.

Pa turned his attention to her. "You got something to say, girl?"

"Wade told me you were a tyrant. I'm not afraid of a strong man. My father was strong. But Wade was wrong. I come here and see a man whining."

"Abby." Wade stepped to her side.

She tilted her nose up at Pa. "I see self-pity and stupidity. Your son comes home with an offer to help and you insult him. Your woman waits on you hand and foot and you snap at her like a yellow dog."

"She's not my woman."

Odd that Pa would think to object to that.

"I will stay here because Wade has asked me to, but I work for a fool and a weakling. Better I should tend a crying child than a man such as you."

"A weakling!" Pa punched the bed.

Flinching from the raised voice, Wade stepped closer to Abby.

"Yes, a weakling. A man in my tribe once lost the use of his legs and he dragged himself around the camp working, helping to skin deer, prepare the food. He knew it was better to work with the women than to not work at all. He refused to be lazy and worthless like you."

Gertie gasped.

Wade braced himself.

Pa's face turned a shade of purple Wade hadn't ever seen on a human being before. "You get over here, you spiteful little shrew. I'll show you worthless." Pa sat forward as if he planned to throw himself at Abby.

She laughed. "Come and get me, old man." She turned to Gertie. "Why is he in bed all day like an infant?"

Pa threw aside his blankets and used his arms to swing his legs around. They dropped, lifeless, bending at the knees. Before he fell out of bed, he stopped and looked at his legs.

Silence iced over the room.

Pa stared as he ran his hands up and down his withered legs.

Tension wrapped like fingers around Wade's neck. He glanced at Abby, every inch Glowing Sun right now, her arms crossed, her eyes too wild and fierce for a lady. But so brave. And honest, too. Wade felt his spine strengthen as if he drew courage straight from her.

At last Pa looked up, straight at Abby. "Get out of my room. Get out of my house."

"A man's house is only his if he can hold it. I have a job here and I'll keep it unless *you* actually throw me out. But I will gladly leave your presence." Abby whirled and left the room.

Wade stared after her then turned back to his father, his spine working better than usual. "I hired her. She stays." He marched out, too.

When he'd prayed to God, *"Whom shall I fear?"* it never occurred to him that God might bring someone into his life who could give him lessons. Or who could be even more fearful than Pa.

"It's that wild woman." Paddy ran into the bunkhouse.

Sid looked up from the saddle he was mending. "What wild woman?" But Sid only knew of one wild woman.

"The one Harv tried to take. She's dressed in gingham now and her hair's tied back neat, but it's her. I just saw her go into the house with a man."

"What man? The one who shot Boog?"

Boog had come riding into the ranch with them, not showing a single sign of weakness. He'd made his excuses then ridden out again, heading for a line shack to spell the men who kept watch over that far corner of the M Bar S. In truth, he was going out there to heal. But if that wild white-haired woman was here, she'd recognize Harv for sure.

Harv lay stretched out on his bunk. They'd made up an excuse about rustlers and Harv getting the worst in a knife fight. Everyone here at the M Bar S was too stupid to know the only rustlers around were Sid and his gang.

This woman could ruin everything. "We'll lay low awhile. Harv's the only one they saw, and Boog with that gunshot might have given 'em a clue. But I can just walk right in that ranch house and give Mort the report like always. It'll look wrong if I don't."

"But how long can Harv stay hidden?" Paddy glanced nervously at Harv.

Sid forced himself to think about the gold. Harv was starting to be a burr under Sid's saddle. Only that treasure kept Harv alive. "I'll have to tell Mort about the rustlers. Then Harv'll have an excuse to stay in the bunkhouse. Maybe the woman and man are just passin' through. They'll stay the night and move on. We're not doing anything to tip our hand."

"And what if she doesn't move on?" Paddy hissed. "You know she's gotta die sometime. She can't be around Divide, let alone the M Bar S."

"Well, we know how to stage a fall off a horse, don't we? When we did it before, no one suspected a thing, not even Mort."

Paddy smiled. Then he giggled and plunked himself down on his cot. "We do know sure enough. This time, I'll come in after just to make sure she's dead. I shoulda never left Mort lying there alive. I heard a wolf pack and figured he wouldn't last the night. I didn't want anyone seeing a bullet hole in him."

"You're the man we want to dry-gulch a woman, Paddy." Sid didn't even try to hide his contempt. Paddy had his uses. There was nothing too low for the man. Nothing too dirty. He enjoyed watching people die. He'd especially enjoy killing a woman, and Sid knew he'd done it before.

Paddy didn't even react to words that would have made Boog draw his gun. Well, Paddy did react. He grinned and started humming an Irish jig.

Sid was tempted to draw his own gun.

CHAPTER 8

So then I got a hoof right in the belly."

Cassie had talked every second since Red had come in for dinner. She hadn't scolded him yet, but he'd earned the sharp side of her tongue several times since they'd left Silas and Belle's. He remembered how quiet she'd been when they were first married. How careful to be obedient.

Those were the good old days.

After a week with Belle, Red's wife was now just looking for an excuse to yell at him.

It was all Red could do not to be ornery, just to let Cassie have her fun. Honestly, it was all pretty lightweight as far as bossiness went. His sweet little wife just didn't have a mean bone in her body.

Cassie gently wiped mashed potatoes off Susannah's face, wrinkling her nose to get the toddler to smile.

Red had added onto their little soddy, made a log house about three times the size of the first cabin. Of course three times the size was still about half the size of a normal home. They still used a cave as their bedroom and a second, smaller cave with a chilly spring running through it for a cold cellar.

MARY CONNEALY

"You think we need to make the house bigger, Cass honey? Does the baby keep you awake at night?" Red took the cloth from Cassie. "Here, let me do that. You've got your hands full. We could add on a bedroom like we did for Susannah and move him just that little bit farther away from us if you're tired. I wake up faster'n you at night, and I'd be able to go cheer him up most of the time."

Cassie finished with Susannah then looked at the wriggling little boy in Red's lap with a fond smile. "He is a terror, isn't he? Why will the child not sleep through the night?" She ran her hand over Michael's curls and Red felt as if she were touching him. She'd been so thrilled when the little boy had his daddy's hair.

Between her cute, newfound toughness and the way she touched little Michael, Red hated to ruin the moment. But he respected her enough to be honest. "Cassie, I've waited until we're about done eating to tell you something important."

His Cassie had a sensitive soul. She looked up straight into his eyes, knowing this was serious. "What is it?"

Red turned Michael against his chest so he could pat a burp out of him, also to stall a few seconds. He wished so much he could smooth out all of life's bumps for his wife and family. "I've. . .I've got cattle missing. Someone from the Jessup ranch stopped in every day while we were gone to do chores and check the herd. Walt, the Jessup foreman, came by this morning, not knowing we'd gotten back. He told me he found a carcass that had been butchered right on the range. Well, a cow can wander off, but Walt thinks several head are missing. It'll take awhile to run a tally, but Walt's a mighty knowing man. If he says he's worried, then I'm worried, too."

A line formed between Cassie's pretty, dark brown eyes. Red regretted laying any trouble on her, but she needed to know. "I'll do some tracking and hopefully pick up a trail and get to the bottom of it. But you need to be on guard." Then Red thought of a way he could maybe cheer her up. "You'd better always keep that blade Belle gave you close to hand."

Cassie sat up straighter as if almost hoping she'd get a chance at having a knife fight with a rustler.

Red wished he could have a long, cranky talk with Belle Tanner...Harden...for putting ideas in Cassie's head. The woman was trouble and that was a fact. Silas had his hands plumb full, and yet he seemed to be a happy man. Which Red wouldn't be if he tussled with Belle. The woman was tougher than a full-grown longhorn and twice as dangerous.

Then he thought of Wade and Abby. The way she'd stabbed that rattler then planned to eat it. Abby had also saved Cassie and Susannah.

The West bred women tough, and his wife was learning to protect herself. No matter how much Red tried never to leave her in jeopardy, he couldn't be at her side every minute of every day. But even if she wasn't as tough as Belle and Abby, well, he couldn't help thinking that, when it came to women, he'd gotten the best end of the deal.

Red stood up and, with no wasted motion, plunked Michael onto the floor then swept Cassie up and sat back down.

She giggled. "Red, what are you doing?"

Red reached out and loosened the towel that kept Susannah secure in her chair then set her on the floor so she wouldn't fall. Leaving Red free to kiss his sweet little wife thoroughly.

"I'm just letting you know I think I'm the luckiest man who ever lived." He gave silent thanks to God that he'd gotten the best of the three women and made sure Cassie knew he felt that way by the strength of his arms and the depth of his kisses.

He only quit kissing his pretty wife when Susannah's slaps on his knee and shouts of "Papa!" got his attention. He wondered how long the little girl had been whacking at him.

Cassie stood; then her knees sagged and Red supported her until she could support herself. When he was sure she was steady, he plunked Michael into Cassie's arms and lifted a fussy Susannah high over his head. She giggled as he hugged her tight and scratched her chubby neck with his whiskered cheeks.

"You know what I think we oughta do, Cass honey?"

She had that wide-eyed obedient look that Red had come to cherish because he saw it so rarely these days. "What, Red?"

"I think while we've still got a little daylight left, we oughta go practice throwing that knife of yours. I think you could teach me a few things."

Cassie's obedience faded to something much warmer and livelier. She threw her one free arm around his neck, and even with both young'uns between them, they managed to while away so much time there wasn't enough light to get any serious practice in before bedtime.

Red was just fading off to sleep when Michael woke. They'd moved his crib temporarily to the kitchen. His howl for attention was the first of what would most likely be four times through the night.

Red went to cajole the fussing baby.

He heard Cassie mumble as she dozed off, "I think another room for our son is a good idea."

Wade came into the house for breakfast to find Gertie and Abby talking and happily working side by side. "Abby, you want to come out and see the ranch?"

"I will stay and help Gertie. We have a full morning planned cleaning this monstrosity. What foolishness."

Gertie snickered. "You go on out with Wade. The hands should be stirring by now, and I'll have breakfast ready when you get back. Something tells me you'll be happier outside than in, but that doesn't mean I'm going to turn down your help."

Wade suppressed a sigh of relief when Abby turned to him, removing the apron Gertie had her swathed in. He dreaded facing the cowhands, knowing he had to earn their respect and knowing he'd never managed it before. But Gertie had said these were nearly all new hands. Maybe they wouldn't have judged him already as a weakling and a coward, a view his father openly held.

Abby hung her apron on a nail beside the kitchen door. She wore the same dress as she had yesterday and had her hair neatly braided. But she still wore her moccasins, and her braid was tied back with a leather thong. She'd packed along her doeskin dress, too.

He could also see the small raised place at her waist, in back, where she tucked her knife. It was an unsettling mix of civil and savage that Wade found wildly appealing.

"I would like to see your ranch. My father raised cattle. I have only flashes of memories from my white family, but I remember a barn with horses and a herd of sandy brown cattle with long horns."

Wade held the door open for her and she stopped to stare.

Gesturing outside, he said, "After you."

"After I what?" Her brow beetled.

Wade smiled. "I mean I'm holding the door open so you can go first."

With a shrug, Abby went outside and Wade followed her. They walked side by side toward the massive barn, one of three huge buildings his father had built, connected by corrals, all set to best block the force of the winter winds.

Wade moved ahead of her and held the door to the closest barn, the one where the horses were taken to foal or heal from injuries. They entered the warm barn. The smell of hay and horses and leather evoked a warm memory of home. He'd always loved the horses best.

As Wade came in behind Abby, he saw five cowboys. Four Wade didn't recognize were mostly loafing around, while one, a grizzled old man who had been with Wade's father for years, was brushing a mare who had a new baby foal at her side.

"Chester, hello."

The old-timer straightened and laid his brush aside. "Wade?" The old man's voice was kind.

Wade had learned most of what he knew about horses from working along with Chester. The man had a kindly way with horses and had always been patient with Wade, too.

Emerging from the stall, he came forward quickly, his hand extended. "Good to see you, boy." The man's grip was solid. He turned to the cowboys lolling about. "Come and meet the boss's son. He's here to take the reins. And about time, too."

The men stood quickly, exchanging glances. One of them, skinny with a weak chin and mean eyes, seemed unable to take his eyes off Abby. Wade could understand that—women were scarce in and around Divide, Montana. That didn't mean he wasn't tempted to punch the guy in the nose.

Then Wade noticed another one staring between him and Abby as if he didn't know which one interested him more. The man had two missing fingers on his left hand. He was broad and running to fat, with blue eyes that looked cold as death. He stepped forward in a way that told Wade this man was in charge.

Chester jerked his head at the leader of the pack of loafers. "Wade, this here is Sid Garver. He's the foreman of the M Bar S now, ever since the old foreman took off."

"Otis took off? He'd been here forever."

"He vanished just after your pa's accident, and then Sid got the foreman job."

Something in Chester's voice made Wade wary of Sid Garver, as Wade was sure Chester intended.

"Sid"—Chester turned to the scowling man—"this is Mort Sawyer's son. His pa sent word that he needed his help, and Wade came home to take up the reins until his pa gets better."

"He's not gettin' better and you know it, Chester. No man gets over a broken back." Garver tugged his Stetson low over his eyes.

Chester sniffed. "Where there's life, there's hope. Somethin' my ma used to say. As long as Mort's alive, there's a chance he can get better. Anyway, he can still rule this ranch with Wade here to be his eyes and ears."

Garver turned to Wade. "Welcome home, boy. I heard you'd quit the country long ago. Heard ranching didn't suit you, that you'd gone looking for a life that didn't get your hands dirty."

The other men, all but Chester, laughed.

The sting of those words sapped the stiffness out of Wade's spine. He wanted to turn away, slink off and hide. It's what he'd have done before he found God. But he wasn't the same boy. He was a Christian. That might not be the same as a rough-and-ready cowhand with a quick draw, but it was a better strength, one that would last.

"Sid, that's the last time you'll call me a boy, and if I hear another insult from you, you'll draw your time and hit the road. Is that clear?" Wade stood straight, holding Garver's eyes.

"I was hired by your pa, and he'll be the only one to fire me." Garver crossed his arms.

Wade turned to Chester. "Have you finished the roundup yet?"

"Haven't even started it." Chester narrowed his eyes at the other cowhands. "And it's plumb late in the season for it."

"Okay, let's go ask Pa if early June is high time to be doing the spring roundup. You want to go in now and explain to him why it's not done? Then we'll see if Pa will back me."

Garver's beefy fists dropped to his sides. "I was starting today anyway."

"I'm glad we agree." Wade watched Garver closely as his hands swung too close to his holster. Wade noticed the man wore his gun on the left, which meant he was left-handed, the same hand that had the two fingers farthest from his thumb missing. "Is there grass in the south canyon?"

"Yep, plenty," Chester answered.

With a jerk of his chin, Wade said to the cowhands, "Let's spend the next three days bringing the cattle in there. We'll take the Lord's day off then be ready to start branding come Monday. Can you handle that, Garver? Have you got any men who'll spend their time working instead of loafing?"

"I can handle it." Garver's jaw was so tight the words were barely audible.

"Glad to hear it. I saw on my ride in that the grass is overgrazed in the west valley. Let's move those cattle first." Wade studied the man for a second longer. "Have we met before, Garver? I can't place you, but something about you is familiar."

"I've never seen you before in my life." Garver made a sudden move with his left hand, and for a fraction of a second, Wade braced, expecting the man to draw his gun. Instead Garver shoved his disfigured hand into his pocket. "Let's get cracking, men." Garver stormed out of the barn.

The rest of the hands tagged along with none of the speed and determination Wade expected to see from cowhands in the spring. Wade watched them closely, still a bit shaken by something he couldn't put his finger on. Once they were out of earshot, he turned to Chester. "We need to have a long talk."

Chester nodded. "I heard you were around, at the Dawsons' and working at other ranches, doing some cattle drives. The best hands have moved on, driven off by Garver and the sluggards he's hired."

"And it's not like Otis to up and leave. He'd stick by Pa."

"There's more, but for now it'll have to wait. I'm glad to have you home. You're dead right that we need to get hustling on the roundup. I've tried to start it, but Garver's been against me every step. And you're looking fit. I've heard you've made some good changes in your life."

"I'm glad to be here, Chester." Wade realized with a start that he was telling the truth.

Chester headed for the barn door then turned back, his eyes somber and steady. "Watch your back, Wade. There've been too many accidents on this ranch, and that includes your pa's."

Nodding his head, Wade said, "I've never known the man to fall off a horse in his life."

"I don't want the next accident to happen to you or your pretty

Wildflower Bride

woman here." Chester tugged his hat down low over his eyes and left.

Wade glanced at Abby, who had stood quietly through the tense meeting with Garver. He noticed she held her hand tucked in the folds of her skirt. "You can put the knife away now." He couldn't control a flicker of a smile.

"For now. But those men look evil." Abby shrugged and returned her knife to its carefully concealed sheath. "Don't be surprised if I keep it close to hand."

Chuckling, Wade said, "I'd be surprised if you didn't. Let's go see the rest of the buildings. Then we can go turn you and your bad attitude loose on Pa."

CHAPTER 9

I'm not taking orders from that whelp." Sid saddled his horse as he watched Wade and that half-wild woman snoop around *his* ranch.

"The kid wasn't supposed to ever come back." Paddy mounted as he whined. "He was long gone before we came here to work. His pa never spoke of the boy except to say he was dead to him."

Sid had only heard bits and pieces of the disappointment Mort's son had been. A lazy coward and a drunk. The only real detail he'd heard was that the falling out between Mort and Wade was final. "I heard the boy disgraced his pa until Mort disowned him. Mort sure enough announced that loud and clear."

"And here he is back." Paddy rode alongside Sid.

Sid was tempted to knock the man out of his saddle just to relieve his temper, but it would draw attention, and the four of them—Sid, Boog, Harv, and Paddy—had been careful not to appear too friendly. "And giving orders like it was his place."

It churned Sid's stomach to think he might lose the ranch if the youngster inherited it. "A kid could die as easy as an old man. And, shame though it is because she's a pretty little thing, the blond wildflower has to die, too."

Paddy gave Sid a hungry look. "I'll take care of her, pard. I'm already watching for my chance."

"It's gotta look like an accident."

Paddy shook his head. "No, it don't. If she disappears, everyone'll just think she went back to the wild, took up with the Flatheads again. I'm tempted to keep her alive awhile, have some fun with her."

"And Harv can't be seen out now." Getting rid of one little woman wouldn't be much trouble. Sid wasn't going to wrangle over how Paddy handled it. "It's possible both Wade and the woman would recognize him."

"We can take him into Divide and leave him with the doctor. He probably oughta have his cuts seen to anyway."

"But the doc might talk. We've got the story about running into rustlers, but I'd as soon not answer any questions from the sheriff."

"Wade is walking the yard like he owns the place. He won't stay out of the bunkhouse if he don't wanna."

"Yep, we'd better get Harv to town." Sid didn't like it a bit.

What had Wade been getting at when he'd asked Sid if they'd met? Sid had only been visible over that rise for a couple of seconds and masked. But had Wade noticed the missing fingers? It wasn't possible the kid could identify him, but a cold chill ran up Sid's spine at the thought of having all those murders connected to him. They were only Indians, but Montana was haggling right now over tribal lands and forming a state. They didn't want to be seen as a lawless place. Not even outside the towns. Someone could get it in his head that even an Indian deserved justice. What was the world coming to? "Better quit talkin' now, Paddy. Put some space between us."

With a swift jerk of the reins, Paddy dropped back as they rode out to start moving the herd.

It was backbreaking work. Work Sid wouldn't do once this was his place. He'd rule his kingdom from a nice office in that big old house. Bitterly, Sid considered how to get rid of Wade and the woman, and Mort, too, while he was at it. The old man was a tough one. He was taking a long time to die.

It was past time they quit leaving it to God and took over shoving Mort into the afterlife.

Wade spent an hour rearranging the furniture in his father's study. Ready now, he carried the odd-looking conveyance Gertie had ordered from back East up to Pa's room. Wade hated the cruel anger his pa was so famous for. But Wade's days of cowering were over.

"Whom shall I fear?"

Praying for the day he wouldn't have to repeat that prayer constantly, Wade rolled the chair down the thickly carpeted hall then peeked in the slightly opened door, bracing himself for the coming war of words. And there *would* be a war and Wade *would* win it.

Pa lay on his back staring out the window. Wade was struck by the bleak expression on his father's face. Wade loved his father enough to have prayed steadily for the bitter man to find peace with the Lord. He held out little hope that his father would ever change.

But this aching sadness showed a vulnerability Wade had never before seen. God was answering Wade's prayer, but not in the way he'd expected. He wasn't giving Wade endless courage, but He might be weakening Pa's cast-iron will.

Wade swung the door and went in. His father turned. His jaw set as his eyes flickered between the chair and his son. Wade couldn't be sure which Pa hated more.

"What is that thing?"

"Gertie ordered it for you. It's a wheelchair. She said she's tried to get you to come downstairs and have a look at it."

"In case you're too stupid or blind to notice, my legs don't work. And I'll die before I let someone carry me down like a baby. It's bad enough someone had to carry me up."

"I've set up a bed for you downstairs. You're moving there. For now, I get you up and into the chair every morning. But Gertie said there are ways you can learn to swing yourself into it without help. With this thing, you can sit up, move around the main floor of the house, read, and pass the time in less miserable activities than staring out at a ranch you can no longer run."

"Get out of here."

Wade had the urge to laugh. Since it made no sense and he'd been praying for a way to deal with his father, he trusted God and laughed in his father's face. "You can't stop me. You've been wasting away up here. I'm stronger than you and more determined than you. I'll help you into the chair, roll you down the hall, then carry you downstairs, or I can just throw you over my shoulder right now. You decide."

Pa started shouting, as Wade had expected. "I can still tear you apart with my bare hands, you young pup. I'm not going to be carted around like a piece of garbage you're looking to throw in the trash."

Wade sighed. It was a long hallway. Pa riding to the top of the steps would have been easier. "I knew you wouldn't cooperate, but I could hope."

"I'll thrash you if you get near me with that thing!" Pa struggled until he sat up. "Get out! Gertie, get up here!"

"Calling on a woman for help? Never thought I'd see the day." Wade rolled the chair aside. "Gertie is out planting a spring garden. She can't even hear your caterwauling."

Coming toward the bed, Wade dodged his father's fist. The intended blow almost upended Pa. Wade grabbed him before he fell out of bed. Wade hitched his arms around the invalid, now sprawled on his stomach, and gently hoisted his pa into his arms. Grief twisted inside him as Wade realized Pa had wasted away to nearly nothing. Dragging Pa's feet, Wade backed toward the door.

The shouting hurt his ears but nothing else, so it was easier than Wade had feared it would be. He ignored the roaring and dodged the fists flying backward impotently and soon had Pa in the study, settled in bed.

"I'll crawl back up those steps the second you're gone!"

"Why, Pa? Does it make you feel better to make Gertie's job harder, running food up and down the steps? In here you've got a library. You could even get back to work, keeping the books for the ranch. Gertie's been doing it and I'm surprised you trust her. With a little practice, you could get in and out of your wheelchair, come to the dining room for supper, and even go outside once I build a ramp out the back door. The ground is smooth enough I could push you to the barn and you could check the spring foals." Wade crossed his arms and leaned one shoulder on the door frame, staring at his father's face, red with rage.

The old man's chest was heaving, his hands fisted.

"You can't walk, Pa."

"I know that!"

"But you don't have to curl up and die."

"What good is life if you don't have legs?"

"You can run this ranch again, live again. Your life isn't over."

"Yes, it is. I'm worse than dead."

Wade straightened. "Considering you've never spent one second of your life contemplating God, I'm thinking you'll be a *lot* worse off dead, because nothing you've done in this life will ever get you into heaven."

Pa responded with the kind of vile language that only proved Wade right about the state of his father's soul. "I'm going to get your chair down here and you can practice climbing into it. Or you can just lie there like you're dead while you're still alive." Wade stalked out of the room.

"You get back here, you little. . ." Pa continued his tirade.

Wade turned his mind from the sound of his father's hate. He prayed all the way up and down the stairs, wondering as he balanced the heavy wheelchair why he wanted his father to have easier access to the ranch. Between his rage and filthy language— which was now easier to hear—and the shady things going on, Pa might have been better off staying secluded.

Wade's chin came up. Would Pa want to fight for this ranch? Of course! And if Wade could turn his father's anger to something that should've made him mad for *good* reason, maybe he'd let Wade be a part of fixing this place. And maybe turning the ranch around would at least give Pa something to live for.

CHAPTER 10

Red fashioned a bull's-eye using the side of his barn and a chunk of coal pulled out of the fireplace. Then he stood and watched in painful silence as Cassie missed the whole building.

She'd been at it for a week, during the young'uns' nap time. Usually the throw was short, plowing into the ground. Red was afraid to stay too close to her, especially after the time she'd dropped it on his boot. Luckily the handle had hit, not the blade, but it had taught him not to get too close beside her. Once she'd dropped it only inches from her own foot. And she'd gotten into the habit of losing it on the backswing. So Red had to make sure he wasn't behind her because he wasn't safe there. He also didn't like to get too far away in case she stabbed herself.

So he couldn't get behind nor beside. Not close nor far. In all honesty, the safest place might be right in front of the bull's-eye. Wherever else she'd hit since she'd started knife throwing, it had *never* been close to the place it was supposed to go.

She was getting better, though. The knife was going forward over half the time these last couple of days. It almost never went so wide it missed the barn. A couple of times, starting yesterday, she'd made contact with wood, but often the knife would hit on

86

its side then slide to the ground.

"Maybe you should step a little closer, honey. Most knife fights are pretty close up. You don't need to stay back this far." They were about ten feet away, and if anyone ever got closer to Cassie than this, Red wasn't going to wait around for her to fight. He'd take over and save the day. But since the barn was no armed killer, Red encouraged her to move up.

"But this is how far away Abby was when she killed that snake." Cassie got a mule-stubborn look on her face. She was so cute when she scowled at him it was all Red could do not to hug her.

Red didn't know how to break it to Cassie. "Abby is okay as an example to follow, but until you're a whole lot better, I wouldn't compare yourself to her. She's about the best knife thrower I've ever seen. Way better than me or Silas. . .or even Belle."

Cassie stayed right where she was, and this time she held the knife by its tip instead of the hilt and threw it like she was mad. There was a solid *thunk* when the knife embedded in the barn. Her eyes lit up like stars. "I did it!" She launched herself at Red.

Knowing not to make light of her accomplishment, plus always being happy to hold his pretty little wife, Red swung her around in a circle until she giggled. "You did great! Look at it. It's almost to the outside ring of the bull's-eye and it's sunk deep in the wood. You are such a tough cookie." Sweet cookie, too. He bent down and stole a kiss and, for a second, distracted her from practicing mayhem.

Deepening the kiss, Red heard her catch her breath, a sound that always sped his heart. He'd begun to consider just how long the young'uns would stay asleep when she pulled away and looked at the barn.

Red let her go, digging deep for patience as his single-minded, knife-fighting wife headed for the barn to jerk her blade free. "I think I've learned the secret. I've gotta be *mad* when I throw."

Since Cassie didn't have much of a temper—despite Belle's best efforts to help her develop a killer instinct—Red figured she might as well give up now. But oh no, thanks to Belle's bloodthirstiness and Abby's hostile confidence, Cassie-the-marshmallow was determined to learn knife throwing.

She was pestering him to let her help with the branding, too. So far two young children and her barnyard chores and spring garden had kept her distracted while Red branded calves at top speed. He hoped to be long done before she found a spare minute.

She squared off facing the barn and raised the knife again just as Silas and Belle and their brood rode into the ranch on horseback.

Waving to draw the Hardens' attention, Red dropped his hand when he saw a grim expression on Silas's face and an even more serious look on Belle's. This was no social visit.

Belle had Tanner on her back; Silas had Betsy riding in front of him. Emma and Sarah rode their own mustangs right behind their parents.

Silas swung down, handing Betsy to Emma, who'd come up to hold the horses. "I've got cattle missing, Red. We set out to track them and found evidence of cattle from your herd being run off, too."

The pleasure of the day faded as Red nodded. "I've been keeping a close watch, but I can't light out hunting rustlers and leave the family home."

"We were close enough to your place we turned away from the trail." Belle jerked her gloves off as she stood shoulder to shoulder with Silas. "It's pretty clear they're headed into some rugged timberland on Mort's range. Mort isn't up to hunting them down, and I doubt Wade is, at least not this soon after getting home."

Red admired Belle for a lot of things, none more than the way she stood by her man.

"Didn't you say you'd found evidence of thieves?" Cassie asked Red as she tucked her knife into a little pouch Belle had sewn to the inside of her skirt's waistband.

Red flinched, always afraid she'd stab herself in the stomach. Belle wanted the knife concealed. Red thought a nice, sturdy leather pouch *outside* her skirt would be better. Guess who Cassie listened to?

Silas pulled off his Stetson and ran his fingers through his hair to get it to stop drooping over his eyes then settled the hat back in place. "We've been snowed in, so we hadn't had any trouble until the spring thaw."

Red looked at Sarah. "Susannah should be up pretty soon. You want to go check on her for me?"

"It's been a long drive," Cassie said. "Sarah, we've got ham in the cold room."

"Eggs, too? I could make up some ham and eggs." Emma slid Tanner out of the pack on Belle's back while she balanced Betsy on her hip.

"You don't have to cook for us." Cassie looked embarrassed. "I'll make the meal. I just thought if you or Betsy were hungry you could make sandwiches."

"I'll take care of supper for all of us." Sarah reached to take Betsy from Emma.

"Emma, go help, will you? The grown-ups need to talk." Silas didn't order her. It sounded more pathetic than that. Red wondered how often Silas had any luck getting his womenfolk to mind him.

"Like any one of you is tougher'n me." Emma rolled her eyes then headed for the house with Tanner while Sarah carried Betsy.

Red shook his head. The girls would take care of supper and watch four active babies and not turn a hair. He got annoyed with Belle for a few things, like teaching Cassie to be bloodthirsty, but he had to admit the woman raised terrific—though somewhat fierce—children.

"Red and I need to talk a minute, ladies." Silas jerked his head to indicate Red needed to follow him. They'd gone one step before Belle fell in beside Silas. Red glanced back and saw Cassie directly behind him. "Belle, please let me talk to Red alone for a minute."

"No."

"Yes. This is man-to-man."

"No."

Silas stopped and frowned at Belle. "I distinctly remember you promising to obey me, woman."

"That was a long time ago."

Leaning down so his nose almost touched hers, he continued, "But your promise was *forever*."

Silas was a hard man. Red had seen that on their trek to find Wade. He rode long, never asking for a rest. He read tracks like they were the written word. He packed light and could live off the land without breaking a sweat. And now, looking as fiery as a Montana sunset, he scowled at his wife.

Red was pretty sure, if it'd been him, he'd have backed down right away.

Belle took a step forward. "I've hardly ever obeyed you, Silas. Why would you expect me to start now when you're going to talk about stolen Tanner cattle?"

"*Harden* cattle." Silas jabbed Belle in the chest. "And don't you forget it."

Red's spine tingled with fear. Not because of the warrior's gleam in both their eyes, or because he was afraid there was going to be a real live fight between these two, but because Cassie might be taking notes.

Belle caught Silas by the front of his shirt. "I never forget it. Even though I built the herd"—she pulled him down closer, but he didn't move so she ended up standing on her tiptoes—"I trained the horses and—"

"You are going to mind me!" Silas grabbed Belle by her slim waist and yanked her hard against him. "You promised, and your word oughta be good. You still want to live in that pretty house I built you, right?"

"You'd never kick me out and we both know it."

They glared at each other until Red thought the tension might snap both of them in two. Then suddenly Silas swooped down and kissed Belle. His arms slid around her waist and he lifted until her feet dangled off the ground.

Silas let up his kissing and whispered something in Belle's ear. She giggled.

Red shook his head in shock. He'd have never dreamed Belle Tanner—Harden—was capable of making such a feminine sound.

Silas whispered some more, and this time Red caught the word *Cassie*. It was low enough that Red wouldn't have heard if he hadn't read Silas's lips. Which brought to Red's mind the possibility that he was watching these two a little more closely than he should be, but it fascinated him to see Silas work his way around stubborn Belle.

With a quick nod, Belle said, "Okay, you've got ten minutes. Then Cassie and I are coming."

"Thanks, honey. And you still don't obey worth a hoot."

"Sure I do. As long as you order me to do what I was gonna do anyway."

"And you're right. I'd never kick you out of that house. I've gotten real used to having you around." Silas kissed her again, soundly.

Once her feet were back on the ground, Belle turned, strode over to Cassie, and linked their arms. "Just because we disagreed and he won doesn't mean anything I told you about how to stand up for yourself is wrong." They walked toward the house.

Red almost followed so he could hear what advice Belle was giving his sweet Cassie now.

"Let's head toward the watering hole."

Red hated to let the two women go. His life might depend on his being ready for Cassie's next round of independence. But since it was about cattle rustlers, he followed Silas.

"I just wanted Cassie away from this. I wasn't worried about Belle." Silas glanced behind him as if to check that the women were gone. Then he lowered his voice. "Okay, I'll admit I'm a little worried, but I can't let Belle know that, and my woman has ears like a nervous mama cougar. Belle gets the bit in her teeth and there's no stopping her. Here's how it goes, Red. I've found a solid trail leading into some rugged land on Sawyer's range. It was mighty bold the way they came into our valley—that gap is close to my house—and drove off about ten head of cattle. I only know it was that many because of the tracks. Then I back-trailed 'em and found a little canyon where they'd held the cattle not more'n a couple days. Then they drove 'em out and met up with another small herd, another ten cattle maybe."

"You think those came from my place?"

"I know they did because we followed the trail back this way."

"I've come up short in my tally. But we always lose a few head to winter kill. Still, it was high enough I was sure there'd been some thievin'."

Nodding, Silas went on. "If I take you with me tracking the cows, that'd leave Cassie alone here. I don't like that idea at any time, but especially not if a pack of rustlers as bold as these are close to hand. But I didn't want to leave the children at our place or here with you and Cassie. So I want Belle here and Emma. They're tough ones. They'll keep everyone safe and be better here than they would be in our cabin. 'Course, Belle is fit to be tied that I'm not letting her come along. I swear the woman would take on a whole gang of outlaws with a baby strapped on her back, and Emma and Sarah are game enough to go along. But I can't stand the thought of them in danger."

Red wondered if Belle wasn't an abler saddle partner than he was going to be. Which made it pretty easy to accept Belle's staying here with Cass.

"So I think Belle will stay behind here if we make it about Cassie, but Cassie will pitch a fit and try to come, too, if she knows it's for her own good. Which then means we'd have to take all the children."

"We might as well be taking a wagon train with us." Red shook his head.

Wildflower Bride

"We can go and leave the women and put an end to this gang once and for all."

"I'd have had it to do pretty soon anyway," Red said. "But I couldn't leave Cassie home with the young'uns. Besides, I'm pretty sure she's got another babe on the way. She hasn't admitted it to me yet, or maybe she hasn't noticed."

"How could she not know if she's expecting a baby?"

"It don't surprise me none. Cassie's led a real sheltered life."

"Keep her with child as much as possible." Silas nodded with satisfaction. "It slows Belle down some, gives me a few months off her scaring me to death busting broncs and hog-tying thousand-pound longhorns."

With a grin, Red said, "I oughta tell Belle you said that."

Looking terrified, Silas said, "You wouldn't!"

Red laughed. "Let's go join the women for a quick supper then hit the trail. There isn't room in that house for us anyway. We might as well put some miles behind us on the trail since we're gonna get banished to the barn."

"Ain't that the truth?" Silas headed for the house like a man who wasn't the least bit scared of his feisty wife.

Red followed along, deeply impressed.

CHAPTER 11

Abby worked on the house, disgusted by the time that was wasted wiping away perfectly natural dust. Didn't the land have a right to be part of every home? Strange people, these whites.

Obeying Gertie's orders, Abby ignored the shouts she'd heard from the weakling tied to his bed—or he might as well be—as she finished her assigned tasks. Turning to her own needs, she found a whetstone and sat at the kitchen table sharpening her knife. The roaring from the bedroom finally got on her nerves to the point she slapped the whetstone on the table, returned her knife to its sheath, and stormed into Mort's room.

His face was bright red. He lay on his side reaching for the strange contraption Wade had called a wheelchair, which, since it was a chair with wheels, was a fair name. His ruckus stopped and he glared at her. "Help me get into that chair."

Sneering with contempt, she said, "And will you need me to bring you warm milk and a baby's bottle to suck?"

Mort's eyes narrowed. "Get out of here. Get off my ranch. You're fired. Fired, I tell you."

"I do not work for you. Wade offered me the job and only he can fire me."

"He's paying you with my money and he has no right to spend it."

"He spoke of this money. I told him I would need food and I accepted the roof over my head, a room next to Gertie's, even though it is a roof held up by your monstrosity of a house. I refused any other money. It would be just something to carry around, another burden."

"Money isn't a burden. It makes life easier. You can buy your own roof."

"I'll build a bow and arrow and shoot a deer or two, skin them, and make a tepee. I need no money for that."

"What about food?"

"The deer that provides my home will also give me food."

Mort waved a fist at her. "What about when you need clothes? Your deerskins are on your tepee."

"I will shoot another and dry the meat into jerky so I can survive for a long while before I have to hunt again. For the cold months, I will find an animal with fur for a warm coat—a buffalo or bear. What good would money do me for that task? Why did you come to this wild beautiful land, overrun with food, clothing, all the things you need to live, then shut yourself away from it inside these ridiculous walls?"

Mort snorted like an enraged buffalo. "Help me up. Come over here. I try to keep the chair from moving but it won't stay put."

Abby narrowed her eyes at him. Their gazes locked. As if they were in a fight, neither of them broke the contact. Abby felt her temper rise, her patience shorten.

Finally, when she'd decided to just walk out, Mort looked away. "Please."

"What?"

"Please. I'm asking you *please* to help me get in my chair."

That word, *please*. It went with *thank you*. Wade had reminded her of these white men's manners. Mort said it like the word was painful to force from his lips. She realized that, to a stubborn tyrant like Mort Sawyer, saying please was an act of humility. And she knew how much a tyrant hated to ask for anything.

Her Wild Eagle had been like that. He didn't ask; he ordered. Abby was used to it, but Wade's kindness had been a surprise and a delight to her. Was this man like Wild Eagle? Would Wild Eagle have been any better if life brought him so low?

"Fine." With a deep breath, Abby rolled the chair to the side of Mort's bed.

They made several attempts to get Mort transferred to the chair, and finally, using his arms and with Abby supporting him almost completely, they made it.

Gasping, Mort finally caught his breath enough to say, "Thank you."

"You're welcome." The words came almost as a reflex, without thought.

"Can. . .can you push me to the kitchen? There's a window there. I'd like to look out over my ranch."

"Use your arms. Push the wheels. Can you not do a thing for yourself?" Disgusted and ashamed that she'd had a moment of sympathy for the weakling, she stalked out of the room.

Before she'd gotten her knife's edge to suit her, Mort was in the kitchen studying the huge piece of the earth he so foolishly claimed as his. The earth was the Lord's, given to everyone, teeming with food, fuel to burn for warmth, and beauty to soothe the soul.

White men seemed to understand none of that. What a strange breed.

"What's that idiot son of mine doing?" Mort punched the arm of his chair.

❧

What were these idiots doing?

Wade saddled up and met the first bunch of cattle the men drove into the yard. They'd been at it for hours and Wade should have gone out to help, but he'd made a quick trip to town instead to arrange for the lumber to make some changes to the house that would make his pa's life easier. Sam Jeffreys, one of Libby Jeffreys's mule skinner sons, usually had a few days between hauling loads. Wade needed to focus on the spring roundup, so he'd asked Libby to have Sam ride out next time he was in Divide.

With that all in order, he'd returned home to find his men just bringing in the first herd. Watching, Wade knew why it had taken so long. The herd milled and broke away.

Wade charged his horse into the fractious cattle. Chewing on dust, Wade cut this way and that to force the critters forward. It was almost as if the men here had no idea how to handle cattle or run a ranch. Or if they knew how, they didn't care enough to break a sweat trying.

The bawling cattle and the thundering hooves of Wade's horse kept Wade from thinking too much about his incompetent cowhands. When he got the herd headed in the right direction, Wade watched. He drove the whole herd with the help of about three of the old hands. A dozen other men spent their time making the day harder for everyone.

They got the longhorns herded into the lush valley. A few of them found the gushing spring. The rest waded into the belly-deep spring grass. They all settled in quickly, as Wade knew they would.

Wade waved his drovers in. He'd seen his father operate long enough to know what he needed to do. Run most of these men off, including the foreman. But that wasn't what God wanted from him. He saw some laziness but mostly incompetence. "I want you, you, you, you. . . ." Wade jabbed a finger at ten of the men. He skipped Sid Garver for now. The man had to go, but not in front of the whole crew. No use humiliating him.

"Team up, each of you. Everyone needs to learn a few cowhand tricks." Wade turned to the oldest hand. "Chester, pick who you want to work with from the men I've pointed out." Noticing

Chester's disgruntled face, Wade said, "Let's head for the high pasture to the west. It's next closest. I want to move at least three more herds today."

The men turned to ride out.

"Chester, wait a minute."

Turning his horse with only the pressure of his knees, the old cowpoke dropped back to Wade's side. "Well, you got part of it. You saw what a bunch we've got here. But instead of teaming them up with the older hands, you should have shown them the road."

Taking a quick look around, Wade made sure no one was within earshot. "I did it that way because not all of these men are no-accounts. Some of 'em are just new. I don't want to fire a man when I can teach him a skill. If I'd have run ten men off, with rustlers in the area, they might have thrown in with outlaws. They might have headed to Divide with their pay and a grudge and drunk all their money away. That'd leave 'em mad and broke, and in some men that adds up to dangerous."

"Some of these men are just bums. All the training in the world isn't gonna help."

Nodding, Wade said, "In a week I'll decide who's a bum and who's just new at ranching. The ones who don't shape up will get run off my range. Fair enough?"

"A week is too long."

With a bark of a laugh, Wade said, "I'll bet we know enough to tell who's gonna at least try to work hard by the end of the day. So maybe I won't give 'em a week."

Chester scowled. "I always knew you were soft, boy. To my way a'thinkin' you're just provin' it the first day."

"I know how to handle a horse, Chester. And I know a cowhand when I see one. Have all these men been hired since Pa was hurt? I can't believe he'd've been fooled by them."

"Sid Garver hired them. So they're loyal to him. And Garver ain't loyal to anyone but himself. Watch your step, Wade."

"Watch yours, too, old man, because I'm naming you the new foreman."

"I'm doing the job anyway; I sure had oughta get the title. And if I'm the foreman, then you'd be better off listenin' to me and just get the worst of these drovers off the property. Instead you've hurt their pride by askin' 'em to pair up like they were greenhorns. Now you'll have a bunch of cowboys carryin' a grudge."

"Maybe, but that's the way it's gonna be." Wade met Chester eye to eye. "That's the way God wants me to handle it."

Chester wasn't a bad man, not much of a talker. A grizzled gray beard, lean and brown and tough as leather. He'd never joined in the harassment of Wade as so many of the hands had. But there'd been plenty of contempt in the old coot's eyes back then. Wade had a lot to prove before the wrangler gave Wade any respect.

"I didn't understand your pa, Wade. He rode you hard, held you up for a fool, and he was too ready with the back of his hand. I have my own beliefs when it comes to the Almighty, and I can see that there's been a change in you. But I've lived long enough to be sure God ain't gonna send lightning bolts to run off a bad bunch'a cowhands. Without your pa here to rule the roost, we're all looking to you. But no one's gonna hand you the reins. You're gonna have to take 'em. And the best way would be to run off the no-accounts and the malcontents."

"Which would leave us about fifteen men short for spring roundup." Wade quirked a smile.

"Not really." Chester looked around. "If all of 'em are worthless, we're shorthanded anyway."

"I'll give you that. I'll decide soon who stays and who goes, and I'll listen to your opinions when I decide."

"I already know who I'd pick. I just hope you figure it out before it's too late." Chester reined his horse around and took off after the cowhands.

Wade rode up beside Sid, who was teamed with one of the men who'd been lazing in the barn this morning. Paddy, that was his name. An Irishman for sure with that name, but nothing about him looked Irish. He was just another Montana cowboy.

"Paddy, mind ridin' ahead? Sid and I need to make some plans."

Paddy looked as if he was planning to refuse. Something about his expression sent a chill up Wade's spine. It wasn't anger but rather vicious amusement laced with a hunger to hurt. Wade decided then and there he'd watch his back whenever Paddy was around. And if Paddy was friends with Sid, then Wade would keep an eye on Sid, too.

Especially after Wade gave him the bad news. "I'm naming Chester foreman, Sid. He knows the way things work on the Sawyer range."

Sid's eyes flashed fire. For a second Wade wondered if Sid would throw a fist. He controlled his rage. "I've been running the Sawyer range to suit your pa."

"You're nearly a month late with the roundup, Sid. That doesn't suit my father. I'll be interested to see if he knows when I get in tonight. Maybe where you're from the winter doesn't let loose of the land until now, but that just proves you don't know how we work here on the M Bar S. Stay on as a cowhand if you like. But if you have any influence on the men, you'd better tell 'em to pick up the pace, because I'll decide who stays and who goes by week's end."

Sid's brow arched. "You want me to push the men after you took away my job as boss?"

"I do. Because one of the men who may stay or go is you. And I can make decisions before week's end if I need to. I'm watching close." Wade turned away from Sid and picked out an inept pair of cowhands who had paired up with each other. Had they deliberately defied him, or were they just that stupid?

Wade rode over to find out, and out of the corner of his eye, he noticed Sid and Paddy riding together, talking up a storm.

CHAPTER 12

Abby caught herself watching out the window for Wade to come in.

Not Wade really, all of them. It was her job.

Gertie had spent the morning working endlessly in the kitchen. Along with a huge baking of bread, she'd made pan after pan of apple cobbler and a mountain of doughnuts. When a bawling, shoving herd of cattle appeared out of a cloud of dust a short distance from the ranch yard, Gertie carried the warm sugary doughnuts out to the men, and Abby hurried along behind her with two huge pots of ink black coffee.

The milling cattle, their horns long and sharp, their coats brown and white and black and red, all colors, all sizes, were shaggy and mean. Baby calves kicking up their heels in the lush grass bawled. Their mothers answered with low crooning moos as their pace sped up to the smell of water.

Abby realized that Mort Sawyer had built his own herd, but longhorns instead of buffalo. But there were no fences. How did the man keep them from heading south when the weather turned cold? Shaking her head, she searched the crowd for Wade.

He emerged from the chaos and came riding toward them.

101

He called over his shoulder, "Coffee, men."

All the riders began trotting their horses toward Gertie and Abby. Gertie reached a waist-high flat rock near the entrance to the canyon, set her huge tray of doughnuts on top, and pulled off the cloth towel. Abby set one tin coffeepot on the ground and the other one beside the doughnuts.

Wade swung down and fished a tin coffee cup out of his saddlebag. His eyes met Abby's, but he didn't come toward her. Instead he dropped back and waved all the men in first. They ground-hitched their horses and dove into the food.

"Why do the cattle stay around, Gertie?" Abby asked. "And why do the horses stand without being held?"

Gertie smiled. "We'll talk ranching once this mob is fed. Or maybe you oughta ask Mort. That man, grouchy as he is, knows more about running a spread this size than any man around these parts. Talking might get him to let up on his self-pity." Gertie focused on the men.

One grunted, "Thanks," and moved toward Abby.

She didn't like the intent shine in his eyes and moved close to Gertie. A quick exchanged glance between the women was all it took to keep Gertie from telling Abby to move over.

The other men took their turn speaking to her, eager to say, "Thanks for the coffee," and a few words more. She felt them all staring at her.

Wade came around the back of the flat rock and stood by her side so that he and Gertie had her surrounded.

"You want coffee?" She did her best not to glare at him. Just another man who prized her fair skin and pale hair.

"In a minute. I'll wait." Wade said no more, but Abby, despite being annoyed at Wade's nearness, realized she felt safe with Gertie on one side and Wade on the other. How could she think she'd be safe in the white man's world? Of course, she had turned out *not* to be safe in her Flathead people's world, too, now, hadn't she?

Wildflower Bride

When Wade finally got his turn, he drank his coffee while Gertie asked questions about the progress of the roundup.

"We'll have lunch in the bunkhouse. You don't need to feed this mob." He watched his men ride back to the next herd as he told Gertie about the morning. He decided to wait until the men were out of sight to make sure none of them bothered Abby.

"I've been talking to Cookie. He's got a pot of stew going, but I've baked a day's worth of bread this morning, so I'm taking that and enough apple cobbler to give every man a bite. While roundup is going on, we'll keep your bellies full."

"Sounds great, Gertie. Thanks."

Looking at Abby, Gertie said, "I need to hustle back to the house. Do you mind waiting until the men are done then bringing along the tray and coffeepots?"

Abby nodded.

Gertie did hustle. In fact, Abby didn't think she'd ever seen the older woman move so fast.

Realizing that while she'd stared after Gertie, the cowhands had swung up on horseback and headed out, she stood alone with Wade. She began collecting the pots as Wade went to his chestnut, the last animal still standing idle.

Wade tossed the reins over the gelding's head. He grabbed the pommel then paused. "If...uh...the men...ever bother you, Abby, you should let me know. I...I don't like the looks of some of them, and...well...I..."

Abby looked away from the tray she reached for. "What is it?"

"I suppose I made 'em mad. Some of 'em at least."

"What did you do?" Abby had a flicker of memory when she spoke the scolding words. She thought maybe her white mother had taken that exact tone with her long ago.

Wade dropped the reins again and stepped close. "I changed foremen. I didn't like the looks of the one we had. And a lot of the cowhands are new since Pa got hurt. The foreman looked mad enough to take my head off when I told him. But he's not runnin' the ranch to suit me nor my pa. And I teamed up my better cowhands with the ones who weren't up to snuff. I suppose I stepped on some pride with that. But it was either that or send 'em down the trail to hunt work somewhere else. Anyway, they might be mad, maybe fightin' mad, and I want you to stay well away from them."

"It suits me to stay far away from all of you." Abby tossed her braid over her shoulder. "I will gladly avoid your men."

"Well, okay then, good. I'll be going." Wade went back to his horse.

Abby turned away to gather the rest of her things. She heard the leather creak as Wade swung up. She wasn't quite able to stop herself from sneaking a look at him—lean and strong and kind— mounting his horse.

As he landed on the saddle, the horse went berserk. Exploding in noise and motion, it launched itself straight up, neighing and fighting the bit. The chestnut's head jerked back. Its head would have smashed Wade's face if Wade wasn't off balance and leaning to the side.

Stiff-legged, the chestnut landed hard. Abby heard Wade's teeth click together. Rearing and squealing, the normally gentle gelding rose up and up. It looked certain to go over backward.

Wade threw his weight forward and the horse landed on all fours. Wheeling, it lashed its heels high in the air, and the iron-shod hooves whizzed past Abby's face.

"Abby, look out!" Wade's voice roared over the shrill whistles of the maddened animal.

She threw her body backward, trapping herself against the rock.

Wade fought for control.

The horse whirled again then lunged forward. Its front hooves raked at her.

Throwing herself sideways, Abby watched as the horse missed her by inches. As she landed, she saw an arrow protruding from the sleeve of her dress, but it didn't hurt. It must have missed her arm. Without a split second to think under the hooves of the maddened horse, Abby regained her feet then timed her leap to the horse's jumps. Swift as a pouncing cougar, Abby grabbed the horse's bridle.

The horse lifted her off her feet. Her weight brought the horse back to the ground as a second arrow whipped by so close that feathers attached to it swiped her face.

With the horse still, Wade leapt from the saddle. "What are you doing?" He raced to the horse's head.

"Holding your horse." Abby gasped from exertion, pulling the horse around so its big body protected them from the arrows.

"You could"—Wade's chest heaved—"have been killed."

Abby seriously doubted it. She caught the fabric covering Wade's shoulder and dragged him out of the line of fire. "What happened to him?"

Wade's eyes flashed in temper, seemingly directed at Abby. But at her question, he turned to the horse. It stood trembling, its eyes wide with fear or maybe. . . "He's in pain."

Abby shoved the reins into Wade's hand and went to the horse's side, keeping her head low, still mindful of those deadly arrows.

"Let me do that."

"Hang on to him." Abby unfastened the cinch. An odd contraption. But there had been a saddle or two in their village. She knew how one worked.

The horse skittered sideways, and Wade dug in his heels. "What's wrong, boy? What's hurting?"

The quiet murmur of Wade's voice made Abby realize she was skittish, too. Those hooves had barely missed her. A quick look around revealed no one who might have sent an arrow her way. A glance at it protruding from her shoulder revealed markings similar to those of her people. Had someone from the Flathead village tried to kill her? What lies and poison had Wild Eagle's mother spread?

She lifted the saddle away then swept a blanket aside to find a small, jagged rock and two heavy burrs tucked under the blanket. "Look." Scooping up the painful objects, Abby patted the chestnut's shoulder as she came to stand beside Wade.

Wade stared for two seconds then looked up at her. "There's no way I was riding all morning with those things under my saddle."

Nodding, Abby said, "Someone shoved them in while you were having coffee."

"And no one was around here except the cowhands."

"How many of them did you say had dented pride?"

With narrow eyes, Wade looked in the direction his men had ridden. "Most of 'em."

Abby couldn't quite control her sarcasm. "You've had a full day, then."

"What is that?" Wade's eyes narrowed on her arm. Quickly, his expression grim, he reached for the arrow. "You've been shot." He touched the arrow. Abby heard his sigh of relief as he realized it hadn't embedded in her skin. "When did this happen?"

"While the horse was going wild."

Wade pulled the arrow gently loose from her dress.

Abby glared at the weapon. "If I'd had my doeskin dress, that arrow wouldn't have even torn it. Why do you whites wear these..." What white word described it? "Weak dresses?" She went back to soothing the horse.

"Abby, I'd like to remind you that you're just as white as I am. Whiter actually, considering the blond hair."

Furious to be reminded, she ignored him to tend to the horse.

"Where did the arrow come from?"

Abby tilted her head in the direction the cowhands had gone. "It's got the markings of a Salish arrow, but none of my people sent an arrow my way."

"How do you know?"

"It's not their way to shoot at a woman from cover. That is the coward's way, the white man's way."

Wildflower Bride

Wade stared at the rocky outcropping that the cowhands had rounded. "It wouldn't be very hard to hide in those rocks. My cowpokes could ride right past a bushwhacker and never see a thing."

Abby looked at him. "Let's go see if the back-shooting coyote has run away."

"You can be sure he has. But he might have left some sign."

Wade fastened the horse's saddle again; the horse now stood calm and steady. Wade stroked the horse's neck, and Abby was struck by his kindness. So different from Wild Eagle.

Thinking of Wild Eagle made her remember something else. "In the madness of the massacre of my village, I remember the men getting off their horses. . .to torch the tepees and club a few of the wounded." Abby glared at the arrow. "Whoever shot that arrow at me just now might have stolen it from my village. He might be the same one who killed my family."

Wade looked as grim as death. "Could be. If that's right, he may still be after you."

"Or you. Or both of us. We both were there when I pulled off that man's mask."

Frowning, Wade reached his hand down for Abby and she swung up in front of him. It was her designated place, after all.

"If you're right and it wasn't one of your people, then who else would know how a Flathead arrow looks?" Wade asked.

"My village is. . .was solitary, and only a small group of us spent summers in that valley. Years ago my Flathead father and Wild Eagle's father defied the rest of the tribe. We would go with our tribe for the winter, but in the summer we returned to our ancestors' hunting grounds. The rest of our people live far to the south all the time, but the land is not so fair as our high mountain meadow. We hunt and fish and live quietly there. We don't run off livestock or steal horses. We have never harmed anyone, but neither do we mix with the whites or trade with them. Knowing how we make our arrows wouldn't be common knowledge."

They reached the outcropping of rock. "There's a very good chance then that there is only one group of whites who would have access to one of your arrows." Wade swung off the horse then reached up to lift Abby down before she could tell him she'd manage fine on her own.

"The men who killed my people."

"Yes." Wade lowered her to the ground. "And I've made men angry enough that they might want to harm me here on the M Bar S, so somehow my ranch hands might have knowledge of your people. A lot of 'em are new. If they rode the mountain trails, they could have come upon your people. Their anger could explain the burrs under my saddle and even someone taking a shot at me. But why you? Why both of us together? The only thing we've done together is see that man and face your angry mother-in-law."

Abby frowned. "What is that word, 'mother-in-law'? What does it mean?"

"Your husband, Wild Eagle—his mother is your mother-in-law."

Abby nodded slowly. "But Wild Eagle wasn't my husband. We were to be wed at midsummer."

Wade stopped studying the crags above and turned to her. "You told me he was your husband. Was he or wasn't he?"

Abby shrugged then pointed upward. "He would have needed to be about there?"

Wade caught her by the shoulder and turned her to face him.

"What?" She scowled, annoyed at being interrupted from her search for a path up the steep rocks.

"Were you married to Wild Eagle or not?"

Abby tried to sort the vague meaning of his words. "We were... to be married. He had spoken for me and the marriage was coming very soon. As soon as we settled in our summer grounds."

Wade's hand stayed on her shoulder. He looked into her eyes in a way that made Abby allow his touch when she should have shaken him off. "I. . .I'm sorry for your loss. You must have loved him very much."

Wildflower Bride

"Love is. . .it is not a reason among my people to marry. At least not for me. I was treated well by the Flatheads, but I was not one of them and they never let me forget it. It was not a choice for me to marry him. Even less so because of my white heritage. In fact, I am much too old by my village's standards to be marrying for the first time. And I might not have ever been accepted as a wife if Wild Eagle hadn't wanted me after his first wife died. I was given an order. Wild Eagle was to be the future chief of our village. He could have any woman he chose. It was an honor that he chose me."

The concern and kindness in his eyes drew Abby in, made her want to look closer, deeper. Her body swayed, and possibly Wade helped her along because she was closer to him. His grip, with those gentle hands, was firm and compelling.

"Abby." His voice was a whisper, so soft it seemed to come from inside her, from her own thoughts and feelings. "Do you mourn him?"

Against her will, her head shook just a bit, just enough to warm his gaze.

"Did you let him into your heart, or is there room in there for another?"

She opened her mouth to reply, not sure what that answer would be, but his lips touched hers, brushing softly as if a butterfly had passed by.

Drawing in a sudden breath from the enticement of those lips, Abby waited, watched. Then her eyes drifted closed and the butterfly returned and landed.

After seconds passed, Wade lifted his head and studied her. "I'll take that for an answer that there is room. For me."

Her eyes opened and her mind began to work again. . .and her ability to reason. She took two quick steps back and crossed her arms. "That should not have happened."

"You're right."

"You will stay away from. . . I'm right?"

"Yes, you're a guest in my home. It's not proper that such as that kiss passed between us. I will explain things to Gertie when we get home, and she will become more than the housekeeper. She'll become a chaperone. I won't dishonor you, Abby. But my feelings for you…" He looked back at his hat. "I won't ignore them either."

At the sight of Wade's bowed head, something far away and faint trickled into Abby's head. The image of her father. He'd had a way about him of protecting her, sheltering her. A flash of his face, browned from the sun, came to her mind. He was tall and wore a hat as battered as Wade's. Blond hair instead of Wade's darker shade. Then the memory widened and Abby saw her mother, too, her parents together in the kitchen smiling at each other across a table. And one other child sitting in a high chair near her mother.

"Lind. I…I think my name is Abby Lind." Abby straightened as more memories flooded in. "We lived far from here, I believe. I traveled a long way with the Flatheads. It seemed that we traveled for days on end, but I'm not sure. When their hunting party found me, my family was dead." Abby's voice broke.

"And the hunting party came…" Wade urged her to continue, saving her from that most horrible memory of being alone with her father's body. "And…"

"My father, my tribal father, took me to live with his people. Walter Lind, maybe. I think that's right."

Abby looked up. "I could find them, I believe, now that I know my father's name. And maybe I have family somewhere back East. I had an older brother. He was grown up and gone— married I think—when we moved West." Abby closed her eyes as she tried to force the memory. "Why can't I remember? I wasn't that young."

"I suppose your life with the Flathead people was so completely different than what you'd had before, there was nothing to remind you of your early years."

Wildflower Bride

Frustrated, Abby exhaled hard. "Maybe that's it, but it seems wrong, sinful, that I forgot my family."

"You want to search for your brother? Maybe go back East and live with him?"

The tone of Wade's voice told Abby that he was dismayed at that news. It pulled her out of her discouragement at the blank wall where her memories ought to be.

She couldn't quite manage a smile, but her heart lightened. "I have no place in the East. Montana is too settled to suit me. There were great cities back there. I don't remember living in one, but I was told. No, I have no wish to go, but I might want to learn of my white family, let them know I am alive."

"I can help you with that. I'll send some telegraphs the next time I'm in town. If your pa bought land, or homesteaded, there'd be a record of it." Wade settled his hat back on his head firmly. "So your Flathead father took you to his village and raised you as his daughter?"

"He was a good man. But I remember now that my white father was a good man, too. I remember I loved him and my ma and little brother. It's all so vague, though, the memories and the feelings."

"You'll remember more with time, I reckon. For now, let it go. It's just upsetting you. Let's see if we can find any evidence to identify our attacker."

Abby pointed to an outcropping of rock. "He must have been up there."

"How do you figure that?" Wade lifted his hat with one hand and smoothed down his hair with the other.

Abby noticed his hair was past his collar. Belle Harden had taken her scissors to it, but she hadn't cut deeply. Not as long as Wild Eagle's, but neither was he shorn like so many whites.

He'd been living in the mountains all winter. Near enough to her to hear gunshots. Roughing it nearly as much as. . .maybe more than. . .the people in their winter hunting grounds in the Bitterroot Valley.

"The arrow was slanted downward, but not arcing down. He couldn't have been higher or lower than that ledge."

Scowling, Wade turned from where she pointed. "You got all that while you were under my horse's hooves?"

Abby snorted. "How do you whites survive in the West?"

"So were they shooting at you or me? Whoever put those burrs under my saddle couldn't have known where you'd be standing, so maybe he was hoping—"

"Hoping to blame it on the Flathead people?"

"Or hoping in the distraction of the rearing horse he'd get us both at once."

"I have done nothing to deserve murder."

"Oh, well I suppose I have," Wade said sarcastically.

"You've come home. It looks to me as if some among your people might have thought this ranch was free for the claiming with your father hurt and maybe dying."

"It's a fine welcome home, isn't it? I've only been back one day."

"And someone's already trying to kill you."

"No one tries to kill a man with a few burrs under a saddle. I've been thrown off many a horse in my day while breaking broncs. Sure, a man could die, but it's not a reliable way to kill. Most often, you just get up and walk away."

"Your father didn't."

Freezing where he stood, Wade seemed to look beyond what lay in front of him. "True. Someone could finish me off and make it look like a fall killed me."

"But that would only work if there were no witnesses."

"Like you." Wade pulled the burrs and stones from his shirt pocket and glared at them. "Someone tried to kill my pa."

"Not my people. We'd only moved to our summer grounds recently, long after your father was hurt. And now my whole village is dead or gone back to the larger tribal settlement. There are no Flatheads about to try and kill either of us." Abby raised the arrow to eye level.

Wildflower Bride

Throwing the burrs and rock on the ground, Wade stomped them with his boot. "So welcome home. It's good to be back, huh?"

"It's not my home, white man."

"Lucky girl."

CHAPTER 13

Sid missed.

He had a chance to end this all at one time and blame it on the savages, but he'd missed. He'd done his share of bow hunting, so he was good, but he hadn't counted on that horse being so close to her when it exploded.

Then that half-wild woman turned the horse so it blocked his next shots.

Furious at wasting the opportunity and putting Wade on guard, Sid jumped down from the rocks where they'd hidden the bow and the arrows they'd made to look like the Flatheads'. Ready for a chance to finish this and lay the blame on the Indians, Sid ran for Paddy, who waited just around the bend with his horse. They were far enough behind the cowhands that no one paid attention when they caught up to them in the mountain valley, lush with thick grass.

"We can't stick together." Sid glared at the incompetent cowhands he'd hired. He hadn't wanted trail-savvy men on the payroll, but now hiring this pack of fools and running off so many of the experienced drovers would likely cost Sid his job. And he needed to be here, on the spot, to take the reins when the old man died. . .which was going to be soon.

Paddy knew cattle, Sid would give him that. "Let's split those two up." Paddy nodded toward a pair of half-grown boys, brothers who looked to be running away from nursery school. The pair didn't know the kicking end of a horse from the biting end.

"They must have come West on the train. They don't have a lick of horse sense." Paddy snickered as he watched one of them fighting his well-trained pony when the pony was smarter than the kid. The sandy brown longhorns that dotted the flowing grassland ripped grass from the ground and chewed while the cowboys tried to get them moving.

"And try 'n' teach 'em something, Pad. Wade isn't man enough to run me off, but there are enough of the old hands left that, if Chester tells 'em to back that young whelp, I won't be able to hold on to this place." Sid grunted when one of the boys nearly fell off his cutting horse. "Maybe if we bring a few of these men along, we can put off that fight. I want Boog and Harv here backing me when that happens."

Paddy nodded and spurred his horse toward the pair.

Sid looked back to see Wade riding through the narrow canyon mouth. Sid scanned the lay of the land, figured where he'd perch to take a shot. He needed to finish this soon with the boy then take out that old he-coon Mort Sawyer. He should have shot him where he lay that night. Instead he'd left him for dead, preferring to make it look like an accident. He could have crushed his head with a rock, though. Or run his horse over the still form until there was nothing left of him.

He'd outsmarted himself that time.

Before Wade could ride up, Sid went and took one of the boys Paddy was working with under his own wing. The fool kid was game, Sid would give him that.

❧

Silas dismounted and crouched by the half-gone hoofprint.

"The cattle passed this way for sure." Red stayed on Buck and rode forward, patting his loyal old horse to encourage him. "They had to, but it looks like a solid wall of rock ahead."

Silas swung back up. "Let's go over that area really closely. These cattle were headed somewhere."

They were surrounded by rugged scrub pines and tightly bunched groves of quaking aspen. Some still small, others much taller. They were just leafing out for the spring, and they grew like an impenetrable wall in front of the rock wall that seemed to have erupted straight out of the heart of the earth.

The ground was pebbles and stone, and if cattle had come this way, the trail had been concealed by a master. The occasional rare bit of a hoof would have been lost if Red was alone, but Silas knew the trail and had an eagle eye. They urged their horses forward as the slippery rocks underfoot gave way to the scratching branches of the scrub pines. "How did anyone get cattle to come through here?"

"Yeah"—Silas eased his sorrel forward—"through here to nowhere." Silas pointed.

"I see it. Another print." Red marveled at the skill of the man. He was good on a trail, but Silas humbled him.

Reaching down, Silas snagged a tiny tuft from one of the sharp branches that tried to claw them to a stop. He held it up. "Fur. A couple of my cattle are red. Herefords. Weirdest thing. We found Herefords in among our herd."

Silas held the fur so it gleamed orange against the brownish red of his sorrel gelding.

"Those probably are descendants of the cattle Cassie's first husband owned." Red studied the fur. "He had some dumb idea about red cattle being the future of the West."

Silas snorted. "Maybe if the land was lush everywhere and water plentiful. There are places those animals could thrive, but not out here."

"It wasn't the only dumb thing the man did."

Silas smiled and continued urging his unhappy sorrel gelding forward.

Red saw Silas's eyes sharpen, and Red followed his gaze.

"A game trail. Right here, going. . ." Silas lifted his eyes.

The rock wall was almost sheer. Red studied it as they drew nearer. Their horses were single file with Silas in the lead, but they moved calmly forward now, no urging necessary. The stone was streaked with shades of brown.

Suddenly, only a horse length ahead of him, Silas vanished.

Gasping, Red leaned forward and saw it. The wall wasn't solid. The game trail veered into a crevice, disguised by the streaks in the stone and the overlapping of one side of the split in the rock. Red found himself in what would have been a tunnel if it wasn't open on top, nearly fifty feet overhead and less than four feet wide. It twisted and turned like a sleeping rattler. Red's throat closed in the tight passageway. There wasn't room to turn around. If this was a dead end, Red would have to back his horse the whole way out.

The scratch of hooves ahead said Silas was still making progress. Buck walked forward without hesitation.

"Silas?"

The response was only a whisper. "Quiet."

Falling silent, Red began to study the ground and saw clearly that many animals had passed this way. A hairpin turn in the canyon brought Red to Silas.

The trail widened for a few feet, and Silas waited silently. "The cattle are in here somewhere sure as you're born. All these cattle prints go in; none come out. The horses, though, go both ways."

"Must be some kind of dead-end canyon in there with enough grass to feed at least a few head of cows."

Silas nodded. "The trail coming up to this gap couldn't be that well covered if it was a big bunch."

"And there could be a back trail out, too."

Silas's eyes narrowed as he considered that. "Then why do the horses come and go this way so often?"

"We'll soon find out." Red could see ahead twenty feet before the gap twisted and went out of sight again. "What are we going to face when we catch up to these rustlers? A band of armed men?"

Silas shook his head. "They've quit covering their trail since we got inside the canyon. Tracks from four different horses. I'm thinking only two of them are in there right now." Silas pointed to a distinct print. "Those two horses walked over top of the rest. And one set is even fresher than the other. I think they've settled in for a few days, letting the cattle heal from rebranding maybe before they drive them off and make a sale somewhere."

Red's eyes met Silas's. "Do we take 'em?"

Silas was dead serious for a few seconds. Then a slow smile crept across his face. "I kinda wish Belle was here. She's a mighty fine help in a fight."

Shuddering to think of Cassie showing up, Red shook his head. "I guess that's a yes, then."

"A definite yes."

"But let's go slow." Red swung down off Buck and led the way to the next twist in the gap.

The trail narrowed and they went single file.

Red saw the first glimpse of sky ahead and knew they'd gotten to some kind of canyon. Then a chill cut through him so hard he jerked his horse backward. The poor horse danced back, and Silas had to step lively to keep from getting trampled.

"What's wrong?" Silas's voice carried, but just barely.

Red kept backing his horse, and Silas had no choice but to do the same. When they reached the wider spot, Buck backed until he was even with Silas's sorrel; then Red pulled him to a halt.

"What happened?"

Red opened his mouth. Nothing came out. Finally, feeling foolish, he said, "I just, well, honest, Si, I felt like God jabbed me in the belly with an icicle. Something told me loud and clear not to go into that canyon."

Silas stared at Red then turned to look at the passageway. At last he nodded. "If someone's on watch, we might walk right into blazing guns. Okay then, what do we do?"

Red almost heaved a sigh of relief that his gut instinct didn't bring him ridicule. He knew, though he'd be hard pressed to explain it, that God Himself had just sent him a message. A life-saving message. Emerging from that gap was walking straight into the teeth of a gun.

Silas was a man of the West, used to the odd ways of a trail. He was also a man of faith. Red had talked to him enough to know that. But not all men of faith did a good job of walking in that faith. Not all believers managed to live up to trusting God with their lives. Apparently, Silas did.

And finally, just as sure as the cold poke in Red's belly came to him, so did something else. "I have an idea."

CHAPTER 14

I have an idea." Belle quit the lassoing lesson. Cassie was getting just plain dependable with her rope. "Let's go throw your knife for a while."

Cassie grinned. "That'll be fun."

Belle almost groaned at the woman's complete lack of killer instinct. "This isn't about fun, Cassie Dawson. How many times do I have to tell you—"

"Yes, ma'am." Folding her hands meekly, she hunched her shoulders a bit. "This is about self-defense."

"Cassie!"

Cassie froze then scowled at Belle in such a phony way that Belle had to fight back a laugh.

"Don't you take that tone with me, Belle Harden. I've got all the...the..." Cassie's scowl faded to a frown. "What'd you call it?"

Emma was pulling her own razor-sharp knife from the sheath on her hip as she walked past Cassie heading toward the target drawn on the barn. She whispered, "Killer instinct."

Smiling her gratitude, Cassie said, "Thanks, honey. That's right. Killer instinct. I've got a lot of that."

Belle rolled her eyes, looking to heaven for mercy for this little marshmallow. How had Red kept her alive this long? Of course, Cassie had survived with her first husband, that worthless Lester Griffin, for three years. So she had to have some toughness in her.

Cassie lined up beside Emma and Belle. Emma sent her knife whizzing, and it landed square in the dead center of the big charcoal circle with the black dot in the center for a bull's-eye.

"Ouch." Cassie flinched.

"What?" Emma turned. "Did something hurt?"

"No, I just wish we could call it something besides a bull's-eye. Just thinking of that knife stabbing a poor defenseless bull right in the eye. . . I mean the bull didn't do anything to deserve—"

"I'm next." Belle cut her off, unable to stand this complaint for the fortieth time. Belle's knife hit with a dull *thud*, a fraction of an inch above Emma's. "I aimed a little high so our knives wouldn't scratch. That's hard on the edge."

Emma nodded.

Cassie squared off and drew her knife.

Emma stepped back four long, quick steps.

So did Belle. She felt there came a point when it wasn't cowardly to protect herself, and Cassie's knife throwing was—no pun intended—that point. "Act like you're mad at it, Cass."

Cassie threw with all her might, and it hit the barn. True, the knife hit on its side rather than the tip, but it was progress.

"You've got the range down. Good. Try again."

By the time the afternoon had faded to evening, Cassie had gotten the knife to stick right in the wood nearly ten times. Ten successes out of one thousand throws wasn't great, but. . . "A journey of a thousand miles begins with a single step." Cassie jerked her chin in a determined nod.

"What's that?" Belle thought it sounded true, though.

"An old saying of my mother's." Cassie pulled her knife out of the barn.

Emma and Belle had split the chores so one of them could stay near Cassie to stem any bleeding she brought on herself. . .

and protect the children. Sarah was doing her best to keep the young'uns in the house and well out of harm's way.

"What's it mean?" Emma asked.

"It means that if I have to throw this knife wrong ten thousand times to learn how to throw it right, then it's a good thing I've gotten past the first one thousand throws today. Because I am going to learn to defend myself better."

"At that rate, considering you're just making up that ten thousand number—but still, it's a good guess—you'll be throwing your knife like a pro in ten days." Belle thought that was wildly optimistic, but she didn't tell Cassie so.

Cassie beamed. "Maybe I'll throw it two thousand times tomorrow just to speed things along."

"You've got to leave time to feed your baby."

"True, suckling a baby does slow a woman down from learning to knife fight."

Belle laughed just as Sarah called them for supper. She rested one arm on Emma's waist and the other on Cassie's. "Let's go eat."

The three happy knife wielders walked into supper together.

"I found out today Sid hadn't started spring roundup." Wade served himself some mashed potatoes.

Abby noticed Wade's casual tone, but his shoulders tensed as if he braced himself for Mort's reaction.

"What?" Mort's fist slammed on the white cloth. The heavy silverware jumped, and Gertie's water glass tipped on its slender stem. She caught it so deftly, Abby wondered how often Mort punched the table.

"We started today." Wade spoke calmly considering his father's face was so bright red. Abby wondered if a head could explode.

"It's a month late! We'll be pushing to get the roundup done in time to cut the herd and get a drive to Helena." Mort shoved against the table and his chair rolled backward. Abby hoped he stayed there, away from the breakables. But Mort rolled himself right back up to the food. "If you'd have been here, this wouldn't be happening." Mort backed his rolling chair away from the table, heading straight for Wade, who sat on his left. Lifting his fist, Mort seemed determined to throw a punch.

Wade stood, positioned his chair between himself and his father, and stopped Mort in his tracks. "You think I'm going to sit there and let you hit me? You really think I'll put up with that from you ever again?" Wade laughed.

It sounded like an honest laugh to Abby. But "ever again" sounded like Wade had known his father's fists before. There was nothing to laugh about here.

"You'd never have the guts to stand up to me if I wasn't in this chair. You're taking advantage of an injured man. You're a weakling! A little, worthless fool." Mort grabbed at Wade's abandoned chair as if he would throw it aside.

Abby flinched and glanced at Gertie. Gertie stared down at her lap, the sorrow on her face telling Abby clearly that this was something that had gone on many times before.

"I know what comes next." Wade held the chair in place with little effort, his strength far exceeding his father's. "You're ashamed to call me your son." He said the words in a singsong way as if they bored him. "I've heard it a thousand times before."

"I am! How did I raise such a coward? If you'd been here—"

"Pa, stop!" Wade's voice was clear but calm.

Abby could hear no anger in it. Only strength underlaid with kindness. But this wasn't a kind of strength she understood. Strength was Wild Eagle's skill with bow and lance. It was riding a horse, racing across the rugged hills. It was battling hand to hand and winning. It was anger and physical domination. Mort's strength seemed more familiar, except being bound to that chair stole any true strength.

"You know why I left this place and you know I only came

back because you were hurt. We've had this out."

"Don't start with your preaching."

"There'll be no preaching. You're not a stupid man. I've spoken to you of my faith and I won't speak of it again unless you ask. It's yours to accept or reject. But know this—if it hadn't been for your accident, and what I believe is my God-given duty to honor my father, I would *never* have come back."

Mort glared.

"I know what you want to say. I can see it in your eyes." Wade stayed on his feet with the chair a barrier Mort couldn't cross. "You want to throw me out. But you can't, not in your condition. Not now especially, now that you know your foreman is incompetent. So you're stuck putting up with me for now. Just as I'm stuck putting up with you. I give you news that makes you furious, and as usual you have no control over yourself. Not something I consider strength, Pa."

The truth of that resonated with Abby. Yes, much of Wild Eagle's strength had instead been simple anger, a tantrum suited more to a small child.

Wade held Mort's eyes, refusing to look away or back down. "All your temper is doing is letting our dinner get cold."

Mort's hands tightened on the chair between the two men.

The moment stretched.

Abby noticed the gravy on her potatoes had quit its lovely steaming, and she resented missing out on the savory food while it was piping hot. She could stand it no longer. "Roll yourself back to your place at the table, old man, or I'm throwing your meal out to the dogs. That's what we do in my village when the two-year-olds act up at mealtime."

Mort's head snapped around.

Wade inhaled so sharply he started to cough. It almost sounded like laughter, but that wasn't possible.

Gertie looked up from her hands, her eyes wide with fear.

Abby took a quick look at the others then glared at Mort.

"What? Am I supposed to pretend that this noise is anything but weakness? Am I supposed to respect a man who would insult and threaten his son, when his son is the only one who can save his ranch? This is some white man's game I don't know how to play, and I refuse to learn. Eat. Both of you. Now."

They obeyed her.

She expected them to, but Gertie seemed stunned. Abby ate her food quietly, ignoring everyone else. The clink of silverware on plates annoyed her as she considered with contempt the ritual involved in a meal. "How many travois does it take to move on if the water goes foul or the herd dies off in a blizzard? You could never take the house. Explain to me why you built this huge structure."

Wade looked up from his plate and smiled at her. A warm smile that reminded her of the moment that had passed between them this afternoon. And another such moment a year ago, when Wade had saved her from treacherous men. He'd done that twice now.

"It keeps the snow off our heads."

Abby rolled her eyes. "The plates, the tables and chairs, such a burden. Eat out of a communal pot. Sit on the dirt floor. Why would you box in such a huge part of the outdoors then be left to clean it and heat it and build useless pieces of furniture to fill it? Why not just leave the outdoors. . .outdoors and let God keep it hot or cold to suit Himself?"

"You told me you believe in God, Abby. That your people believed in Jesus."

"Yes, we were visited by the Blackrobes."

"Blackrobes?"

"Our word for men who came talking of the white man's God. The first such man came years ago, long before I lived with the Flathead. A man named DeSmet spent a long while with our people. We respected him greatly and embraced his teachings. Other Blackrobes have come since, including one last winter. There are many believers in the one God among my people."

"I've heard of DeSmet." Mort spoke, sounding almost polite.

Abby braced herself for his cruelty. It was nearly all she'd heard from him since they'd met.

"He walked into a hostile Sioux gathering of five thousand warriors and demanded to talk to Sitting Bull. He convinced them to sign a peace treaty when they were talking war. I never knew he'd been around here. Imagine the strength of the man—facing down Sitting Bull."

"He walked with God. That was his strength. My people told me so. My Flathead mother knew him well. She was a young girl when he lived among them. There was a greatness to him that led us to embrace his words when we would have driven off another white man. And we have passed that belief in his faith down over the years."

Mort stared at her. "You're saying you believe in this God stuff, too? You, raised as a savage?"

"You were the one who lifted your fist to your son. Neither my Flathead father nor my white father ever did such to me or *anyone* except in self-defense. You are the only savage at this table, old man."

Mort glowered at her.

"Do you now wish to strike me? Is that what makes you feel like a man?"

Mort shook his head. "I'm done with this meal and this company." Mort, his head shaggy with overgrown white hair, turned to Wade. "Move aside, boy, so I can get to bed. Been a long day, my first to be moving so much. I'm tired."

"Do you need help getting settled for the night, Pa?"

At first Abby thought Mort would shout and threaten again. His fists clenched and his face reddened. For a long, taut minute he seemed to fight a battle within himself. Mort said at last, "I might. I'll call you in later if I can't manage."

Astonished, Abby remembered that in her village she'd been taught that the elders of the tribe were to be revered. Her dealings with Mort to this point had been anything but reverent.

Wade, however, had spoken of honoring his father. Ashamed of herself, Abby watched Mort nod, his eyes downcast, as he waited for his son to politely move the same chair they'd used as a wall between them earlier. Mort rolled past that side of the table.

Laying one hand on his father's shoulder, Wade said, "I'll get things straightened out fast with the roundup, Pa."

"Thanks." Nodding, Mort headed for the office they'd converted to a bedroom.

CHAPTER 15

"Belle, honey, I might need you to shoot a man."

"Now, Silas? Or can it wait until after lunch?"

"After lunch is probably soon enough. The Jessups are sending three men over. They'll sleep in the barn and watch over Cassie and the children. I need a couple of sharpshooters, though. Can Emma come, too?"

"I want to go. I'm a good shot." Cassie smiled eagerly.

Suppressing a groan, Red went to his newly bloodthirsty wife's side and slid an arm around her waist. "You are a good shot. But someone's gotta stay here with the young'uns."

"We can take the children."

Silas shook his head and scrubbed his face with his gloved hands. "No babies allowed in our posse. That's final. Belle, tell her. I'm going to get something to eat." Silas marched inside.

"You go eat, too, Red," Belle ordered. "We can't leave until the Jessups get here, so there's time."

Cassie turned, her hands fisted and plunked on her hips, as Red, recognizing a will stronger than his own, obeyed Belle. As he went in the house, he heard Cassie say, "Don't you tell me what to do, Belle Tanner."

128

"It's Harden," Silas yelled from inside the house. "Try and remember her name, Cassie."

The Jessups showed up, three of the six brothers, who batched with their pa on a nearby ranch. They were a rough bunch, with no female influences to soften their manly ways, but decent men and the Dawsons' closest neighbors. They often rode over to share church services when the weather wasn't fit for them to all get to Divide.

Red was pretty sure they were believers, but he didn't kid himself that they were coming for his sermons. They liked looking at his pretty wife and two little children. The men were as fascinated by the young'uns as they were by Cassie. . .well, almost. Close enough Red hadn't had to punch anyone yet.

Despite her nagging, Red, Silas, Belle, and Emma left Cassie behind.

"I can't thank you enough for teaching Cassie to stand up for herself more." Red considered Belle to be an uncommonly intelligent woman. No chance she missed the sarcasm.

Belle worked the lever on her Winchester as her horse galloped smoothly along, the four riders abreast.

They made good time closing the distance to the gap. It had been slow going to keep up with the faint trail before, but now they knew where they were headed.

"You may not like her standing up to you—"

"She's never had much trouble standing up to me anyway. Maybe a little bit at first, but it didn't last."

"But she needs to stand on her own two feet. What if something happened to you? You want her to be trapped like she was last time, when that worthless Lester Griffin died? Forced into a marriage she doesn't want? The next time she might not get as lucky as to have a kindhearted man at the ready to save her."

"What do you want us to do, Pa?" Emma slipped her rifle into the boot on her saddle and settled in to take the long ride to the gap.

"Red's idea. Let him explain." Silas rode with Belle on his left and Emma on his right. Red was beside Belle, probably so she was handy to protect them both, trusting Emma to take care of herself.

Remembering how Belle had taught Cassie to sass him, Red couldn't bring himself to break the news of what Belle's part of this plan entailed.

"You want me to scale that mountain?" Belle stared at the sheer rock. "Emma, too?"

"This is the steepest part." Red pointed to his left. "There's an easy place to climb farther down that way." Relatively easy.

Silas pointed right. "And Emma, you can climb that tree. It'll take you up to that rock shelf." Silas raised his hand, his finger pointing almost straight upward. "From there you can get a clear view of the canyon inside. Be mighty careful when you get up there. Keep your head down. We think there are two men in there, and they're wily. They most likely are watching the gap, but they could see some movement on the rim, too."

"They had to be wily to find that gap." Belle studied the almost invisible fissure in the sheer rock wall.

A low rumble turned them around in their saddles. "And here comes the rest of my plan." Red settled his hat firmly on his head and turned to see cattle of all colors, but mostly brown with dust, tromping up the trail.

Jessups, the three sons who weren't staying to protect Cassie, herded twenty head of cattle up the trail.

"You think they'll find that gap?" Emma reined her horse aside to make way for the oncoming cattle and to help funnel them toward the rocky gap. The girl knew more about horses, cattle, and ranching than Red ever would.

"Get to climbing, girls. We'll hold the herd till you give us a signal." Silas rode with Belle to make sure her horse got tied up tight when Belle started climbing. Red followed Emma, though the Harden horses were so well trained Red suspected they'd both stand untied and riderless for hours.

As Emma stood on her horse's back and reached for the nearest branch on the twisted pine tree growing out of the rock, she said to Red, "How'd you come up with this plan anyway?"

"Well, my first idea was to dynamite the gap."

Emma swung herself up to sit on a branch then looked down at him. "That seems kinda mean hearted."

"I s'pose. But in a way, it's no different than putting those outlaws in jail. If we catch 'em, they'll be hanged or end up in the territorial prison. They'd probably be happier in that canyon."

"I didn't say it was bad, just mean. I like it. If this doesn't work, Ma and I can ride to Divide for the dynamite."

Red sincerely hoped it did work, or chances were he and Silas and the Jessup brothers wouldn't live to tell the tale. Belle and Emma would be all right, though. No one was going to get them up on those rocks. And between the two of them and Cassie, there would be three remaining Jessup men to marry.

The more Red thought about his own sweet Cassie married to one of the Jessups, the more determined he was to win this showdown.

Emma scrambled up the rock wall like a mountain goat and vanished over the rim. Red turned to see Belle swing over the top with her rifle strapped on her back.

Red and Silas rode out to meet the Jessups. All three cut from the same cloth, dark hair windblown and too long for respectability. They all were lean, running to skin and bones, with weathered skin and eyes, wise to the trail.

"Let's get this over and done." Red fell into a semicircle with the Jessups and Silas, urging the cattle forward, hoping that a sudden rush of cattle and gunfire from above would give them the seconds they needed to breach this outlaw fortress.

"We're short a couple of men, Chester." Wade looked up from the list he'd made when he went over the ranch books late in the evening.

Chester slapped leather on a feisty black mustang Wade had always admired. Chester was a steady hand, and with that bright-eyed little cutting horse under him, there was no cow that could best him. "Boog's at the line shack and Harv's in at the doc's. Sid left him because he needed some care and we don't have time for it."

"Harv's the one that came up on the rustlers, right?"

"Yep, caught a man kneeling over a calf, using a running iron. Leastways that's what Sid said. Harv wasn't talkin'. The outlaw knocked him cold. Sid couldn't get anything out of him, a description of the man or the horse."

Wade stared at his notes for a long second. "I went in to the doctor's office to talk to him and he's taken off. So that's another hand we've lost. We've been losing cattle all winter, it sounds like."

"Yep, nothing big, but more than can be explained by wolves and blizzards. And we've got more than two men missing; three of the hands you picked out yesterday as no-accounts were gone when I woke up this morning. Payday was last week. They didn't have cash coming and they didn't want to work, so why wait around?"

Wade got their names and marked them off his list. "That leaves us shorthanded, but those men weren't pulling their weight anyway. We're no worse off. I don't want to take the time to ride to Divide and hire more help. We can get by until the roundup is finished. Who sent Boog out to the line shack?"

"Sid. Bad thinking, too, because Boog's a top hand. Too fast with his gun, but he knows cattle. Did the work of two men. Harv wasn't so good. Knew the job but didn't push any harder'n he had to."

"What was my pa thinking to hire Sid?"

Chester shrugged. "You want my opinion? Your pa wasn't right in the head when he made that decision. Sid rode in a couple of days after Mort was hurt. He went in the house and came out with the foreman job. I'd have accused him of lying about being hired except he went in that house every day, a couple of times a day, and did a lot of the heavy lifting work for Gertie."

"Pa must have just not cared after he fell. I think he's coming out of the worst of that black mood and starting to show interest in the ranch again." At least a little. Most of it rooted in anger. But Wade didn't think those words would encourage Chester.

"Whatever Sid said, Mort must have agreed to hire him. I accepted that Mort was out of his head. First because he was knocked cold. Then, when he realized his legs wouldn't work, he was half crazy. Sid knows cattle, I'll give him that, but he did a poor excuse of hiring hands and a worse excuse for bossing them. He's as lazy as the rest of this lot."

"One hard week, Chester, we'll have the cattle branded and can start cutting out the stock for a drive. We'll put them in the valley with the lush grass and let 'em fatten up then drive 'em to Helena."

"We'll have to push it to give 'em any time at all on grass before market." Chester swung up on horseback. The mustang danced and crow-hopped a little, but it was just spirit and Chester knew how to stick a saddle. "There'll be no break between roundup and cutting the herd like most years. And even if we push, there won't be as much time to fatten the cattle as we'd like."

"Sittin' here talkin' doesn't add any more days to the year." Wade finished saddling his own horse. "Let's get on with it. We're burning daylight."

CHAPTER 16

It took considerable work to get the first of those stubborn cattle into the gap.

For a few minutes—which seemed like an eternity—Red thought he'd come up with a real poor idea.

The cattle balked inside the gap. They tried to turn.

Red had worked cattle for years, though, and he knew a thing or two. He and the rest of the men kept them crowded against the rock wall but didn't push. Instead they waited, letting the herd sniff around and calm down.

When the herd was settled and quiet and a few had milled close to that narrow gap, Red began threading his way in, quietly, so as not to stir them up. He walked his horse straight into that gap without a moment's pause. He went in just a few feet and stopped and poured a small bag of corn out on the ground.

It took about ten seconds for a steer to come sniffing. He licked up the corn and followed Red straight on in.

Silas and the Jessups would work from the rear.

Red kept moving until he got to the slightly wider section of the gap and then eased to the side to let the cattle come on past him. Because others followed the first, the lead steer was pushed along, though he balked when he passed Red. Red used Buck's big body to crowd the animal forward. Dust churned underfoot as the animals bawled and slashed with their wide horns.

Choking on the dirt, Red forced the recalcitrant longhorn forward until they both pushed past the wider spot. Then Red dodged to the side and dropped back to push the next cow forward. In here they could walk three abreast. A few tried to turn and go back.

Silas pushed up beside Red, and the two of them had a few uneasy moments as the cattle wallowed in dirt they were churning up from the canyon floor until it was nearly blinding. At last they moved forward, and the rest followed, pushed by the herd. They picked up speed and began trotting as Red had hoped they would, straight into the rustlers' canyon.

A single shot rang out when the first steer charged through. Then gunfire exploded from overhead.

Red kicked his horse into the line of cattle, dodging those vicious horns. The gunfire from inside the canyon stopped before Red reached the opening. But the shooting from overhead, from Belle and Emma, rained down like hailstones. Red, Silas right behind him and the Jessups a few jumps after that, charged into the valley.

Red leaned low over Buck's shoulders to make less of a target. Eyeing the terrain, high and low, for likely lookout spots, Red brought his gun level as Buck's hooves thundered. Exploding bits of rock drew his eye to an outcropping about fifty yards straight ahead. The perfect spot to keep watch on that canyon mouth.

Judging by the boulder being battered by gunfire, Belle and Emma had seen the outlaw take a shot when the first longhorn came through. Then they'd pinned the shooter down. He must be crouched at ground level, so he'd never get a clear shot at the womenfolk. And the women made it impossible for the varmint to get a shot at Red and the rest of his posse. Perfect.

The focus of the gunfire was so exact Red knew Belle hadn't seen a threat from any other direction or she'd have aimed at one man while Emma took care of the other. It struck Red as just a bit amazing to have such complete confidence in a woman and her skill with a rifle. Amazing but true, because Red had no doubt Belle wouldn't make the mistake of being careless. But there were two men in here. Red knew it from the tracks. One had yet to show himself. Which meant he still posed a threat.

In the melee of bawling cattle and guns, Red raced his horse for cover, hearing the beating of shod hooves behind him. Swinging down, Red saw Silas alight right beside him. Silas had a look of such satisfaction as he threw himself against the rocks, Red knew the man was button-popping proud of his wife and daughter.

Red, Silas, and all three Jessups had made it into the canyon without a scratch. The women had things so well under control they hadn't even had to duck any gunfire. A quick glance told Red that none of the cattle were even wounded. The bad *hombre* who'd done the shooting had fired a single time, and he'd missed. Or maybe he'd pulled his aim when he recognized a longhorn was coming through. But that one shot had alerted Belle, and that had been the end of the shootout.

"Spread out," Silas yelled. "We can get the drop on him, if Belle hasn't filled him with lead."

The five men fanned out, slipping along the scattered rocks of the canyon entrance. There was plenty of cover in the rugged mountain canyon once they'd cleared the opening. They drew steadily nearer the rustlers' hideout boulder, each taking turns providing cover, although Belle and Emma had pinned them down so well there was no sign of a man.

At last Red found a place on the canyon wall slanted enough he could climb and get a good look at the hiding place. A lone man lay flat on his back. Red leveled his Winchester and shouted at the bloodthirsty women. "I've got a bead on him."

The thunder of bullets ended.

Red looked down on a pathetic excuse for a desperado. Bleeding, scratched to bits by chunks of flying rock. "There's only one man back here. Be careful. There's another here somewhere."

The man raised his hands. "I'm alone. No one with me. Don't shoot."

"Stay up there and keep us covered," Red hollered at his two faithful sharpshooters.

While Red kept his eye on the outlaw, the rest of them scoured the canyon, lush with grass, holding nearly a hundred head of cattle, all with fresh brands.

There was no one.

While the Jessups continued to search, Silas quickly trussed up the outlaw.

"Where's the other one?" Red asked.

"I'm alone." The man had an ugly cut on his chin, sewed up but still raw and red. He was clean shaven, except for close around his wound, and his hair looked like he'd cut it himself with a bowie knife and no mirror.

"I'm not talking to you." Red raised his rifle in what he hoped was a menacing fashion. Truth was he'd never so much as aimed a gun at a man. The thought of pulling the trigger made him sick.

Thank You, God. We ended this without any killing.

"We saw tracks from two men, so we know there's someone else."

"No!" The man's clothes were battered and slashed as if he'd gone a few rounds with a grizzly. "The tracks were just me riding two different horses."

Red didn't think so, and he wasn't about to take the word of cattle-stealing scum. "Silas, are you sure the canyon's empty?"

Nodding, Silas rose from beside the man he'd just hog-tied. "I was careful. But remember how that gap opened so you could barely see it? There could be a back way out of here just as hidden.

I found his camp. Two men have been here, but one's gone."

"Are Belle and Emma in danger? Could the other one have gone out over the rim?"

Both men wheeled to stare up at the women. The rocks the women stood on were so sheer from this side of the canyon that no one could have gotten within a hundred yards of them.

Emma waved down when they looked at her, but the girl was uncommonly smart. She kept low to the ground, never relaxing her guard.

"I've got me a family of women, don't I?" Silas blew a soft whistle through his teeth.

"They're the kind of women who can help tame a wild land and make no mistake about it." Red turned back to the outlaw and prodded the vermin with his toe none too gently. "They work their hearts out. They put in long hours in the blazing sun. They work in the bitter cold. They miss meals and get knocked around by longhorns and feisty mustangs. Then you come along and steal from the labor of their backs. You're going to hang, or if you're lucky, spend a lot of years in prison. Let's get you to the sheriff. Maybe if you help us catch your friend, and any others of your gang, the sentence won't be quite so long. The judge who comes through Divide likes a cooperative prisoner."

The Jessups rode up. Huey Jessup, the oldest of the brothers, seemed to be the spokesman for the taciturn family. "I think we found where a man went out on foot over the west rim. It'd be a scramble, but a man could make it and stay low enough not to draw attention. He couldn't pack things with him, though. He left on foot and his bedroll is still here. I found two horses and leather for both of 'em. We might find a name."

"Let's gather everything up," Silas said. "I'll start heading the whole herd out of here. It'll be slow going, but we need to drive them into Divide then put out the word that we've recovered stolen cows. The area ranchers can come in and identify them best they can through those altered brands."

"We'll let the law sort it out." Red untied the outlaw's feet and nudged the man to stand. "What's your name?"

Glaring through mean, animal black eyes, the man refused to answer.

Red didn't wait around to try to get it out of him. That job he'd leave for the sheriff.

CHAPTER 17

"I want this step fixed!" Pa's fist hammered against the door frame. "I want to get out of this house."

Wade had only moments ago strode into the kitchen out of the dark, up the three steps that formed a back stoop. He had a ladle full of Gertie's delicious chicken noodle stew ready to dump on a plate full of biscuits.

Wade lowered his plate and the ladle. He was starving, exhausted, frustrated, filthy, saddle-sore, and grouchy. Not a good time to have to handle his father. "How do we fix the step, Pa? Got any ideas?"

There, dump it back in Pa's lap. Wade figured the old man would rant and rave steadily for about ten minutes while Wade ate. No trouble tuning out the sound of Pa's yelling. Wade had become a master over the years. He returned to dishing up his dinner, his stomach growling nearly as loudly as his father.

"Someone with any brains would know that."

Abby came in with Gertie right behind her.

"Sit down and let me get that for you, Wade." Gertie immediately began flapping at him, shooing him aside.

Grinning, Wade escaped with his full plate and sat at the small kitchen table. It was a relief to not have to sit in the formal dining room and eat off china. Instead he had a tin plate and quick access to seconds. "Sit down with me, ladies. It's been a brutal day and I could stand the sound of a woman's voice or two."

"We're going to fix this door or I'm ripping the whole back of the house down with my bare hands." Pa grabbed at the door frame as if intending to begin right now.

Sighing, Wade said, "You ladies are gonna have to talk loud to drown out Pa."

Gertie gave Pa a wide-eyed look. Had he taken his nasty temper out on the housekeeper? In earlier days, after Wade's ma had died, Gertie had protected Wade to the extent she was able, and Wade had never seen Pa use his fists on her. But Pa's temper was out of control at times. Why else would Gertie be so scared?

Wade felt heat climbing his neck—temper. If Pa had hit Gertie. . .

"And if I can't get my own son to help me, then I'll find someone who—"

Abby laughed and jabbed a finger at Wade's plate. "You eat your food. Keep your mouth busy so we women can talk."

Pulling his thoughts from violence, Wade looked from his raging father to Gertie to Abby. "I think I'll say a prayer before I eat. Would any of you like to join me?" Prayer was what he needed very badly right now.

Pa continued shouting. Gertie stared at her entwined hands, more fearful than prayerful. Abby bowed her head.

Wade prayed quietly, ignoring his furious father, who was too wound up to even notice they weren't listening to him.

"God, thank You that the roundup is going well. Bless the hired cowhands I have. Let those who want to learn find skills here on the M Bar S that they can use all their lives. Keep us safe, help Pa get better, bless this fine food Gertie and Abby made, and let me use the strength I gain from this meal to be a good servant to You, Lord. In Jesus' name I pray. Amen."

"I've got enough money to buy and sell all of you ten times over. If you don't get this door fixed—"

"We already took a mountain of cake over to the bunkhouse. You kept the men out for such a long time." Abby braced her elbows on the table and plopped her chin on her fists. No manners at all. Wade had never seen anything so beautiful in his life. And she lived here at his house, with him.

"I'm trying to get three weeks' work done in one, and short-handed, too. But the worst of the hands quit right off, and the ones who stayed are working their hearts out trying not to lose their jobs at the end of the week. Some of them are pretty unskilled, but they're game, and they're making up with effort what they're lacking in experience."

"Stop talking and eat." Abby pointed at Wade's plate.

He couldn't help but smile at her bossy ways.

She smiled back. "I've thought that maybe we could build a ramp of dirt to the back door. Your father could be free to come and go as he pleased."

Pa quit trying to yell and jerked around to face Abby. "Really? That's a good idea."

"I may let you roll out of here then knock down the ramp so you can't get back, old man." Abby smirked at him.

Wade was appalled—and thrilled—at her disrespect. He had never dared talk to his father this way. Of course, his father had been quick with punishment, but that was when Wade was a child and had no ability to defend himself or escape.

The fear Wade battled every day, with the help of his Savior, faded, replaced with confidence that if Abby could face down his father, so could he.

"Instead of a dirt ramp, how about I have a wooden ramp built. Less work than piling up dirt. It'll be smooth and that wheelchair will roll right down it." Wade cut one of his fluffy biscuits and scooped it up with a spoonful of the savory stew.

"Quiet, eat." Abby flicked her fingers at him. "Good idea,

though. I have some practice with building. I could cut down saplings, lash them together. It wouldn't be hard." Abby turned to glare at Pa. "You could even make yourself useful and help."

Pa lifted his chin, his eyes shooting bullets.

Abby's eyes narrowed and didn't waver.

Wade watched the byplay between the two, memorizing Abby's courage and his father's impotence.

"I think we could build a special wagon without much trouble, too." Abby stared at the wheelchair. "If we tore the seat out of the buckboard and could somehow roll your chair into place, you could probably handle the reins. You could make yourself useful."

Pa slammed his fist on the arm of his chair and made a noise similar to a hissing rattler.

Wade swallowed quickly to interrupt the attack. "I asked Libby in town to send Sam out here when he's home. I thought we could widen some doorways so Pa could get to all parts of the house. Sam's a good builder. He could help with the ramp and any other ideas you've got. Pa, if you could work the buckboard, maybe you could run to Divide to pick up supplies. If we sent a list, the storekeeper would fill the order and load the wagon. You wouldn't have to get down. Your arms are still strong enough to drive. You could get out of here, see your friends."

Wade paused for a moment to consider if there was a man alive who would count Mort Sawyer as a friend. A neighbor, even a friendly acquaintance, maybe, but a friend? No one with any sense would count Pa as a friend. He had always been too ruthless to trust.

"I'm not going to town in the buckboard." Pa battled the wheelchair to roll it to the table then slugged the arms of it hard. "People would see me and pity me."

Remembering Abby's calm disrespect, Wade scraped his plate clean, chewed, and swallowed. "They probably pity you already, Pa. And you break that wheelchair, I'm not buying you another one, so calm down."

Gertie gasped.

Pa's face turned an odd shade of purple.

"Maybe if you got out, proved you can still do some work, they'd pity you less." Wade waited to see what form his pa's explosion would take.

"Probably not." Abby studied Pa as if he were an interesting species of bug. "I think they're going to pity him no matter what. But if a man were strong, strong in his guts, in his heart, he could ignore misplaced pity. Only a weakling would prefer to be useless."

Gertie slid from the table, and for a second Wade wondered if she was going to leave or maybe fly to Pa's defense. Instead she took Wade's plate and refilled it.

Good thing—he was still starving and this conversation had given him an appetite. "What do you say, Pa? Interested in any of this? The ramp? I don't know how well that chair rolls."

"The ground is hard packed. Not too many ruts, except right after a rain. He might be able to get to the barn and even do some work out there." Abby looked doubtfully at Pa. "It'd probably take a lot of strength to get out to the barn, but it might work. It'd probably be good for your arms."

"There are some rough places in the yard, but the men could spend some time smoothing them starting tomorrow. And if we built the ramp right, we could make one part slope down and a second part at the right level to roll right into the buckboard. We could have you free to ride the range in no time."

A sudden look on Pa's face had Wade regretting, just for a split second, that he'd been unkind. The hunger on his pa's face, when Wade said the word *free*, reminded Wade of the best things about his father. His willingness to work long, hard hours. His skill as a horseman and cattleman, never asking hired men to do a job he wasn't willing to do.

Pa had a brutal streak, and no amount of hard work made up for that, but Wade couldn't take away from his pa the incredible strength of will it had taken to move into this country and take and hold this land.

Wade would have called it strength of character except Pa's character was so badly, miserably flawed by cruelty. Watching now, knowing how badly Pa wanted to control his own property, Wade asked quietly, "What was it that made you think turning your fists on me was a decent thing to do?"

Pa's expression of hope and hunger faded, replaced by sullen anger. "I raised you the way my pa raised me."

Abby laughed scornfully. "And look how well you turned out. Is that your point? A broken, lonely old man in a wheelchair? With one child, a son who had left you and only now returned home, not out of love but out of duty? You call your life a success?"

All good questions, but Wade wanted to ask something else. "You mean my grandpa Sawyer hit you when you were growing up?"

"Some. When I had it coming." Pa's defiant eyes slid away from Wade's. "My. . .my ma was tough, though. She put a stop to it. Most times. But I got the message that I had to be strong. Same as I tried to teach you. But you came out weak. Weak like your ma."

"Weak because of what? She died? She couldn't turn aside your anger? She wasn't mean enough to pull a gun on you to drive you back?" Wade remembered his mother. She'd been a gentle soul, trapped like Wade. "What do you mean by weak, Pa?"

Pa scowled, and Wade saw the lines cut into his father's face by years and years of steady hate. "She was always at her Bible. Always praying. She tried to ruin you with that stuff, too. A man has to depend on himself. God respects a man who makes the most of what he's been given. God gave me strength and a sharp brain and He expects me to use it."

"You used your strength to tame this ranch land, Pa. But you also used it against me. Why?"

"I wanted you to stand up for yourself. I wanted you to grow up as strong as me. To be worthy of this ranch I built for you."

"You sit there now, in that chair, a broken man, and claim to have had a reason for how you acted, but I don't think you really thought it through, Pa. I think you have a mean streak and you took it out on someone smaller. That isn't what I think of as strong, Pa. It sounds weak to me." Wade stared at his pa for a long time, and for the first time in his life, he saw a man to be pitied. A boy who'd been battered. A weakling who was maybe, in his own way, just as fearful as Wade.

" 'Whom shall I fear,' Pa?"

"What's that?"

"It's a Bible verse I say to myself all the time. Psalm Twenty-seven. 'The Lord is my light and my salvation; whom shall I fear?' I've spent my whole life fearing you, Pa. But no more." Wade slashed his hand downward. "Because with God, I don't have to fear anyone." Wade turned his attention to his supper.

"I–I'm sorry, son."

Wade looked up from his meal at the words he'd never heard before. He had no idea how to react to an apology from his father. He'd never gotten one before.

"It was never my intention to make you afraid."

Somehow Wade found it easy to respond to that. An excuse. The old man wasn't really taking responsibility at all. "As if the way you acted wasn't meant to frighten me? As if the fact that it did is somehow my fault?"

"No, that's not how I meant it."

"That's what you said. And you know, I think it was your intention. I just can't figure out what pleasure you got from terrorizing a child." Wade went back to eating.

"No pleasure." Pa stared at his hands, folded in his lap, subdued. Not himself at all. "But power, I guess. Some kind of satisfaction. I thought I needed to run the whole world, control every bit of it. Dominate every acre and tree and cow and rock. And that stretched to people, too. Including you. Just know that I'm sorry. I know I done wrong by you. I'll probably do wrong again, but maybe now I can at least admit it when I do."

Wade stared at his plate of cooling supper. When he spoke, it was quietly. "I appreciate the words. It isn't enough, it doesn't make up for much, but thanks for at least saying it."

After a long stretch of silence, Pa rolled to the kitchen door and opened it. "We could do it. We could fix up a ramp and adjust the buckboard. I could oversee this place again."

"Good—the sooner you take back control of this ranch, the sooner I can leave." Wade chewed thoughtfully on his biscuit.

Gertie gasped and rose from the table to begin cleaning the kitchen.

A cow lowed softly in the distance. Crickets chirped, and a night owl whooed. A cool breeze reminded Wade that summer came late up here and left early.

"I'm for it. Mort and I will start work on it tomorrow morning." Abby took her knife out of its sheath. "It will get him out of this house, and good riddance." She rose and picked up a whetstone lying on the kitchen counter, and soon the soothing rasp of metal on stone filled the silence.

The first thing Red saw when he came riding up was Cassie, running out of the house to meet him, a smile on her face and her long dark hair flying.

Red had pushed all night to get this rustled herd home, just so he could see his pretty wife. Silas and his women were agreeable, and the Jessups were too quiet to voice an opinion.

The Jessups who'd come to see to Red's place stepped one by one out of the rocks here and there, lowering their rifles as soon as they recognized Red, Silas, Belle, Emma, and the three other Jessup brothers.

It gave Red a deep pull of satisfaction to know his family had been so carefully guarded. Good men, the Jessups.

Red spurred his horse ahead so he could keep Cassie from getting run down by the herd, but the cattle were tired after a long trek and they probably would have just walked around Red's careless little wife. When he pulled his horse beside her, he bent down and lifted her off her feet to settle her on the saddle in front of him.

"Hi." He looked at a smile warm enough to melt the Rockies in January; then Cassie flung her arms around his neck and gave him the hello kiss he'd been dreaming about. The herd headed straight for the pond south of his house while Red greeted his wife enthusiastically.

Then Cassie noticed the prisoner. "Is that man draped over the horse one of the rustlers?"

"Yep. There were two, but one got away."

"Does it hurt him to have his head hang down like that?"

Red sure hoped so. He wasn't about to forget the man had a rifle trained on that gap. "He's fine. We'll take him on into Divide after breakfast. You think we've got enough food to fill this crew up?"

"I'll start scrambling eggs and frying potatoes right now. We've got plenty." She kissed him again and said with a pert tilt of her nose, "Now take me over to the house and quit distracting me. I've got work to do."

Red loved it when she sassed him; he'd made sure she knew it, too. He rewarded that pert little mouth with another kiss.

Belle's daughter Sarah had breakfast going before Red could walk Cassie back to the house. She dished out enough eggs and ham to fill up the whole crew of them, and it was a considerable crowd. The little redheaded girl did it all with one baby on her back, another on her hip, and one clinging to her ankle.

"We're not riding into Divide with you, Red," Belle said as she drained her second cup of coffee. "We've been away from home too long as it is."

"With another rustler still on the loose, I don't like leaving my place for so long." Silas looked at Belle. "We ought to start standing a watch on both gaps into our place. We've never hired any cowhands, but maybe it's time we did."

Belle frowned. "I don't like strangers around the place. Especially men when we've got young girls."

Emma looked up from where she was wolfing her food. "Ain't no man around I can't handle, Ma." Red saw the narrow eyes and quiet determination in Emma and suspected the girl had it exactly right.

"Let's wait a few days on it, Silas. See what Red finds out about the rustler he caught. Maybe he can get the man to talk and we can put an end to the trouble without adding hired hands at the ranch."

Silas nodded. "Gonna go cut our cattle out of that herd." He rose from the table, the legs of his wooden chair scraping against the floor. "You womenfolk gonna help or sit in here having tea and cookies while I work?"

Red watched a brave, brave man leave his house, Belle and Emma right on his heels.

Silas and his family were soon heading down the trail, pushing their cattle toward home.

The Jessups found a few of their own herd, and Red cut out the ones that belonged to him. It was a smart operation, taking a few cattle at a time. Red wondered if the rustling hadn't been going on for years.

Three of the Jessups drove their recovered animals home. Red was left with around fifty head to drive into Divide.

They were ready to set out by midmorning. Cassie rode well enough now to actually help with the drive, but she had Michael strapped on her back and Red had Susannah on his lap, so the Jessups got to do more than their share of the work.

The normally three-hour ride took the rest of the day, and as they confined the cattle in a holding pen, the Jessups hit the trail in three directions to area ranches with the news that cattle had been recovered. A man was in town from the Linscott place and rode out for his boss.

Before Red escorted his prisoner to jail, he turned to Cassie. "Cass, honey, go get us a room at Grant's, okay? We'll have to stay the night in town and wait for the ranchers to ride in and sort out their cattle."

"Yes, Red." The polite obedience was like sweet balm to his soul. There once was a time the little woman would hardly say anything other than "Yes, Red." Ah, he loved remembering those days. Cassie scooped Susannah off his lap; then, loaded down with children, she skillfully turned her horse toward the hotel. Watching her reminded Red how far his wife had come since they'd married. His overly submissive, fumble-fingered little wife had turned into about the best rancher's wife in the whole world.

He noticed the knife sheath at her waist and felt a little chill of terror.

Later, Red got his family settled in Grant's Hotel and gave them each a good-night kiss, going down the row, sweeping Susannah up to eye level and listening to her giggle. Red next gave Michael a noisy smack on his drooly chin then ended with a longer kiss for his pretty wife.

"I'm going to stay with the sheriff, at least for a while. He'll need to keep watch all night, and we can spell each other."

Enviously, he watched Cassie tuck the children into bed then join them. If he stayed, he could climb in, too, and be surrounded by comfort and warmth and love.

Instead, feeling a mite sorry for himself, he went to jail.

CHAPTER 18

"Harv's in jail." Boog slipped into the small cabin Sid was allowed as foreman. Chester had yet to kick him out.

Sid looked up from his whittling. "What? How?"

Judging by the way Boog moved, Sid knew his arm was still hurting him, but no one else would have noticed. Boog wasn't a man who showed weakness.

"Someone must have tracked us." Boog positioned himself so he wasn't visible through the single small window in the shack. "I didn't stay around to learn their names. They posted marksmen on top of the canyon wall and pinned Harv down. I could see I'd never be able to pick them off from the angle I had, so I told Harv to keep his mouth shut and we'd bust him out of jail as soon as we could. Then I climbed out on foot over the west wall."

Sid felt his throat tighten at the memory of that treacherous trail. He and Boog had scouted it, knowing a way out might be necessary. But that trail was a terror. And Boog had managed it with only one good arm. He'd had to go out on foot; no horse could make the passage. Then he'd made it all this way. Sid raised his already sky-high respect for his saddle partner's toughness.

"I walked ten miles before I found a horse. I rode hard then

151

set it loose and swatted it toward home. I hope it just goes on back and no one asks too many questions."

"So the cattle are gone, too?" The very careful cattle thieving they'd done was a prison offense, but a man could get hanged for stealing a horse. Sid steered clear of hanging offenses until he had no choice. That was one of the reasons Sid hadn't killed Mort Sawyer that night. A decision he'd regretted ever since.

"I didn't stay around to watch, but we gotta figure they took the herd." Boog wasn't so squeamish about killing, but then, he'd ridden a hard trail for a long time and was a known outlaw in parts of the West. Boog figured he could only hang once and he'd done his worst, so nothing he did now made any difference. His only goal was to stay out of the hands of the law.

Sid's pockets were empty of cash money. He'd enjoyed himself a bit too much after their last sale, with whiskey and women and poker. He'd been counting on those cattle. "Okay, give me a minute." Sid set his knife and the sharpened stick aside. "Mort's son and that wild woman are here to stay. The only way we're gonna take possession of this ranch is by getting rid of Mort and his son. Getting to that old curly wolf, Mort, took some planning, but Wade's a weakling. I can swat him like a fly."

"Don't count Mort out. He ain't dead yet, and even busted up, he's dangerous. Worse now that he's got his son to back him." Boog eased toward the window and took a long, careful look out through a crack in the shutter.

"He'll be dead soon enough. No one lives long with a broken back. As for Wade, I just need some time to set it up, make it look like an accident or blame it on someone else." Sid didn't admit that he'd tried once already and he'd missed. He didn't want to hear what Boog had to say about that. "Are they taking Harv into Divide?"

"Yep. I reckon."

"Someone there will recognize him as being a hand here. We need to get him out of there fast."

"He don't look like himself without the beard."

Sid met Boog's eyes. The two men knew each other well. Their thoughts traveled the same lines. Harv knew too much.

"Easier just to put a bullet in him," Boog said as if he was discussing the weather.

"We'd lose the gold."

"Yep, 'less'n we find it ourselves."

"Harv said it's where no one would ever find it. He stumbled on it by accident." Sid pondered. "We'll make one try for him. If we run into trouble, we won't leave him alive to talk. We need to go as soon as it's dark and bust Harv out. I told Wade you were at the line shack, the old Griffin place, so he hasn't asked any questions, but if I'm not here for work in the morning, he'll notice sure enough."

"I wouldn't mind a few minutes with the Sawyer kid. I owe him for this bullet." Boog's eyes burned with hate. He rubbed his shoulder hard as if to stir up his pain and feed his desire to get revenge for being wounded.

"You'll get your chance to pay him back."

A quiet shake of the head was Boog's only answer. "Go wake up Paddy."

"Leave him. If I go into the bunkhouse, the hands will remember we left the place."

Nodding, Boog said, "Let me get down the trail a ways and into the woods. Then you catch up." Boog left the cabin as silently as he'd come.

Sid moved furtively to the corral, saddled up, and made tracks for Divide, doing his best to keep the barn between himself and the bunkhouse until he was out of sight. If they were careful, no one would even know Sid had been gone tonight. As he rode, Sid considered that it might be time to just cut his losses and move on. Instead of riding toward Divide, he could head for Helena, hop on the train, and make tracks for Denver. Boog would probably go, but it might be best to travel alone. Sid would have done it if he had enough money to pay for the train ride. Instead he'd have to go on horseback, live off the land, find some way to make money as soon as he got to Denver, because no one lived without money in the city.

The M Bar S was going to be hard to claim now. The gold was lost if they didn't pull Harv out of that jail. Sid was probably going to lose his job by the end of the week anyway, unless he broke his back working for Wade. And working that hard for a young whelp grated until Sid wanted to start unloading his gun at someone.

This had seemed like a way to strike it rich when he'd ridden in. One old man working a huge, successful ranch. Easy pickin's. But there wasn't much easy about it now. He should just ride out, leave Boog, Paddy. . .Harv, too. Start over in California. Easy pickin's out there, he'd heard.

But he thought of Wade coming in here and taking what Sid thought of as his, and it made him mad clean through. No, he'd stay, and he'd get Harv out, too. He wanted the ranch, the gold. . . and at that instant greed took him by the throat, and he decided that he even wanted that pretty wild girl. He'd break her spirit, crush her for causing all this trouble, bringing Wade home, being in the way when they'd attacked that village. She was the only survivor, and if she hadn't been there, no one would know what had happened. The massacre, if it was ever discovered, would have been blamed on one tribe attacking another. Yes, he owed that spitfire of a girl, and he'd make sure she paid.

As he savored his hate, he felt fire for a second, fire in his soul. Painful fire telling him, not for the first time, his life fit him only to spend eternity in a burning lake.

Even knowing that, he heard a whisper from his black heart that it was his *right* to take by strength. This was the West. Strength won in the West. And he was strong. The feeling of fire in his soul had been with him for years. He remembered long ago; the first few times he'd felt it had scared him, made him doubt the path he'd chosen.

Wildflower Bride

Not anymore. As he spurred his horse toward Divide, he basked in the warmth.

❧

"Why don't you get some sleep, Red. No sense both of us being up all night." Sheriff Dean had his feet up on his desk and was rocked all the way back in his heavy wooden chair. His hands were folded over his stomach, and Red suspected that with about ten minutes of silence the sheriff would be fast asleep. He wasn't used to much trouble here in Divide. It was a quiet little town for the most part.

Red was tempted. Of course, he'd have to lie down on the hard floor. "It's been a long day, Sheriff. I think we both need to stay alert. I'll keep you awake and you do me the same favor."

"Fine, let me get a stack of wanted posters, then."

"I thought you went through them already."

With a dry laugh, the sheriff pointed to a stack of posters knee high against one wall. There was an ankle-deep stack right beside the bigger one. "I set the ones to the side I've looked at."

"Tell me it's the short pile we have to study."

"Nope, 'course not. I've looked at the ones on the left."

Red sighed and thought of Cassie, asleep and warm and sweet. And his beautiful children. "Catching outlaws is almost more trouble than it's worth, Sheriff."

"Tell me about it. I thumbed through 'em until my eyes crossed and all the men started looking alike."

"Fine." Red got up and picked up all the posters he could get in his hands. He took them to the desk.

The sheriff sat up straight, the hinges of his chair shrieking like he was killing them. "Give me half and pull your chair up to the desk."

Red dragged his chair over, and as he got it in place, he felt a little rush of cold chill. Not from a gust of wind so much as from nerves.

"You ever had a jailbreak from this place, Sheriff?"

Shaking his head, Sheriff Dean said, "Nope. I've mostly just arrested cowpokes that drank too deep in their monthly pay. Let 'em sleep it off and sent them on their way with a scolding. Usually half-grown boys get into nonsense like that."

"You checked that the back door is locked, right? That man we arrested has a partner out there."

"Like as not his partner ran for the hills. It's a cowardly bunch that rides the outlaw trail."

"They struck me as a savvy bunch. I'll ride you out to that canyon sometime. Hard to believe a man ever found it."

"If they were real savvy, they'd be honest. Being a rustler is just plain stupid."

"Well, I'm not saying they're wise, but they just might be smart. I think we need to stay on edge all night. I'll feel better when we've had a chance to question the prisoner a little better."

"Well, he's asleep for the night. He's cut up and so exhausted from being hauled over a horse for two days that he ain't makin' no sense." Nodding, the sheriff said, "In the meantime, let's see if one of these posters looks enough like him to give us a name."

Red's neck still felt cold, like God in heaven was sending a warning. He bent over the posters but kept his ears wide open.

Sid rode side by side with Boog, and the moon was high in the sky by the time they reached the sleeping town. A light shone in the window of the sheriff's office. Sid nodded toward it. "Sheriff Dean must be keeping watch."

Boog muttered in the cool spring night, "Looks to be the only light in town."

"Let's circle around. Come in through the back. You still got that key that works on most doors, Boog?"

"I got it."

"Then let's go in quiet, get the jump on the sheriff, then knock him cold and leave him in a cell. No shooting if we can help it. We'll be in and out before he knows we're there."

Pulling their kerchiefs over their faces, the two men circled like patient vultures. There was no sign of life anywhere in town. It was long after midnight and even the Golden Butte had closed up.

Sid saw a dim light showing under the back door of the jail. Sid had made a point to know the layout of every building in Divide he could gain access to, always planning for a robbery or escape. He silently swung down off his roan and hitched him beside Boog's gray mustang and the horse for Harv.

They moved toward the door. Boog quietly produced the key he'd filed down until it would open all but the most expensive locks. The jail hadn't bothered with expensive.

The lock gave with a single scratch of metal on metal. The door opened with an almost inaudible creak. Boog slipped in. Sid knew his saddle partner well and let Boog lead the way. The man knew more about sneakin' and thievin' than anyone Sid had ever known.

It was what Sid liked best about him.

"What's that?" The voice coming from the front of the jail froze them in their tracks.

A second later, trying to be silent, they slipped out the back, and Boog swung the door shut. He turned the lock with aching slowness, and then they hurried into the shadows, pulling their horses along. An outcropping of rocks that edged the town about a hundred feet to the south was the nearest cover. Sid led his horse with Boog right behind him and they waited.

Looking carefully around the rocks, Sid saw the back door open.

Red Dawson poked his head out. The town parson.

Sid had seen the man once, right after he'd struck Mort down and taken the job. Hard to forget the preacher with his flaming red hair. Sid had heard of the Dawson ranch, too. A well-run operation, and he knew of Cassie Griffin Dawson because the Sawyers used that fancy, neglected Griffin house as a line shack.

The older cowpokes on the Sawyer place liked swapping stories about what a worthless, no-account Lester Griffin had been and how beautiful and spoiled his wife was. The stories were laced with envy that Red had gotten her and apparently taken a firm hand, because now she was the hardworking-est woman any of them had ever seen.

Boog nudged Sid then spoke in an almost silent whisper. "He's who came into the canyon and took Harv. I could look back once I got myself clear. They had two men scale the cliffs outside the canyon and pin Harv down. Sharpshooters, the best riflemen I've ever seen. Probably fought in the War Between the States."

Sid had fought in that, too. Then he'd stayed on and fought after Lee had surrendered because he'd gotten a taste for shooting men, and it suited Sid to take what he wanted. Let weaklings work for their bread.

"I wasn't on watch, or they'd have had us both. I yelled to Harv to lay low and if they caught him I'd bust him out of jail; then I ran. I saw that red hair for sure."

"Name's Red Dawson," Sid said. "He's a rancher, but he's the town parson, too."

Boog grunted in disgust. "He must be staying the night with Sheriff Dean."

"You sure it was him in the canyon? Preachers don't run with riflemen."

"This one does. Maybe he converts people by threatening to send them to Hades. It was him for sure. How could it be anyone else? You think there's any chance someone else would offer to stay with Harv, someone with bright red hair?"

Dawson, the sheriff just behind him, stared into the darkness. It was too far to see Red's eyes, but his whole body spoke of alertness. He wasn't going to let Harv go without a fight.

"Let's ease back and wait 'em out." Sid thought of the long, brutally hard day of work he'd had and another one coming tomorrow. He needed that gold. He was sick of breaking a sweat to earn a living. But to just go charging in there with guns blazing would bring the whole town down on them. "They'll be easier to take when they're asleep."

Sid and Boog faded a bit farther under the trees and settled in.

"I'll take first watch. Get some sleep. You can spell me later." Boog sat and leaned his back against a tree so he could keep an eye on the back door.

Sid dozed until Boog jarred his arm. "It's gettin' on toward daybreak. We've gotta move on the jail now or forget it."

"Let's go." Both men pulled their handkerchiefs up and eased forward in a silence so thick the hoot owls didn't even breach it.

Boog led the way back to the rear entrance of the jail. Again he unlocked the door with his filed-down key. They stepped into the quiet murmur of voices and the loud roar of Harv's snoring. Sid stayed close. Despite the narrow confines of the hall running along the front of the two cells, with Dawson and the sheriff to deal with, it was a two-man job now.

The hall was about two feet wider than the door leading to where the sheriff and Dawson sat talking. Slipping up that hall, the sight of the iron bars sent a chill up Sid's spine. He'd cheated prison so far, and he had no intention of ever spending a night in jail. If he ever found himself cornered by the law, he'd decided long ago to go down guns blazing rather than be locked in a cage like an animal.

Harv lay snoring in the cell farthest forward; the other cage was empty and its door stood slightly ajar.

Sid didn't wake him, afraid the cessation of the deep roar of Harv's sleep might be the same as sounding an alarm. Sid ducked behind the slightly ajar door and peeked through the crack between the door and the frame.

The sheriff sat there, hands behind his head, feet propped up on his desk with the ankles crossed, talking cattle. Dawson's chair was closer to Sid. He sat just inside the door, holding a cup of coffee in both hands, rocking his chair on its back legs.

Sid knew his blow to Dawson's head had to be brutally hard. Sid wanted him down and out with one quick move. Whether Dawson survived the strike or not didn't matter much. A witness could bring trouble. Then Sid would get the drop on the sheriff and tie him up. Hoping to avoid the noise of gunfire, Sid knew he'd shoot 'em both, grab Harv, and run if he had to.

Sid glanced at Boog then drew his gun and turned it so the butt end was forward. Boog nodded, understanding Sid's plan. Dawson's chair swayed as he sipped his coffee.

Raising the gun butt, Sid prepared to storm into the room and strike.

Dawson stood suddenly.

Sid whirled his gun around to take aim.

"I might as well get some sleep. It'll be dawn in a few minutes."

The sheriff lowered his hands and took his feet down off his desk. "I'll make it the rest of the night."

"Just remember he had a partner. Someone out there knows we caught him and could be looking."

"I appreciate the company. Stop by before you head out of town and we'll try and get some information out of him." Dawson left without a backward glance, and the sheriff settled back into his reclining position at his desk.

Sid and Boog exchanged glances; then, less than a minute after Red's exit, a soft snoring sound came from the front. Boog's cold eyes gleamed. He slipped through the door into the sheriff's front office.

Sid heard the dull *thud* of something hard striking flesh and bone.

Boog backed into the room, dragging a bleeding sheriff by his feet.

Enough light came from a single lantern in the sheriff's office that Sid saw the trail of blood. Vicious satisfaction uncurled in Sid to think of hurting any lawman. They were the enemy. "Harv, wake up."

Dropping Dean's feet, Boog went back up front and returned with a key hanging from an iron ring as big around as a saucer.

"Sid, that you?" Harv sat up, groggy but jumping to his feet the second his eyes focused.

With a rasp of metal, Boog unlocked the barred door.

Harv rushed out.

"Let's go. Get clear of town fast." Sid led the way. The three of them scurried through the night to the horses—they'd brought a spare for Harv from the M Bar S.

The three of them kept to the woods as they swung a wide circle around the town. "You and Boog go stay at the Griffin place. As soon as Boog is healed up, he can come back in. No one's paying too close a mind to who's there working because of Wade being back. He don't know how things were before. So no one's gonna notice you gone for awhile longer. Harv, you might need to lay low until I get shed of Wade and that wild woman he brought home."

Staring out of the thick trees of the rugged mountainside Sid studied the trail. It would split about two miles ahead—one trail well traveled, leading to the Sawyer place, and the other only a faint depression in the grass heading toward the abandoned Griffin house.

"The going gets hard in the woods from here on." Sid nodded at the tumbled stretch of slippery shale ahead. "Let's get on the trail. We won't meet up with anyone out this late."

"Hold it." Boog's quiet voice stopped Sid. "Look down the trail."

In the gray of predawn, Sid heard more than saw someone approaching from the direction of the Sawyers'. "A bunch of riders."

Harv spoke up. "I heard Red Dawson sent men out to the

Sawyer place and every other ranch around. He told 'em to put out the word that he'd brung in rustled cattle and to come claim their stock. The Sawyers must be sending a party into Divide to fetch their cows."

Either Sid's eyes adjusted or the sky lightened or both, because he could make out one blazing white head in the midst of five riders. An unmistakable head of hair. That wild woman was riding with them.

"There's that woman." Harv had a hungry tone to his voice.

Sid didn't like the sound. He'd gotten to thinking of that untamed woman as his. "Keep quiet until they pass."

As the group rode closer, following the trail, Sid realized they'd come within fifty feet of where he hid with Boog and Harv. He could take them now. With Boog's gun and Harv's and his own, they could end it in a blaze of bullets, then ride to the ranch, get rid of Mort, and settle into the Sawyer place right away.

"Don't do it." Boog must have read his mind. Sid looked sideways and Boog nodded at the group of riders. "That's the saltiest bunch on the Sawyer place, and look, the woman—she heard something."

"Quiet!" Sid hissed.

The wild woman stopped. She sat on a barebacked pinto mare that few at the M Bar S ever rode because she was so feisty. The horse paused without any visible direction from that wildflower on her back, almost as if the horse had read her mind. The woman turned and stared into the woods straight into Sid's eyes.

He knew she couldn't see him. The woods were too thick, and with the barely lightening sky, the forest was impenetrably dark.

Impossible.

But those eyes. Chills sprang up on Sid's arms. Her eyes crawled over him then glanced left and right as if she not only saw him but made out Boog and Harv, too.

All three of them sat their horses motionlessly. Even their mounts seemed frozen as if they knew danger lay in the slightest movement.

Wildflower Bride

At last, as the Sawyer hands left her behind, the wildflower looked forward and her horse, as if the two were one creature, started walking again.

Spooky, that woman. Seeing into the dark, maybe seeing into Sid's mind.

After the Sawyer riders vanished from sight on the winding trail to Divide, the trio stayed still.

"It's safe." Boog urged his mount forward. "Let's go."

Deciding to trust Boog, because Sid was tempted to stay hidden for a good long time, the three moved on.

"I'll be in by the weekend. My arm's almost healed up and I'm sick of sitting around. Should have spent the last few days driving those cattle south into Idaho. Now we've lost 'em." They reached the fork in the road and Boog paused. "Maybe we oughta cut out of here, Sid, and go collect that gold. It's been long enough for those Indians to bury their dead and go home."

"Forget it." Knowing he had to face a long day's work without a minute of sleep, Boog's wanting to quit fired Sid's temper. "Come back from Griffin's when you're ready, but the plan doesn't change."

Sid spurred his horse toward the Sawyer place. As he rode alone toward the spread he planned to make his own, it occurred to him that Boog and Harv were free as birds. They could sleep the day away. They could even head out and collect that gold and make tracks for California.

Refusing to look back, Sid decided this whole plan had taken too long. Mort was supposed to die outright. Arrogance had goaded Sid into letting the fall and the long cold night kill the old man. Now he needed to finish off the old man and the son and deal with that wild woman.

He'd give Boog and Harv a few more days to heal up; then it was time to make his move.

CHAPTER 19

I have no wish to see your white village, Wade. I should have stayed with Gertie."

"I'm sending a telegram to Helena asking about settlers named Lind, from back a few years. They can pass it on to land offices, and maybe we'll find where your pa lived. Don't you want to be there if we get an answer back?"

Abby scowled. She'd done more frowning since she'd come to live with the Sawyers than in her entire years with the Flathead. This long trail ride in the predawn darkness was unsettling. She'd smelled something back in the woods. Men. White men. Even riding with this group of them, she knew more were watching from the woods. But white men were always about. She'd learned to fear them, hate them, but mostly ignore them.

They'd taken everything from the Flatheads, all tribes in fact, but her people had found fertile valleys and lived in remote places. They were far from the whites who spread like a disease across this land. Until that massacre of her village, they'd left Abby's people alone in their rugged mountain valleys.

Wade rode his horse a bit closer to Abby's side and lowered his voice. "The more I think about it, the more I'm sure that arrow

Wildflower Bride

was aimed at you, not me."

"You don't know that."

"Or maybe they were going for both of us. If that arrow was shot by the same men that massacred your village, then they might count both of us as witnesses."

"You're just trying to scare me."

"Maybe you need to be scared. If I'm right, Abby, then we're dealing with the worst kind of yellow dog."

"You've just described all white men." Abby waited for Wade to defend his people. When he didn't, Abby felt bad about it. Wade had been nothing but kind, even sweet, so all white men except Wade.

Instead of defending his honor, he went right on pestering her to be more cautious. "We're talking about a man who'd shoot at a woman from cover. When you're in the house with Gertie, I think you're safe. A coward like that wouldn't storm the house. But that's with me and my best hands working close enough to be here in minutes. But today I have to go to town and I needed to take my best hands with me. I didn't want to ride off and leave you and Gertie without any protection. If they're really after you, then Gertie's in danger, too, as long as you're there. I couldn't ride off to town without you, so you had to come."

He'd used this same argument to nag her into going. She had agreed to come along and now she regretted it. Mainly because of that sense of being watched. "Fine, I will see this village and help drive your stolen cattle home."

His eyes narrowed as if she'd insulted him somehow, but he didn't say why, and she made no effort to coax his reasons from him or soothe his feelings.

"Let's pick up the pace now that it's light. We need to make a fast trip. The roundup is going well, but I want to get back."

As she guided her pony with her knees, Abby looked at the men, loaded down with their iron guns and their heavy leather saddles, and wondered how the poor horses stood it.

❦

"That's Tom Linscott and his drovers." Wade drew Abby's attention toward a group coming into town the same time as the Sawyers.

He and Abby and his cowhands rode into Divide just as the sun finally cleared the horizon.

"Red must've sent word to him, too. Our range butts up against the Linscotts'. Pa and Tom have been wrangling over water holes and grazing land ever since Linscott came in here nearly eight years ago. The man isn't an easy neighbor, but truth be told, Pa was always more at fault than Tom."

Abby gave the riders a disinterested look and turned back toward the corral ahead of them. Wade saw the yard full of cattle standing quietly as if they hadn't gotten out of bed for the morning yet, but he turned back to study Linscott. Wade had picked up his father's attitude toward the stubborn Swede, but now Wade was determined to be friendly if Tom would allow it. There was considerable bad blood between the families.

It was easy to resent the blond giant because Wade knew Tom was the kind of man Mort wished Wade would be. Being a Christian now, Wade admitted that the hostility he felt toward Linscott had a lot to do with jealousy, and it wasn't right.

Wade rode up to the corral just as Tom got there. Tom had a wary gaze on Wade. It was hard to look the man in the eye, remembering drunken insults Wade had hurled at him only a couple of years ago. Wade knew God had forgiven him, but he had no such hope about Tom.

"Morning." Wade swung down off his horse and wrapped his reins around the hitching post. He noticed Abby swing one leg over her horse's neck and drop lightly to the ground on her moccasin-covered feet. He saw her legs almost to her knees and looked away quickly just because he didn't want to see any more. He could not convince the woman it was important to keep her ankles covered. But proper manners or not, all the gingham in the world wasn't going to dull her skill as a horsewoman.

"Sawyer." Tom looked at Wade; then his eyes were drawn on past.

Wade glanced behind him to notice Abby striding toward them. Abby was as white-blond as Tom, and it occurred to Wade that the two would make a likely pair. For some reason that reminded him of why he'd hated Linscott. "Looks like we're on the same errand."

Linscott rode a black thoroughbred with a white blaze and white stockings on his front feet. The animal was huge and feisty, rumored to be so dangerous no one went near him but Tom, and no one else had ever been on his back. He'd made Linscott a fortune as ranches paid top dollar for stud fees. And Linscott used that fortune to buy up land and build up his herd.

As Wade stepped close, the stallion snorted and shook his head, jingling the metal of his bridle. The bared teeth were ample warning for Wade to stay back.

Linscott rode the black to a hitching post well away from the other horses and lashed the reins tight.

"Can I talk to you for just a minute, Tom?" Wade knew Linscott was a brusque, short-tempered man, a good match for his horse.

"Make it quick." Tom walked toward Wade, his spurs jingling, his stride long and impatient. He faced Wade almost as if squaring off for a shootout.

Wade couldn't blame Tom for expecting the worst, but Wade wasn't going to give the man trouble. "I spent most of the years since we've met being a first-class coyote and I'm sorry. There, that fast enough?"

Linscott's shoulders slumped a bit, and his eyes narrowed. "That's what you wanted to talk about?"

"Yep, that's it. I don't expect you to trust me after some of the things I pulled, but I've changed. I quit drinking. I'm back on the ranch with Pa. I'd like there to be peace between us. No more pushing Sawyer cattle onto your range, no more fighting about those two water holes Pa liked to wrangle over. They're yours and always have been. I'll keep my cattle away."

Linscott scowled. "I've wanted to put my fist through your face for years."

"You have a few times, if I recall."

"It wasn't ever enough." Linscott crossed his arms as if to keep his fists from flying.

"It'll take time to prove to you that I mean what I say." Wade made a point of looking Linscott straight in the eye. If there was anger, even fists, Wade intended to take it as his due. Linscott wasn't an evil man, just a grouch with a short temper. "But I do. After a time, you'll believe me, I reckon."

A soft nicker from Linscott's stallion drew Wade's attention.

"Such a good boy." Abby caressed the beast's nose, standing directly in front of the horse.

"Get back!" Wade took one step.

Tom's hand clamped on his arm like a steel vise. "Don't move!"

Releasing Wade, Tom eased himself the ten feet or so toward Abby. "Miss, step away."

Abby looked up from the horse's muzzle. "Why?"

"He's dangerous. Step slowly back."

Abby smiled then gave the stallion a kiss on his nose. "Dangerous, are you, boy? I'd say you're just looking out for yourself. I know how you feel."

She stepped away from the horse and walked toward Tom without a bit of fear or caution. She was easily within reach of the stallion's iron-shod hooves.

Wade held his breath until she was far enough away from the horse to be out of biting and kicking range.

Tom took two long strides toward her, put that iron vise of a hand on her arm, and jerked her nearly off her feet. "Are you crazy?" He dragged her about half a step before she kicked him in the back of the knee, twisted her arm loose, and rammed a fist high into his belly. Tom was flat on the ground on his back, sucking in breath like a backward scream, with Abby kneeling on his chest with her knife pressed to his neck.

It all happened so fast Wade hadn't even reacted before it was over.

"You put your hands on me again, white man, and I'll see you don't get your fingers back."

Linscott was too busy trying to breathe to do much else.

Several of the Linscott drovers turned to defend their boss.

Wade was at her side and raised a hand to Linscott's men. They might not obey a hand gesture from him, but they might hold off on shooting the woman who was threatening to slit their boss's throat. "Don't hurt him, Ab. Tom was afraid his horse would attack you. The animal's got a reputation as a killer."

"Hey, my stallion's never killed anyone." Linscott defended his horse from his position flat on his back.

"Not for lack of trying." Wade prodded Tom with his toe, not too hard, to remind the idiot that he was one swift knife slash from death. Not that Wade thought Abby would kill him. Unless she really had to. Or Tom was really stupid in what he said in the next few minutes.

"The horse never put his hands on me." Abby leaned forward and put all her weight on the knee she had rammed into Tom's chest. "He never dragged me around or shouted at me. I'd say the stallion has better manners than his owner."

"He was trying to save you." Wade knew Abby was just having fun now. The time to cut was long past.

Abby gave him a look of such doubt that Wade added, "No, really, he was."

With motions so quick the human eye couldn't follow them, Abby whipped her knife away, back into its hidden pouch. Wade still wasn't sure where exactly the woman kept the knife, and it was rude to study her skirt long enough to be sure.

Abby shoved off Tom's chest far harder than necessary, and she dusted off her knee as if Linscott had gotten her dirty.

Wade reached down, and Tom, his eyes locked on Abby, didn't notice. Wade kicked him, no gentle prod like last time.

That Tom noticed. He grabbed Wade's hand to get to his feet.

Wade pulled maybe just a tad harder than was absolutely necessary, and Tom, back to looking at Abby, almost fell over forward.

"S—sorry, I didn't mean to mistreat you. . .uh. . ." Linscott looked at Wade.

That wide-eyed fascination with Abby set Wade off. But he'd just told Tom about turning over a new leaf, so he refrained from gaining Tom's attention with his fists. "It's Abby." Wade tried for a minimum amount of good manners. "Abby Lin—"

"What?" Tom reacted as if a lightning bolt had just landed slap on him. "Abby Linscott? That's my sister's name."

"Not Lin*scott*." Wade resisted the urge to swat the man in the back of the head, just to see if he could make him blink. Tom was riveted by Abby. "Lind. Abby Lind, this is Tom Linscott."

Tom moved closer to Abby.

Abby seemed to be focused unduly on Tom, too.

Wade needed his gun.

Suddenly Tom was fumbling with something on his shirt.

Wade stepped closer. He'd have stepped right between them if there'd been room.

"Linscott?" Abby paid rapt attention to the man. "Tom Linscott?"

Tom produced a large gold pocket watch and pressed the stem winder. The watch popped open to reveal a picture. "This is. . ." Tom looked from the picture to Abby and back. "This could be you."

"Who is it?" Abby leaned close, studying the picture. She took it from Tom's hands even though he tried to hang on, but he didn't try hard. He tried like a man who was numb all the way to his fingertips. She lifted it close, and long seconds passed as she stared at the likeness. "Mama."

Barely able to hear the words, Wade leaned closer. "You recognize this picture?" Wade looked, and there was no way to deny that the woman in the picture bore a stunning resemblance to Abby.

"They died. My whole family died." Abby's eyes rose to meet Tom's. "Except my older brother. You stayed back East."

"When you all went West, I stayed behind. I had a girl I was sparking and a good job working in a lumberyard." Tom's lips curved down. "You forgot you had a brother?"

"No, not forgot. But that life seems so far away. Almost like it happened to someone else." Abby looked deeply into Tom's eyes.

"She's been living with the Flathead all these years, Tom. Speaking their language, living by their customs. She's remembering her old life only in bits and pieces."

"Indians kidnapped you?" Tom's brows slammed together. "Savages? I never knew. I never even considered you'd lived or I'd have come to save you. We heard the family died of the fever. I inherited Pa's land and my girl married someone else, so I came West."

Wade saw a flash of temper in Abby's eyes. He jumped in to head off her drawing her knife again. "The Flatheads found her alone, her family dead. They didn't kidnap her. They *saved* her. Took her and cared for her and raised her as their own." Wade added in a whisper, "She doesn't like it when you call them savages."

Tom started shaking his head. "My sister. I. . .I never thought one of you might have lived. I was t–told. . ." Tears welled up in Tom's eyes.

Wade looked around quickly, knowing Tom wouldn't want anyone to see him crying. Once the danger was past, his men had moved away. They were in the corral separating the stock.

Suddenly Tom launched himself forward and grabbed hold

of Abby in a bear hug. Startled, Abby looked to Wade as if asking for help.

Wade shrugged. "He's happy to see you. Aren't you kinda happy to know you have a brother?" For some reason, Wade was extremely happy to find out Tom was Abby's brother. He didn't bother trying to decide why exactly. Of course, there was bad in it, too. Tom couldn't spark her, but he could take her home.

"Yes." With a quiet cry of distress, Abby flung her arms around Tom and hugged back. "I'm very happy to know I have a brother. Tom, I do remember you. I was so young when we headed West."

"Seven." Tom let her go, stepped back a bit, and kept his head down as he fished a handkerchief out of his pocket. He blew his nose and made a quick swipe of his eyes then looked up. "You were seven when Pa threw in with a wagon train. I was sixteen and not about to leave my best girl behind. Stubborn kid. If I'd have come, maybe I could have helped."

Wade clapped his hand on Tom's back, enjoying slapping the man a bit too much. If he wasn't careful, he was going to lose Abby because of this. "You two have a lot of catching up to do. Why don't you send your hands home with the cattle and ride out to the M Bar S with us, spend the day."

Tom suddenly bulled up, got a mean look on his face that Wade remembered well from the old days. "I'm not coming out there. Abby is coming home with me."

Wade froze. Then he melted; in fact, he got a little hot under the collar. "No, she's not."

"My sister is coming home with me." Tom dismissed Wade's comment and turned to Abby. "We'll give you a ride. You don't need a horse or anything else from Sawyer."

"She's got a job on our ranch." Wade wasn't about to let Abby ride off with anyone, least of all Tom Linscott.

"She doesn't need a job. I can support her." Tom reached for Abby.

Wade stepped between them. "I know how you live out there."

"I live just fine." Tom's jaw clenched.

Wade could see the man remembering, but just in case, Wade reminded him. "Your cabin is falling down and your ranch hands live in it with you. She'd be more comfortable in a cave of bears. Safer, too."

"So I'll build a house." Tom's hand seemed to sweep aside the problem of where Abby would stay in the meantime. "I didn't have a reason to before this."

"Come out to the Sawyer place after the house is built. We'll talk about her going with you then." That gave Wade plenty of time to convince Abby that she needed to stay with him forever.

"No. She comes now." Tom squared off in front of Wade, turning sideways to Abby.

"It's not right nor proper." Wade took a step closer to Linscott. "At least at my place we've got Gertie. Plus, Gertie is run ragged trying to take care of Pa and cook for the hands doing roundup. We really need Abby's help."

Tom jerked back. "You don't have your roundup done yet?"

Wade thought the heat in his cheeks might be a blush. Blushing, at his age, in front of Tom Linscott, while the man swept Abby off to live with him. Could things get any worse? It was not *his* fault that he'd come home and found chaos. "No, we don't. And that's not what we're talking about. Abby's reputation will get dragged through the mud if she's out there with all of your bachelor cowhands."

"No one will say a word against my sister or they'll face me." Tom jabbed a finger straight at his chest.

"Oh, now you're going to shoot anyone who raises an eyebrow." Wade snorted. "Instead of just letting her come to the M Bar S like you should."

"She's my responsibility. She's my sister." Tom shoved Wade's shoulder.

Wade took a step forward. "You're a stranger."

"She's mine."

"No, she's not. She's mine!" Wade clenched his fists.

"Shut up!" Abby shoved herself between them, one hand flat on each of their chests. "Just shut up!"

Dead silence reigned. She looked from one to the other. " 'She's mine'? Did I hear those words come from your lips? Both of you?"

Neither answered.

"I belong to no white man. I belong to no *man*!"

Wade watched Tom's eyes focus on Abby with confusion and fondness. Then those eyes shifted to Wade and narrowed. Wade wondered what in the world the man was thinking. "Any fool can see she can't stay out there with you."

Abby's blade flashed right under Wade's nose. "I said shut up."

Tom's narrow, dangerous eyes widened. Then he smirked. "You ever meet a man you didn't pull a knife on, baby sister?"

Wade thought it over. "I can't remember her skipping anyone so far."

Abby glared.

Tom studied Wade as if taking his measure. . .maybe for a pine box.

Wade wasn't sure what the stubborn idiot was hunting for.

Suddenly Tom's expression eased, and he shook his head and smiled. "No more fighting, Abby girl. You're a woman grown, easy to see. You can decide where you go all on your own."

"Of course I'll go with Wade. I have a job, and I don't want to live in a single house with a crowd of cowboys. At the M Bar S, I only have to put up with him and his whining yellow dog of a father."

Tom jerked a little then started to laugh. "I'm starting to really like you."

"And Gertie," Wade interjected. "Don't forget her. My housekeeper makes a perfect chaperone. Tough, no nonsense." Abby might not be getting the undercurrent here, but then, the woman was busy putting her knife away in some secret hidey-hole. Wade

Wildflower Bride

knew Tom got it just fine.

"But I do want to spend time with you, Abby." Tom rested his hand on her arm, sounding as sincere as a man ever had. "I've got enough men in town to drive my cattle home. I think I'll come on out to the Sawyer place with—"

A bloodcurdling scream cut Tom off, and they all turned to face the sound.

A woman ran out of the sheriff's office. Bright red blood on her hands. "Doctor! I need a doctor!"

Wade dashed forward. He heard other feet running, all charging toward the bleeding woman.

CHAPTER 20

The sound of screaming bolted Red straight out of his chair. "Stay inside, Cass." Shouting that order, he hoped Cassie picked today to be obedient and ran.

He saw Libby before he'd gotten out the door of the diner. Libby Jeffreys, his good friend who only minutes ago had left the diner with a tray of food for the sheriff and his prisoner. Libby now staggered onto the board sidewalk covered in blood.

He sprinted toward her and almost collided with Wade Sawyer, who reached her at the same moment from a different direction. Red caught Libby's shoulders, looking for the source of the bleeding. "Wade, get the doctor for her."

"No." Libby's voice shook. "I mean yes, get the doctor, but not for me. It's Merl."

"I'll go." Tom Linscott was a single pace behind Wade. He wheeled and raced for the doctor's office.

"He's knocked cold, bleeding, maybe dead." Libby burst into tears.

Red took one more hard scan of Libby's bloody but uninjured body. Then as Seth from the general store came up beside Red, he thrust the sobbing woman into Seth's capable hands.

"Take care of her." Red let her go and headed for the jail.

Wade beat him in the door.

The two went in to find a trail of blood leading from the single front room of the sheriff's office through the swinging door to the back room. A room where Red's prisoner had spent the night in one of the two small cells.

Red rushed to the door and swung it open to find Sheriff Dean facedown on the floor, lying in a pool of blood. The cell where Merl had locked up Red's prisoner last night stood empty, the door swung open.

Dropping to the floor, Red felt sick to think the prisoner he'd brought in had done this. Red looked up at Wade, who was kneeling on the other side of Merl, and said, "It didn't happen long ago. The blood is too fresh. I didn't hear a gunshot."

"Let's roll him over. Be careful."

Red and Wade eased the burly older man over, and he groaned. With a rush of hope, Red saw what looked like a single blow to the head, a nasty gash, swollen and bleeding into his salt-and-pepper gray hair, but not a bullet wound.

Merl's eyes flicked open, and he struggled to sit up.

"Lay still." Red pressed on the older man's shoulders. "The doc will be here in a few seconds. You're all right. Just got knocked cold."

Red prayed silently. A quick glance at Wade's moving lips told him Wade had joined in with his own prayers.

No other wound showed up. Merl reached for his head with a moan of pain. "What happened?"

"Just stay quiet. Looks like your prisoner or maybe his partner knocked you cold and escaped." Red had hoped the prisoner would talk, especially after he'd been locked up overnight.

The man didn't seem possessed of any great supply of courage, judging by the way he'd lain frozen under the onslaught of Belle's and Emma's gunfire. And if the man talked, then the ring of outlaws could be broken up for good. Now the area ranchers had their cattle back and the hideout uncovered, but they didn't have a line on the outlaws.

Frustrated, Red turned back to Merl just as the doctor hustled into the narrow hallway that ran along the front of the jail cells. Red got to his feet to make room for the doctor. He studied the little area and moved toward the rear of the building. That's when he noticed the alley door standing just barely ajar. "Wade." Red strode the last few feet and examined the latch. "They must have gotten in this way." Red stepped outside, knowing it was far, far too late. He crouched down and studied the dirt torn up with hoofprints.

"Look at this door. The knob isn't broken. They must've had a key."

"Door probably takes a skeleton key. Easy to find." Red stood and rubbed one hand into his hair. "I should have stayed all night instead of going back to Grant's Hotel to sleep. We knew he had a partner."

Wade tugged the brim of his hat low over his eyes. "Tell me how you caught him."

Tom Linscott picked that moment to round the building. Glowing Sun—no, Abby—was right behind him. Red was struck by how the two resembled each other. Not many folks had that unusual shade of white-blond hair. "The doc is taking Merl over to his office. Looks like he just got a hard blow to the head. He should be okay."

"Morning, Tom. Find any cattle of yours in that mob we brought in?"

"My men are checking. We were just in town a few minutes when Libby started screaming. She's fine, by the way. Upset but not hurt at all. This gang's been hitting us for a few head all winter. Probably gathers a few up then drives them somewhere to sell. Tough call with the brands, but it's hard to do a perfect job of covering the old ones. We should be able to identify ours."

Red looked from Tom to Abby again then shook his head to focus on what was important. "I brought in a man to the sheriff I found holed up with the cattle. He had a partner with him who got away."

Red quickly told them as many details as he could. Then they started studying the tracks. In the lightly traveled alley, they could tell which way the gang went, straight for a clump of trees that led into the rugged hills around Divide.

Abby did a better job of tracking than any of the rest of them. Finally, the ground turned to rock and the riders seemed to vanish. Frustrated, they turned back to Divide.

"At least we got these cattle." Wade slapped Red on the shoulder. "Maybe with their hideout found, they'll move on. But I hate passing our troubles on to some other ranchers. I've got to get headed for home now. We're in the middle of roundup."

"You're still doing roundup?" Red was amazed.

Wade scowled. "Yes, we're still doing roundup."

Red was sorry he'd said anything. "Send your men on home and take a few more minutes to decide if there's anything to be done about these rustlers. It won't take long."

Wade agreed.

The group headed for Libby's Diner, where Cassie was now waiting tables with Susannah hanging from one ankle and Michael strapped on her back. Red marveled at his wife. She just would not stop working.

"How's Merl?" Cassie came up with a coffee cup and a pot as Red settled at the table. Michael blinked sleepy eyes at Red over Cassie's shoulder and smiled.

"He's at the doctor's office. Doc said he's making sense and sitting up, so he'll be okay, but someone must have come up behind him, because he can't remember a thing." Red got up to relieve Cassie of her burden and also because he couldn't get enough of holding his little redheaded son. He settled Michael on one knee, Susannah on the other, and still managed to drink his coffee without burning tiny fingers. He was getting real good at this father stuff.

Wade came in next, holding the door open for Abby. A cranky-looking Tom Linscott tried to come in with Wade still holding the door, but Wade stepped in front of Tom and dropped the door in Tom's face. The two shoved at each other for a few seconds as if fighting to see who could get in the door first.

"I told you I'll start building a cabin today." Tom was talking to Abby. Was Tom trying to convince Abby to marry him?

Red's eyes slid to see how Wade was taking that. It hadn't taken any leap of great genius to see that Wade was sweet on this woman.

"Come and talk to us when it's done." Wade wasn't taking it a bit good.

"You can move out to my place in a week if we push hard." Tom ignored Wade and talked to Abby. "And we will push hard."

Abby ignored both of them and looked down at Susannah.

"She's not coming out there, Linscott. She's got a job at the M Bar S."

Red looked at Abby, obviously the object of this discussion.

"Let me help you." Abby swooped in and plucked Susannah off Red's lap and began talking to her as if there wasn't a wrangle going on behind her. . .about her.

"Why're they fighting over you?" Red jerked his head at the two men.

Abby studied Red for a few moments as if he'd asked her to explain the mysteries of the universe. "I am Tom Linscott's sister."

"You are?" Red lowered his coffee to the table, clicking it hard.

Abby rounded the table to sit straight across from Red. "It would seem so. In fact, I believe I remember him. Of course, he was much younger."

"No sister of mine is going to work for a living. And especially not for the Sawyers." Tom headed for the seat beside Abby, but Wade beat him to it. Scowling, Tom went to sit on the bench next to Red, right across from Wade. Handy—now they could glare at each other full-time.

"Are you sure of this sister thing?" Red asked.

Cassie appeared with more cups and the steaming pot. "What sister thing, Red?"

"Abby and Tom Linscott are brother and sister."

"Family." Cassie smiled at Abby. "That's so wonderful for both of you."

"She's not working for an outfit so worthless they haven't even gotten spring roundup done yet."

Abby snorted.

Tom bared his teeth.

The soft sound of pouring liquid and the chatter of others gathered in Libby's Diner weren't enough to draw Red's attention from this new development.

"He has a pocket watch with a picture of my parents." Abby's brow furrowed. "I resemble my mother closely. And I. . .I remembered. . .earlier with Wade. . .that my last name was Lind. But now that Tom says Linscott, yes, I know that's right."

"Well, I'm happy for you. Finding out you've got a family has to be good."

"Good? To have more white men wanting me? I do not see how that is good."

Red laughed.

Abby relaxed a bit from her frowning, and her eyes went to Tom, who was so busy arguing with Wade that his sister might as well have not existed.

Red had noticed the resemblance, the pure blue of their eyes, the white-blond hair. But now he saw that Tom had a lot of features similar to Abby's, a more rugged, manly version of course, but no one would be surprised to find out they were kin.

"Well, you're welcome to come out to our place." Cassie was still serving coffee, but she'd heard the end of the exchange. "I need more help with my knife throwing. Belle spent a couple of days working with me, and I've improved. But I can't seem to hit the target dead-on."

Susannah reached for the blazing hot stream of liquid Cassie was dispensing into Abby's cup. The two women moved together in a way music could have been put to it to keep Susannah from burning herself and still get done what they wanted.

The door swung open and Sheriff Merl Dean walked in with no color in his face and a bandage on his forehead. "I need a posse."

"We already tried to track them." Red stood and guided Merl, still pale and shaky, to the seat Red had just vacated. "We lost them in the foothills just west of town. Nowhere for a posse to go."

"I want to check myself. Can you three help?"

"Wade can't," Tom said with his usual cocky smirk, his only real expression except for anger. "He's still doing roundup."

"You're not done with roundup yet?" The sheriff's brows disappeared into the bandage on his forehead.

"No." Wade's stony expression didn't encourage further comment.

Red changed the subject. "Did you question the prisoner any more last night after I left?"

"No. I think I got hit minutes after you left. I don't remember anything past you saying good-bye. Figured I'd have another crack at him this morning. Are you sure you didn't find anyone in that stack of wanted posters we thumbed through?"

Shaking his head, Red said, "The man had no scars or anything else that would identify him. That cut on his chin is too new."

Abby turned on the sheriff like a hungry cougar who'd just spotted a three-legged buffalo. "Cut on his chin?"

"Right here?" Wade asked as he sat up straight and ran a finger along his jawline on the right side. Then he rose and stood behind Abby, resting his hands on her shoulders.

"Yep."

"Get your hands off my sister." Tom half rose from his seat.

Wade's hands stayed where they were. "Long beard, dark hair?"

Sheriff Dean shook his head. "His hair was dark, but short, looked like he'd hacked it off with a knife to me. And no beard."

"He could have done all that to change his appearance." Red looked at Wade and Abby. "Probably had to if his face needed stitches. What's going on?"

"I told you about the man who tried to take Abby after the massacre."

"Massacre?" Tom slammed his coffee cup on the table. "My sister was in the middle of a massacre?" He jabbed a finger at Wade's nose. "You didn't say anything about a massacre."

"I told Red." Wade dismissed Tom, which struck Red as very brave or very foolish. Tom Linscott was notorious for his bad temper and quick fists. A match in every way for that famous black stallion.

"He did tell me." Red felt the need to back his friend.

"And where exactly were you when my sister was in the middle of a massacre?" Linscott rounded the table as if to put himself between Wade and Abby, as if it were Wade's fault the girl had been in a massacre and she was still in danger. And just maybe Tom had some massacre plans of his own.

Wade, rather than backing down, which most sensible people learned to do when Linscott's temper flamed, took a step forward, lifting his chin as if daring Tom to land a fist on it.

"Shut up, both of you." Abby stood and, as if this was nothing new, shoved her way between the two men. "Red may have captured a murderer. You fight like squabbling children. We don't have time for your foolishness."

Tom jerked back as if Abby had cut *him*. Which she probably would, given time.

Wade smiled and moved out of Tom's reach. "Yes, Abby fought back and managed to cut her attacker with her knife. She got in several good slashes. I think his clothing was cut up. His face she laid open bad. He let her go and ran. She saved herself. I only came along afterward."

"That's not true. You put a bullet into one of them."

"One of them? How many men had their hands on my sister?" Tom's face turned beet red.

"There were four," Abby said.

"You shot a man?" The sheriff's brows lowered and he glared at Wade. "You should have reported it."

Wade shrugged. "He rode off. He couldn't have been too badly hurt."

"Which means you took a shot at him and missed, of course," Tom sneered.

"This rustler I brought in could be the same man." Red ignored Linscott. Everyone was used to his cranky ways. He pulled up a chair from another table and sat by the sheriff. "And if he had four men at the village, then there are more rustlers around than we figured."

"What village?" The sheriff was looking irritated. Red couldn't blame him. The man was finding too many things out by chance that they should have reported to him from the start. And all while nursing one beauty of a headache.

"Abby was living with the Flathead in a high valley past the Tanner ranch." Wade settled back in his chair.

"It's the Harden ranch," Cassie said as she poured more coffee for them all.

All the men grunted.

"Oh, only Indians." The sheriff turned to his coffee.

"Only?" Abby turned on the man, and Red thought her hand was going for her knife. "Only Indians?"

Wade grabbed her arm. "Don't pull a knife on the sheriff, Ab. He can arrest you for it."

"He'd have to be alive to arrest me, now, wouldn't he?"

The sheriff was concentrating on his coffee and missed the ensuing struggle.

Wildflower Bride

"Abby really liked her Flathead family," Red told the sheriff, hoping to avert yet another massacre. "They saved her life. Found her when her family was dead from the fever and took her in. They treated her far better than many whites have."

"Sorry for the insult, miss." The sheriff rubbed his bandaged head. "I'm sorry about your village, too. I'd pick your village over the scum that are running these hills any day. And I'll help you catch them, too, and see them hanged for what they did to your people."

Abby quit trying to arm herself and sank with a disgusted snort into her chair. "Your prisoner destroyed my village, he and his three friends. And now he rides away from your jail cell free as a bird."

Merl lifted the coffee cup and took a long sip. "I thought I could handle him. Red stayed for most of the night, but I should have brought my deputy in, too. We've never had a jailbreak before."

Abby's eyes softened as she looked at the battered man. It reassured Red some to note that the woman wasn't always bloodthirsty.

"Maybe you oughta go on home, Merl." Red studied the man's ashen face. "You look white. You couldn't stick your horse even if we did know which way to ride."

Merl sighed. "No one reported this massacre to me. Where'd this happen?"

Red, Wade, and Abby took turns filling the sheriff in.

Tom seemed bent on yelling every time one of them added a new detail.

"Try and describe these men more carefully." The sheriff looked between Wade and Abby. "Do better than heavyset, thin, masks. Think hard. Picture them. You've left a scar on my prisoner and a bullet wound in another one of them. Did they have any other marks, scars, anything we could use to identify them? Did you notice their horses? Were they branded?"

Wade considered things quietly for a time. "One of them had a funny way of holding a gun. I can't put my finger on just. . . Wait! His fingers, that was it. He held his six-shooter in a stiff way." Wade pulled his own Colt and checked the load to make sure the hammer was on an empty chamber. Wade pointed the gun at the ceiling and stared at his hands. "Two fingers on his left hand stuck out." Wade demonstrated. "Usually they'd be curled around the gun butt, like this."

Wade seemed to be looking into the past, trying to picture the scene. He closed his fist, his index finger on the trigger, the next three fingers wrapped around the gun handle to meet his thumb. The normal way to hold a gun. "But instead his little finger and the one next to it stuck out straight. He had leather gloves on, tight, not like the buckskin gloves you see. Normally a man would take his gloves off to handle a gun, but this one didn't. Of course, it all happened so fast, and the massacre was over. Maybe he was leaving and it was a cold morning. He didn't have time to remove his glove when they came upon me."

As they finished the telling, Abby added, "I smelled the stink of a white man in the woods this morning. I believe there were three of them, certainly more than one. Maybe it was the escaped prisoner heading north."

"You smelled a man?" Tom looked at her as if she'd sprouted elk antlers.

Red would have looked at Abby strangely, too, except Red saw right away that Tom's comment made Abby mad. So Tom's big mouth saved Red from making himself a target.

"What did you learn living with those savages all these years?" Tom asked. "It'll take me forever to teach you better."

"Teach me better?" Abby's voice got so high it threatened to shatter glass. "A white man teach me? I will fight learning the white ways to my *death*."

Cassie reached for Michael, probably to save the little tyke's hearing, and she started choking.

Wildflower Bride

It took some doing before Red was satisfied Cassie had recovered enough to hand over the chubby little boy. He helped tuck the boy into Cassie's carrier on her back then kissed the child on his cheek and spared a quick kiss for Cassie, too.

She smiled, ran one finger down Red's nose, and then went back to waiting tables.

"What do you mean a white man stinks?" Tom demanded.

Red couldn't imagine the idiot really wanted to hear Abby's answer.

Red noticed Wade's eyes followed the exchange between him and Cassie. He knew Wade envied the Dawsons' happy marriage. There'd been a time when Wade's interest in Cassie was an obsession. Wade had gotten past that when he'd put his faith in God. But Wade was lonely. He'd told Red he wanted a family, a wife like Cassie who would be gentle and funny and sweet. Then Red watched Wade's eyes go to beautiful Abby, and Red thought maybe his friend had finally found himself a woman.

"You are a fool, brother"—

Well, maybe not quite as sweet.

—"to ask me what I mean when I say white men stink."

And not really all that gentle.

Abby drew her knife and tested the blade. "Better to live amid skunks."

But she was pretty funny, Red had to give her that.

CHAPTER 21

Sheriff Dean rose from the table. "I'll ride with you partway home, Wade. Abby can show me where she thought she. . .uh. . . smelled. . .someone."

"You should bring more riders." It made Abby furious to see how the man doubted her. Her fingers itched to reach for her knife, but she knew that was getting to be a bad habit. At least the sheriff was going to check. "You'll find tracks and maybe catch these murderers before they harm more of my people or steal more of your *cows*." It sickened her to think of these brutes running free while her Flathead family lay dead.

Wade came to her side, and his hand rested whisper-soft on her lower back.

Abby wasn't sure if he was showing his support and offering her comfort or blocking her from getting to her knife. "Tell me, Sheriff, what are you really hunting for, rustlers or murderers? Would you even stir yourself from your chair if there weren't cows missing?"

"Now, miss"—the sheriff's brow beetled and he pulled his hat from his poor wounded head—"I didn't know about the village massacre. Someone has to report a crime before I can arrest someone for it."

Wildflower Bride

Abby had to admit that the sheriff couldn't arrest a man for a crime that no one had even told him about. And from the look of his bloody bandage, the lawman had his own reasons to want these men caught very badly. It wasn't all about cows.

"You and Wade didn't even bother to ride into town and tell me about it." The sheriff shifted his eyes to Wade. "I saw you in town, Sawyer. You've ridden in at least once since you've been back. You didn't say a *word* about murder."

"You don't go out to the countryside, Sheriff. And Abby's village was located at least two days' ride away from town. I didn't even consider telling you about it."

"I reckon you're right. I wouldn't have gone out to try and catch an outlaw that far from Divide." The sheriff sighed and rubbed his head. "I'm sorry to admit that's true, Miss Linscott. But I don't really have jurisdiction in the countryside. I don't worry about trouble unless it comes into my town."

It burned Abby to hear him say it, but she had to admire the man for looking her in the eye and admitting the truth. How was she ever going to find her place in this white world? Abby's eyes went to Tom Linscott. "You really are my brother, aren't you?"

"I do believe I am, Abby girl." Tom turned to Wade. "I'll be riding out to your ranch with you, Sawyer. I want to spend some time with my sister. Meanwhile, I've told my men to start building a cabin."

"She's working for me, Tom." Wade got that bulled-up look in his eye, and he had the same tone she'd heard when Wade had snarled, "She's mine," to Tom.

Insulting. Yet Abby felt a softening in her heart to have two men wanting to take care of her. She didn't need them for protection, but maybe she wanted them to care just a little.

"Come on out, though. We'd love to have you." Wade's hand stayed on her back, more firmly pressed against her spine now. Definitely support, since she suspected Wade wouldn't mind one bit if she pulled her blade on Tom.

Abby thought of Mort Sawyer and sniffed in disgust. A clear lie—Wade wasn't even bothering to fake honesty. She marveled at finding a brother, even an arrogant, unpleasant one. Couldn't she have found a better family than him? Wade would have made a better brother to her. But thinking of Wade as a brother wasn't comfortable. She didn't care to examine why.

"Come in to services on Sunday morning." Cassie gave Abby a huge hug.

Abby found herself nose to nose with the little redheaded boy on Cassie's back while receiving her hug. The boy blew a spit bubble at her and smiled. Abby smiled back. After receiving the prolonged hug from Cassie, which Abby found she rather enjoyed, she mounted her horse and they headed for the M Bar S.

Wade, Tom, the sheriff, and five others from town rode along.

"This is the place." Abby pressed her knees into the sides of her pinto and turned the horse to the wooded area by the trail. "Judging by the stench, I'd say there were three of them."

Tom shook his head a bit hard. Abby had seen dogs around the Flathead village shake themselves that way when they'd come out of the river, and yet Tom was bone dry. White men made no sense.

When Abby reached the edge of the woods, she saw immediately the tracks of three men coming out of the forest onto the trail. A trail that had been trod heavily by the cattle Wade's cowhands had driven home.

Tom and the sheriff and his men all swung down and began studying the tracks.

"They could have shot us dead, three men. We had some riders with us, but we'd have been sitting ducks." Wade rode up to her side, his eyes examining the ground. Then he looked sideways at Abby and spoke softly, his words only for her. "If these are the men who kidnapped you after the massacre and attacked us at the ranch, why did they pass up a chance to finish things this morning?"

Abby looked from Wade to the tracks and back again.

"Cowards, I'd say. They could probably have killed us all shooting from cover and not gotten a scratch, but they didn't want to take that chance. These men have proven themselves to be cowards with every move they've made. Attacking defenseless women and children, kidnapping a lone woman."

"You weren't exactly defenseless." Wade smiled at her. "I'm glad you fought them. I'm glad you hurt the man who put his hands on you."

"Are you glad you put a bullet into one of them?"

Wade's smile shrank to something grim. "It had to be done. That's not the same as being glad."

"Then that's a difference between us, Sawyer. Because my only regret is that he wasn't hurt worse and that he was gone this morning and I didn't get my hands on him in that jail cell."

"We'll never follow tracks in this rocky soil." The sheriff rubbed the white bandage on his head.

Elders were respected in her tribe, and she had to force herself to mind the sheriff. Men had pride, and Abby doubted the sheriff would thank her. But he wasn't up to chasing outlaws and that was a fact.

"Let's follow the trail back toward Divide. Study it, see if we can get a feel for their horses," the sheriff suggested.

"You don't even know it's the right men." Wade raised his Stetson and ran one hand through his hair before putting his hat back on.

"No, and that's the plain truth." The sheriff stared at the tracks. "But why sit in the woods and watch you go by? It's suspicious behavior, enough to make me wonder. I'll follow the trail back into the woods, see where it leads."

Abby watched the sheriff and his men leave. Wade, Tom, and Abby were left alone.

Wade nudged his horse forward, and the three of them rode abreast. "I didn't go into details yet, Tom, because we just haven't had time, but someone tried to kill Abby after she came to the

M Bar S. He shot an arrow at her, tried to make it look like an Indian attack."

Wade and Tom exchanged a long look that excluded her, as if they were in charge of her protection. As if she couldn't protect herself well enough. As if, when things got bad as they were sure to do with murderers on the loose, she wouldn't probably have to save herself and both of them, too. It made Abby want to bang their heads together.

"So does this have to do with the massacre or the rustlers?" Tom looked at Abby as if he was counting all the reasons someone would want to kill her.

Wade shrugged. "I don't know. I brought her to town with me today mainly because I don't like her being alone out there, even with Gertie. I think someone tried to kill Pa and make it look like an accident. I've been trying to never let her go anywhere alone. That's another good reason she should stay with me. With the house she's got some protection. At your place she'd be out in the open all the time."

"She could stay inside at my place." Cranky Tom was not a woman's dream of a brother.

"Your house is a falling down shack." Wade sounded as bristly as a porcupine. "She'd go crazy in there before the first day was over and be outside doing something."

"Don't talk about me as if I'm not here." Abby was tempted to smack them both in the back of the head.

"I've already told my men to start leveling ground for a bigger house."

"Good for you. About time. I hope you'll be very happy living there alone."

"Shut up, Sawyer. It's for Abby. And I can afford to make it real nice."

"Better make it a tepee or she'll start insulting you just like she does my pa."

Wade smiled at Abby and she shook her head. Why did her

insults to his father cheer him up?

"It won't be a big dumb house like the one you built."

"My pa built it, not me."

"But it'll have plenty of room. I've just never bothered when it was only me and my cowpokes." Tom turned and studied Abby with eyes that surprised her. Kind eyes. They didn't go with the gruff man. "I want to talk to you about our life. I'll help you remember everything. Leastways everything I know about. And that falling down shack I'm in is where you lived. It's the house Pa built before he died. I—I—" As Tom fell silent, Abby wondered what it was he couldn't say. He'd shown no shortage of words up until now.

"You what?"

"I love you, baby sister." From the strained look on Tom's face, Abby sensed that the man didn't talk much about feelings. In that way he was far more like Wild Eagle than Wade.

Abby stared, trying to absorb the words. "I remember you so slightly and all in bits and pieces. I know I loved my white family. I imagine that includes you. I would love to talk with you about the early days of my life."

Tom jerked his chin in a satisfied nod. "Good. I told my men I might be a couple days coming home, so we can really spend some time together."

"Well, have fun," Wade said. "I'm going to be busy with roundup."

Tom did a poor job of covering a laugh. "I can't believe you're not done with roundup. . . ."

Wade kicked his horse into a ground-eating gallop, leaving Abby and Tom in his dust.

"I wonder what's the matter with him?" Abby decided to ride faster, too, rather than be left with her grouchy, confusing brother.

CHAPTER 22

"Are you still here?" Wade came into the house and his mood dropped so low he'd need to get a shovel and dig for it. And he'd been cheerful a second ago. The roundup was finally done.

"You said I could stay and get to know my sister." Tom smiled, as content and lazy as a housecat. The lazy lug was sprawled in one of the kitchen chairs watching Abby and Gertie get supper.

"Did you get done, Wade?" Gertie tapped a heavy metal spoon against a pot bubbling on the massive black stove that took up an entire corner of the kitchen.

Shaking his head, Tom said, "I can't believe you're just now done—"

"Yeah, yeah, yeah, done with roundup, I know!" Wade jerked his gloves off and tossed them onto the floor below a row of elk horns. He hung up his hat and turned back to the room, running ten fingers through his hair to smooth it, and since his hands were busy, it also kept him from strangling their houseguest. Vermin could have moved into the house and been better company than Tom Linscott.

Pa rolled his chair into the room. Wade noticed that the old grouch was getting around pretty well in the contraption. "You about done with the roundup, Wade? I can't believe you're still—"

"We're done, Pa." Wade cut him off and slid his eyes between his father and the king-sized rodent who had moved in. "I haven't been nagged like this since you tried to teach me how to rope a maverick calf."

"You were hard to teach roping?" Tom rolled his eyes heavenward. "Why doesn't that surprise me?"

"I was five years old at the time. And Pa's idea of teaching was mainly yelling his head off and swinging the back of his hand. Roping lessons aren't exactly my favorite childhood memory."

Tom looked sideways at Pa with contempt. Wade's mood further deteriorated. A stubborn, short-tempered grouch like Tom Linscott knew better how to raise a child than Wade's pa. Didn't that just beat all?

"Supper's ready." Abby brought a stack of plates to Gertie, who began scooping beef stew, thick with potatoes and carrots and onions.

Working from can-see to can't-see for all this time had left Wade thin and hungry and cranky. Right now that stew smelled so good it was all he could do not to dive headfirst into the boiling pot.

He washed up quickly at the kitchen sink, and his heart warmed when Abby brought his plate first. By rights she should have served Pa first, then Tom because he was company. Abby wasn't too interested in polite ways, and anyway, it was fitting he got the first plate. He was the only man at this table who'd worked a hard day.

"Abby and I are done with your pa's ramp now," Tom announced.

Okay, so maybe they'd done a little something.

Abby put a plate in front of Pa next.

"And we got the old buckboard out and tore out the tailgate and the seat so Mort can roll right up and grab the reins." Tom watched Abby with the affectionate eyes of a brother, a grouchy brother.

Maybe Tom had done more than just a little. Wade started eating to reassure his growling stomach that his throat hadn't been cut.

"And with the ramp done, Mort can roll straight out the kitchen door onto the thing and drive easy as you please."

Fine, they'd put in a good day, then. Big deal. How many thousand-pound longhorns had they wrangled?

Tom got his food and dug right in. "And Mort took the buckboard for a ride around the yard, didn't you?"

"Sure did. Felt great." Pa sounded happier with Tom than he ever had with anything that Wade had done since birth. "I might ride into town in a few days. Oughta build up some strength in my arms first, though. Hard to get back to working when a man's been sitting around for weeks on end."

Wade sat at the foot of the table, Pa at the head. Tom was on Wade's left with his back to the wall. Gertie and Abby took up two seats on Wade's right. Abby next to Wade. He could have reached out and touched her.

Tom might have pulled his six-shooter and killed him. It was obvious the man was watching their every move. But it was nice to know she was within reach. Now if Wade could only get a few minutes alone with her, just to talk. He'd little more than exchanged greetings with her since Tom had as good as moved into the house. And he'd thought Gertie was a tough chaperone.

He sighed and continued shoveling in the stew.

"So how soon until we can do the drive?" Pa was a mighty bossy man for someone who'd been outside for the first time all spring just today. "It's almost time now."

Wade had to quit wolfing down his food to answer. "We'll leave the cattle on the closest pastures for the next week. We'll move them around so the grass stays thick for them, try and get the yearling calves fattened up before we cut the herd and drive them to Helena."

"They should have been on those pastures a month ago." Pa glared at Wade.

"Yes, they should have, Pa. Why weren't they?"

"Because you weren't here." Pa pounded the table with his fist, but the silverware didn't jump. No doubt the man would build up to that if he kept talking.

"No, because you hired someone incompetent to be your foreman. What'd you ever sign Sid on for?" Sid was still living in the foreman's cabin, too. Wade and Chester both had been too busy to evict him. But that was no longer true. Wade could see to that right away.

"He looked good to me." Pa picked up his fork and scooped up a savory helping of stew. He clearly didn't want to take any responsibility for the mess Wade had found, so having his mouth stuffed full of food seemed like a good way to stop talking. "I was hurting. If my son had been here, if you hadn't gone off in a pout—"

"Do I eat my meal here, Pa, or should I go out to the bunk-house? It's not enough I'm working eighteen-hour days—I've got to come in and get whined at by all of you? I swear, sometimes I feel like I've got four nagging wives."

Pa slammed his fist on the table.

"You're comparing *me* to a *wife*?" Tom roared.

Gertie let her head fall back so she could stare at the ceiling. Abby laughed.

Wade wished he could get rid of Tom something fierce. But he loved having Abby here at his table. She wasn't exactly his dream woman, true. Not one bit like Cassie Dawson to be sure. But her strength drew him as well as her reckless disregard for what anyone thought of her. He needed to learn that. She could teach him. He noted that she was sitting sideways to the table, faced toward him, with her legs crossed and in her bare feet. Beautifully arched feet. He could see her ankles again, too. She had one elbow on the table, and she plucked a chunk of meat out of her stew with her hands, sucked the gravy off it, and then ate it.

He could maybe teach her a few things, too.

"Tomorrow's Sunday. Red will be in town for church services. Anyone want to go with me?" Wade looked at Tom. He'd never heard a word about believing from Tom Linscott, and he'd never seen him in church. The man was a heathen and that was a fact.

"Waste of time, church." Pa hit the table again. Wade wondered how the furniture stood up under the assault.

"I'll take that to mean you're not going." Wade expected it. In fact, he was looking forward to a day that included neither backbreaking work nor his pa's endless complaining. But as much as he wanted a day of peace, it always hurt to think how lost his father was.

"I'd think a man who's had a brush with death like you oughta figure out where he wants to spend eternity. If you ever decide to ride along, you're welcome. I'd even let you drive us."

Pa turned back to his plate with a scowl, eating with the grace of a wild dog.

"Have fun, Sawyer." Tom's refusal hurt, too. "I want another day or two here with Abby before I head home." As annoying as the other man's company was, Wade had a burden on his heart for any unbeliever.

"I'll go." Abby reached for the biscuit plate and helped herself.

Tom frowned.

Pa muttered.

Wade smiled. "Good. Gertie, you in?"

Pa stiffened visibly. Wade could see he was worried Gertie would leave.

Gertie shook her head. "Your pa shouldn't be here alone."

Wade knew Gertie refused the offer of church to keep peace in the household. But he wasn't so sure of where her soul stood with God. Not that it was his place to judge, but Gertie spoke of God and there was a Bible on a shelf in her room. But he'd never seen her read it, and she'd steadfastly refused to attend church.

Now Wade had the whole ride to town and back alone with Abby. His mood lifted.

"I guess I'll go, too." Tom as good as tossed a bucket of brackish pond water on Wade's mood. "If Abby goes, I'll go."

Wade's sogged-up mood fell straight back down with a splat. Tom wanted to attend church. Wade should be glad of that.

One look at Tom's smirk told Wade that big brother threw in to keep an eye on his sister, not out of any desire to worship God. Well, fine. Maybe Red would say something that would drill its way into Tom's hard head.

Wade quickly washed up and headed for bed, hoping he could get enough sleep to keep going through another day.

Thank You, Lord, for a day of rest.

CHAPTER 23

Wade came into the kitchen the next day in his best black pants, wearing a black leather vest and his newest white shirt. He'd found the clothes in his old room or he'd've had nothing after his winter in the mountains.

He should count it a blessing his father hadn't dragged his clothes out onto the ground and burned them to ashes.

After he'd worked four hours on the morning chores, taken a bath in the spring, dried off, and dressed, he'd come in to shave and comb his hair at the kitchen sink.

"I've got water boiling and your razor laid out, Wade." Gertie was at the stove scooping eggs and bacon onto a plate. The house smelled so good, Wade decided to eat first and then shave. No sign of Pa or Tom. It was too much to wish they were gone for good, though.

Abby added two biscuits to Wade's plate and set a ball of butter and a dish of preserves on the table beside him.

"Gertie tells me there is a proper way to dress for church." Abby frowned but she didn't go for her knife, so Wade took that to mean she'd cooperate. "I can see that you've put on special clothes, so I must, too, then."

Wildflower Bride

A cup of coffee was added to Wade's meal by Gertie; then the two women hurried off, with Gertie talking, possibly giving Abby pointers on church behavior. No one had ever threatened to stab anyone at church before. It might be a day to remember.

Gertie and Abby disappeared into the back of the house where they slept.

The food went down fast and Wade shaved quickly, not wanting anything like a weapon in his hands lest Tom Linscott made an appearance. Could the man be sleeping this late?

Up in his room, Wade found his best Stetson, the one with the shiny silver hatband and a small feather on the side of the band. The feather made him think of Glowing Sun—Abby—as she'd been in her doeskin dress and moccasins. She was dressing in gingham and calico now, but she wore her civilization very lightly. Wade would like to see her in that beaded dress she'd had on the day he'd found her after the massacre. He'd fallen in love with her in that dress.

There was nothing left of this day, until evening chores, except to attend church and do his best to find a few minutes alone with Abby. He held out little hope he could accomplish the latter.

Abby came out of her room seconds later, her hair untied from its braid, curling about her shoulders with the shine of sunlight. She was wearing a dress Wade had never seen before. The fit wasn't perfect, but the sky blue gingham sprigged with yellow flowers made her sun-bronzed skin and white-blond hair glow like—Wade couldn't see it any other way—like a glowing sun.

Wade pulled his eyes away from Abby when Tom entered the room. He'd only brought one set of clothes, and he didn't seem inclined to go home anytime soon and clean up. "Is it time for church yet?" He sounded like a choir boy, eager, good, sincere.

Wade wasn't fooled. "Don't you have a ranch to run?"

Tom just smirked. "Good thing I got done with roundup. . . about a month ago."

Wade had no response to that fit for a Sunday morning—or any day.

They headed for the corral. The three of them, always together.

As they approached the nearest horse pen, Abby whistled to the pinto mare grazing in the far corner of the corral. The half-wild pony perked her head up, whickered, and trotted toward Abby.

She'd done the same thing the morning they'd ridden to town to inspect the herd Red brought in. Wade had to keep his mouth clamped shut. He'd ridden that pinto. It was small, but it was mean and fast. Blue blazes as a cow pony, if you could stick on her back long enough to calm her down.

Catching the pinto usually involved a fast-moving horse and a cowboy with a lasso. Now Abby had the little stinker eating out of her hand. And she hadn't lost a finger yet.

Tom's shining black stallion lifted his head, too, in a neighboring corral. Wade had taken to moving his best mares into the corral with the stallion. Maybe he'd get some good foals out of the beast.

He'd pointed out what he was doing to Tom, hoping the man would throw a fit and go home. Tom didn't seem to care one whit.

The beautiful killer whickered at Abby as if he was being slighted and moved in his pen to the closest point to her.

The mare came to her. Abby slipped on the bridle she'd rigged to have no bit. Leading the pinto out of the corral, she mounted up bareback with one supple leap while Wade was still leading his horse to the barn for a saddle.

Abby's skirts flew about, her ankles clearly visible. She batted at the fabric impatiently. "Stupid gingham dress."

Tom's stallion was busy trying to commit murder, though his heart wasn't really in it or Tom never would have gotten leather on the brute. The stallion reared toward the sky then landed stiff-legged and crow-hopped sideways. Tom hung on expertly. "Abby, you need to put a saddle on that horse."

Wildflower Bride

When Wade and Abby had ridden to town to check the cattle Red had brought in, Wade had taken this same position.

Wade had lost.

Now it gave him pleasure to stand back and watch Tom lose.

Abby made an incredibly rude noise for such a pretty woman and started for town without a backward glance.

Wade, thinking of the dry-gulchers gunning for her, raced through his preparations and was on the trail while Tom was still letting the black work its kinks out by jumping and rearing.

Wade caught up to Abby quickly, and soon Tom came along. Wade had hoped to visit with Abby on their rides to and from church. Maybe risk asking her if she might one day have feelings for him, but with Tom along that was impossible. They set a swift pace and made it to town in record time.

The church in Divide was so new it still smelled of wood shavings, but it was painted bright white, as clean as a new penny. Wade had noticed it in passing when they'd come in for the cattle, but now he could really appreciate the tight little building the town had erected.

They tied their horses to the hitching post alongside a dozen other horses and scattered buggies and buckboards. Inside were tidy rows of oak pews. The church was packed, and Wade, Tom, and Abby stood, leaning against the back wall with several other worshippers.

Church was its usual informal affair. The service was different when the circuit rider was in town. Parson Bergstrom ran a very proper, orderly service, and Wade enjoyed that well enough. But he much preferred it when Red was in charge. Red was far more casual. He had told Wade that he was working on getting himself named a real legal minister so he could perform weddings. Wade doubted Red's style would change much, though, if he got papers calling him a real live parson.

Today he talked on one of Wade's favorite verses. It was from the first chapter of John.

"'In him was life; and the life was the light of men. And the light shineth in darkness; and the darkness comprehended it not.'"

It reminded Wade so much of the dark world he'd lived in before he found his faith. Wade found light once he understood about Jesus dying for him. But Pa still lived in that dark place. And just as the verse said, he couldn't comprehend the Light. It grieved Wade to think how lost Pa was, but Wade also battled an angry, sinful part of himself. He bitterly resented the abuse he'd taken from his father's hands. It was a battle to pray for his father. A cruel voice inside of Wade said Pa deserved a terrible afterlife for the way he'd lived this one. Most of Wade's petitions for God to open his father's heart ended with Wade begging God's forgiveness for himself, not his pa.

When the service was over, Wade, Abby, and Tom stayed to visit. Abby took a turn holding Michael, but all the women wanted to hold the baby. A fair number of the men wanted turns, too.

Wade loved Cassie and Red's children, although he'd been gone for most of little Michael's life. He knew Susannah well from all his time spent at the Dawson place, so she giggled and demanded a hug as if he was a beloved uncle.

Wade hoped Tom had really listened to what Red had to say. The ruffian had seemed to be listening attentively to Red's talk and asked some good questions. Even feeling like Tom was a leech who was determined never to let Wade and Abby be alone, Wade prayed silently for Tom to hear this truth.

Standing outside the church, Wade saw a rider galloping into town on a horse wearing Tom's brand. The rider pulled his racing mount to a halt when he spotted Tom. "I thought I'd have to ride all the way to the Sawyer place. We've got trouble out at the Double L. Big Black ran afoul of a grizzly."

Wade recognized the name of the prizewinning Angus bull Tom had brought out from Kansas City at great expense. It was the first pure black breed anyone in these parts had ever seen.

Angus cattle had only just been imported into America. They

were reputed to be as hardy as a longhorn but faster growing with tender meat where a longhorn tended toward gristle. Wade was skeptical. He figured some snake oil salesman had gotten the best of Tom. But Tom had a good head for ranching, and he loved to talk cattle more than any man Wade had ever known, so he might have heard of the breed somewhere, even before he came West. Wade had seen the bull a year ago, and there was no denying he was a beauty.

"Is he dead?" Tom slapped his Stetson on his head and started for the hitching post in front of the closed general store, where his black stallion stood tied. Tom had left the temperamental horse well away from the other horses.

"The grizz had him down and tore him up, but he's got a chance. You're the best hand with hurt animals, Tom. You've gotta come and come fast."

Tom jerked his chin in agreement and started to mount up. Then he halted and looked back at Abby. "Sorry, Ab. I'll be coming around again as soon as I can." Tom gave Wade one hard glare that promised swift, brutal retribution if any harm came to his sister.

Abby watched as Tom galloped out of town behind his cowhand, but she didn't look particularly sad to see him go.

Wade was outright thrilled.

The fellowship outside the church broke up with a lot of conversation about that magnificent blue-black Angus bull. Red even led them in a prayer for the big animal.

Wade and Abby rode out of town with Wade on top of the world. "Let's not go directly home, Abby. I want to spend some time away from Pa and his bad temper."

Abby gave a harsh half-laugh. "I feel no excitement to return to your father's side."

"There's a house I want you to see out here. You think my pa's place is foolish—this is even worse. But it is beautiful."

"More beautiful than the trees they cut down to build it?"

Wade laughed. "Maybe not. And definitely not now that it's

abandoned. We use it as a line shack. I think it will be safe. No one can waylay us because they can't know we'd ride that direction."

When they came to the fork in the road that led toward the old Griffin place, Wade guided his horse down the faint trail. "So are you happy to have found a brother, Abby?"

Abby looked sideways at Wade, barely touching her reins, so comfortable was she on her barebacked horse. "I remember Tom just a bit. I have felt so separated from memories of my white family here in Montana, remembering back to living in the East is even more confusing. I have this image of rushing wagons and people and noise. I need to ask Tom more about our home back there, but I can tell. . .he's. . .angry that I can't remember."

"Hurt, I think, not angry. But Tom is a Western man now. He's going to cover his hurt with gruff words."

"My Flathead father was like that. Once, my little brother fell into the water and had to be pulled out. He wasn't breathing, and for a few minutes we thought he was dead. Once it was over, my father was furious. But he was scared, I know. He just saw those feelings as weak, so he covered them with stronger emotions."

"I spent a lot of my life doing that." Wade felt the warm breeze and knew that summer had come to Montana. It came late up this high and left early, but for now it was here and he enjoyed it. The season of growth gave Wade the nerve to say more about his life before he'd become a man of faith. "My father punished me every time I showed fear or cried. Pa saw that as weakness. So I became rude and insulting and arrogant to cover my fear. I managed to pick a few fights with your brother along the way, too."

Abby sat up straight. "Really? You punched Tom?"

"Well, not so much punched him. Insulted him, threatened him, but I always had M Bar S riders with me. I thought I was being brave, but I always knew they'd step in if I got into trouble I couldn't handle."

They rounded a curve that followed a rockslide at the base of a mountain. Wade could see the clump of pines that surrounded Cassie's old house. Wade had come visiting many times before Cassie's first husband had died. There was a twisting trail up into the rocks they'd just skirted. He would lie in wait. When Griff would leave, as he did nearly every Saturday to ride to Divide to waste more of Cassie's money, Wade would go see Cassie. "This curve in the trail marks the end of your brother's property and the beginning of the Sawyer holding."

"My brother lives near here?" Abby looked around as if she expected to see a house.

"No, this is the far north edge of his ranch. His cabin is a couple of hours away, but he holds a lot of rangeland. The house is right behind those trees. It's only a few yards from a spring that never dries up, which makes it as valuable as gold. Cassie Dawson lived here with her first husband. When he died, Pa and your brother had a dustup deciding who would own it, and Pa paid a big price to win."

"Tom is so much younger than your father. I'm surprised he'd enter into a fight like that."

"He's one tough hombre, your brother. He's a respected man in these parts. Age doesn't have that much to do with earning respect."

"And you, Wade, are you a tough hombre?"

"No." Wade laughed to even think of such a thing. "Far from it."

Wade's eyes narrowed as the chimney came into view above the trees. Smoke curled up into the sky.

CHAPTER 24

"Hold up, Abby." Wade pulled his horse to a stop. "Why would we staff a line shack this time of year? The cattle are all moved close to home for the roundup."

Abby stopped beside him. Wade saw her suspicion and her unwillingness to approach the house. He decided then and there she was about the smartest, trail-savviest little thing he'd ever seen. One tough hombre for sure. Tougher than him by a long shot.

"I know an overlook where we can study the place before we ride in." Wade turned his horse and went easily to the barely existent trail. There'd been a time when he'd worn quite a path.

That old obsession and his weakness of character haunted him to this day. He knew he was forgiven. And that forgiveness helped him keep his heart open to his father. The man's cruelty had driven Wade to believe Cassie needed saving from her first husband and Red. Wade could understand and explain away the shame. But there remained a ghost of wonder that a man could be so confused and steeped in sin and still find God. That wonder urged him on after his father's soul. Pa had done nothing worse in his life than Wade. If Wade could find God and change, then so could he.

Wildflower Bride

With Wade leading, they moved to a high, well-concealed spot with a clear view of the house. Abby rode up beside him, gasped, and pulled her horse to a stop.

Wade smiled as they looked at the ridiculous, crumbling monstrosity.

White clapboard, three full stories high, stained glass windows shining from gables in each side of the roof. A second-floor balcony above a whitewashed porch, both wrapping around the whole building.

Abby turned to Wade. "Who would built such a. . .a. . ."

"Castle?" Wade suggested. "Mansion?"

She looked back at the house. Wade saw a missing board on the porch and broken windows that made him think of a gap-toothed old crone. The paint was peeling and weathered.

"A real fool of a man built this house about. . .five years ago." Wade swung down from his horse, ground-hitched it, and leaned on the massive stone that had a lower spot just perfect for spying.

"It's only five years old? Why is it. . ." Again words seemed to fail her. She dismounted and came to his side. "Who would build such a thing then just let it die?"

"A man who had no sense. Simple as that." Wade didn't want to talk about Cassie's first husband and how he'd wasted her money and left her destitute and pregnant at the mercy of the Rockies. . .a mountain range that had no mercy.

"It's a shame, though." Wade hated to see the waste, but he wasn't going to pay the money to keep up this monument to a man's foolish pride. "It's a beautiful thing. The owner hired some guy to come all the way here from Denver to build it. Shipped the building material in, too."

"Where is this foolish man?" Abby asked.

"Where most foolish men end up. . .especially in the West." Wade settled his hat lower. "Dead."

The smoke had thinned then vanished from the chimney. No

movement in or outside the house was visible. Wade studied the place then asked Abby, "What do you think?"

"No horses around. No movement or noise from the house. And if the fire has burned out already, it was most likely left from the morning meal. I'd say whoever was in there is gone."

"Can you smell them?" Wade turned and grinned at Abby.

She lowered her brows to a straight line and reminded him so much of Tom Linscott that he smiled bigger. "The only white man I smell is you."

He smelled her, too, but she made it sound like a bad thing, whereas Wade had no objection at all. "Abby, I want to ask you something important." He barely whispered the words, afraid he'd scare her away like a half-wild mountain creature. "We haven't known each other long enough, but I want this thought to be in your head."

"What is this thought?"

"Me. The thought is me. I want to be in your head and in your heart, Abby. Because you are in mine. Could you consider letting me court you? Might the day come when you could see yourself agreeing to spend your life with me?"

"Marry a white? Never!" Her words were cutting, but she didn't back away. No, in fact, his wildflower stepped a bit closer, studying him as if there was a speck of dirt in his eye and she was considering doctoring him.

And maybe she noticed a smudge on his lips, too, because her eyes went there as well.

Wade leaned down and touched his lips to hers.

Abby jumped back, reminding Wade of a startled horse. A beautiful, golden-maned. . . He shook his head. The woman was nothing like a horse.

She kept her eyes locked on his, and the little jump was only her straightening away from him. In the silence, Wade saw her fascination and fear. He decided to ignore the fear and take ruthless advantage of the fascination. He captured her lips again, and this time she wrapped her arms around his neck with the strength of a warrior.

The kiss deepened as Wade's future unfolded before him with perfect clarity. Abby, the ranch, six sons and three daughters. Maybe they'd live here. He could restore the old Griffin place. He kind of liked the idea of all the children's names starting with the same letter. Having a name that came at the end of the alphabet, Wade was partial to *A*. Like Abby. Maybe Adam, Andrew, Alan—

Abby slammed the heel of her hand into Wade's stomach.

Staggering back, Wade gasped for breath that wouldn't come. "What'd you do that for?"

"Keep your hands off me, white man." She flashed that wicked blade right under his nose.

Okay, so maybe a little early to be actively naming their children. Finally, he dragged in some air on a high whistle, and his lungs decided they'd let him live. "*My* hands?"

By way of an answer, she waved her knife close enough to draw blood if Wade made one wrong move.

Backing off would have been the sensible thing to do. Wade never had much sense. How many times had his father told him that? "You had your arms wrapped around me like a thousand feet of vine, Ab. Don't pretend like you didn't like that kiss. You may hate that you liked it. You may be surprised that you liked it. You may even want to stab me because you liked it. But you liked it just fine."

He actually heard the air whoosh past the blade as she swung the knife. For no reason on earth, her fierce resistance to something neither of them could deny made him smile. Raising his hands like a man surrendering, Wade backed away—not too far on the narrow, rocky slope, but enough to get her to lower the weapon. He still wasn't perfectly safe. The sharp, angry, downward slash of her white-blond brows could have cut him.

"Okay, no kissing. You're right anyway. You're right for the wrong reason, but I shouldn't have taken such liberties, especially without your permission. I apologize." He noticed he still had his hands up like he was surrendering and lowered them, since he wasn't giving up at all.

She sheathed her knife. When had she found time to add a hidden sheath to this dress? Did she stay up late at night planning to stab people? "Your words mean nothing when your actions presume so much. I do not want your hands on me."

Wade suspected she did, but he didn't mention that. "Abby?" He stood silently until she quit attending to her knife and faced him.

"What?" She nearly shouted her impatience.

It was with a bit of pain he gave up his dream of a perfect, gentle, Cassie Dawson–like wife. But his feelings were stronger than the dream. "I want your permission to court you."

"No." She crossed her arms that had been warm and fluid around his neck only moments ago. Now they were a flesh-and-blood fortress wall between them.

"I want to spend the rest of my life with you."

"I will never tie myself to you." Her head shook with absolute denial. "To no man."

"What are you planning to do, then?" The woman had to use her brain if she intended to get on with her life. "Stop being angry and think for a minute. You've got no home with your Flathead people now. You're the one who told me that."

Abby lifted her chin defiantly. She'd left her hair down for church, and the sunlight of it curled and danced and swayed around her shoulders and all the way to her waist, alive and beautiful in the gentle mountain breeze. "I will strike out on my own. I will hunt for deer, skin them, and build a tepee."

"I'll help you. We can live in your tepee together."

"You will *not*." With a silent stomp of her moccasined foot and a derisive snort, she went on. "I'll make a buckskin dress instead of this foolish thing I'm wearing now."

Her dress was the color of the Montana sky behind her. It brought out the blazing blue of her eyes. Or maybe the only blazing was caused by her temper.

"You can wear a buckskin dress if you wish. You had one when I found you. You brought it along to my house. Wear it. Or make another if you want. I'll find you beads if you want to add them. Sturdy clothes make sense on a ranch. I'm not trying to change you, Abby. I think you're wonderful. I wish I had half your strength."

Her arms dropped to her sides. Her jaw went slack, too. "You do? No man should look to his woman for strength."

"Why not?"

"Because it's weak."

"Jesus said, 'My grace is sufficient for thee: for my strength is made perfect in weakness.'"

Abby narrowed her eyes. "What is this? How can strength come from weakness?"

"It's a Bible verse. One of my favorites. You're strong and independent, but that's never been true of me." Wade sighed and looked at the ground. It was hard to confess weakness to anyone, even himself. But almost impossible to do it now, to this woman. He was sure he would only deepen her contempt for him if he admitted just how weak he was.

Then he remembered her graceful arms enfolding him. That wasn't him stealing an unwanted kiss. That was the two of them stealing a kiss that shouldn't have been, not between two people who weren't committed to each other and intending to marry. Wade had made that commitment. Obviously Abby wasn't ready to admit that she had feelings for him.

"I was a bad man. I shamed myself. I failed God." He shoved his hands into the back pockets of his pants to keep from reaching for her again then raised his head to meet her gaze. "My strongest sense of failure, not that long ago, was that I'd never had the guts to kill a man."

"Killers are weak. There's no strength in taking a human life. The strength comes in controlling yourself, doing right, even when it's hard." Abby's pretty brow furrowed. At least she was listening.

"Thank you. I agree."

"Unless they need killing, of course."

Wade shook his head. He was in love with a savage. It was hard to get used to. "Before I made my peace with God, I convinced myself that all the worst things in the world were strong—drinking, fighting, lying, killing." Wade slid his hands out of his pockets and wished he hadn't because now he didn't know what to do with them. He'd never felt this awkward in his life. "I lived the life of a fool because I was trying to live up to my father's standards. He called me weak, and I did terrible things to prove I wasn't."

"Your father is a foolish old man."

Nodding, Wade said, "I can feel sorry for Pa now, but that's because I've found peace, and I've found a Source of real strength." Wade raised his eyes to meet hers. "You know, I think it was easier for me, always drunk, obsessed with evil, to find God than it is for my father. I knew I was ruining my life. I knew I needed help. But how does a man like my pa ever admit he needs help? His whole life has been lived on pride and the strength of his will and his back."

"Well, his back has failed him now." Abby seemed to have forgotten wanting to kill Wade. He was thankful for that mercy. "Maybe this weakness you speak of has finally come to him. Maybe God's strength can reveal itself with your father laid so low."

"I keep hoping. I keep trying to be a light shining in the darkness of his life. But he's thrown my words back at me so many times, I feel like I'm casting pearls before swine."

"You speak in riddles." Abby shook her head. "Light shining, pearls and pigs. . ."

Wade smiled. "We got off the subject."

"What subject is that?"

"The whole reason I was glad we'd have a chance to ride together for a few hours. You say you will refuse to belong to a white man, but then what will you do?" He fell silent. Let her think for a while.

"Gertie has no ties to a man. She has a job. She belongs to no one but herself."

"So you'll be getting a job, then? Doing what? You can stay on at our ranch. But if you're going to stay there and be with me every day, see to my food and wash my clothes, then you might as well. . . marry me." He'd said it. Point blank.

Marry me.

His heart started thumping so hard he hoped she couldn't hear it.

"Wade. . ." Abby fell silent, and she stared at him as if lost for words.

Well, that might be a good sign. "No" had come easily before. "If you can't say yes, at least say you'll think about it. We'll get to know each other. I can help you hunt your deer and skin it for you to make your dresses."

It wasn't what Wade wanted, because, though she hadn't said no, she was far from saying yes. But well he remembered that moments ago her clinging arms seemed to shout yes.

"Perhaps—I don't know. It—it's true I have no home. And we get on well together."

"We do." Wade didn't mention that she'd pulled a knife on him only moments ago. He could live with an occasional outburst of mayhem if it suited Abby.

Abby stared at him as if trying to look inside his head. What was it she searched for? A warrior's bravery? The cruelty of some of the white men she'd known? He possessed neither.

She slowly leaned forward, and Wade was so busy worrying about her refusing to even give them a chance, he didn't realize her intent until her lips brushed against his. He resisted the urge to grab her. She pulled back and gave him a sad smile.

"What is it?"

"I've lost everything that mattered to me in my village. I don't know if I can be comfortable in your world."

"We don't have to live in Pa's house." He was very close to

begging, and that wasn't showing strength. "We could set up a tepee. They're kind of cold, but I'd live anywhere with you."

"Tepees are easier to keep warm than a house. No one could burn enough wood to keep your father's house comfortable."

It was the absolute truth that Pa's house was drafty and the floors were freezing no matter how huge the fire in the three different hearths. "We could build a snug cabin." Wade felt such hope that he could barely speak. She was actually talking about what their lives might be like, where they might live. "Strong log walls to keep out the winter wind but small enough that a blazing fire will warm us up like toast."

"I do like kissing you." She didn't sound all that happy about it. "It was so with my tribal parents. They were very affectionate with each other. And I remember my white parents kissing, too. That is an important thing for a man and wife, isn't it?"

"Very important, Abby. Vitally important." Wade brought his hands up to cradle her face. "May I kiss you? Will you give me permission this time?"

Abby didn't speak.

Wade didn't move. He'd never felt such closeness to another human being as they stood there, her nose almost touching his as he waited and waited until finally he heard the faintest of whispers.

"Yes."

He cherished her with his lips for long moments. He had never dared hope for so much. Or rather he'd hoped, but he'd never dared believe.

When they drew apart, he watched her with hopeful eyes and felt the breeze waft past them. Aspens quaked and danced. The warmth of the sun shone like a halo off Abby's beautiful hair. It was a beginning. She was going to give them a chance. The kissing needed to end now. It was surely the only proper thing to do.

Then her arms slipped around his neck, and Wade didn't have a proper thought in his head.

CHAPTER 25

"Honey, can we have lunch before you start stabbing the barn?" Red knew he was whining, but the woman was obsessed with that knife.

Cassie pursed her lips and scowled at him.

Red fought a smile. He knew she liked to scare him. So he did his best to act scared and begged sweetly. "I promise we can work all afternoon on making you dangerous."

"Red!"

"Oops, sorry, I mean *even more* dangerous. You're already a real tough character, sweetheart."

She smiled as if he'd offered her roses.

"But I'm starving after the ride home from church."

With a little huff, she stuck her nose right up in the air as if she were put upon mightily. "Well, all right, but don't expect me to help you with your chores."

Covering a sigh of relief to not have Cassie risking her life in the barn, Red nodded, perhaps just a bit too frantically. "That's fair. And with the herd culled, I don't have that many cattle to check. I can manage without your help."

Her eyes narrowed a little.

He gulped. "But it won't be easy. I'll miss the extra pair of hands."

Cassie had come a long way helping with chores, but often as not she did the chores with Michael on her hip and Susannah clinging to her skirt. It scared Red to death to watch her try to feed Harriet—his very angry sow—with the children in hand. To be fair, she hadn't set the barn on fire in months.

"I'll help you get the meal on, too. I won't leave it for you to do alone." Red saw that sweet smile break out on her face again.

She looked like every kind of fragile there was, with her ivory skin and her endless dark hair. The roses on her cheeks might have been painted on like those on a china doll. Her brown eyes, circled by lashes as long and soft as a mink's fur, shone with kindness. It was just the plain truth that the woman didn't have a mean bone in her body, no matter how hard she tried to be fierce. He still thanked God a dozen times a day for the precious gift of Cassie.

They ate quickly, and the young'uns, worn out by the long ride home from Divide, went down for their naps without a whimper. Well, Susannah did a little bit of screaming, but Red could see her heart wasn't in it. Michael fell asleep in his mashed potatoes.

They went outside to get to work. Red with chores, Cassie with stabbing the barn. Red stayed for a few nervous minutes, scared to death she'd somehow throw the knife and stab herself. But she was getting purely good. The knife stuck in the barn wall nearly half the time now, and the rest of the time it splatted against the barn and fell to the ground. He decided it was safe to do chores. Except for one little problem.

"I just can't get the bull's-eye, Red." Cassie went to dislodge her knife from the barn wall, right near the ground. It always hit there. Always. "How come I can't get more accurate?"

Red lifted his Stetson from his head and ran one hand through his unruly red hair before clamping his hat down to corral the mess. He studied the circle of charcoal on the red barn with the single black dot in the center. It was the pure undeniable truth.

Cassie had never made a single knife hole in the bull's-eye. Red could see where Belle and Emma had stabbed it up pretty good.

"Um—have you tried aiming higher? Maybe if you aimed at the top of the circle—"

"But that's admitting failure." Cassie crossed her arms and pouted like Susannah did when the cookies ran out. "I want to hit what I aim at."

Red deftly plucked the knife from her hand and pulled her into his arms. When he'd kissed all the pouting out of her, he rested his forehead against hers. "Have I told you lately how proud I am of you?"

Her eyes, which had fallen shut—as if the kiss had robbed her of her thoughts—flickered open. That warm gaze made Red feel like the richest man in Montana. And it was the truth—he was. Not a whole lot of money, but rich in the things that endured.

"Thank you. I love you, Red."

"Aw, Cassie, honey, not half as much as I love you." Wrapping his arms around her waist, he lifted her to her toes. Then her toes must have curled, because she was all the way off the ground. The richest man in Montana swept his ten-thumbed, knife-throwing wife up into his arms.

She giggled, and he silenced her with his lips.

Red, with a herd to check and a cow to milk, chickens to rob of their eggs and a hungry, killer sow and her ten piglets to feed, enticed his beautiful, precious Cassie into following him into the hay mow and forgetting all about throwing her knife for a long, long time.

While they passed an hour together, it occurred to Red once, briefly, that he should tell Cassie a baby was most likely on the way. She was as innocent as a babe in these matters. But he knew she'd be excited. But then he lost all track of his thoughts, too, and never got her told.

Red whistled while he milked in the dark. Rosie, his black and white Holstein who'd come West with him, kicked him to punish him for being late, but despite her best efforts, Rosie couldn't knock the smile off his face.

"We'd best have a look at that house." Wade's voice was hoarse as he pulled away from Abby, his wildflower.

She was acting purely tame just now.

He'd made his point with this kiss, and the few before. Well, honesty forced him to admit it had been more than a few. Abby was going to marry him. He wasn't going to take no for an answer.

He had a sweet feeling the answer wasn't going to be no.

With a grin, he slid his arm around Abby's waist and turned to study the old Griffin place.

Abby leaned against him.

The happiness filled his heart until it barely fit in his chest.

"I don't"—she cleared her husky throat and went on—"see any sign of life."

Wade smiled down at her. "And if there's someone sleeping there, just passing through, we'll let 'em stay."

Abby nodded then stopped cold.

He felt the tension in her body. "What is it?"

"We've had a jailbreak, cattle rustling, and a massacre within days of each other."

Wade couldn't find a single smile now. "And someone tried to kill you."

"Or you."

"Or both of us." Wade knew his woman well.

"And these bad men must be staying around here somewhere."

Wade studied the obviously recently occupied house then looked at the wild woman he'd taken up with. "How good are you at sneakin'?"

The tension left Abby's body, and she smiled and arched one brow. "I'm *real* good."

"With the stand of trees around the place, we should be able to come up on it quiet, get a closer look. I don't think anyone is there, but they may be back, so we'll be careful."

Nodding, Abby said, "Let's get the horses to a place they can graze and go check that house."

Sid stirred the cool ashes and looked sideways at Boog. "It's time we get that gold."

Boog grunted as he sipped the last of his coffee.

Paddy couldn't sit still. He was on his feet, moving, twitching, pacing. "Good, good, let's go. I'm tired of sitting."

"We can find the gold and get back to the ranch. With me out as foreman and so many of the men fired or new, Wade doesn't seem to realize you and Harv are gone. Why would he? He never knew you were there."

Harv sat forward with a groan. A lazy man, Harv. Never stood when he could sit. Never walked when he could ride. Sid would be glad to get rid of his edgy, bad-tempered, do-little saddle partner.

Boog froze, so suddenly, so completely, Sid was instantly alerted.

"What?"

Boog hissed at him and slashed a hand inches from Sid's face. No one talked or moved. Finally, Boog said, "Someone's coming."

Sid grabbed for his gun.

Paddy let a tiny giggle escape. His eyes shone with a hunger to shoot someone.

Sid knew of the four of them Paddy was the one who had a real appetite for murder. The rest could kill and had killed their share. They were hard men in a hard land, and Sid prided himself on being willing do to what he needed to do. But only Paddy smiled while he emptied his gun.

They turned to cover all approaches, guns cocked, eyes peeled, every sense alert.

CHAPTER 26

The sharp *snap* sounded loud as a gunshot.

Abby looked back and scowled at Wade's clumsy foot, now square on a brittle stick. Then, on her belly on the ground in her foolish gingham dress, she continued sliding through the tall grass, hunting shadows to use like hiding places.

Thank heaven he'd let her go ahead. Abby stopped her forward progress when she caught herself falling back into that kiss. What had come over her? Why had she let Wade, a white man, hold her close and tempt her into believing she could be happy in his world?

He had let her go ahead with her sneaking, though. With a twinge of pleasure, she thought of how Wade had not only admitted she was better at sneaking; he'd admitted she was a master. She knew it chafed him to admit she was the better woodsman, but he'd done it. It filled up a strange, empty place in her heart to be respected like that.

Wild Eagle had certainly never conceded that she had skills superior to his. He had seen her ease her way up close enough to slap the children during games of hide-and-seek. When she was young, she was the best of all the children when they'd played

222

at hunting. But older girls weren't included in the hunts. She'd known she could help feed her family, but Wild Eagle's pride had been too great to consider letting her come along. Instead he'd forbidden her to go along on the hunts. Ordering her to stay in the village where a woman belonged.

But truth was truth. Wade knew who was better in the woods. Now he stood there, not moving, and managed to be noisy. Abby wanted to growl at him through the knife she had clenched in her teeth. He grinned at her, apology and admiration in one sweet smile.

She looked away to keep her, attention on her sneaking. Easing forward, using swells in the ground and the waist-high prairie grass to conceal her as she inched forward.

That sound bothered her but she didn't turn back. If there was anyone in the house, Wade had very possibly alerted them.

She heard another sound, much softer, the hush of iron on leather, and turned back to see Wade pull his Colt revolver and take careful aim at the house. Abby was approaching from the south. There were two windows on the ground floor and more on the second. She knew that if Wade saw someone at those windows, he'd cover her.

Protect her.

Kill for her.

Die for her.

Abby hesitated to admit it, even to herself, but she felt the same. She knew a fraction of how much Jesus must have loved her because of the determined look on Wade's face and the deep resolve she felt in her heart to protect him.

God, please let me be worthy of his love. Please help protect us both. Please, please, please don't make it necessary for either of us to kill or die.

Abby inched forward. The moving grass would hopefully be mistaken as the blowing wind. She prayed.

Wade aimed.

God, please hear the praying and forgive the aiming.

❦

Nothing. No movement. No sound. Minutes passed. Then half an hour.

Sid could see Paddy twitching with impatience. Sid wasn't far behind. He hadn't heard a thing but that one snap of a twig. "There's nothing out there, Boog."

Boog turned narrowed eyes on him, and Sid froze as surely as if he'd been hit with a high mountain blizzard. Those eyes threatened slow, painful death, and Sid had no doubt Boog could deliver that death without a qualm if it meant protecting himself.

Sid hunkered down again. His partner was woods savvy, no doubt about it. But there were animals in the woods, the wind gusted, trees sometimes had a branch snap and fall to the ground. He dropped his own vigilance and let Boog play his game.

Suddenly Boog, already taut with acute attention to the area in front of him, stiffened even more, raised his gun, and took careful aim.

❦

"Abby, get down!" Wade felt an icy chill of fear, and he had to stop her.

She dove low, invisible behind the waving grass.

Silence stretched.

Wade stared at the seemingly empty house. What had scared him? Had God Himself given that warning? Or was Wade reacting to some subtle movement at the window? A faint noise? Or was he scared of his own shadow?

There was nothing.

Then there was Abby. She hadn't gotten down at all. She'd continued forward, so smoothly that Wade hadn't noticed until she emerged from the grass right next to one of the south windows and pressed her back against the house. With a look at Wade, a smirk it had to be, she moved closer to the window as she silently took her knife from between her teeth and eased her head past the glass.

Wade couldn't believe she'd ignored him.

No, no, no. Please, God, don't let her die.

Waiting for a gunshot to end Abby's precious life, Wade snapped. He screamed loud enough to impress Abby's Flathead family at a medicine dance and charged from behind the tree. Waving his arms and shouting, he rushed the house. He could draw their fire if someone was inside.

"Wade, no!"

Boog, on his knees crouched low, suddenly reared up and brought his rifle to bear. Then he twisted his body. "Get down!"

His low, harsh order drove the three other men to the ground.

"Not a sound. Nothing! Flathead hunting party!" Boog had barely whispered, but the terror in his voice was enough to make Sid obey him without question. Boog was scared right down to his belly, and Sid had never seen the man scared before.

Not one of them moved. Sid didn't think he even breathed.

Seconds passed. Minutes.

A whisper of noise reached Sid, and he stared through the grass that surrounded their camp.

They'd been riding since before dawn, pushing hard after the gold. He'd let Boog and Harv rest at the Griffin place while he'd ridden in for Paddy and made an excuse to Chester for why they'd be gone a couple of days.

Pushing as hard as four hardened men could, they'd brought spare horses and switched saddles to keep going. They'd made good time and now were near the mountain valley where they'd killed off those interfering Flatheads.

There shouldn't have been anyone here. It had been long enough for the larger tribe to come, bury their dead, and return to the Bitterroot Valley. But Sid saw through the tall grass a group of warriors. These riders, ten in all, were armed with rifles as well as bows and knives, unlike those they'd attacked earlier.

If Boog had fired a shot, the Flathead warriors would have been all too ready to fight. It was one thing to come upon a sleeping village with only a few armed men, none of them bearing rifles. It was another to take on ten adult warriors. That was certain death.

The hunting party was far enough away and upwind. They didn't notice Sid and his gang. Pure luck, because Indians were a noticing kind of people.

Each rider had a deer slung over his saddle as the group rode up the mountain, undeniably on their way into the valley Sid had just cleared of Indians.

His fury grew in direct proportion to the terror he'd felt a few minutes ago.

The Flatheads vanished into the trees that covered the mountainside most of the way to the top, before it dropped off into the lush green bowl of a valley that hid Harv's gold.

Once they were gone, Boog turned to Sid as if he needed to work his fury off on someone. "Cleared out that valley, huh? It don't look like they're gone. It looks like there're more of 'em than ever."

"Just shut up! Give me a minute to think!" Sid saw Boog's mouth close, but it wasn't because Boog obeyed. No one ordered Boog around. So Boog must've decided to be quiet for reasons of his own. Probably doing some thinking for himself.

"Let me shinny up there," Paddy offered, his eyes bright and sick to think they could massacre again. "I'll find out how many there are. I'll count 'em and come back and report."

"They'll have lookouts, you fool!" Harv sat up, looking after the hunting party. Then, as if he'd heard something, he began scanning in all directions.

Sid controlled a snort of disgust. Of course there might be

more. He'd been scanning from the moment he'd spotted the riders.

Harv was a bigger fool than Paddy.

"Let him go." Boog wasn't suggesting; he was ordering.

Sid should have called him on it. Sid was the boss. But calling Boog on anything could lead to shooting trouble, and neither of them dared fire a shot. It'd bring those Indians right down on their heads. Sid jerked his head toward the upward slope. "Go scout, Paddy, but watch your back."

Practically drooling with excitement, Paddy slipped into the heavy woods surrounding them and vanished.

Paddy was good, Sid had to admit it. If anyone could get up there, get the lay of the land and come back alive, it was the Irishman. But once he was there, if anyone was stupid enough to open fire on someone, it was Paddy. Then they'd all die.

"I've gotta make sure he doesn't do anything stupid." Practically growling, Sid stood, crouched down, and headed after Paddy.

"No one there."

Abby's terror exploded in something she felt a lot more at home with—rage. He'd run out into the open to draw fire to himself. She grabbed Wade's shirtfront and yanked so hard he stumbled forward. "You could have been killed! Are you crazy?"

Suddenly she wasn't pulling him forward. He was coming forward all on his own. His arms went around her waist and he lifted her right off the ground. "Why, Abby Linscott, you were afraid I'd get hurt."

"No, I wasn't!"

"You care about me."

"I'm tempted to hurt you mysel—*mmpph*!"

Her words were cut off by Wade's lips, and her terror, flipped to rage, now flipped by this kiss to. . .to. . .God help her. . .to love. She'd been unable to resist kissing him on that overlook, but she'd held back her heart. But now it tumbled free, falling into love.

No, no, no, God. I will not be in love with this man.

It was already too late. She wrapped her arms around his neck until she might have strangled him.

The man didn't show a speck of fear as he kissed her senseless.

Then, so suddenly she thought her head might be spinning, he put her down and pushed her away. "You behave yourself, woman." Then a ridiculous grin spread from ear to ear on Wade's face. "Kissing me like that isn't proper until we're married."

Married! Married? No, no. She'd be in that stupid house with his grouchy father, surrounded by the horrible whites for the rest of her life. Wearing gingham, of all disgusting things. She'd reached for her knife several times today planning to slit the skirt up the sides like her doeskin dress, but so far she'd controlled the urge.

Abby was back to wanting to kill him. She dove at him, but he was too fast for her.

He rounded the house and was up on the porch. The only reason he got away was because her knees were wobbly from that kiss. He pulled open the mansion's door and vanished inside.

She went charging after him. Yes, he needed strangling, but she was sorely afraid if she got her hands on him again, it would be to grab another kiss.

Sid caught Paddy just as he clambered up the last of the steep rise.

Paddy poked his head over the canyon rim then jerked it back, flipped over on his back, and slid down a few feet. "Injuns, hunnerds of 'em."

Sid took one look at Paddy, his eyes wide with fear. He lay flat on his back, his arms spread a bit as if to cling to the ground.

Sid inched upward for his own look.

"Careful." Paddy's voice was hoarse. Paddy was a man who liked to kill, and he never seemed too afraid of dying himself, like the danger was a drug he was addicted to. But right now, Paddy found no fun in what he'd seen.

Slowing down, Sid picked a spot where a gnarled pine grew only a few feet high, its long needles lying on the ground. He lifted his head the bare minimum over the ridge, slowly, careful to make no sound or sudden movement. And he saw.

The entire Flathead nation must have moved into this valley.

Before, there'd been a handful of tepees and only a few adult warriors, no guns that Sid had found when scouting. Now there were dozens of armed men. Tepees filled nearly the whole bowl-shaped valley that topped this mountain, lining both sides of the rushing stream that poured down from a higher mountain to the north.

They'd waited too long and now they were locked away from the gold. Maybe forever. The tribe might leave for winter hunting grounds, but this was no hunting party. They'd put up their tepees. Women stirred pots. The hunting party was already skinning the deer they'd brought in. Women were tanning hides, probably from yesterday's hunt. Children shouted and played along the water's edge. They were here to stay.

Sid turned just as Paddy had and lay on his back, his plans tasting like ashes in his mouth.

"There's no chance we'll find the gold. Not until they move on." Paddy said what Sid already knew, and Sid had a strong urge to slam his fist into Paddy's mouth until he shut up forever.

The gold was out of reach. Sid realized in a moment of perfect clarity that he now needed the M Bar S more than ever. He needed a place nearby to stay until the Flatheads moved on. His defeat turned to bitter determination. "Let's go. Let's get back to Sawyer's and finish what we started. This tribe'll move on come cold weather and we'll come for the gold then."

"It looked like a permanent settlement to me."

The only reason he didn't put a bullet in Paddy right then was the noise it'd make.

Sid started back to Boog and Harv fast, because one more stupid word from Paddy and even a village of Flatheads coming down on them wouldn't stop Sid from shutting Paddy's mouth permanently.

∼≈∽

"No one here. But someone's been here recently." Wade jabbed a finger at the pile of tin cans. The jagged edges of the lids looked like they'd been hacked open with a knife. "He cleared out. Nothing left. If a drifter went out hunting for an hour or two, he'd probably leave his gear behind."

"Maybe."

Wade smiled up at her. He could still see that anger when he had been reckless. Now why would a little woman who claimed to hate him care one speck about a man getting hurt?

She didn't hate him half as much as she wanted to. Of course, he'd suspected as much when she'd let him kiss her silly up on the mountainside while they watched the house.

God, I can see she cares, and I can see she doesn't want to. Help her. Help me to say the right thing. Ease her grief for her Flathead family and her hurt at their rejection.

Wade realized that Abby's rejection by her Indian world was far too similar to his rejection by his father. It was no wonder they had turned to each other. Two people alone in the world.

Despite the fact that Wade was now back at his father's house, Wade felt adrift. Abby could be his anchor.

"Enough adventure for one day. Let's be on our way." Abby crossed her arms and glared at the huge front room they stood in. A stairway swept in a graceful arc upstairs on one side of the room. Doors opened off the other side of the mammoth entrance. "This house is even more ridiculous than yours. I didn't think that was possible."

"My father's house, not mine."

"Wade"—Abby let up her glowering for a second—"how can

you stand the way your father treats you? Why don't you stand up for yourself?"

"The Bible says to honor your mother and your father."

Pursing her lips, Abby studied Wade. "I know this verse, but I don't think God asks us to let our parents heap cruelty on us. Do you?"

"I've struggled with that, for a fact. What do you think?" Wade prayed silently, wishing she'd have the answer to the question of his life—how to honor his pa.

"I think that we can honor our parents from a position of strength."

Considering, Wade shrugged. "But what does that mean, exactly?"

"Do you feel God urging you toward calm? Or do you want to fight your father, demand his respect the only way he understands, with your own anger?"

Wade crossed his arms. "I've never been able to demand a thing from Pa. He's always treated me badly and I've never found a way to change it, short of leaving."

"Then why did you come home to him?"

"You were there. He sent for me. He was dying, Red said. I had to obey that summons. I didn't expect to have to live with the old coot. I expected to be on hand to bury him."

"And now it looks as if he'll live, probably for years. Are you going to accept that and let him pour hatred on your head for the rest of your life?"

She sounded so kind. Not like his Abby at all. A fighter by nature and by upbringing, she was more likely to go for her knife than to coax cooperation out of anyone. That was one of the things Wade liked best about her.

"So you think I should. . .what? Yell back?"

Rubbing her mouth as if considering just that, finally Abby said, "You'll do as you see fit. But I don't believe it's honoring your father to let him get away with the things that make his son hate him. In fact, you're standing quietly by while your father commits a terrible sin."

Stunned, Wade could only stare at her. His heart, already soft toward the whole world, softened even more. "I think you're right." Wade's spirits rose as he thought of his father and the hate that festered in him. It was indeed a sin for Wade to patiently accept his father's sin. He smiled. "Say, when we're married, we can build a tepee and stake it out anywhere you want. We can go up into the mountains and live off the land."

"We won't be getting m–mar–married." Abby closed her eyes tight then seemed to force them open. "I will bind myself to no white man."

Wade had to admit that was a long, long way from "I do." But he had time. "We can start out with a small tepee then work on a bigger one when the babies start coming."

Abby turned and stalked toward the door.

Before she reached it, Wade, in a strange mood of utter confidence that he was going to change Abby's mind, with God's help, followed, tormenting her for her own good. "I'm a crack shot. I'll keep us in deer meat. You can plant a garden. . . ."

Abby moved faster across the thin stretch of overgrown weeds, away from the house and him.

"I saw a really nice valley not too far from the cabin where I spent the winter. . . ."

Abby vanished behind the clump of trees, heading for the horses.

Wade decided to shut up before she pulled that knife again. And he ran in case she stole his horse.

He thought he was getting to know his little wife-to-be pretty well.

CHAPTER 27

Mort met them at the front door roaring. As usual.

"Old man—"

Wade caught her around the waist and dragged her past the beast at the door. "Ignore him, honey." He grinned at her.

She could have taken a swing at him, but it just didn't seem worth the effort.

"You know we need to work on that reflex you've got to pull your knife every time you're the least bit aggravated."

Looking down, Abby saw she had it in her hand. Reflex must be right, because it hadn't been a conscious choice. But she'd been raised to loathe and fear whites. Nothing she'd seen had convinced her to forget that raising. Except she'd learned she liked kissing one white man very much...too much. "I don't need to work on it at all. I'm very good." She tucked her weapon away.

"I didn't mean that." Wade had her nearly through the front entrance area, heading toward the kitchen. Any part of the house where they wouldn't have to listen to Mort's growling. Honestly, the man belonged in a cave. "I meant—"

"You called her 'honey'?" Mort followed in his chair. They never should have put wheels on the man.

Abby was going to lose the hearing in her ears if that grizzly man didn't stop roaring like a trapped bear.

"Pa, did you have a good day?" Wade talked pleasantly, quietly. Abby doubted if Mort heard him. She also doubted that Wade cared if his pa heard him. "I took a ride after church. Abby 'n' I needed some time alone. With the roundup over and the men free on Sunday, it was the perfect time."

"Sundays free, bunch of nonsense." Mort rolled his chair forward.

Abby heard the gentle rolling of the wheels on wood as Wade dragged her into the kitchen. Gertie was pulling a roast out of the oven.

Wade was planning to widen a few doorways so Mort could get around more easily. Abby was tempted to ask if he could narrow a few of them so she'd have a place to escape.

Wade dropped Abby's hand and rushed forward. With a quick grab for a thick towel, Wade protected his hands then relieved Gertie of the massive roasting pan. Abby had to admit that growing the cattle and keeping them nearby was far handier than going hunting. Except of course Wade had spent nearly every waking moment since he'd been home working with his cows, so how much easier was it, really?

Wade slid the black pan, with its domed lid, onto the top of the massive iron oven. He pulled off the lid, and a faint sizzle got louder. Steam that smelled like a lovely dream billowed from the pan.

Abby realized she hadn't eaten since breakfast, and now the sun was low in the sky. "Did you expect us for the noon meal, Gertie? I never thought of discussing it with you."

"No, Wade said you might be late. If he could get your brother to go away."

"Oh, he did, did he?" Abby's head swiveled to look Wade in the eye. He'd planned their little afternoon ride, then. Most likely with the intent of stealing a kiss. The truth was Abby had never been touched by a man in such a way. Wild Eagle had walked with her, but they had been mindful of the proper distance between an unmarried man and woman. Wade had no such consideration. Or rather, he'd spoken of propriety then ignored his own dictates.

"He never mentioned it to me until after church."

Wade helped Gertie get the roast and vegetables out of the pot, and Gertie went to work turning the drippings into her wonderful gravy. Abby knew she should try to learn how Gertie made that delicious concoction, but it was hard. She'd tried once and nearly destroyed the meal. Quitting seemed wiser, but Gertie said she needed to learn.

Wade was taking a deep breath, bent over the meat, inhaling the savory smell. He straightened and grinned at Abby, unrepentant. "I didn't think you'd go, and I had almost no hope of running off your leech of a brother."

Mort bumped into Abby with his chair.

Startled, Abby jumped out of the way.

"Pa, you're a menace with that thing. If you don't be careful, I'm going to hang a bell on it so we hear you coming." Wade stepped to Abby's side, gently caught her upper arm, and pulled her out of the doorway when Abby would have preferred to snarl at the rude old man.

She wondered if their talk at the Griffin place had taken root. Wade exchanged a look with her and she knew he was thinking the same thing—how to handle Mort.

Abby gave him a barely perceptible shrug. The decision had to be Wade's. She would have been crushed to her soul if either of her fathers had spoken to her the way Mort spoke to Wade.

Abby saw sorrow in Wade's green eyes as if he pitied his father. Pity she could maybe manage. But never would she allow this old man to run roughshod over her.

Mort rolled to the head of the table then slammed his fist so hard a glass on the table toppled over. "Get supper on the table, Gertie. I'm hungry."

Gertie began bustling around.

Wade went to a cupboard on one side of the sink and took plates out.

Abby reached for her knife.

Looking over his shoulder, Wade caught her eye and winked at her, as if he knew she wanted to attack.

That calmed her for some reason. She went to the cupboard, shoved Wade aside, and took over his job.

Wade laid out the heavy pottery plates carelessly, noisily, then went to the side of the table closest to the wall, around the corner from Mort's left hand, and sat. Once he was settled, he turned to his father. "Pa, do you want me to stay on here?"

Turning with her hands full of silverware, Abby looked from Wade to Mort, bracing for a flood of cruel words.

Mort, busy centering his plate, froze. Then slowly his eyes went to Wade. "I don't—"

"I know what you're going to say." Lifting a hand, Wade stopped his father with a motion. "You don't need anyone, least of all me. You are ashamed to call me your son. I'm a coward, I'm lazy, I'm clumsy." Wade said the words in a singsong chant as if they bored him to death. "What else, Pa? I've heard it all before."

"You've never been—"

"Know this, Mort Sawyer"—Wade cut him off with a hard voice Abby had never heard before—"I am ready to leave. I don't suppose I've convinced her yet, but I have hopes of persuading Abby to marry me."

"Marry her?" Mort's white brows arched to his hairline.

"Marry me?" Abby set the cups on the table with a sharp *click* of glass on wood, the fistful of forks clattering against them.

"You're getting married?" Gertie set a platter on the table, heavy with roast beef, ringed with bright carrots and white potatoes and whole baby onions.

"Like I said, she hasn't agreed yet."

"That is an understatement." Abby crossed her arms and glared. "In fact, I've told you—"

Wade cut her off. "Whether or not I can convince you doesn't change the fact that Pa treats you terribly."

"He treats everyone terribly. I'd feel left out if he was nice to me."

"I don't treat anyone terribly. If you'd all act right, I wouldn't have to say a word."

Wade snorted.

Abby exchanged a dark look with Gertie.

"I can put up with a lot, Pa, because I see it as my Christian duty to honor you. For me, that means not letting you waste away in your bed for the last few pitiful months of your life stewing in hate."

"Now, Wade, Mort's getting better." Gertie put a bowl of gravy on the table then helped spread the utensils and glasses.

Abby chipped in setting the table.

Even Mort pulled his glass and silverware into place.

"Well, that's the problem, Gertie."

"What?" Mort roared. "Me getting better is the problem?"

With a kind expression completely at odds with his words, Wade said, "If you were going to linger a bit then die, I'd stay on for sure. Least I could do."

"Wade, shame on you." Gertie fetched a loaf of bread, still warm from the oven, and set it on a breadboard next to the roast. She added a tub of butter and a pitcher of milk.

"But since you seem to be surviving pretty nicely, and in fact it looks like you could live ten more years, I'm not going to stay on"—suddenly Wade's calm voice began to darken as his pleasant expression faded to grim anger—"if you don't find a way to get a civil tongue in your head and treat Abby and me with some respect! I'm not going to put up with it!" Shouting, he pressed both hands flat on the table and pushed himself up from his chair.

"You've been a tyrant all your life. I've talked with you about my faith and you've thrown it in my face. So fine, make that choice, cut yourself off from God. But do not think for one moment"—Wade slammed his fist on the table—"I'm going to live my life with your hate and spite! Decide now, Pa." Wade's hand slashed only inches from Mort's face. "Right now. A man with no self-control is a weakling. So have you got any control over your mouth or not?"

Silence reigned in the kitchen.

Wade breathed as if he'd just completed a long race up a mountainside. His eyes flashed with angry fire.

For the first time, Abby saw a man she'd think twice—or three times—about making angry.

Wade's breathing slowed, and he lowered himself to his chair. With a huge, razor-sharp knife, he began carving the roast.

For a while Mort was frozen, his face beet red. Mort's eyes, as green as his son's, locked on Wade's and they held in a battle of wills. Abby suspected Mort had a thousand horrible things to say, but Wade's crack about his being a weakling had obviously started a war in the old man. Finally, Mort ate in sullen silence.

No one spoke a word through the entire tense supper except an occasional "Pass the bread" or something else necessary to complete the meal.

As they finished Gertie's hot apple crisp, swimming in cream, Wade finally spoke. "It'll do no good to give me an answer, Pa. Your promises mean nothing even if you could bring yourself to make them. The next time you're deliberately unkind to me or Abby, or Gertie for that matter, I'm leaving. Chester is a good foreman. You'll be fine without me." Wade rose from the table and began gathering the dishes.

As he slipped past Gertie at the foot of the table, Mort spoke. "You're right." Mort sounded tired and defeated.

Wade turned, a wary look in his eyes. If his father had threatened him, he wouldn't have flinched, but Abby thought Wade actually looked a little scared of this version of his father.

Abby had certainly never heard this tone. From his reaction, Abby guessed Wade had never heard it either.

"I'll try. That's the best I can do." Mort's hands gripped the arms of his wheelchair until his knuckles turned white.

Abby held her breath. She'd never expected Mort to give an inch. She still didn't really believe he would admit he was wrong about anything.

"I've been wrong about everything. You've done a good job with this ranch since you've been back. I'll watch my mouth, and you can take over the ranch I broke my back building out of nothing." Mort jerked the wheels backward to roll away from the table. "While I wither up and die in my room." Mort nearly ran over Abby as he left the room.

Good survival instincts served Abby well as she stood and pulled her chair out of the way for Mort's exit. She watched him leave, and then her gaze went to Wade's. "Maybe you should go after him?"

The door to Mort's bedroom slammed so hard Wade's Stetson fell off the elk antlers by the back door.

"Better let him cool off." Gertie looked after Mort, regret plain on her face. "You were pretty hard on him, Wade."

"Yeah, and he's been pretty hard on me all my life, and you, too, Gertie. Why'd you put up with it all these years?"

A frown turned down the corners of her mouth, and from the lines on her aging face, Abby was sure frowning was something Gertie had done a lot in her life. Why had Gertie stayed? Why had she put up with Mort's vicious temper?

"I stayed to protect you." Gertie's eyes brimmed with tears. "I knew how he was to you, but I couldn't stop him. But I could be here and comfort you after it was over."

Wade looked at Gertie in silence.

The silence was too much for Abby. "You couldn't stop him? Why not? Did he hit you, too?"

"No, he's never laid a hand on me. Oh, I got the same yelling as everyone else. . .but never a fist."

"Well, I'd say you did a poor job of protecting Wade if that was your goal."

Wade gasped. "Abby, Gertie was always good to me. No one could control Pa."

"Two adults in a household." Abby sniffed. She liked Gertie, but the woman had failed Wade just as Mort had. "One of them an abusive tyrant, the other a kind and decent woman who stands by while the tyrant beats a child. You could make a case that the tyrant is out of control, even crazy. But the decent adult has no such excuse. To me, that makes the one who stands by more evil than the one who swings his fist."

Gertie lifted her chin and glared at Abby. The kindness that was usually there had vanished. "I did the best I could."

"She wasn't to blame." Wade set his plate down as if he needed his hands free to defend Gertie from Abby's unkind truth.

"The best? The best you could do is cower in the kitchen and come out with hugs and sympathy afterward? A true defender would throw herself between the child and the tyrant."

Gertie turned her face aside as if Abby had slapped her. "I was too afraid to protect the closest thing I'll ever have to a son. You're right."

"Being right in a family of whites isn't hard." Abby stepped away from the table and turned her eyes on Wade. "I can't sleep in this house of grief and anger tonight. I can't even breathe. I need the wind blowing to cool my body and the night sounds to soothe me to sleep."

"It's not safe out there, Ab."

"And it's safe in here? This home is a haven from danger? I don't think so, Wade. All the danger is locked inside with you. Your father built a fortress to keep happiness out."

"Now, Abby, just settle down and we'll talk about this."

"The time for talking is past." Abby turned toward the door.

"Don't go out." Wade rushed across the room and literally threw himself in front of Abby, blocking her from the door.

"Get out of my way."

"Calm down. It's dark and damp. Don't just go storming off.

We'll talk this through like two reasonable adults."

"You want to talk, you come outside."

"No." Wade got a stubborn look on his face that reminded Abby of how he'd stood up to his father. "You stay in. You don't get to win all the fights, Abby. A man is to be the head of the house. The Bible says so. You're going to mind me, and that's the end of it."

It was a lovely night for a walk in the woods. And Wade knew he was going for one when Abby snarled at him, dodged past him as spry as a mountain goat, and slammed the door on her way out.

He had to go after her, but first he needed to comfort poor Gertie. "She's wrong."

Shaking her head, tears welling in her eyes, Gertie said, "Maybe. I did what I was able to do for you, Wade. But we both know it wasn't enough. I was a coward. I still am one." Gertie turned and left the kitchen.

Wade was left alone. The silence was so profound he could hear his heart beat in his chest.

They'd all left him. It came to Wade then that he'd been alone all of his life. His pa had never been with him, not in any sense of affection or support.

Gertie's arms had comforted him, but only when it was too late.

Now here was Abby, a woman he wanted to marry and bring into his home, into his heart. She didn't want him, either.

Oh, she was drawn to him. Wade was sure of that. But it was against her will. If he married her, would her untamed ways just be another kind of loneliness? If he did convince her to marry him, would he spend his life bending to her will? Was that God's vision of a good marriage? His trying to keep her happy, hoping and praying she wouldn't dash off into the night and return to the life she loved far more than she would ever love him? Leaving him alone again.

She'd just this minute made that choice, and now she was in danger. There were dangerous beasts, four-legged and two-legged, outside this house. He'd lived in fair harmony through the winter out there, with a mountain and the bitter cold seemingly bent on killing him five times a day. He'd liked the barren life. The time with his Bible had been good for his soul.

And now he was back with Pa and Gertie and more confused than ever. Not about his faith. He needed the comfort of God more than he needed his heart to take its next beat. But what was he supposed to do with his life? What did God want for him?

Wade walked to the door and went out onto the back step, now a ramp sloping down to ground level on the left and a section that went straight ahead for several feet so Pa could roll right onto the buckboard. Wade went to the end of that section and sat down, his legs swinging, staring out into the night.

He prayed.

As the silence of the night embraced him, he saw a light in the bunkhouse and another in the foreman's cabin. Everyone was abed for the night. . .or would be soon. Except Abby, his Glowing Sun, who was no doubt using that confounded knife of hers to kill and skin a buck so she could build her own house.

He was an idiot to hunt for her. She was tougher than he was by far. Yes, she'd been caught by white men, twice. So she wasn't invincible. She'd been kidnapped once last year when Wade had found her while on his way to help Belle Tanner—it had still been Tanner back then, before she'd married Silas—with her cattle drive and once this spring.

But the honest truth was she'd been running from the first men, already free, and she'd been slashing away at the second man. She'd saved herself both times before Wade ever got there.

Dew had formed on the ground, and he could see footprints leading around the house as clearly as if they'd been outlined by lantern light. With a sigh, he followed them. He'd just talk to her. Find where she was sleeping.

Wildflower Bride

She'd said, *"All the danger is locked inside with you. Your father built a fortress to keep happiness out."* He looked at the house he was right now rounding and knew she was right. He could never ask her to live in this house. So he'd make sure she knew he was ready to leave. To live anywhere as long as she was with him.

Shoving his hands in his pockets, he followed her trail toward a wooded area to the north of the house, hoping she'd just gone in there to fume and cool down. He stepped into the woods and felt an arm go around his neck and a pointed blade jab into his neck.

Either someone was trying to kill him, or. . .he'd found his woman.

Or both.

"Go back inside." Abby needed some peace. She needed time to think.

"I was hoping that was you, Ab." Wade's voice worked, just barely, through her hold. He didn't try to escape. In fact, after they'd stood there a few seconds, the grip she had on him seemed less like an attack and more like she'd grabbed him to give a hug.

A hug with a knife involved, but still—

"I meant it when I said I wouldn't sleep in there tonight."

"Okay, I'm not going to try and argue. I just wanted to know where you were going to stay. I want you to be safe."

"As if I was safe inside." With a sniff of disgust, Abby let him go, sorry she'd ever touched him. Her arm was warm where it had wound around his throat. Holding her knife felt foolish. She would never harm Wade. Never.

"There are different kinds of safe, Ab. You're right—so right—about my family being an unhappy one. I don't think you can blame Gertie any more than she blames herself, but in the end, yes, I grew up in a sad place."

Abby walked deeper into the woods. The ground was rocky, but that was so everywhere in this part of Montana. She needed to find shelter but didn't worry about it. The mountains and forest would always shelter her.

She found a shattered pine tree, its stump nearly four feet across. It had snapped about ten feet up, and the massive top of the tree had fallen and was long dead and bare. The ground, piled high with the fallen needles, was soft as a feather bed. Sinking to the ground, Abby leaned back against the tree. She could sleep here as well as anywhere.

But Wade needed to go away first. Instead he slid down the trunk next to her. The tree was big enough that there was plenty of room for both of them, especially with Wade sitting so close their arms touched. "You know I care about you, Abby, don't you? I want you to stay here."

"And if I can't?" The needles gently scented with pine seemed to ease into Abby's bones. There was peace for her in the wild places.

"Then I'll leave with you. That home holds nothing for me but responsibility, Christian duty. I needed to come home and see to my father, but I've done that now. I thought for a time we could stay and be happy here, but now I doubt that. We'll go somewhere else. We can leave now, tonight if you want. Go into Divide and have a marriage blessed then head for the mountains, in the direction of your high valley. Build a small cabin, raise a garden, and hunt for food. We don't need the ranch to survive. We've both proved that."

He just would not stop jabbering about marrying her. She couldn't say yes, yet she found herself unable to say no. So she changed the subject. "You really lived in the mountains last winter?"

Wade nodded, and Abby had to look close in the dark night. With the trees overhead, even the bright moonlight and blazing stars struggled to penetrate the darkness, but Abby's eyes adjusted quickly and his sincerity was unmistakable. "I found an old miner's shack, or maybe a trapper lived there. It was probably smaller than your tepee."

Wildflower Bride

"And you liked it there?"

"I—I was contented there. I needed some quiet to get over—"

It took a moment for Abby to realize he wasn't going to continue.

"To get over what?"

The sound of Wade slowly inhaling melted into the soft rustle of the wind and the cry of a hunting owl. Insects chirped in the night, and the leaves overhead sang their own quiet song.

Long after she decided he wasn't going to answer her, Wade finally spoke. "To get over—the—the sight of you—riding away from me with Wild Eagle. It broke my heart."

Now it was Abby's turn not to speak. Abby thought of how Wade had saved her from those men last fall when he was headed for work on a cattle drive for Silas Harden's family. He'd abandoned that job and stayed with her, tried to persuade her to come back with him to his white world. When she'd refused, he'd taken her to her home. And on the way, they'd come to care for each other. Abby thought of these things in the silence.

Wade reached down and took her hand, fumbling for it a bit in the dark. He pressed her knuckles against his lips.

She liked it so much it terrified her, so she wrenched away. "I can't do it, Wade. I can't bind myself to you. I've seen too much of the white men, all bad."

"No, not all bad. Not me." He moved suddenly, rising onto his knees. He caught her shoulders and turned her, pulling until she knelt to face him. "You trust me, Abby. I know you do. And my father and the trouble that goes with him doesn't have to be part of choosing me. I will go with you wherever we have to go to find a peaceful home, full of happiness. Say you want that. Please, at least tell me there's a chance. I need to hear that."

She hesitated to speak the words that he seemed to believe would bring him happiness. But there was no way for them to be happy with her dislike of all his people.

His lips settled onto hers. In the darkness, she hadn't seen him lowering his head. For this reason only, she didn't duck away. And then she couldn't. She couldn't end the kiss that she knew was all wrong for both of them.

He drew her closer, all his loneliness pulling at her own.

At last he raised his head. "You know we could find a way to be happy together, Abby. Your kiss tells me the truth even if your words deny it."

"Oh, Wade. . ." Abby rested one palm on his face. He had whiskers, bristly from neglect. She remembered her father would come in cold from checking cattle and scratch her cheek with them and she'd giggle. She'd loved her father, a white man.

"Just a chance, Ab. I'll give you all the time you need to decide if you can live here with me, or we can leave here right now if you can't bear life in this house. I'll walk away with you, not even go inside to say good-bye. We'll find a preacher and say our vows to God. I'd pledge myself to you forever."

"You offer to give up your family for me?"

"You'd be my family. We'd begin our own." Wade kissed her deeply. "Have children." The kiss came again, longer this time.

He turned then and sank back down to lean against the tree. He pulled her down, tucking her to his side. "You don't have to answer me now. I know you're still confused and grieving and angry. But say you'll give me a chance, please. Here or in the mountains or anywhere else you'd like to go."

Knowing it was a mistake, Abby rested her head against Wade's broad shoulder. Through the trees, she could see the lights in the big house. She hated that house. It represented all that was wrong with the whites. Its foolish size and the unhappy people who inhabited it. Now she was forcing Wade to do something he might regret all his life. It wasn't yet time to leave. "I will give you this time you want so badly, Wade."

His arm tightened around her, and his sigh ruffled her awful yellow hair. The light in Mort's room extinguished. Moments later, a light farther to the back of the house came on, in the room where

Wildflower Bride

Gertie slept. There was still a lantern burning in the kitchen; the light spilled out and illuminated the bit of backyard that Abby could see. Gertie had left the light on to guide Wade home.

"I will stay here and try to adjust to this world while I decide if I can risk a life with you."

A soft kiss on the top of her head made her smile and admit the truth. "I, too, felt my heart break when I rode off with Wild Eagle. I did not want to leave you."

His other arm came around her, and he hugged her until she thought she might have to pinch him so she could breathe. Then he laughed and pulled back enough that they could see each other. "Do you really want to sleep out here tonight? I could go in and get you a blanket."

"No, I'll come back in. But there may be times when I need to get outside, to clear my head and breathe clean air and think without the noise of your father ringing in my ears."

"I was dead serious about leaving if he speaks rudely to you again. If he is unkind, just tell me and we'll go. I give you my word."

Abby nodded, thinking he'd just put yet another burden on her. Now if his father was cruel, which he was bound to be, she would have to keep it secret unless she wanted to send Wade from the house.

They stood and Wade took her hand, his fingers sliding between hers. "Are you ready to go back in?"

She would never be ready, so why wait? "Yes."

"Do you mind if we pray before we go? I need to ask God to be with both of us."

"I need that, too." Abby took Wade's other hand, and he quietly said many things that were in her heart, but not all.

He couldn't begin to imagine all. And she couldn't begin to tell him.

CHAPTER 28

I'd like to go see Belle, Red." Cassie had Michael on one hip, and Susannah was clinging to Red's right leg singing as the two adults washed the supper dishes side by side in their new, bigger kitchen.

Cassie had tried to stop him from making it too big. Heating a large house was too much work. But Red had a stubborn streak and a bit of a temper to match his red hair. He'd pushed for more space when he'd found out Michael was on the way, and Cassie admitted she liked the children having their own room.

"Now, Cass, honey, we've been doing so much running lately I'm not seeing to the cattle like I oughta."

Cassie grinned at him. She could get the man to do anything and that was a fact. It was a power she tried not to abuse. Michael slapped her on the face and she probably deserved it. But she was determined to get her way. "We've only been to Belle's once."

"Yes, but she came here once, too."

"Not really. She and Emma went off with you. I want to talk with her about why I can't get the hang of knife throwing." It was a plain fact that no amount of practice seemed to improve her skill.

"It sticks in the wood almost every time now. You're doing great."

"But it's always too low."

Red opened his mouth.

"And no"—she wasn't listening to any more of his nonsense—"I'm not going to just aim higher."

"Why not?"

She could be stubborn, too. "Because—" It pinched to admit the truth. "Because—" So she rushed it out in one long, frustrated shout. "Because I've already tried!" She slammed a metal pot onto the counter with a loud *bang*. "I still can't hit what I aim at."

"Oh." Red subdued himself after that and picked up the pot to dry it.

"It doesn't work." She pouted. Pouting was one of the best things she'd learned since she'd gotten married. She loved the way Red teased her out of her bad mood. She could hardly sustain the down-turned lips when she thought of how sweet he was while he cheered her up. But that really wasn't why she'd started this. "Please, Red."

Susannah hollered, "Pick me up, Papa!"

"We've been to the Tanner Ranch."

"Harden, Red."

"Right, right. Sorry." Red nodded. "The Hardens have visited us here. I went hunting for Wade. Then later I had to track down the rustlers. I took the herd to Divide. We went in for church. Why, we've been gone more than we've been home. Good thing we got the roundup done early. I can't believe the Sawyers are just now finished." Red shook his head as if it was incomprehensible.

Cassie had felt sorry for Wade with the roundup still ahead of him. He hadn't been home, so it wasn't his fault, but none of the other ranchers would see it that way. "I didn't get to go with you to hunt for Wade."

"You were with Belle. I thought you liked Belle." Red swiped a bit of drool off Michael's chin with his shirtsleeve. Michael, content on Cassie's hip, swatted at his papa and giggled.

"I didn't get to go hunt the rustlers with you."

Red gave her a very dry look. "You're saying you *wanted* to be part of the posse?"

It was all Cassie could do to maintain her pout. She was really crazy in love with her husband. "I'm just saying you feel like you've been out and about a lot, but I haven't been. I want to go see Belle. A woman with a baby on the way needs the company of other women from time to time."

She stamped her foot and almost felt ashamed of herself. Reminding Red of the coming baby was very dastardly of her. He was so excited about it and so kind to her. She could barely lift a finger around the barnyard these days.

Susannah stamped her little foot and giggled.

The reminder about the baby he'd had to tell Cassie about earned her a very long, sweet kiss. The man was a marvel the way he figured out a baby was coming.

"I'm wondering which of us this'n'll look like. We've got a matched set now. Maybe we'll have a redheaded little girl or a dark-haired boy. I can't wait, no matter which it is." He kissed her again until Michael started trying to poke his little fingers between their lips.

"I can't wait either, Red. And I want to tell Belle about it."

"She probably knows."

Jerking back from him, Cassie narrowed her eyes. "How would she know?"

"I told Silas."

"Before you told me?" Cassie felt herself blush. How *had* Red figured it out?

Red just laughed in her face. "Yep, and he probably mentioned it to Belle."

She really did need to wheedle his secret out of him. The symptoms she knew of—a round belly and lots of kicking—came quite late.

Wildflower Bride

"Red, I insist we go see Belle. I want to visit with her and I'm not letting up until we do things my way. Especially now that I'm carrying your child." Cassie fluttered her eyelids a bit and rested one hand on her flat stomach. She'd win now. Red was just too sweet; he wouldn't be able to resist giving in.

"Nope. We can't. I've got too many chores."

Cassie's mouth fell open.

Red hung the last pot on the hook beside the kitchen sink then set his dish towel aside and used one finger to push up on her chin to close her mouth. "And that's final."

Michael grabbed at his finger.

"Pick me up, Papa!" Susannah put both her tiny feet on his big boot and started bouncing up and down.

Red swooped Susannah into his arms and lifted her to the ceiling.

We'll see about final. Cassie narrowed her eyes and considered which of her womanly wiles to use on her husband to get her way.

Before she could bring out her arsenal, Red tucked Susannah onto his hip. Then he plucked Michael out of her arms, bent over, and kissed her with a low smack on the lips. "How about next week? Give me that long to catch up on a few things, move the herd to better pastures, and clear the deadfalls out of the spreader dam. I'll get the Jessups to ride herd and we'll go and stay awhile so you can work with Belle and get all your female talkin' out."

Cassie grinned until she thought she might laugh out loud. "Next week would be fine, Red." She said it in her best submissive wife voice. The one Red loved.

"You're such a good, obedient little wife." He kissed her again as a reward. As if he didn't realize she'd gotten her way, as usual. "I love it when you pout, honey," Red whispered.

Startled, Cassie pulled back and glared at him.

He laughed and turned away, bouncing the children around the room, singing a silly, lilting Irish song about wearing green, while Cassie contemplated whether she was controlling her husband or he was controlling her.

Since it didn't matter, and she was going to see Belle regardless, she didn't contemplate it too long before she snatched Susannah away from him and joined in their play.

⤙⤚

Sid pushed the men hard to get back.

Boog had seemed to be completely well, but he was pale and tight-lipped by the time they got back to the derelict Griffin house. Harv was practically asleep in his saddle.

Sid and Paddy decided to split up so no one would connect them. Paddy would ride in first, then Sid. Boog and Harv would stay away for one more week.

As long as that girl was alive, she could recognize Harv. Maybe without the beard he could get by, but Sid wasn't going to risk it. And if Red Dawson had a reason to come to the ranch, it would all be over.

The trail from the Flathead valley back to the M Bar S was brutal. It should have taken two days to cover, but Sid didn't want the men to make note of his absence. Lots of the hands had taken off for the day, with Wade announcing Sundays would be for rest from now on.

As Sid hitched his horse at the old Griffin place in the early hours of Monday morning, he felt the whole weight of the long weekend. First pulling Harv out of jail, then riding for the high valley, and now coming home. And all for nothing. They had to leave the gold behind. He ached until it felt like someone had taken a club to him.

He gave Paddy fifteen minutes to get to the ranch well ahead of him. Sid would barely beat the sunrise home. He stood watching Boog and Harv unsaddle their horses as Paddy rode off toward his bunk.

"We've got to finish this." Sid got out the makings for a cigarette.

Boog lifted his saddle off his gelding's back. "Yep. Someone's gonna identify Harv sooner or later."

"We'll do it this week," Sid said as he dumped the tobacco and rolled the fine paper, counting down the time until he could head back.

"Let's hit 'em all at once." Harv rubbed his chin. Sid could see his hunger for revenge against the wild woman. "We tried to make it look like an accident before, but why bother trying that again? With that woman dead—the only one who saw me—no one will be able to prove we had a hand in the killing."

"A lot of the hands rode off to town yesterday morning." Sid remembered the exodus when he'd gone in to get Paddy. "They went to church with Wade. That leaves Mort home alone with only his housekeeper. He's vulnerable then. We can do it next Sunday."

"Then we'll waylay Wade and the woman on the trail. Finish it in one stroke." Harv pulled the bridle off his horse and swatted his rump. The horse trotted away with a thud of hooves on grass in the small corral Mort kept up at the Griffin place.

"But let's keep our eyes open this week," Boog said as he rubbed hands full of grass on his gelding's sweat-soaked side. "If we have a chance, catch one of them out alone, we'll take it, thin the herd a little."

Harv snorted. "Herd? A cripple, a woman, and a coward. No herd to thin there. I'd like to keep that woman alive for a while, though. If I caught her out alone—" A chuckle broke up his big talk.

Sid drew on his cigarette. Harv always talked big, when he wasn't whining. He was a weak link in every job they pulled. If he hadn't grabbed that girl to begin with, no one would be able to identify him now. Harv wouldn't have cuts as good as shouting his identity. Sid did his best not to glare at the fool. He mentally repeated that Harv held the secret to a hidden shipment of gold that had been lost in that valley.

Even with the gold in mind, Sid was afraid of what he'd say. Deciding he'd given Paddy enough time, Sid tossed his cigarette butt on the ground, climbed into the saddle and spurred his weary horse toward the ranch. No roundup to face this morning. Maybe he could steal a few hours of sleep.

He'd stolen a lot bigger things in his life and paid no price.

CHAPTER 29

It almost pained Abby to admit it, but Mort was trying.

It was almost killing him. Watching Mort try to be nice was funny. He quit most of his barking. Not all, but Abby didn't say anything about the times he snapped at her and Gertie. And he was doing really well with Wade.

They sat at the table enjoying a fairly civilized supper of fried chicken. It was delicious, but Abby missed the smoky taste of a wild bird cooked over an open fire. Turning the spit was one of the first jobs she'd been allowed when she lived with her Flathead family.

Mort sat eating as if he were starved. He'd regained some muscle in his arms from rolling his chair around, and he spent enough time outside these days that he had lost that sickly pallor.

Wade always discussed the ranch thoroughly with his pa, and Mort seemed hungry for details about the preparation for the cattle drive and how the hands were doing. Wade listened to Mort's opinions, too, and seemed to respect his father's ranching skills.

When the daily report was finished as well as the evening meal, Abby reached for Mort's plate to stack it with the others for washing, but his words stopped her.

"Have I been doing well enough to suit you, Wade?" Mort turned to his son.

Abby let her hand sink back to her lap, afraid Mort might be getting ready to snap. She'd seen the uncertain hold he had on his temper at times.

"It's been a good week, Pa. I hope I've been doing well enough to suit you, too."

"You're running things right. I can see that. Or hear it at least. I can't get out like I'd like to. I know, from this week of watching... well, I'd like to say...to say..." Mort gave Abby a leery look.

There'd been a couple of times when, if Abby had wanted to, she could have tossed the last kerosene on the fire and burned up this family. She knew Mort feared she'd mention that now. But she had no wish to break the family apart. If that happened, it wouldn't be because of her. She'd leave alone before she left with Wade and bad feelings.

"I can—well, it's been hard. Harder than I've ever imagined. And—what you said about my own pa awhile back, I can see now how my ma protected me from him. He was angry all the time, but Ma could handle him. I saw her take his anger on herself when he'd come home mad. She'd always shoo me away. I know he hit her. I think—" Mort fell silent. "I'm sorry. I can't promise I'll never lose my temper again. But I'm going to try." Mort refused to meet anyone's eyes as he quietly rolled himself out of the room.

Wade stared after him, a longing in his eyes that Abby's heart hurt to see.

"Go after him," she whispered.

Wade looked up, hopeful and scared. "Should I?"

She nodded, feeling like she might be sending Wade away from her by encouraging him to choose to draw closer to his father. "He may be ready to talk for the first time in your life. Don't miss it."

Wade turned and smiled at her. "You're right." He came around the table and kissed her, a hard, fast smack. "And I *am* going to marry you." He hurried after his father, following him into Mort's converted bedroom.

Abby and Gertie looked at each other in wonder. Then Gertie pressed a shushing finger to her lips, and they eavesdropped shamelessly while they cleaned the kitchen.

⬸⬹

Wade watched his father swing himself from his wheelchair into an overstuffed leather chair that he'd always used behind his desk. It was huge and comfortable. Wade had liked sneaking in here to sit in it when he was little. Until the time he'd been caught.

Pa knew how to teach a lesson.

"You're getting good at that, Pa."

Pa looked up, startled. Then he leaned back and stared down at his useless legs. "You really think I can live ten more years like this?"

Wade shrugged. "Or twenty. I don't see why not. You seem healthy enough to me."

The tight line of his jaw was so rigid Wade was afraid his pa's teeth might crack. "I've always prided myself on being tough."

"Pride's a sin, in case you need a list."

A humorless laugh escaped Pa's throat. "I probably do need a list. I think I've done everything exactly backward in my life. And nothing more backward than the way I treated you." Pa raised his eyes until they met Wade's.

"I think this is the first time in my life you've ever looked at me without anger or contempt." Wade shook his head, and it was only his faith in God that kept him in the room. He wanted to run outside and cry.

"I think those are words God would use to judge me at the Pearly Gates. An awful thing for a son to say such about his father, that he'd never known a moment of kindness. My duty to you is to protect and love you. I failed at the second, and at the first, well, you needed someone to protect you from me."

"I agree…God would judge you harshly for that." Wade wasn't inclined to pretend a lie. He prayed silently for wisdom.

Give me the words to speak, Lord. Give me love in my heart that he beat out of me years ago.

His stomach twisted as he realized just how fully he hated his pa. Yes, an awful thing for a son to feel for a father. God would judge Wade for that.

They faced each other in silence.

"I'm not going to throw out a bunch of words now that I spent my life destroying. I'm not going to cheapen a father's love by claiming it for you, because I don't think I know what it means."

Sick to his stomach that, even now, his father couldn't say, "I love you," Wade turned to leave. The room, the house, the ranch. Everything. He couldn't stay.

"I will tell you this, boy." Pa drew his attention and Wade watched the defiant old man square his shoulders. "You're a better man than I am."

Wade gasped. He couldn't have been more shocked if his pa had slugged him in the stomach. In fact, that wouldn't have been a shock at all. "You mean that?"

Pa nodded. "I've known it since before you left. Since you got ahold of your drinking and carousing and came back here to work. I could see then you'd finally grown up. And grown into something better than I could have ever created with my yelling and hitting. I was ashamed that Red Dawson had done something I could never do."

"It wasn't Red, Pa. It was God."

Nodding silently, his father took a long time to respond. "I know that, too. But it's easier to see what's there in front of my eyes and not try to figure out some distant God that I've never seen the need for."

"Everyone needs God."

"Not me. I never did."

"You needed Him more than anyone I've ever known."

"How can you say that?" Pa shifted in his chair, his eyes furtive, not meeting Wade's now.

"Because you're so strong."

Pa jerked his chin up. "In the kitchen you called me a coward. That's a weakling. And you were right. Only a coward hits someone littler. A child." Pa rubbed his face as if he wanted to scrub away twenty years of bad memories. Or maybe, if Grandpa Sawyer was as mean as Pa, the bad memories went back much further.

No way Wade could think to deny that. "A strong man—measured by Western standards—can carve a good life out of a hard land, and you've done that. No one on earth would call you anything but strong." Struggling for the right words, Wade continued. "But that kind of strength needs to be tempered. A man that strong needs to—to put limits on himself. Or accept the limits God puts on a man."

"Like the Ten Commandments."

"Except Jesus gave us new commandments, did you know that?"

His brow furrowed. "I've never heard they threw out the ten."

"Jesus gave us two. Love God; love your neighbor. That's it. He said that if you followed those two, you'd be keeping all the rest."

"Instead I've broken them and all the rest."

"You've as good as stolen land from Tom Linscott. I told him we wouldn't run cattle on his spring anymore."

"You what?" Pa's eyes flashed, and he lurched forward. Then he caught himself. "Yes, of course we can't do that. I always knew where my land borders were. But I'd used those springs before Linscott came in and bought them."

"And you've coveted those springs, and the Griffins' water, and—"

Waving one massive hand, Pa cut in. "I've coveted everything.

Things I didn't know I wanted until someone else had them. My neighbor's land and water and wife."

That one almost flashed Wade's temper back to life as he remembered the things his pa had said about Cassie. The way Pa had tried to force a marriage against Cassie's will.

"And none of it had a thing to do with loving God or your neighbor," Wade snapped. "You didn't accept that there was any limit on right and wrong. And there was no one around strong enough to back you down. So you became a tyrant."

"Red Dawson backed me down, didn't he?" Pa looked up sheepishly, as if he was ashamed of that fact.

"Good thing he did, Pa. Good thing Tom Linscott came in and stood up for himself. You were beyond the laws of God and man before those two stepped in. I hate to think what would have happened if you'd have gotten your way and brought Cassie here. It makes me sick to think of it. That's why a strong man needs some power over him—God—or terrible things happen."

Pa looked reduced by more than the wheelchair and his weight loss. His spirit looked crushed. "Things are going to change, son."

"Like I said earlier, I'll decide if I stay or go. No assurances from you will make a bit of difference if you start in on me or Abby again."

"That's as it should be. You *are* a better man than me." Pa reached for his wheelchair and rolled it a bit, back and forth, staring at it as if there were answers in those moving wheels.

Maybe they were the answer. "Maybe God struck you down to get your attention."

"I don't think much less would have worked." Pa looked up from his chair, and Wade saw longing in his father's eyes. Longing for something better between the two of them.

"How about this, Pa? How about I fetch my Bible in here for you? For the first time in your life, you've got time stretching out empty in front of you. Days and days of idleness. Spend them reading the Bible. Hunt for the Ten Commandments and the two.

See if you can find Someone stronger than yourself. Someone you can respect enough to give Him charge of your life. You'll be a better man for it."

Pa nodded. "I want you to stay, son. I want to try and fix things between us. I promise you I'm going to try."

"It's more than I ever expected to hear from you." Yet it wasn't enough. Even though it seemed hopeless, he wished Pa could find a way to love him. "I'll be right back."

Wade ran upstairs and was back in Pa's bedroom in minutes. He handed over the heavy book. Wade had bought it new from Bates's General Store in Divide. Muriel had helped him pick it out. He'd nearly worn it out in the last couple of years.

Pa accepted the book, and then an almost-smile quirked his lips. "So you really gonna try and get that little wild woman to marry you?"

Wade did smile. He couldn't stop himself. "Oh yes."

"So have you asked her yet?" His pa caressed the Bible while he spoke in a friendly way to Wade.

It was already more of a miracle than Wade had ever dreamed of. He should have started yelling at his father years ago. "I mention something along those lines just about every day."

"And what does she say?" Pa ran his hand over the leather.

"As a matter of fact, she usually pulls her knife on me. She's done it so often I've kinda quit keeping track."

Pa chuckled. Then that wasn't enough and he laughed out loud. "I liked that girl from the moment she walked in this house and started threatening me."

"We're going to hit the place next Sunday," Sid whispered to Paddy. "We'll let Wade and the girl, plus all the hands, ride off to church. Then we'll just go in the house and finish Mort."

Paddy snickered as he nodded. "Then waylay the rest of 'em on the trail home."

Nodding, Sid stared at Wade, riding the herd, cutting out the older steers to drive to market.

"We'll be pushing cattle to Helena after next Sunday, so if we don't get it done, we'll have to make that long drive."

Paddy narrowed his eyes. "If you're taking over the ranch, you'll need to make the drive anyway, boss."

"No, I won't. I'll order the hands to go. I'll stay here and they can bring me the money."

"You'll trust this crowd to bring the money home?" Paddy stared at the half-trained cowhands Sid had so carefully hired for their incompetence and lackadaisical attitudes, so when the moment came for him to seize the ranch, he wouldn't have much resistance.

Sid snarled. He didn't, now that Paddy mentioned it, but it burned to have Paddy point out something so obvious. "Okay, then I'll go along."

"Better to let Wade take the drive. The girl will be left home with Mort. Maybe we go on the drive, finish Wade off on the way home. Lots of places for accidents to happen on a cattle drive. Leave Boog and Harv to handle Mort and the girl."

Sid rode his horse, pushing a docile, fat-bellied bunch of longhorns along toward new pasture, and considered the plan. No plan was perfect; some risk was involved in all of them. But dry-gulching Wade on the trail was no sure thing. There wasn't a good spot to shoot from cover. And walking straight into the house to murder Mort was as cold-blooded as Sid had ever been. They'd have to kill Gertie, too, because she'd be a witness, and it bothered Sid to kill the old woman. Her cookies reminded him of his ma's cooking. It made him sick to think of someone killing his ma just because she was standing beside a man who needed killing.

Maybe the drive was best, leaving the women and cripple to Boog and Harv. "We'll wait." Sid looked around to make sure no one had ridden up on his flank. "Unless I find a likely chance. We don't have to kill 'em all at once, you know. We could space it out.

Wildflower Bride

But I want this done. We've been too careful. It's time now to act."

"It's past time." Paddy had to wipe his chin.

Sid could see he was so hungry to hurt someone he was drooling. Just the kind of man Sid needed at his side.

CHAPTER 30

Abby tied the apron on around her clothes. It was a good idea to wear it. How many times had she gotten her soft leather dress stained while she worked over a cooking pot? It was a fact, though, that gingham made her skin itch. She missed her doeskin, the easy movement, the split skirt that made riding so easy. Foolish whites and their fussy dresses.

Even so, she was beginning to adjust to the ways of the white man. With disgust, Abby realized she was getting soft. Remembering Wade's confident announcement that he was going to marry her, she'd gone to ridiculous lengths to avoid being alone with him all week. She needed to figure out what was the matter with her that she could hate his kind and his skin color and his ways. . .but still like the man.

Wade wasn't like the rest of the whites. Abby knew that clearly enough. She forgave herself for her fascination because of that. She might have even considered marrying him if they could get away from the ranch and live somewhere in the mountains, away from her Indian family and his white world. He was an especially kind man—look at the way he grinned when she threatened him with her knife. Although, truth be told, she was almost certain she could never really stab him.

When had she become such a weakling?

"Time to punch down the rising of bread, Abby. Do you want to do it and shape the loaves?" Gertie smiled, and Abby felt another pang of guilt. She'd come to care about this elderly woman, too. When they worked on the house or the meals or the garden, Abby felt almost like a daughter being taught by her mother. It helped shake loose memories of her own white family, and with the memories came love. Yes, she'd loved her family. They were good people, and they'd tried to take care of her until the sickness had made that impossible. Not all whites were evil. She knew that.

The smell of the yeast and flour made her mouth water. Another thing Abby had begun to like—the easy food. Yes, there was hard work to making a meal, but the choices were plentiful and the garden was yielding a rich bounty of vegetables. The beef supply never ended, and there were chickens and eggs, ham and bacon, milk and coffee laced with thick cream. And sweets. Gertie was a hand with the sweets.

Punching the soft, puffed-up mound of dough with more force than necessary, Abby admitted the disgusting, unthinkable truth. She was starting to like this place.

Mort rolled himself into the kitchen, and Abby almost cheered up. Finally someone she really couldn't stand.

Mort was trying, Abby could see that. But he was failing—a lot. More this week than last. The man had a short temper, and he liked things done his way and right now.

So far, Abby had followed Gertie's example and kept the hard words Mort said to them from Wade, not wanting to cause the final break between Wade and his pa. Especially since Mort *was* trying. He only yelled his orders part of the time these days.

"Get me a cup of coffee and some of those gingersnaps, Gertie." Mort wheeled around the table to his place at the head.

Abby was working near that end with the dough, but there was plenty of room for the old tyrant.

"Why didn't one of you women bring them into my room?" Mort swept his hand across some flour that scattered too close to him.

Abby started kneading harder, pretending the dough was Mort's yammering face.

"You used to care that I was stuck back in there alone, Gertie."

Abby felt her temper rising. But was it really Mort, or was she panicked because she felt herself weakening to the white world?

"But now you'd let me starve to death if I didn't come and fetch every bite I eat."

Bam! Abby slugged the dough with her fists, her jaw clenched shut.

Mort jumped a little, and his eyes narrowed. "You act like a savage. You need to learn some woman skills if you're going to stay around here."

"And you're like a whining dog that used to sneak around the edges of our camp." She punched the dough again. "Worthless, begging for food but never doing the few little things a dog can do to help."

"You got something you think I should do, say it. You think I like sitting in my room all day reading Wade's book?"

Abby felt a pang of remorse over her temper. She knew Wade wanted his father to come to his own faith in God. After his outburst the other night, Wade had gone back to being patient with his father. But his father had behaved himself with Wade.

The man really didn't want his son to leave. And wasn't that a good thing? Wasn't that loving? Wade finally had a father who loved him after all these years. Abby didn't want to ruin that, and she knew she could with a word. She'd tell of Mort's behavior and announce she was leaving, and Wade would come with her. He'd follow her into the rugged mountains to her valley.

She longed to go there and live. With her Indian family gone, she'd be able to have the place to herself. All alone. Forever. No, she couldn't bear that much loneliness. She knew herself well enough to admit that. But with Wade, maybe they could make a life up there in the thin air among the mountain peaks.

"I do know something you could do, old man." Abby jammed her fingers deep into the dough.

Mort's eyes widened as she swung her hands toward him. He snatched his coffee cup out of the way just in time.

She slammed the dough onto the table in front of Mort. "This takes no brain nor skill nor legs. Knead this dough for two more minutes. Then shape it into loaves."

Mort shoved his chair back two feet from the table. "Woman's work." He might as well have spit when he said it. "You think I have no pride left?"

"Now, Abby. . ." Gertie had endless patience with this old curmudgeon. Abby knew confrontations distressed the older woman. If she hadn't known she had to leave sometime, she might have kept quiet.

Abby put both fists on the table and leaned down to Mort's face, his teeth nearly bared. She kept her jaw clenched so she wouldn't shout the next words. "If you want to be useful"—no, she wasn't shouting, more like hissing, which still wasn't good—"there are things you could do. You might not think they are worthy of your great manliness, but they would help. And there are more *manly* things we need done. There is a chair we set aside in the pantry because the leg is loose. You could repair that. Surely that is a manly pastime."

Mort's face was turning red. His breathing was loud. Abby had a sense that he, too, was struggling to control himself. He hadn't forgotten Wade's threat. And yes, he'd lashed out a dozen times this week. But Gertie had jumped to do his bidding and he'd calmed down. There'd been no drawn-out string of insults and shouts. Too bad he'd been closer to Abby this time. "I'll do any work you have for me. Don't pretend like you've asked." Mort's voice started climbing.

"Now, Mort. . ." Gertie stepped to the foot of the table, wringing her hands.

Abby knew she should stop for Gertie's sake. For Wade's sake. But the satisfaction grew. She'd been spoiling for this fight. For the first time she really knew what she wanted—to leave and take Wade with her. This would be a real chance for happiness. The only one she could see.

"Don't pretend like I've refused to help you." Mort pounded the side of his fist on the table and hit the dough, plunging his hand into the soft, sticky mound.

"Don't pretend like you've tried, old man." Abby reached for the dough and jerked it away from him.

"Please, let's not fight." Gertie took the dough from Abby, clearly hoping they'd just let her do the work.

"Always you leave women's work for us and men's work for Wade while you roll around this house like a. . .like a. . .worthless object, a child's toy on a string, making everyone's life harder."

"I want this fight to stop now. You're both being unreasonable." Gertie for the first time sounded stern.

His temper blew. "A child's toy?" Mort grabbed the wheels of his chair.

Satisfied, she gloated that she'd ignited that temper. Now he'd say words he couldn't take back. And she'd tell Wade and they'd leave.

"I want peace!" Gertie shouted and clutched her hands together as if begging.

Until now Abby had been calculating in her pokes and jabs at Mort's ego. But when Gertie said "peace," and Abby knew she meant peace no matter the cost, Abby went over the edge of her temper, right after Mort.

Suddenly she saw Gertie and Mort in a way she'd never seen them before. Peace at any cost. "That's right. That's what we've all been doing, having peace at the cost of our self-respect. Taking Mort's abuse to try and maintain some kind of peace in this house."

Abby turned on Gertie. "Is that what you did when Wade was

growing up? You let Mort hit him, then rushed in and bandaged his wounds when it was over, all for peace?"

"You leave Gertie out of this, you little wildcat."

"Well, if a man hit a child I loved, any child"—Abby glared at Gertie, sorry that her temper had turned on the older woman, but not sorry she spoke the truth—"he'd have himself a *war*."

Abby knew then that she wasn't going to find a place in this house and she wasn't going to go tattling like a child to Wade, either. She'd find her beloved mountain valley. She'd find her home alone in the wild. With no man, no people, white or Indian, no peace but the peace she found in God. She ripped the apron off her body and flung it aside.

Mort and Gertie seemed frozen by her hateful words.

She stormed out of the room and was changed into her deerskin dress and moccasins and out of the house before either one of them had moved from the kitchen. The two of them were stuck in a twisted relationship of anger and placating, wounding and bandaging. For all she knew, Wade didn't have the will to leave it all behind either.

If he couldn't break free of this sickness, it was best that she found out now before she was foolish enough to fall in love with him.

She took no horse. She had only her knife and knew she could live very nicely with nothing else forever.

"We've got the herd rounded up and ready for the drive, Pa." Wade pulled his Stetson off his head and wiped his brow.

The days were long and hot now. Spring had come so late up in the mountains where Wade had wintered that he was having trouble adjusting to the full summer heat. Add to that, he'd only a few days ago finished roundup, and it didn't seem right at all.

Gertie set a glass of cool water on the table as Wade hung his hat on the elk antlers on the wall beside the kitchen door. Wade noticed her setting a plate of cookies on the table, too. She always had some on hand for him. Wade had to admit this was a more comfortable life than the one he'd lived in his mountain cabin during the bitter winter.

"Where's Abby?" She'd been avoiding him ever since Sunday. Wade had to bite back a smile. A spirited little thing, his Abby, but she'd come around.

Gertie and Pa exchanged a look, and for the first time since he'd come in, he really looked at them. Two very worried people.

Wade's head swiveled to nail his pa to the wall with his eyes. "What did you do?"

Pa got a stubborn look on his face. "I've been trying to do better; you know that, son. But that woman is just plain contrary."

"Tell me right now." His pa got a sullen look that Wade knew only too well—stubborn, mean old man. But Gertie wasn't so tough. He turned to her. "Well?"

Gertie's hands were clenched together, her eyes wide with fear. She'd always been the peacemaker in this house; Wade wondered how she could have stood it all these years. "She left, Wade."

"Left? Left for where? When?"

"We don't know. She was okay and then Mort came in. He didn't say that much, nothing that should have set her off like that, but she took exception to it."

He felt empty inside. Lost. She'd left him. Or had she ever really been with him?

"Let her cool off for a time, son. If she wants you, she'll come back. If she doesn't want to stay in the white world, you can't make her."

Turning to study his father, Wade prayed silently, wondering what exactly had happened. Pa could still bark well enough. But he'd been so much better. He'd been reading the Bible daily. Why hadn't Abby been patient and given his father more time to grow in the Lord?

Sinking into his chair, Wade stared forward, seeing his future stretched out in front of him without her. He slapped the table and stood. "No, I can't make her stay. But I can go with her."

"Wade, you can't leave us." Gertie grabbed his arm. "We need you here."

Stopping at that familiar weight on his arm, Wade looked down at the only person who'd ever loved him all the while he was growing up. The woman who had come to him after his father's rampages and bandaged his wounds, held him, prayed with him. She did need him. He saw that now. Looking back, he saw that, in her mothering, Gertie had needed Wade as much as Wade had needed her. They were both Pa's prisoners.

If he left with Abby, he'd be abandoning the only mother he could remember. And would his father fall away from his first steps toward faith? Could Wade's actions now be directed by the devil himself to knock Pa off his path back to God? Why had Abby left? She knew he loved her. She had nowhere else in the world to belong. Wade shoved his hands deep into his hair as his thoughts chased themselves in circles.

The answer came to him quietly.

Prayer.

That was the only answer.

"I need time in prayer." Wade grabbed his hat and went outside, knowing there'd be no peace to pray in that house. There'd never been any peace.

He'd been in prayer three minutes before he knew where she'd go.

"What do you mean she's gone?" Tom Linscott grabbed Wade by the shirt collar and lifted him onto his toes.

"Get your hands off me." Wade knocked Tom's hands aside. He'd come charging into this little wreck of a cabin lined with bunks. Tom and all his hands lived in this hovel. Now Wade stood in the doorway shouting. "I don't have time for this. Abby left. She had a fight with Pa—"

"I'm going to find your father and shoot him dead." Tom rammed his fist into his palm with a loud *smack*. "He's a complete waste of human skin. I should have—"

"Will you shut up? Fighting with my pa won't help me find Abby. I was sure she'd come here. Where else could she be?" Wade turned and strode away from the cabin.

"To town?" Tom followed on his heels.

"There's no one in town she knows at all." The sun was setting. Wherever Abby had gone, she'd spent at least one night alone in the wilderness. Wade was half crazy thinking of the danger.

"Muriel would take her in. Or Libby."

"She might have seen Libby, said hello. And she met Muriel at church, but she doesn't know them at all, and she hates whites. She'd never go to them. She'd see it as begging." Wade stopped beside his horse, ready to mount up and ride, but to where?

"How about the Dawsons'? She sat at the table with us the day of the jailbreak. Red and Cassie were both there. And you said the two of you stopped by the Hardens' on your way home, with Cassie and Red there. She knows them."

Shaking his head, Wade tried to think. His mind spun around. "It doesn't sound right. But I don't know where else to try."

"Let's go check the Dawson place first." Tom whirled and charged toward his corral. His black stallion stood there, proud, watchful.

Wade called after Tom. "I'm not going with you. No sense both of us trying the same place."

Tom stopped and turned back. "Where else then, the Hardens'?"

Wade couldn't answer that. "I'll head that way. Then I'll see where I'm led."

"Where you're led? What does that mean?"

"It means I'm praying as hard as I can for inspiration. But if she did what I'm afraid she did—"

"What's that?" Tom's eyes sharpened, reacting to Wade's obvious dread.

"Headed out to live in the mountains alone."

Clenching his fists, Tom said, "No, no one's that stupid. A woman can't live out there alone."

"Abby could. On her own she'd be fine. Your sister is the bravest, toughest woman I've ever known. She could live off that land, even in those rugged mountains. It's just that—"

"Just that what?"

"Lonely as it is up there, there are still men who might hurt her." Wade thought of the rustlers who had escaped. He thought of the men who had massacred her village. "If someone finds her before we do and gets that knife away from her, she'll be at his mercy. With all that wild country to cover, the two of us will never find her."

"There'll be more than two of us. My men and I will split up and go south and west of town, toward the Dawsons'. You go north." Tom whirled toward his horse, yelling for his men as he ran.

"Did you hear that the wild woman ran off?" Paddy sidled up to Sid at the breakfast table. Paddy heard a lot more living in the bunkhouse than Sid heard in the foreman's cabin.

"No. She's out alone?" Sid knew this might be his only chance to catch that woman. He'd been watching her all week and she never strayed farther than the garden. He'd planned to waylay them on Sunday morning, but he hadn't liked the plan any too well.

"Yep, and Wade took out after her. Mort told Chester when he went in to give the week's accounting last night."

"So they're together?"

"Nope, don't sound like it. She went without him and he went hunting her."

All their targets were separated, alone. Even Mort in the house with only Gertie was defenseless. Sid wanted to charge into that house and put a bullet in that stubborn old man. But he couldn't do that now. Too many cowhands around. The West was still untamed, but even out here there was a limit to cold-blooded murder. Killing Mort Sawyer in front of twenty witnesses was well beyond the limit. He'd have to pick a better time. For now, he had his chance at Wade and the wildflower.

"Saddle up. I'm telling Chester we're riding supplies out to the line shack."

"Are we really going there? Boog's the best tracker among us."

Nodding, Sid said, "I think that little woman wants her wild life back. And if she ever gets to that high valley and sees her Flathead tribe is there, she might just move right in with them."

"Well, then let her go. If she goes off with the Indians, our problem is solved."

"Not as long as she's out there, able to recognize Harv's face. And Wade's sweet on her. He'll be going to try and bring her back. No, we can't have her running around. This is our chance to finish Wade, too. Then we'll come back and pick our moment with Mort. If we find the wild woman first and use her to set a trap for Wade, then kill Mort, we can take over this ranch in a couple of days."

Paddy's eyes narrowed. Hunger and greed glowed like lantern light out of his beady eyes. "Let's go." He whirled to saddle up their horses while Sid told Chester his "plans" to go to the line shack.

Chester didn't like it, but Sid wasn't interested in what Chester wanted. Firing Chester was the first thing Sid planned to do when he took over.

CHAPTER 31

Abby felt as if she shed her white skin as she strode along in the early dawn.

She had days to walk to return to her high valley, but she'd learned to walk tirelessly with her nomadic tribe. And time mattered nothing to her.

No one waited. She simply needed to care for herself, only herself. The very thought was like a huge weight lifting off her shoulders. She could breathe again.

The summer day promised heat, but the early morning air had a bite to it. She loved the breeze that cooled her muscles, and she rushed along, her long legs swinging under her doeskin dress. The pretty beads she'd sewn around the neck reminded her of the quiet time spent with her tribal family, learning at her mother's side.

She was at peace.

Except for Wade.

She missed him.

At the same time, she was glad to be rid of him. She never should have allowed him to lure her with his confusing kindness and tempting kisses.

She remembered the path they'd taken from her high valley.

Her dead reckoning told her she might cut the distance by striking out straight north. But the mountains she had to pass in that direction were daunting. Better to veer west a bit and take the trail past the Griffin place, through the gap into the Harden ranch and out the other end of that. If she was careful—and Abby knew how to be very careful—no one would see her as she quietly walked home.

If she set a fast pace, the Griffin house would be an easy point to reach by dark. Abby glanced to the west and knew a storm was possible. The sky was gray and overcast, but no rain was falling so far. Rain didn't scare her. She could move along soaking wet as well as dry. She admitted to herself that if the house was empty and the night was stormy, she might set aside her contempt for the foolish house and wait out the storm.

Increasing her speed to a ground-eating lope, she smiled as her muscles stretched and became fluid. She felt at one with nature like any other wild thing running free.

As the hours passed, the overcast sky grew heavier. Abby could see rain streaking to the ground in the distance. She could run tirelessly for hours, and she picked up her pace from the comfortable lope, knowing she'd never get to the Griffin place in time but feeling pushed to hurry anyway.

At last, as the wind grew cool and the midafternoon turned dark as dusk, Abby saw the white of the house through the stand of trees. She heard the first sprinkles of rain on the trees overhead, and she made a dash for shelter. She raced under the drooping porch roof with a laugh of triumph and fell against the front door, gasping for air, turning to watch the rain. She'd beaten it. A rare victory against nature.

Suddenly the door behind her opened and she fell backward. Hard hands grabbed her around the waist, and she looked up into the evil eyes of the man who had destroyed her village. His face was nearly healed, but the cut she'd given him had formed an ugly scar and she was glad. She'd enjoy adding to his marks.

Wildflower Bride

She reached for her knife, but a viselike grip on her wrist stopped her. She lashed out with her feet, but a blow to the back of her head stunned her. The world wavered. She shook her head to clear it and only faintly felt the shock of another blow.

The man let go of her, and she sank to the floor. She was fumbling for her knife, but her fingers were stupid and clumsy. Her vision seemed to narrow as if she were looking through a tunnel. The man loomed over her, scarred and victorious, holding his gun so the butt end was handy to use as a club.

As the light faded from her eyes, he smiled at her in evil pleasure to have her in his power.

Wade threw his covers off an hour before dawn.

He'd had to give up the search when darkness fell. He'd hunted the trail to Divide and asked about Abby there then ridden back to the ranch and tried to pick up a trail. Not wanting to sleep in Pa's house, he'd headed in the waning light for the Griffin place and made a cold camp in the woods, knowing he had to stop. He could ride right past her in the dark. Precious little sleep came his way for worrying and praying.

He circled, trying to pick up a trail, but none was there. Abby was too light on her feet, too woods savvy to leave a single footprint.

Chafing at the delay, he slept a short night then set out for the place that kept coming into his head. The place she thought of as home. That high mountain valley. It was so far away that if he was wrong, Wade would be wasting days in the search.

Lord, let me find her.

Darkness was catching him as he drew near the Griffin place, planning to spend the night there. A storm seemed bent on crashing down on his head when he heard someone coming along the trail. He pulled his horse to a stop and eased off the path to watch.

Red and Cassie rode into sight, and Wade came forward. Red caught sight of him and instantly put his horse between Cassie and trouble to shield her, reaching for his pistol.

Red's lightning-fast reflexes reminded Wade that his friend, for all his gentle heart and good nature, was as tough as any rancher around, and that included Pa. This was the kind of strength Wade wanted. Strength used to protect and defend rather than tyrannize and terrorize.

Red visibly relaxed as soon as he recognized Wade in the fading light. "What are you doing out here?"

Cassie leaned around her husband and smiled. "Hi, Wade."

Susannah was riding in front of Cassie, and the little girl waved and bounced as if she wanted to kick the horse into a gallop. The wind was rising and the setting sun was blanketed by gray clouds.

Letting go of his screaming tension for just a second, Wade allowed himself to smile at the Dawson family.

Michael, carried on Red's back like a papoose, whacked at his father's hat, and Red grabbed it before it fell. He did it so naturally Wade knew the child had tried that stunt many times before.

Then Wade's moment of relaxation was over. He pulled up beside Red. "Abby's run off. She had a fight with Pa last night and she stormed out. No one's seen her since."

"She was out overnight?" Cassie's fair skin seemed to pale in the sunset.

Nodding, Wade said, "Linscott's whole crew is out hunting for her. I'm riding back to the valley where we found her, hoping she went there. She's threatened to take off and live by herself in the mountains. She could go anywhere. So I'm trying to pick up a trail, but there's nothing."

Red frowned. "We're on our way to visit the Tanners."

"Hardens," Cassie whispered.

"This late?" Wade looked around. "You've got hours of riding yet."

"We got a late start. Trouble with the cattle, then a couple of other little things."

"I let Harriet out." Cassie grimaced.

Red smiled at her. "It was an accident. It could have happened to anyone."

"Big mean piggy." Susannah's eyes were wide as the full moon.

Wade could hardly stand to imagine it. That old mama sow was a killer. "You plan on trying to get through that pass tonight with the little ones? The gap into their ranch is pretty steep. You might have trouble with it in the dark."

"We almost waited until tomorrow to leave, but we finally decided we'd make it. Now, with the storm brewing, we've decided to ride as far as Cassie's old house tonight and bunk there."

Nodding, Wade said, "Mind if I ride along and stay? There's no trail to be found this late anyway."

"Glad for the company." Red smiled. "It's your house anyway."

"You're welcome to the shelter anytime you need it. You know that."

"Thanks. I appreciate it. And we can pray together for Abby."

"We'd better move or we're going to get wet." The panic Wade had been riding with all day eased a little now that he wasn't alone. Maybe he'd go as far as the Hardens and take Red and Silas along with him to search for Abby. Their help might make all the difference.

"You wanted her—now you've got her."

Sid glared at Harv. Then his eyes wandered to the still female form in the corner. She lay with her back against the wall. Her hair had mostly fallen out of its braid and now covered her face in long white curls. She had her wild woman dress on, the deerskin she'd been wearing when they'd taken her after the massacre. It even had stains on it from Harv's blood.

Sid itched for that woman. Seeing her lying there unconscious gave him a feeling of such fierce power that it was all he could do not to pull his six-gun on his gang, drive them out of the house, and have her to himself.

None of them looked eager to give her up.

Cool-eyed Boog wasn't a man Sid could read. So maybe he didn't care, but that woman was a feisty little thing. They'd watched her attack Harv after the massacre. Subduing her, dominating her, appealed to Sid, and he couldn't believe it didn't appeal to every man.

"We don't have time to fool with the woman." Nothing about Boog's voice gave anything away.

"I wouldn't have grabbed her if she hadn't come right to the door," Harv said. "I didn't have time to get out. I knew if I didn't get her under control, she'd run for help and bring a posse down on our heads."

"She wouldn't have run for help." Sid wanted to backhand Harv. "She'd have carved another notch in your face. You hit her because you were scared, not because you were afraid of the law."

The lump on the back of the wild woman's head told Sid that Harv hadn't fought fair. Not even with a woman. He'd come up behind her, knocked her cold, and tied her up while she was unconscious. Harv had a wide coward streak.

Sid had been around enough cowards that he knew to watch his back. The four of them sat cross-legged in the first room of the big house. They needed to get rid of the woman somehow and then turn to hunting Wade, but no one stepped forward and volunteered to pull the trigger, mainly because she was too beautiful a woman to want dead. "Boog, I want you and Paddy to ride toward the south."

"Now?" Paddy looked out the window. There was little light left, and the storm kept threatening, though it hadn't dropped any rain yet.

"Yes, now. This is our chance. Wade headed that way and we need to finish him."

"Who's gonna take care of that wildcat?" Boog jerked his head in their captive's direction.

"I owe her. I oughta do it." Harv looked at her and wiped his mouth.

Sid nodded. It suited him to let someone else do it. Not that he was squeamish, but he'd never killed a woman before. No sense starting now if Harv would do it. "If you can catch up to Wade and kill him, and Harv finishes the girl, we only have Mort left. We'll meet up in the morning and have that ranch in our hands by tomorrow night." Thinking about the land grab gave Sid more pleasure than thinking about the woman.

"Bury her deep, whatever you do." Boog stared at the woman's still form. "Women are mighty scarce out here. Some folks get mighty riled when someone mistreats one of 'em."

"I'll bury her deep." Harv's eyes shifted between Sid and the woman. He looked like a rat, making filthy plans.

Boog stood. "Let's get it done, Paddy." Something about the tone of his voice told Sid that Boog wanted no part of killing this girl. But as usual, Sid couldn't be sure.

Grumbling and looking at the woman with no attempt to disguise his unhappiness with the assignment, Paddy stood and left the room with Boog.

Sid relaxed when he heard the hooves of their horses pounding away down the trail.

"You know I don't want her dead, Sid." Harv stood.

Sid got to his feet, not wanting Harv towering over him. "You want her dead in the end, don't you?"

"Yeah." Harv rubbed his finger over the scar on his chin and stared at the unconscious girl. His eyes flashed as he touched his wound. "But I want her to beg to die."

Sickened, Sid was tempted almost beyond control to put a bullet in his saddle partner. But if he did, the woman would still need killing. If instead Sid turned his back, walked out into the night, Harv would do his worst and Sid wouldn't have to get his hands dirty. Harv's knowledge of where that gold was tipped the balance, even if getting to the treasure seemed impossible.

"I'm gonna go looking for a deep hole to dump her body in." Sid turned and strode from the room, forcing himself to hurry before he did the foolish things that were rattling around in his head. He almost ran off the porch, pushing himself to make a clean break from his hunger to hurt Harv, hurt the woman, hurt the whole world. It was like a thirst for whiskey and it rode Sid harder all the time.

Leave the woman for Harv.

As Sid walked away from the Griffin place, he rounded the side of the house and looked back. He could see into the room. The last traces of the setting sun found their way between two trees and the billowing clouds and sent a single shaft of light into that room. Sid saw Harv staring at the woman, and Sid stopped. His heart seemed to beat at half the speed and twice the strength as Harv slowly advanced on the woman. Swallowing hard, Sid watched Harv bend down, out of sight, but Sid could picture Harv's filthy hands reaching toward all those miles of golden hair.

With a grunt of self-contempt, Sid turned away toward the corral to saddle his horse and ride away. Give Harv some time then come back and everything would be taken care of. The wild woman who could identify Harv and bury them all would finally be dead.

CHAPTER 32

Abby'd be fine. Wade hated that she was out here alone. But she was tough. She'd take good care of herself.

Her only real trouble would be loneliness.

Same for him.

Wade thought of that long, bitter cold winter in his shack. The cold was relentless and brutal, but compared to the loneliness, it was nothing. Wade had needed that time. Maybe Abby needed some, too, but it was a hard way to live, and Wade wasn't going to even consider leaving Abby alone. She needed him whether she knew it or not.

Having Red and Cassie along cheered Wade up. With his friends along, nothing could go wrong. They'd hunt for Abby however long it took, and in the meantime, she'd protect herself, probably better than Wade could.

The trail to the Griffin place wound through woods and mountains. It was too narrow to ride abreast, so they strung out single file with Red leading, Cassie going next, and Wade bringing up the rear.

The rain was holding off, but the night was wild with wind and scudding clouds playing peekaboo with the moon and lightning and thunder in the distance.

Wade had taken Susannah in his lap, and the little one had chattered away for a long time before she'd passed out in his arms. She went from fully awake to limp between two sentences. It would have scared him if he hadn't seen her do it so many times before.

"She's sleeping," Wade whispered.

The wind was at his back and carried his voice over the thrashing limbs overhead and the soft *clop* of horses' hooves to Cassie. She looked back and smiled. Her teeth gleamed in the twilight.

They kept their horses at a fast walk. In the darkness, pushing their mounts would have been dangerous.

Wade saw a glimpse of the moon overhead as the clouds rushed across the sky. A jolt of lightning lit up the east. The thunder sounded next, but not for a long time. The storm might be going to the south. Wade could only hope.

Red's fist went up in the air, and even in the dark, Wade knew there was trouble. He goaded his gelding forward, coming alongside Cassie on the slender ghost of a trail. He caught her reins just as Red glanced back. Red jerked his chin, giving Wade his approval, and Wade pulled Cassie's horse toward a barely existent break in the surrounding woods.

"Wade, what—"

"Shh." The single sound brought Cassie's question to a halt.

The woman was too obedient for her own good, but right now Wade was thankful for it.

Red's horse disappeared off to the left of the trail. Wade went right, wishing fiercely Red didn't have Michael strapped on his back. But there wasn't time to snatch the little boy. It was just as well. Red and Cassie would protect their children, leaving Wade free to handle whatever trouble was coming.

The only problem was Wade wasn't half as good at handling trouble as Red.

When he had Cassie well hidden behind a nearly impenetrable line of ancient oaks, Wade helped her down from her horse and urged her behind the massive trunk. He leaned inches from her ear. "Take Susannah and stay here."

Cassie was sweet and pretty. She was a city girl born and bred. But she'd lived in the West for a few hard years, and Wade saw every one of those years in her knowing eyes as she took her little girl.

"Red's got Michael, so I need to handle this. You make sure you and Susannah are safe."

Cassie caught Wade's sleeve. "Be careful."

With a quick nod, Wade left his horse with Cassie and inched forward until he saw the trail through the brush and low-hanging limbs. He wondered where Red was, knowing his friend wouldn't hide from trouble. But the man had a baby with him, and protecting that child had to come first. Wade prayed Red thought of his son first and stayed out of the action. Wade was the one without a child. He was the one who should take the risks. Even if he was killed protecting his friends, he'd leave no one behind to mourn. Not even Abby, apparently.

On that sad thought, he drew his gun with a soft *whoosh* of iron against leather, a sound he could barely hear in the rising wind. He waited, prepared to give his life for his friends. The trees danced and swayed, reaching out for him like skeletal fingers clawing at his neck. A night for danger and nightmares. A night for fear.

"Whom shall I fear?"

He wasn't afraid of any harm to him. Instead, he feared for Abby in danger. And that his friends might come to harm. His own life he would gladly, fearlessly lay down to protect them all.

As he prayed in the howling wind, Wade heard the soft whinny of a horse.

"He could be anywhere." A man's voice, high with nerves, carried over the sounds of the approaching storm.

Iron jingled. Horses' hooves clopped quietly. An eagle screamed high overhead where it soared, playing on the downdrafts.

Another voice, lower, was audible, but Wade couldn't make out words.

"She shoulda been mine!" The high-pitched voice sounded again. "I'd've liked to get my hands on all that long white hair. I'd've tamed the wild outta her." The voice droned on, complaining, making sickening suggestions. The man raved on and on about a wild woman with white hair. It had to be Abby. Some of the words were lost when the wind struck just so and carried them in another direction.

Wade didn't need to hear them. He'd heard enough to know they had her prisoner somewhere.

"I say we go back." That whining voice started again. Wade recognized it, but he wasn't sure from where. "Just 'cuz she cut Harv don't make her his. I want that wild woman."

"I don't care what you want."

Chills of terror almost drove Wade out onto the trail, gun blazing. He fought a terrible battle with his desire to charge out to confront the men. Wade knew better. Getting himself killed was no way to save Abby and no way to protect Red and his family. But still he felt his legs tense to jump forward. His hand tightened on the butt of his gun, ready to open fire.

God, they have her. Protect her, Lord. Help me find her. Get us there on time.

Two men here at least, and they'd left Abby behind with someone else. Could it be four men? Could it be the ones who'd attacked Abby's village? Knowing how vicious those men were made it harder to stay hidden.

The voices were closer. A bend in the winding trail hid the riders, but Wade knew they'd appear any second. He swallowed hard. He gripped a low branch of the tree he knelt behind, partly to hold himself in place, partly so when his chance came he could use the limb to catapult himself onto the trail.

Wait. Wait.

The wind held him in place as if it were the hand of God. He itched to move, to act, to fight and punish, but he controlled himself, biding his time.

The lightning flashed so often the trail was lit almost constantly. An especially bright slash lit up the trail enough that Wade caught sight of a horse's nose just as it appeared from around the bend. He leveled his pistol. He wouldn't shoot, though. Instead he'd charge in once they were closer, get the drop on them, and make sure they were disarmed, with Red backing him up but staying hidden well enough to protect Michael and make sure they survived for Cassie's sake. Wade would stop them, and they'd find out where Abby had been taken. Repeating that in his head gave him hope that he could do the right thing when he was killing mad.

Suddenly, to his left, a noise scared Wade into nearly jumping out onto the trail. A swift hand grabbed his arm or he might have run forward right into the men's path.

"It's me. Hang on." Red appeared by Wade's side on foot. It took a second for the lightning to show that Red didn't have Michael. He must have circled back, crossed the trail, and given Michael to Cassie.

Wade hated the thought of Red risking his life, but the odds had just gotten a lot better.

Their eyes met. Then Red nodded at the approaching men. "Now." They rushed the trail.

"Stop right there or I'll shoot." Red cocked his gun, the sound clear and chilling in the stormy night.

The men shouted. One of their horses reared up.

Wade rushed the riders, eager to get his hands on them and beat the truth out of them, to find Abby. He caught the closest man and, from the cry of alarm, knew he'd gotten the man who'd uttered such horrible threats against Abby. Jerking the man to the ground, Wade snatched at his holster and relieved the villain of his gun.

The other horse landed four-legged, and Wade saw its back was bare. The quiet man was gone.

Wade yanked the man he held to his feet and used him for a shield, searching in the darkness for the other man. There was no sign of Red, either.

"Let go!" his prisoner shouted then began flailing his hands and feet.

To subdue him, Wade flipped his gun around and crashed the butt down on the man's head. The fight went out of him and his legs sagged. Wade crouched low, looking for the missing outlaw and now for Red. Wade didn't dare shoot at someone coming toward him because he couldn't be sure who it was in the dark.

Underbrush thrashed and snapped.

Wade heard it and turned. They were on the side of the trail where Cassie was hidden with the children. Like the seasoned rancher he was, Wade snapped the fringe from his buckskin jacket and used it to hog-tie his prisoner.

A crack of gunfire split the night, followed by a flash of light deep in the woods. A man's sudden cry of pain that Wade hoped didn't come from Red was followed by more commotion in the trees.

Wade's attention focused on a spot close to him. He quickly dragged his limp captive to the side of the trail and stashed him out of sight then rushed toward the oncoming noise. Slipping behind a tree, Wade bided his time, drawing his gun but knowing he didn't dare shoot.

A dark form leapt through the last of the cover, and Wade tackled him. The second he made contact, he was sure he had the other outlaw. They tussled, Wade searching wildly for the man's gun in the darkness. A fist slammed into Wade's face. He stumbled backward, losing his grip.

Another gunshot split the night, then another. In the chaos,

Wade knew he'd pulled the trigger. Sickened, he didn't waver. He rushed toward the man. It wasn't Red, Wade was sure of it. But that bullet could have gone wild.

The man, facedown on the ground, groaned in agony.

Wade knelt and rolled him onto his back.

"You got him?" Red reached Wade's side, sounding desperate.

"Yes." Wade bound this man's legs and hands just as he had the other's.

"He fired his gun too close to Cassie. I've got to see if she's okay." Red vanished.

Scared to death, Wade saw a gun within the outlaw's reach and kicked it aside then searched the man for hideout weapons. As he frisked the attacker, he became aware of wetness soaking the man's shoulder. Blood. Wade ripped another long fringe off his jacket and bound the man as quickly as he would have bulldogged a calf.

Seconds ticked by as Wade waited, hoping and praying Red would come back and tell him Cassie and the children were okay. The time crawled.

Finally, Red emerged from the woods.

"Everything okay, Red?"

"Yep."

"You weren't hurt? Your family's okay?"

"They're fine."

"Did you shoot him?"

"Nope, I never even fired my gun."

"Then this must be my bullet in his shoulder." Wade reached for the bleeding shoulder and ripped the shirt aside. A flare of lightning revealed not one but two bullet wounds. A new one and an old one. Instantly, Wade was sure he'd put the old wound in this man near the Flathead village.

"This one was in on the massacre of Abby's people."

"How do you know?"

"Because I shot one of them that day near Abby's village, and

I can see the bullet wound right here." Wade jabbed a finger at the two wounds.

"And if it's like it sounded—" Red didn't continue because it was too sickening.

Wade knew someone had to say it. "They've got Abby." Wade stood. His foot slipped, and he accidentally kicked his prisoner.

The man howled in pain in a way that struck Wade as ridiculous for such a minor bump.

Then Wade looked closer and saw a knife sticking out of the man's boot. Shaking his head in disbelief, he looked closer. He'd seen that knife before.

"Can I have my knife back?" As polite as a schoolmarm, Cassie approached Wade's prisoner. She had Susannah in her arms and Michael on her back, and she held the reins of all three horses.

Wade remembered that man's cry of pain in the woods. A sound he now realized was wrung from this man when Cassie's knife had embedded in the leather and obviously gotten some toes. Honestly, they'd made the little woman do more than her share of the work tonight, and now it looked as if she'd taken a big hand in bagging an outlaw.

Wade hoped there was a reward. "You have got yourself a handy little woman, Red."

Red reached down and retrieved Cassie's knife with no oversupply of gentleness. The outlaw howled in pain.

He handed the weapon to his wife and took Susannah. "You should get out of here, Cassie, but I can't leave Wade, and I can't let you go off alone."

"I'm fine, Red. I'll be careful."

"Like you were this time?"

"I'd say stabbing that man was real careful of me."

Wade would have laughed if he hadn't been so scared for Abby.

"This trail doesn't lead anywhere but to your old house, Cass. I'll bet they've got Abby there."

Wildflower Bride

In a tearing hurry, Wade and Red made short work of dragging the two men well off the trail, making sure they were trussed up tight and had no concealed knives to cut themselves loose.

Red held Susannah and helped Cassie to mount with little Michael on her back. Then he and Wade swung up on horseback, and the three of them moved swiftly down the trail.

Wade kept hearing those men talk. Kept thinking of Abby in the hands of these brutes.

Wade took the lead this time, leaving the Dawsons to bring up the rear with their children. He set a dangerously fast pace. It was so dark now Wade could barely make out Cassie when he looked behind him.

One thing did bother him about that attack. . . . He dropped back beside her. They were far enough from the Griffin place, and the wind whipped wildly enough. He decided it was safe to talk. "Why'd you stab him in the foot, Cassie? That's a pretty small target."

There was no answer except Red's laughter. A shocking sound considering what had just happened and the danger that lay ahead.

"It's not funny, Red." Cassie sounded huffy. It was too dark to see her face and no handy lightning bolt supplied illumination, but the little woman sounded for all the world like she was pouting.

"It's a little bit funny," Red said quietly from behind them.

"It is not!"

"What's funny?" Wade asked.

"Nothing." Cassie said no more.

"Then what's *not* funny?"

But Red wasn't done talking. "She wasn't aiming for his foot."

"You don't know that for a fact. I might well have been aiming for his foot." Cassie sounded like she was trying to threaten Red into silence.

Wade's good friend Red apparently wasn't scared at all. "She was aiming for his. . .uh. . .his bull's-eye."

291

❧

"You're mine, you wildcat." Harv sank his fingers deep into Abby's hair. "And I'm gonna make you pay for this cut on my face."

She slashed out with her knife and gave him a new cut to worry about.

Harv stumbled back.

Abby, her feet bound, dove at him. Her weight slammed into him, and she jerked his gun out of his holster as he fell backward. His cry of fear gave her a purely sinful surge of satisfaction. She flipped the gun so it faced away from the filthy pig and brought a clean, hard butt stroke down on his head.

His turn to hurt, his turn to be overpowered.

She felt the vicious pleasure of that blow. She really needed to talk with God more about this desire she had to hurt, or threaten to hurt, white men. It wasn't biblical, she was nearly certain of it.

She didn't think it was a sin to defend herself, but enjoying it was most likely not something God approved of. She decided then and there that once she was sure the stinking outlaw was knocked into a sound sleep and she'd gotten well away from here, she'd spend serious time in prayer and repentance.

He slumped to the floor unconscious on the first blow.

Infuriated that she had no excuse to keep beating on him, Abby quickly slit the bindings on her ankles and jumped to her feet. "One of your men is still around," Abby said to the still figure in front of her. She wasn't going to stand around waiting for him to come back.

Eyeing the gun with distaste, she decided there was no reason to leave it behind for him to use on her or another innocent. She took it and ran out the front door, dashing into the woods, hoping the second man wasn't watching.

The trees surrounded her. She crouched down, watchful, worried about the location of the other outlaw. The first two who'd left would be on their way far down the trail by now. But the second one was close at hand, and he'd intended to return after Harv did his worst.

The fools had tied her hands behind her back and not taken her knife. The slim weapon was hard for others to find in its pouch. The stiffness of the blade was concealed by the beading, so if they searched her at all—she'd been unconscious at the time, so she wasn't sure—they'd missed it. But she'd awakened in that room and watched them through eyes opened just a slit while she'd found her knife and cut her hands free.

Then while they plotted, she prepared to make them sorry they'd touched her. These were the men who had massacred her village. The man's injured face was testimony to that, and his threats to make her pay for his scars were as good as a confession.

She would have to do some serious work on the state of her soul to find an ounce of regret in her that she'd hurt that dreadful, stinking man. But she'd do it. She promised God.

Not now but soon.

She expected no white lawman to exact justice for the murder of a village of Flatheads, so she didn't consider trying to take the men to the sheriff, even if she could have figured out a way.

Staring at the house, she tried to decide what to do. These men were dangerous, and though she'd hurt this one, he'd be fine and all four men were still free. She'd heard them plotting to kill her and Wade and Mort and take Mort's ranch. It made sense to kill her because she'd witnessed them committing murder, and Wade had seen this man's face. But Mort? What did he have to do with this? Was he just another victim, another chance to do evil?

Crouching there in the woods like a frightened rabbit didn't suit her. But what should she do? Where should she go? The forests weren't safe, and she needed to warn Wade. She could have lived in the wilderness alone. Hadn't she just proved that she was tough enough? But did she want to be this tough? Did she want to fight for her life every day?

Abby had lived through a disease that killed her white family.

She'd survived a brutal massacre that finished her Salish family. She'd never been allowed time to grieve for either as she'd been torn away from both of those lives. Twice now her life had been broken into pieces. And now, with her aching head, fresh blood on her hands, and the man she now knew she loved in danger, she couldn't make a decision.

She had to protect Wade. She had to leave the white world.

God, I belong nowhere.

Wind whipped around her and laughed as if the devil himself mocked her.

She was utterly alone. The whole wide world seemed closed to her. A moment of loneliness so profound it nearly choked her held her in place. Go forward. Go back. Every choice was hostile.

Abby knew this was the lowest moment of her life. The utter loneliness sank into her bones until she knew things could never get any worse.

A crack of thunder proved her wrong.

The heavens split open and slashing, frigid rain poured down on her head.

CHAPTER 33

"Hold up." Wade lifted one gloved hand.

The trail widened enough that Cassie and Red were able to come up beside him just as the rain began slashing his face. They stared at the dark house. Cassie and Red had both donned oilcloth ponchos, and the children, sleeping under the waterproof cloth, were still and comfortable. Red and Cassie looked okay, too.

Wade hadn't taken the time to pack anything. He was miserable, cold, wet, and within seconds of pure panic.

The house was dark. No sign of life anywhere.

"Let me go in alone." Wade spoke low, his voice barely audible under the sounds of the storm.

"No. Cassie, lift up your slicker and let me hand Susannah over." Red tented his poncho and shifted around to slide Susannah off his lap and under Cassie's rain gear without awakening the little girl or getting a single drop of water on her.

"I don't want you hurt." Wade's fear for Abby and guilt at putting Red and his family in danger were making him twitchy.

Turning to Wade, Red said, "Give me a minute to scout the outbuildings. I'll signal you when I'm ready. Then you go in the front, and I'll go in the back."

"No, I'm not waiting. I need to get in there. You stay back. Protect your family."

"It's all quiet now, Wade. If she's in there, she'll be no worse for a few minutes' wait. If we go in stupid and get ourselves shot, she'll be a lot worse off, and so will Cassie and the little ones."

Red was right. Wade knew it. He forced himself to do the smart thing. He nodded in agreement, keeping his eyes fastened on the old house. She was in there, maybe hurt, maybe dead. And if she wasn't in there, then where did they look?

"Cass, honey, you drop back into the woods and mind the young'uns and the horses."

"Yes, Red."

Wade tried to imagine Abby saying, "Yes, Wade," in that obedient tone of voice. It would never happen, and Wade would never care. He'd let her say anything and do anything as long as she was all right. He'd never ask for more than her safety.

The drenched horses obediently followed Cassie into the dark woods as wind buffeted them and thunder rumbled overhead.

"Stay back until you hear from me, Wade." Red vanished toward the back of the house. There was a large barn, built with Cassie's inheritance before her first husband went broke and died, leaving her alone, pregnant, and penniless in the unsettled West. Griffin also had several smaller outbuildings erected, too, so it would take time to search them all.

It took every ounce of self-control Wade had to watch and wait. He stared at that house through the nearly blinding rain, trying to burn a hole through the wall with his eyes. Was she in there? Was she hurt or dead?

God, please let us be in time.

Suddenly Wade heard a birdcall—a bird that would never be out singing in this kind of rain. Red.

Inching forward, Wade drew his gun.

Wildflower Bride

❧

Sid stopped in his tracks.

His eyes narrowed as a shadow separated itself from the barn. Moving slowly, silently, someone slipped from building to building, searching.

Sid backed his horse well out of the man's line of sight, dismounted, and tied the animal securely.

A bolt of lightning lit up the yard at just the right second, and Sid got a good look at the man. But as he was swathed in oilcloth, he couldn't identify him. Not Harv, that was for sure.

The man came out and headed in a crouching run toward the house. A flare of light outlined the man's gun. Then a shrill whistle told Sid the rest. This man wasn't alone.

Dying was not part of Sid's plan. He felt his feet itching to take off, to run for the hills, to leave Harv to his fate. Except Harv was the only one who knew where that blasted gold was hidden.

They'd run into that house and see Harv with the wild woman, and there'd be killing trouble and Sid's dreams of gold would die along with his saddle partner.

Inching forward, Sid drew his gun.

❧

Abby couldn't believe her eyes.

Maybe the lightning had left her addled, but she saw somebody huddled in the woods, barely visible because she was covered head to foot with a cloak. Watching closely, a long braid whipped out, and a pretty bow on the braid told Abby that this was a woman. The woman held three horses, and even deep in the woods on this black night, Abby recognized Wade's horse.

Wade was here? Abby sidled closer, hating that she lost sight of the house as she moved closer to the woman.

A high-pitched cry Abby recognized convinced her to forget being quiet, and she walked forward without concealment. It sounded like. . .a baby. And who had a baby with her every time Abby had seen her? "Cassie, is that you?"

"Abby? You're here? You're okay?"

Cassie Dawson, and from the odd wriggling and crying from under her cloak, Abby surmised that the woman had indeed brought a baby along.

"You brought a baby to a gunfight?"

Cassie's smile shone in the darkness. "We didn't set out for a gunfight. We set out for Belle's."

"So how'd you end up here?"

"Mama scary."

Startled at the little voice sounding from beneath Cassie's slicker, Abby looked closer at Cassie's little tent she'd created with her waterproof coat. "You brought a baby and a toddler to a gunfight?"

Cassie shrugged under the wind-battered oilcloth. "Here's what happened. . . ." Cassie finished her explanation quickly.

"Now I reckon I've got to go in there and save Red and Wade." Abby turned toward the house just as a ridiculous excuse for a birdcall sounded through the storm.

"I'd surely appreciate it if you would, Abby." Cassie said it like she didn't have a single doubt in her mind.

Abby didn't have any doubts, either. "You stay here."

Inching forward, Abby drew Harv's gun.

Using every bit of cover, Wade rushed the house. He paused at the porch. The minute he took the first step, the people inside would be warned. There was no way to disguise the creaking of the wood.

He caught his breath then charged up the steps. He threw open the door and swung his gun to cover the dark corners. One lump lay in the room. A human-sized lump. Wade's heart stopped beating.

"Here, Wade." Red appeared in the doorway that led to the back of the house. The frequent lightning flashes helped Wade locate his friend. Red stood alert, pointing his gun toward the floor so no wild shot went in the wrong direction. With Red watching the corners of the room, Wade rushed to the prone figure. Never had he known such terror. It made all he'd felt in his growing-up years, with his brute of a father, fade into nothingness. If this was Abby, if she was dead, then Wade would have to find a new way to live, because nothing made sense without her.

He dropped to his knees, and a helpful blaze of lightning told him it was a man. An unconscious, bleeding man. Another lightning bolt revealed an ugly scar on the man's chin.

"Where is she?" Wade shook the man. "Where's Abby?" The unconscious man didn't seem to be so much as breathing, though Wade had checked and he was alive. And considering that the man was knocked cold, Wade suspected Abby had been here. This looked like her work.

A scratching sound pulled Wade's attention from all the black niches of the room. Red had come all the way into the room, and now light popped to life as he held a match close to the still figure. Red leaned close. "This is the rustler I brought in."

Wade studied the man until he was sure. "He's the man Abby cut at the massacre."

"So it was the same gang." Red lifted the match to look at Wade. "And you said there were four of them?"

"Yep, and we've accounted for three."

Red blew out the match. He and Wade wheeled to face away from each other. The house was as silent as death. The only sound the raging storm.

The rain battered the house. Wade felt awful knowing Cassie waited in the miserable darkness. Where was Abby?

"This must be Abby's doing. Who else would cut the man then knock him cold?" Red asked.

"Unless the two rustlers fought over her and one took her."

"Maybe, but those two men we caught were fast with their guns. Figures their partners might be, too. A knife sounds more like Abby's style. I think she got away."

Wade, studying the corners of the room during the occasional lightning flash, saw something against a far wall. He hurried over and lifted up a rope, knotted but cut through. "She got loose."

"And she knocked this guy cold and ran. He's stopped bleeding, but the blood hasn't dried yet. She didn't leave long ago."

"I'm going to look upstairs." Wade headed up the sweeping staircase.

"I'll check all the rooms down here." Red's voice changed. "Wade, there was only one horse in the corral out back. If there's a fourth man—"

"There is." Wade paused, wishing Red would hurry up so Wade could be doing something.

"Then he's gone. We can hope she got away, but he might have taken Abby with him."

"Maybe he saw his partner, figured out he'd lost Abby, and took off."

"Maybe. I hope so."

Sick with fear, Wade rushed toward the stairs and was halfway up them when he heard a gun cock. He stopped and turned toward the sound, hoping Red's gun had made the noise.

A bolt of lightning told Wade more than he wanted to know. Red stood in the door that led to the back of this rambling house. The black of a gun was pressed against his neck. Wade saw the gun was held in an awkward way, with two fingers of a glove extended rather than curved around the butt.

That's when Wade knew.

Sid.

The M Bar S foreman—missing two fingers. Wade had seen that before. Sid had been at the massacre. And the unconscious man was one of the cattle rustlers, which meant Sid was one, too.

Suddenly, Wade was just as sure that Sid had caused Pa's fall.

This man or one of his partners had shot at him and Abby with the bow and arrow. This one evil man was the mastermind behind all the trouble. He had to be stopped.

"Come out where I can see you." Sid was shorter than Red, and he crouched low like a cowering dog, so Wade couldn't get off a shot.

Wade had fired his gun twice in his life at a man. Both times it had been little more than an accident. It made him sick, still, thinking about his bullet hitting the outlaw, even knowing the man was vermin who deserved to die.

"Let him go, Sid. Abby's gone. You can't get her." She'd probably run on toward her mountain valley. Choosing a life utterly alone over a life with him.

"You think I want that wildflower? Why do you think I left her for Harv?"

Wade might be too much of a coward to shoot a man, but he wasn't a coward when it came to his own life and death. He knew he'd spend eternity in heaven, and that erased all his fear. What mattered was that Red came out of this alive. He had Cassie to care for.

Wade felt God writing a message across his heart with a fiery fingertip:

"In him was life; and the life was the light of men. And the light shineth in darkness; and the darkness comprehended it not."

No, darkness couldn't comprehend the light. But Wade could shine the light of Jesus in the darkness. He'd tried with his pa, and maybe seeds were planted that would someday grow. And maybe that meant Wade wasn't such a coward. Maybe a willingness to shine a light in dark places took a special kind of courage. And if the darkness couldn't comprehend it, as Sid couldn't now, then Wade's willingness to die to save Red took more courage than a willingness to kill.

Wade's spine stiffened. He walked down the last two steps. Then he stepped out and squared off in front of Sid, his heart on fire for the Lord. The light of God was shining within him until Wade thought it might be lighting the room.

A bolt of lightning brightened the room enough that Wade could see Red's eyes. Red had both hands raised slightly above his waist, and Sid's gun was jammed against Red's throat. But Red looked calm, at peace, another source of light.

Wade knew all he needed was for that gun to aim away from Red for a split second, give Red a chance to act.

It was Wade's job to bring that gun around to bear on himself.

"Let him go, Sid." Wade was amazed his voice sounded so confident. "You're finished. We've captured your other two saddle partners, and you can't get this man out of here"—Wade tipped his head toward the unconscious outlaw—"without carrying him. Time to cut your losses. Back out of here and run."

"You've captured Boog and Paddy?"

Wade had heard of Paddy, another Sawyer cowpoke. In the darkness, he hadn't recognized him. Red had taken care of the Irishman, but Boog? That had to be the name of the man Wade had shot. Twice.

Wade swallowed hard to keep his voice steady. "Yes, we've got them. Give it up and run. We won't try and stop you."

"No, I've got too much to lose, and there's still a chance I can win. As long as you're dead." With lightning quickness, Sid turned the gun from Red and aimed at Wade.

Wade went for his gun.

Red grabbed Sid's hand and shoved up.

Sid's gun blasted the ceiling.

A dull *thud* echoed in the room.

Lightning lit up the room, and Wade saw Sid's eyes go wide into a vacant stare.

Red wrested the weapon free.

Sid's knees buckled.

As Sid sank, an inch at a time, to the floor, Abby's golden head emerged behind him. In both hands, she held the gun she'd just used to club Sid over the head. She had her knife clenched between her teeth. She was soaking wet and killing mad.

Wade had never loved her more.

CHAPTER 34

We've got to help Red and Cassie take the outlaws back to town, honey."

"What do you mean 'we'? I don't have to go."

Wade did his best not to let his exasperation show.

"Quit scowling at me, white man."

His best was apparently not very good. "Just ride with us, please, Ab?" Wade was begging. He was planning to spend the rest of his life begging, because he was planning to spend it with the stubbornest woman he'd ever known. He accepted it and looked forward to a lifetime of being overpowered. Never ever would he hear those sweet words, "Yes, Wade."

"Are you okay, Cassie, honey?" Red had brought Cassie inside to drip dry.

"Yes, Red."

That sounded so sweet, Wade felt a little like crying. But there was no use in it, like crying for the moon. He loved Abby and that was that.

They had Harv and Sid tied up, both still sleeping like babies, while they waited for the rain to stop. The other two outlaws were out in the weather, but Wade couldn't get worked up about their being uncomfortable. If they thought rain was unpleasant, wait till they felt the business end of a noose.

"What I don't understand is the massacre of your village." Red interrupted the wrangling that Wade and Abby had been doing for the last hour. He spoke calmly because he had Michael cradled in his arms. They'd made a little bed for Susannah out of a blanket that wasn't soaking wet. She'd slept through everything.

The night was wearing on and they were in no hurry to head back to Divide, especially Wade, because he couldn't convince Abby to go along.

Glaring, Wade said, "You were the only witness to what these men did to your village. You've got to come in and tell the sheriff. The rustling, the kidnapping, the assault on you will send them to jail for a few years, but they need to hang or stay locked up for life. With you as an eyewitness, they'll hang."

"No white man hangs for killing Indians." Abby practically spat the words.

Sorely afraid she might be right, Wade tried another argument. He backed her up against the wall and kissed the living daylights out of her.

She'd kept Harv's gun, tucking it in the belt of her deerskin dress. She had her knife, too.

Wade was through thinking of himself as a coward. He was holding Abby close and she was armed to the eyeballs. That made him a brave man indeed.

She wasn't shooting him, though. And she didn't even go for her knife. Instead she wrapped her arms around his neck and kissed him back like a house afire. With the tiny corner of Wade's mind that wasn't overwhelmed from the feel of her holding him, Wade realized he should have kissed her the minute Sid collapsed.

He'd wanted to, but she'd really had bloodlust in her eyes, and truth be told, he was a little scared she'd hurt him. Also, there was the knife in her teeth. That could have gotten ugly.

Red cleared his throat.

Wade came to his senses. . .or as close as he'd ever get with Abby in his life. He pulled back about two inches, no more. "How could you run off from Pa's like that?"

"Your father is an insulting, cruel tyrant. I couldn't bear another moment in his presence."

"Okay. I know how that feels. That's no excuse for leaving me."

"No excuse? I wasn't going to make you choose between your family and me. I know things are bad between you and your father, but. . .the day may come when you want to return to him, and I will never do that. And I won't make you choose me over him. You'd come to hate me."

Wade looked into her eyes and realized he could see her. The sun was rising; the darkness had turned to gray. The rain had ended. Daylight would come again. "I will *never* hate you. You didn't ask because you knew I'd come. You're making this excuse because—because you love me."

He saw the fire in her eyes. He saw her desire to be her usual blunt self and hurt him. Then he saw deeper, under the hostility, to the hurt and the fear. She'd lost so much.

"You're marrying me, Abby. We will go wherever we need to to find a home, but we'll do it together. Don't you dare make up an excuse about why it won't work. I love you and we will travel through this life together, alone in the wilderness if that's where we're happy."

As she shook her head, Wade saw Abby's fear come closer to the surface, as if she was daring to show what was in her heart. "There's nowhere we can both be happy." Her arms were still around his neck.

"I'm happy now. Aren't you?"

She flinched, tightening her arms as if her mind told her to let go of him but her body wouldn't obey. Well, he wanted all of her, body, mind, and heart. Although right now, her body felt really nice. "Abby, I can be happy by your side. I need nothing else."

Their eyes held. Wade closed the distance between them,

and this time the kiss was pure tenderness. It was a promise. She nearly crushed him with her warrior's grip, and he knew he had her promise back.

When Wade raised his head this time, she smiled. The fear was still there, but she was brave enough to face that fear.

"Um. . .I have a bona fide preacher's license. I can perform a wedding ceremony."

Wade turned to Red and smiled. Wade slid his arm around Abby's waist so they could face Red, side by side.

"I say yes." Wade looked at Abby.

"And Cassie and I can get these men to town. We left the horses with the other outlaws, and we've got horses enough to carry these two. We can manage. You can say your vows and go start your lives together anywhere you want." Red smiled. "But if you'd like to stop by our place once in a while, we'd love to see you."

Cassie came and relieved Red of baby Michael. She slipped the little tyke onto the blanket beside Susannah. "I'll be a witness to the marriage. I think you need a witness, Red. I don't think those unconscious men really count."

Red shrugged. "I've never done this before, so probably having someone witness it is a good idea. Although you'd think me bein' a witness and them being witnesses oughta be enough. I mean, I'm a parson. I should be trustworthy."

"Yeah." Wade nodded. "And why would we lie? But we'd like you to witness our wedding, Cassie." Wade looked at Abby. "If there is one. What do you say?"

Abby sighed and looked disgruntled, but that was pretty much how she looked all the time, so Wade didn't let that discourage him. It just helped him to fully accept the life he was signing up for. And if she stayed by his side, that was all he would ever ask for.

The wait was nearly unbearable. The sun rose a bit more as Wade watched Abby's heart battle her mind.

Finally, she smiled. "I say yes." Her arm around his waist tightened. "And since I can't get shut of you, I'll ride along to deliver these men and tell the sheriff my story. I want the white world to know what happened to my people. I want someone to admit that the true savages are these outlaws."

Wade jerked his chin, a happy, contented, slightly-frightened-of-his-wife man. "So how about we wait and get married in town so everyone in Divide knows I'm the luckiest man alive?"

Abby leaned against him a bit, and Wade started thinking he hadn't plumbed the depths of the happiness he and Abby could find together.

"I wouldn't even mind inviting your odious father. I'd like that horrible yellow dog to see that we are wed to each other. It will make him sick. I'd like to be watching when his stomach turns at the sight of his son's choice of a wife."

"Please, Abby." Red raised his hands as if to surrender. "All this mushy sentiment is too much for me."

"We can invite Pa, but we're getting hitched whether he shows up in town or not." Wade hooked his arm through Abby's and said, "Let's get to town and get on with starting the rest of our lives."

Their future was unplanned.

Their destination unknown.

But wherever life led them, they'd go together. Wade knew that God had at last granted him an end to his loneliness.

"Whom shall I fear?"

And here he was marrying the scariest woman he'd ever known.

And that made it official. Wade was a brave man.

"Whom shall I fear?"

Those old, painful words Wade had battled to hold close and claim as his own now sang like a blessing raining down on his new life with his wildflower bride.

CHAPTER 35

After the outlaws were locked up, a few Linscott hands who happened to be in town rode out to pass on the news of the impending wedding to their boss.

Wade couldn't decide whether it was best to rush the wedding before Tom could stop it or take plenty of time and make Tom sit through the nuptials.

Hands from the Sawyer place had ridden out, too.

Between locking up the bad guys and the sheriff questioning Wade and Abby, as well as Red and Cassie, the day was nearly wound down when Pa came tearing in, riding in his specially built buckboard, driving it himself.

Wade braced for his father to go on a rampage. Instead Pa was subdued. They were standing in the middle of Divide's Main Street, Pa on the high buckboard seat, Wade and Abby on the ground.

"I'd like for you to come out to the ranch and have the wedding out there, Wade," Pa said real polite-like, and Wade wondered what the old codger was up to.

"Ask her." Wade jabbed a thumb at Abby.

"Will you, Abby? And not just for the wedding, but to stay.

I know I can get in an evil mood, but we want you and Wade at the M Bar S."

"No *mood* excuses the things you say and do." Abby scowled.

Wade studied her and realized he was trying to twist his own face into that same scowl. He envied her fierceness. Once he realized what he was doing, he quit mimicking her and looked around, afraid someone had noticed.

Wade realized he was looking up to his Pa, and that didn't sit right. But it wasn't exactly easy for the tyrant to get down. He wondered how long it'd take Pa to realize just how well sitting high above everyone else suited him. "I'm not promising it'll never happen again. I'd be a liar if I did, because I know my temper too well. But just for today, would you. . .please"—Wade thought the old man sounded like he was choking on the word *please*— "come out and be married at the ranch? I'd be honored if you'd let me give you my. . .blessing."

Another word that nearly did Pa in. Wade wondered if the grouch even knew what the word *blessing* meant. He prayed silently for his father. And wished he could love him in any way except as ordered by God. Wade had serious doubts that would ever happen. But Wade was honest enough to know how far he'd come since he'd made his peace with God. If Wade could change, then anyone could. Including Pa.

"We need to send for Belle and Silas." Cassie had dismounted and stood on the street holding Susannah. "They'll want to come to your wedding."

"Uh, honey," Red said, bouncing his redheaded son on his hip. "Belle's no big fan of weddings."

"She'd probably try to stop it if she showed up," Wade told Cassie. "You know how she is. She'd think Abby needed saving."

Everyone did know.

"If I need saving, I'll save myself." Abby rolled her eyes.

"Will you come, Abby?" Pa sounded sincere. He didn't look like he was dying from speaking kindly. That surprised Wade.

Wildflower Bride

He'd have sworn it would have killed the man to be polite.

Wade looked at Abby. "You get to decide." He had a feeling those words were going to be repeated a million times in the sixty years he planned to be married to her. Wade smiled in anticipation.

A horse walked by in the dirt. A door slammed somewhere. A coyote howled in the forest near Divide, all while Abby stared at Pa.

"We'll come out and be married there." Abby somehow made that sound like a threat.

"And will you stay?" Pa didn't even ask Wade. The man had obviously figured out who was going to be in charge of this marriage.

Abby grabbed hold of the buckboard and vaulted up beside Pa. Apparently she didn't like his looking down on her.

"We will stay if Wade wishes it." Abby leaned down until her nose almost touched Pa's. "But he will go the moment I say I can't bear it. And I will go the moment he says *he* can't bear it. We'll take it one day at a time."

Pa's face turned an alarming shade of red, but he kept his mouth shut for once in his stubborn, tyrannical life and just nodded. He managed to squeak the words, "I understand," through his clenched jaw.

Wade doubted Pa's restraint would last long, but maybe, with enough prayer and an almighty, powerful God, things would change.

Red came out of the sheriff's office in time to hear that. "It'll be full dark by the time we ride out to your place, Wade. Cassie is tired. The children have had a long, hard day. Can we put it off until tomorrow?"

The delay chafed at Wade. He'd have preferred to stay out at that house where they'd taken Sid Garver prisoner and let Red speak the vows. He'd be well into married life by now if they had. A honeymoon would have commenced. Wade felt a little dizzy and hoped he wouldn't fall off his horse.

But Abby had been kidnapped today, and all of them could use clean clothes, a hot meal, and a bath. Considering he planned to live a long time as a married man, another day wouldn't hurt. Wade looked at Abby.

She smiled and nodded.

"Tomorrow, then." Wade turned to Red. "We'll go on out to the ranch and see you in the morning." Wade reached his arms up, and Abby let him catch her around the waist and lower her to the ground. She smiled at him, letting him know she'd taken his help not because she needed it but because she liked it. Liked him. Loved him.

They saddled up and were almost ready to head out when Tom Linscott came galloping into town on that brute of a stallion.

He pulled the horse to a stop a few feet away from everyone. "You're marrying Wade Sawyer, then?" Tom's question was for Abby, but he glared at Wade and Pa in equal parts.

"I am. We're having the wedding tomorrow at the M Bar S. Wade and I are planning to stay there until I can no longer tolerate it. Then we'll wander."

Tom swung down off his horse and came to Abby, taking both her hands. "You've always got a home with me, Abby girl. You know that, right? I love you. And if Sawyer ever treats you bad, I'll beat him into the dirt for you."

Abby gave Tom a hug, and for the first time Wade wondered if living with the Flatheads had really changed Abby all that much. She seemed to be a lot like her brother.

"Come out to the wedding, Linscott." Wade couldn't fight the sense of pure satisfaction that he got from marrying Linscott's sister. It felt like he was getting the better of the man for some reason. Of course, that wasn't the reason Wade wanted to marry Abby, but it was a nice little extra.

"Try and stop me." Tom mounted up and turned tail for his ranch.

Wildflower Bride

The next morning dawned clear and warm after the storm of yesterday. When he awoke rested, with the ugliness of yesterday separated from his wedding day, Wade was glad they'd delayed the ceremony. Almost.

He came down to the kitchen to find Gertie humming as she frosted a cake. The woman had obviously been hard at work for hours.

"What's all this, Gertie?" Wade came up behind the house-keeper and kissed her on her round cheek.

Gertie smiled over her shoulder and waved her frosting-coated knife at Wade. "You two are having a nice wedding dinner whether you want one or not."

Wade shrugged. "I reckon we have to eat."

He dipped a finger in Gertie's frosting bowl and she slapped his fingers, but he dodged and got away with the sweet treat.

"Breakfast's warming in the oven, Wade. Fetch it yourself." Gertie turned back to her cake while Wade slipped a plate of hotcakes out.

"Wade. . ." Gertie didn't sound playful.

"What?" Wade braced himself to hear Gertie's misgivings about Abby. His stomach twisted as he wondered how long he'd be able to stay on the ranch. Not that he minded leaving. He just wished there could be peace here.

"I just want you to know. . .I'm sorry."

Wade had done his best not to think about the things that had been said that had driven Abby, and him, away from the ranch. Somehow, he'd never blamed Gertie for any part of the abuse he'd suffered. But when Gertie said she was sorry, he knew he had to think of it.

Wade opened his mouth to say it didn't matter since he had finally taken control of his own life, but the words wouldn't come. "Why didn't you stop him, Gertie? I remember all the times you'd wait for him to work out his temper. Then you'd come to me and tend me. I thought it was love, but you were part of it. I can see that now."

"I thought of just taking you and running a thousand times. But I'd imagine him stopping me, throwing me out. You'd have been left here at his mercy." Gertie turned to Wade. "But there is no excuse good enough for my cowardice."

"I suppose, but there was more than that somehow. You weren't just afraid. You were part of it. Your care of me. . .made you—" Wade couldn't quite put it into words. "It was its own kind of power. You controlled me by being the nice one. You abused me right along with Pa by letting it happen and picking up the pieces afterward."

Gertie was silent, her lips pursed. "We weren't what a child hoped for in a family, were we?"

Wade shook his head. "Not even close."

"I can't go back. I can't do it differently, but please believe me, however badly I showed it, I did love you, Wade. I still do. As for your father, I've seen some softening in him. I think God needed to bring your pa low, break him, to have even a chance of reaching him. But watching your strength, in handling your pa, has reached me. I'm not staying home from church anymore in some worthless show of respect for Mort's feelings. I've asked God to forgive me for my mistakes, and I'm hoping someday you will, too."

Wade nodded, touched and deeply glad for Gertie that she'd found her way to God and that somehow he had a part in her finding that path. "I forgive you, Gertie. You know the sin in my past. What kind of Christian would I be if I was forgiven so much and then wouldn't forgive you?"

"Thank you, Wade. I'm sorry I was always so weak. And I'm so glad you've found a woman who will be kind and gentle with you."

Wade smiled to think of his sweet, beautiful Abby.

"I'm not wearing that fool dress you left in my room." Abby chose that moment to stride into the kitchen wearing her doeskin dress and moccasins, carrying her knife.

Gertie looked at Abby. Then her gaze slid to Wade. The two of them broke out laughing.

Wade jumped to his feet and grabbed Abby in a hug that lifted her off her feet.

"Put me down!" She scowled, but he noticed she was careful not to stab him.

"Good morning." Wade gave her a loud, smacking kiss.

"Let's get on with this wedding." She didn't smile, made it sound like she was being harassed. But it sure sounded like she wanted to get married.

"Red'll be here soon." Wade glanced around and saw that Gertie had turned her back and was now fussing with her frosting again.

Wade took a second kiss, much quieter and deeper. And Abby cooperated something fierce.

"Then we will get on with this wedding." He smiled and tricked a smile out of his woman, too.

Tom Linscott picked that moment to slam the kitchen door open. "Get your hands off her, Sawyer." Tom pulled Wade's arm away and shoved in between Wade and Abby. "You're not married yet."

"We're going to fix that very soon. Have some breakfast."

Red was none too swift getting to the ranch. Pa was behaving pretty well, but Wade was ready to strangle Tom by the time the parson showed up.

It was finally time for the wedding, and Wade practically ran to stand by Red's side in front of the fireplace in Pa's huge living room. Cassie sat in a rocking chair with both her children in her lap. Gertie sat on the sofa next to Pa in his wheelchair.

Linscott finally walked in escorting Abby, smiling down at her. "I'll give the bride away."

"That sounds good, Tom." Red smiled. "This is my first wedding. You come up on Abby's right, with Wade on her left."

"Give me away?" Abby's fingers twitched, and Wade braced himself for her to go for her knife. "As if I now belong to Tom and will soon belong to Wade?"

"You belong to yourself, Abby." Tom took her by the arm and eased her over to Wade's side. "No one here doubts that for a single minute."

Wade watched closely. He didn't mind Abby loving her brother, but there was no sense getting overly acquainted with the cranky, blond grizzly of a man.

He'd feel a lot better when the vows were said and they could get out of there. Wade had no intention of spending his wedding night under his father's roof. Maybe they'd set up camp in the woods, where Abby was happiest. Wade liked that idea. In fact, he liked that idea so well he lost track of what Red was saying.

Red kicked him in the shin. "So do you, Wade?" Red glared.

Wade realized he was missing his own wedding. "I do. I surely do." He hoped Red had asked the question Wade was guessing he'd asked and not something dumb like, "Do you want to go check the cattle before the ceremony?"

Red smiled.

Wade took Abby's hand and she let him, so he must have had the right answer to the right question.

"And Abby, do you take this man to be your lawful wedded husband?"

Abby smiled those blazing blue eyes right at Wade and said, clear as day, loud enough for them to hear all the way back in the Flathead village, "I do."

There was more talk, which Wade mostly missed because he was lost in Abby's smiling eyes. He did catch Red saying, "I now pronounce you man and wife. You may kiss the bride."

And right there in front of his nasty, cranky pa, Abby's nasty, cranky brother, sweet Cassie Dawson, and the first-time marryin' preacher, Red, Wade Sawyer wrapped his arms around his brand-new wife and kissed her until no one in the room could doubt that he was staking a claim. And since Abby was fully cooperative, Wade decided she was staking her claim right back.

When he pulled away, he said for all to hear, but looking at only Abby, "We'll go wherever we need to go to be happy. If it's not here, we'll search until we find it."

Abby ran one finger down his cheek and gave him the tiniest possible nod. "We'll find home in each other."

Wade knew it now as he never had before. "Wherever you are, that's where my home will be."

"And we'll have children to fill that home, whether it's a house or a tepee or we're camped under the open stars."

The thought of those children and what was involved in creating them caused Wade to remember very little of the feast Gertie had prepared. He was polite, he was sure of it. Or if he wasn't, no one pointed it out forcefully enough to get his attention, and both Tom and Pa had a whole lot of forceful they could use on him.

The wedding wore itself out. Their guests all went home, and Wade told his pa and Gertie good-bye.

He and Abby slept under the stars in the woods near Pa's house, but plenty far away. When the camp was set and a warm fire crackled in the Rocky Mountain twilight, Wade finally pulled his brand-spankin'-new wife into his arms. "Abby, this is a new beginning for us. A new life. We'll roam the mountains if it's what you wish."

"I'd like to take a few days and be alone with you, Wade, if that's all right."

Wade felt a little dizzy at the very thought. "Nothing has ever sounded as right." He pulled her close and kissed her.

"I think we will give your whining coyote of a father a chance, Wade. But I want to hunt a few deer, build a tepee out away from his home. Have a place to go when I have to either get away from him or slit his throat."

"That seems reasonable to me." Wade could not have been fonder of his wife. He wasn't sure what that said about him, but the truth was the truth.

"Maybe we can even build a small cabin. That might be better in the winter."

Wade really wasn't that interested in planning their whole future right now. The way Abby was going on, he half expected her to start pacing off the land for the building site.

"And when the children come, we might be more comfortable with four strong walls and a stone hearth."

"About those children..." Wade ran clean out of patience, and for a mild-mannered man who'd spent most of his life fighting fear, he suddenly was almost exploding with courage. But he wasn't a foolish man. He didn't tell her to quiet down. That was a good way to get her to draw her knife, which she most likely had with her, even on her wedding day.

He tricked her instead, distracted her, kept her mouth too busy to talk.

He made sure his feisty little wildflower bride didn't say a single discouraging word.

It was a joyful beginning to a new life that rarely included Wade's prayer of old, *"Whom shall I fear?"*

Because his prayers were now of joy and praise and thanksgiving.

And besides, if he ever was afraid, he had Abby right there to protect him.

ABOUT THE AUTHOR

MARY CONNEALY is a Christie Award finalist. She is the author of the Lassoed in Texas series, which includes *Petticoat Ranch, Calico Canyon,* and *Gingham Mountain*. She has also written a romantic cozy mystery trilogy, *Nosy in Nebraska*; and her novel *Golden Days* is part of the *Alaska Brides* anthology. You can find out more about Mary's upcoming books at www.maryconnealy.com and www.mconnealy.blogspot.com.

Mary lives on a Nebraska ranch with her husband, Ivan, and has four grown daughters: Joslyn (married to Matt), Wendy, Shelly (married to Aaron), and Katy. And she is the grandmother of one beautiful granddaughter, Elle.

Mary loves to hear from her readers. You may visit her at these sites: www.mconnealy.blogspot.com, www.seekerville. blogspot.com, and www.petticoatsandpistols.com. Write to her at mary@maryconnealy.com.

If you enjoyed

WILDFLOWER BRIDE,

then read the rest of the MONTANA MARRIAGES SERIES:

Montana Rose
978-1-60260-142-0
$10.99

The Husband Tree
978-1-60260-143-7
$10.99

Available wherever books are sold.